A' SLAYING WE SHALL GO

Taut with urgency and uncertainty, Macurdy rode a sleigh trail through fresh snow. Night and the trees could not hide him; hoofprints, and the crystal in his pocket, gave him away. Shortly he came to a three-sided woodsmen's shelter. In front of it lay a heap of firewood blocks, with a splitting maul standing beside it.

Stopping his horse, he got down and went into the shelter. A log, hewed flat on top, served as a bench. A splitting wedge lay on it.

He knew at once what to do. Taking the wedge outside, he laid it on the battered maple chopping block, then reached into his coat pocket. The crystal was almost hot! The hunters were near! Alarmed, he laid it on a groove of the wedge, then hefted the maul and swung powerfully, accurately, overhead and down.

The heavy steel head slammed the crystal, and at the impact, a great pain stabbed through Macurdy's skull. At the same instant he heard a terrible cry perhaps a hundred yards back down the trail. Dropping the hammer, he staggered to his horse and pulled himself into the saddle. Then he kicked the animal into a trot, and lying low on its back, fled westward through the forest.

THE LION
RETURNS

JOHN DALMAS

THE LION RETURNS

Copyright © 1999 by John Dalmas

All rights reserved, including the right to reproduce this book or portions thereof in any form.

A Baen Books Original

Baen Publishing Enterprises
P.O. Box 1403
Riverdale, NY 10471

ISBN: 0-671-57824-3

Cover art by Larry Elmore

First printing, August 1999

Distributed by Simon & Schuster
1230 Avenue of the Americas
New York, NY 10020

Typeset by Brilliant Press
Printed in the United States of America

Dedicated to
ELIZABETH MOON

ACKNOWLEDGMENT

Parts of the first draft were critiqued by members of the Spokane Word Weavers, a writers' support and critique group. The second draft was critiqued by two science fiction and fantasy authors: Patricia Briggs and James Glass. And as always by my wife Gail. My thanks to all of you.

The Farside series grew out of an invitation by Jon Gustafson to write a short story for a WesterCon program book a few years ago. I rather quickly realized it was not a short story, but the opening chapter of a novel. Thank you too, Jon.

CONTENTS

PART FOUR — WAR: BLOODY BEGINNINGS

PART FIVE — AN EARLY WINTER

PART SIX — EXPANSION AND INTENSIFICATION

PART SEVEN — CLIMAX AND AFTERMATH

PART EIGHT — CLOSURE

PROLOG

The distance across the Ocean Sea to Vismearc is said to exceed that from fabled Tuago to the River Erg. It took fifty-eight days and nights to sail across, and fifty to return. Of the four ships that set out, only one came back, and very fortunate its mariners, for those days and nights were beset with storms, and sea dragons with necks like mighty snakes. The larger of them snapped men from the deck. And there were monstrous eels whose very stare was venomous, but fortunately they were rarely seen.

And when the sea had finally been crossed, Vismearc itself proved no less dangerous. Great birds dwell there, their hearts as black as their plumage. They are more clever than a man, and large enough to carry a sheep through the air. The women in Vismearc birth many children, in order to have any left after the birds have taken what they wish. Several birds together would attack a man and clean his bones in minutes, so that no one walked out alone, even to relieve himself. While one man voided his bowels, another stood by, sword in hand, to protect him. And there are bees large as sparrows, that make honey of surpassing sweetness, but a single sting causes men to swell like bladders, and die horribly.

1

But most terrible of all are the hordes of savage warriors no higher in stature than the nipples of a man. Short of leg but long of arm, they have bodies of stone, the strength of giants, and no concept of mercy.

Yet it was for Vismearc the Ylver set sail from their island home, those centuries back. For though their mariners had read of the terrors they would face, their fear of the voitusotar was greater. And no man knows whether any of them arrived in that frightful land, or if they arrived, whether any of their progeny yet live.

> *Oiled parchment found in the archives*
> *of Hwilvoros Palace.*

PART ONE
The Plans Of Men

The physical universes are not designed for the convenience or pleasure of humans or other incarnate souls. Intelligence, diligence, and good intentions do not necessarily produce security, comfort and pleasure. There are no guarantees.

One can try and one can hope, but one's expectations are often disappointed. On the other hand, today's victories sometimes lead to tomorrow's woes, while out of today's woes may grow tomorrow's blessings. The roots of joys and griefs can be distant in both time and place. So it is well to be light on your feet, and not too fixed in your desires.

Vulkan to Macurdy,
on the highway to Teklapori
in the spring of 1950

1

Leave

Captain Curtis Macurdy's train pulled slowly up to the red sandstone depot. Through a window he saw his wife on the platform, flowerlike in a pink print frock. Without waiting for the train to stop, he moved quickly down the nearly empty aisle, grabbed his duffel bag from a baggage shelf, and when the door opened, swung down the stairs onto the gray concrete.

Mary saw him at once, and crying his name, ran toward him. Putting down his bag, he caught her in his arms and they kissed hungrily, while the handful of other disembarking passengers grinned or looked away. It was Thursday, June 1, 1945. Servicemen on leave were commonplace.

"You taste marvelous," he murmured. "You smell marvelous."

She laughed despite eyes brimming with tears. "That's perfume," she said, then added playfully, "Evening in Paris." She looked around. The air was damp and heavy; smoke from the coal-burning locomotive settled instead of rising. "Perfume and coal smoke," she added laughing. "And soot."

He picked up his bag again and they walked hand in hand to the car. It was she who got in behind the wheel. That had become habitual. He got in beside her, feasting his eyes.

"Hungry?" she asked.

"For food you mean? Yeah, I guess I am. I had breakfast on the train somewhere west of Pendleton, and a Hershey bar at the station in Portland."

He knew from her letters that she'd moved out of her father's house and rented the apartment above Sweiger's Cafe. He was curious as to why, but hadn't asked. She'd tell him in her own time. She pulled up in front, and they went into the cafe for lunch. Ruthie Sweiger saw them take a booth, and came over with menus. "Look who's here!" she said. "How long has it been?"

He answered in German, as he would have before the war. "Not quite three years. July '42."

Her eyebrows rose, and she replied in the same language. "Your German sounds really old-country now. You put me to shame."

"It should sound old-country." He said it without elaborating.

"Curtis," Mary said quietly in her *Baltisches Deutsch*, "people are looking at us."

He glanced over a shoulder. At a table, two men were scowling in their direction. Curtis got to his feet facing them, standing six feet two and weighing 230 pounds. One side of his chest bore rows of ribbons, topped by airborne wings and a combat infantry badge. Grinning from beneath a long-since-broken nose, he walked over to them.

"Do I know you guys from somewhere?"

"I don't think so," one of them answered, rising. "We came over from Idaho last year. We log for the Severtson brothers."

Macurdy extended a large hand. "My name's Curtis

Macurdy. I used to log for the Severtsons, before I joined the sheriff's department. With luck, I'll be back for good before too long."

Both men shook hands with him, self-conscious now, and Curtis returned to the booth, grinning again. "A little public relations for the sheriff's department," he said, in German again. "And food for thought about people speaking German."

Ruthie left to bring coffee, then took their orders. While they waited, Curtis and Mary made small talk, and looked at each other. Curtis felt her stockinged foot stroke his leg. When their food arrived, they ate quickly, without even refills on coffee. Then Curtis paid the bill and they left. They held hands up the narrow stairs to her apartment, and when Mary closed the door behind them, she set the bolt.

For a long moment they simply stood, gazing at each other. Then they stepped together and kissed, with more fervor than at the depot. Finally Mary stepped back and spoke, her voice husky. "The bedroom," she said pointing, "is over there. I am going to the bathroom, which is over there." Again she pointed. "When I'm done *there*, I'm going *there*. Which is where I want you to be."

After a couple of minutes she arrived at the final *there*. He was standing naked by the bed. She wore only a negligée, and as she walked toward him, dropped it to the floor.

"Oh God, Curtis!" she breathed in his arms. "Oh God, how I want you! How I've wanted you these three long years!"

Their first lovemaking was quick, almost desperate. Afterward they lay side by side talking, talk which was not quick at all. There was much he hadn't written; much of it would have been deleted by military censors if he had. And things she hadn't written, not wanting to send bad news.

He knew of course that Klara, Mary's grandmother, had died of a heart attack the previous autumn. He'd gotten that letter while in France, training dissident Germans to carry out sabotage and other partisan actions in Hitler's planned "National Redoubt." And he knew that Mary's dad, Fritzi, had married after Klara's death.

Mary had moved out of her father's home because she hadn't gotten along with Margaret, Fritzi's wife. Margaret was basically a good woman, Mary insisted, but bossy and critical, in the kitchen and about the housework. And insisted that Mary, as "her daughter," attend church regularly with Fritzi and herself. Even though Mary was thirty years old, and been married for twelve of them. The matter of church attendance was Margaret's only position that Fritzi had overruled—previously his own attendance had been fitful—and Margaret had backed off without saying anything more about it.

Mary's uncle, Wiiri Saari, owned several rental houses. Lying there on the rumpled bedsheets, the young couple decided to let Wiiri know that when Curtis got out of the army, they'd like to rent one of them.

Curtis suggested they spend the rest of his leave on the coast south of Tillamook Bay, where they'd spent part of his leave in 1942. Mary agreed eagerly. She'd already gotten a week's leave from her job at Wiiri's machine shop. She could probably get it extended.

With a slim finger, Mary followed a long scar on Curtis's right thigh. "I wish—" she said hesitantly, "I wish you didn't have to go back. Mostly I felt sure you'd come home, but sometimes I wasn't very brave. I was so afraid for you. And the Japanese? People say they won't give up, that they'll fight to the bitter end. And you're dearer to me than my own life."

Curtis kissed her gently. "Don't worry," he said, "I won't have to fight the Japanese." He paused, sorting his thoughts. When he spoke again, it was in a monotone, all emotion suppressed. "I was never in ETOUSA; that was a lie, a cover story. In the hospital in England, while I was recuperating, I was recruited by the OSS, because I spoke German well. Railroaded is the word. After they trained me, they smuggled me into Germany on a spy mission. In Bavaria I lived with people I had to kill. Kill for good reasons."

He stopped talking for a long moment. Mary looked worriedly at him, waiting, knowing he wasn't done.

"People I saw every day," he went on. "One of them especially I knew and liked; I had to shoot him in the back. Another I killed treacherously, while he was shaking my hand. I needed to kidnap him, but first I had to make him unconscious, and . . . sometimes you misjudge how much force to use. You can't afford to use too little."

He paused, took a deep breath and let it out slowly. "I'll tell you more about those things sometime." Again he paused. "Those ribbons on my Ike jacket—they include the Distinguished Service Cross, the next highest decoration after the Medal of Honor. That one's from Sicily. I almost bled to death there. One of the two silver stars is from Bavaria; they're one step below the DSC. You can read the commendations that go with them."

He reached, touched her solemn face. Her aura matched her expression. This wasn't easy for her, he knew, but she needed to hear it. "Anyway I'm done with war now," he went on. "For good. It may not be patriotic to feel that way, but I'm done with it. I'll tell you more about that too, someday. It's not only this war. It's stuff from before. From Yuulith, stuff I saw and did there that I never told you about."

With his fingertips he felt the rugged scars of his buttocks, and his voice took on a tone of wry amusement. "This," he said, then ran a finger along the longest of the surgical scars on his right leg, "and these will help me stay out of it. Among the things I did to get ready for Germany was, I practiced walking with a limp. Till it was automatic. Along with my scars, and pretending to be weak-minded, the limp explained why I wasn't in the German army. And kept me out of it while I was there."

Again his voice changed, became dry, matter-of-fact. "I'm due to report at the Pentagon on June 19. When I get there I'll be limping, just a little. And no one will question it; my medical records will take care of that. At worst they'll have me training guys somewhere."

That evening they ate supper with Fritzi and Margaret. Margaret questioned him about the war, his family, his plans. His answers were less than candid; her aura, her tone, her eyes, told him she was looking for things to disapprove of. He felt a powerful urge to shock her, tell her about his weird AWOL at Oujda, in French Morocco. About the voitar and the Bavarian Gate; the promiscuous Berta Stark, now a good wife and foster mother; the sexually ravenous, half-voitik Rillissa; the sorceries in Schloss Tannenberg. Instead he recited generalities.

Afterward he told Mary that Margaret might be good to Fritzi, but he himself wouldn't care to be around her. Though he didn't say so, he was aware that Fritzi was having regrets. Curtis saw auras in much greater detail than Mary did.

The next day they got in their '39 Chevy and drove to the coast. There they rented a tourist cabin, and spent ten lazy days strolling the beach, listening to the gulls, watching the surf break on great boulders and basaltic shelves, and hiking the heavy green forest. He left for D.C. on the 13th, planning to spend a couple of days in Indiana en route, visiting family.

❖   ❖   ❖

Curtis's parents, Charley and Edna, had had no further contact with the Sisterhood. Not that he'd asked—all that was behind him, for good—but they'd have mentioned it. Charley's back had gone bad, and he'd sold the farm to his elder son, Frank. Frank was running beef cattle on it because he couldn't get enough help to raise crops, and couldn't afford to quit his job as shop foreman at Dellmon's Chevrolet. Frank Jr., a platoon sergeant, had come back wounded from France, and was training infantry at Fort McClellan. He wanted to farm the place when the war was over.

Curtis left Indiana feeling both good and bad. The farm he'd grown up on had changed, and his parents had become old in just the three years since he'd last seen them. On the other hand, Frank was looking out for them, and when Frank Jr. got out of the army, the farm would be in good hands.

2

Job Interview

At the Pentagon, Macurdy reported to a major in G-2—Intelligence—who looked him over thoroughly and with disapproval. "The OSS," the major said, "has little or no role in the pending invasion of Japan, and some of its personnel, including yourself, are being transferred to other services. You might have been transferred back to the airborne, but you have twice been transferred out of it as medically unfit. And the Military Police"—he paused, then added wryly: "to which you once were assigned but in which you never served, have rejected you on the basis of your subsequent service behavior.

"There is also the problem of your rank. Your captaincy may have been appropriate to OSS activities, but you lack both the training and the experience to serve as a captain in the airborne or other infantry organization. They might have been interested in you as a sergeant, but not as a captain."

He gazed disapprovingly at the large young man across the desk. Having read his service record, Macurdy's surly expression didn't surprise him. "At any rate," he continued, "for some undecipherable reason you have been assigned to us. Perhaps because of certain very limited similarities of function between G-2 and the OSS. We have found your personnel records both interesting and puzzling. Frankly, your history in the OSS is sufficiently odd and undocumented to bring into question your veracity and your mental health. While the irregularities in your airborne history were impractical to analyze, since so many of the people with whom you served were subsequently killed or invalided out.

"Your combat record, on the other hand, is well documented, and impressive if brief. Overall, however, it seems clear that you showed remarkably little respect for standard procedures, and for army ways of doing things in general. Which you might have gotten away with in the airborne, or"—he grimaced slightly—"the OSS. But not in military intelligence. Even your injuries and medical-surgical history, after the traffic accident in Oujda, are utterly incompatible with your subsequent assignments and combat record." The major peered intently at Curtis, as if hoping to perceive the truth. "Afterward, when reassigned to the Military Police, you avoided the transfer by going AWOL from the hospital, and by some still undetermined subterfuge, inserted yourself into the 505th Parachute Infantry."

He looked down at the blotter on his desk, then up again. "My commanding officer has instructed me to ignore all that, since the results redounded to the benefit of the war effort. So now I am faced with the problem of what duties to assign you. Your alpha score was rather ordinary, and your education ended with 8th grade. Your courage is beyond question, and your German passed as native." He paused. "Despite your conspicuously non-German name. But German is now irrelevant. I can send you to military intelligence school, but by the time you could complete it, we're unlikely to have any need for you."

Again the major paused, his gaze intent. "Tell me, Captain Macurdy, what particular skills do you have to offer, which we might build upon?"

Macurdy scowled a dark, ugly scowl at the major. "I can see and read auras," he answered. "The halos people have around them. Tells me all sorts of things about them. And I see better at night than most. Give me a knife, and I can go around in the dark and kill people without anyone the wiser, till they come across the body. And I can keep warm in the cold; I can go naked all day, in weather you couldn't stand in winter uniform." He seemed to sneer, then raised his exceptionally large hands in front of him, opening, then clenching them. "I can take a horseshoe in either hand and squeeze it shut. I can light fire without matches. I can go a week easy without eating, but I need water every day." He stopped as if done, then added: "And I can shoot fireballs out of my hand. Blow a man's head off without hardly a sound."

Without realizing it, the major had leaned back, away from the man across the desk. Now he looked long and carefully at him. "Thank you, Captain Macurdy," he said carefully. "That was an interesting and informative list of talents. Return to your quarters. You'll be notified of our decision."

While limping down the long corridor, Macurdy whistled so cheerfully, people he passed turned and looked back at him.

3

Making
Adjustments

Curtis's next arrival home was on June 25. He had a medical discharge, based on his old injuries, and was on thirty-day terminal leave. He'd draw his captain's pay till July 23. As before, Mary met him at the depot. They went to her little apartment—theirs now—and made love. Afterward he dressed in civvies, clothes he'd left behind in '42.

"This week," he said, "I'll talk to Fritzi about getting my old job back. If it's going to make any trouble, I'll settle for sergeant on an undersheriff's pay. And if that's not possible . . . I'll worry about that when the time comes.

"Or maybe," he added, watching her intently, "maybe it's time for you and me to go somewhere else." They'd talked about that eventuality even before they were married, but she'd lived in Nehtaka all her life. It wouldn't be easy for her.

"Somewhere we're not known," he went on, "where people won't realize I don't age. Back before I enlisted,

15

maybe four years ago, people already commented on it. Axel Severtson asked me if I'd been drinking from the Fountain of Youth—that I didn't look any older than when I'd worked for him. And Lute Halvoy said I better hurry up and start showing my years, or people would call me a draft dodger.

"And tight as manpower's got to be, with so many off in the military, we can go just about anywhere and find good jobs.

"Think about it. We'll have to do it sooner or later, and in a couple years, when the war's over and all the guys start coming home, jobs might get hard to find. Might even be another depression."

That night they had supper at Fritzi's again. "When do you want to come back to work?" Fritzi asked.

"How does next week sound? I'd like to lay around a few days." Curtis paused. "Is Harvey Chellgren still the undersheriff?"

"*Ja*, and he is a good officer. Maybe a little too political. He likes a little too much to please people. You will be better. And he knows you got the job coming to you, by law and by right. I told him if you take it, I will ask the county to approve a raise for him, to what he's getting now, and we will call him senior deputy. He's got so many friends in the county, the board will probably do it.

"Besides, I'm going to retire in '48, when my term is up. I've already told him I might. He will probably run for sheriff then. You should too. You'd make a better one than him. Then whoever loses can be undersheriff. You two always got along good."

The first thing bad that happened to Curtis was the next day, when he went to see Roy Klaplanahoo's wife and children. Roy, she told him, had been killed in Germany, in Bloody Hürtgen. With the war in Europe almost over, and having survived Sicily, Italy, France and Belgium.

It was almost predictable, but Curtis was crushed. He went home and wept before his dismayed wife. Afterward he told her of the battle of Ternass, in Yuulith. Of the thousands killed, all of them his responsibility, his guilt. How many Roy Klaplanahoos had died there? But Roy had been his friend. There'd been a bond, begun in the hobo jungle outside Miles City, Montana, carrying forward to Severtson's logging camp, and renewed in North Africa.

He told her of other things that had happened in Yuulith, too, things he'd never mentioned before. They'd seemed irrelevant, there'd been no need for her to know, and they'd have stretched her credulity.

"Do you believe me—Mary?" He'd almost called her Spear Maiden! Despite the two being so unlike.

"I believe you, darling," she answered. "I know you too well to doubt your honesty or your sanity. And I see auras too, you know. I even saw some of your mental pictures when you talked." She paused. "I want you to tell me more about Yuulith. Sometime soon. Share it with me. I won't be jealous of your other wives, I promise. I want to know more about them. They must have been good people."

He kissed her gently, and minutes later they went to bed.

That night he awoke from a dream. Of the spear maiden, Melody; he hadn't dreamt of her in years. But the setting was different than in earlier Melody dreams. This one was on the battlefield at Ternass. They lay side by side on the grass, talking. Then someone—Varia, he thought—blew a trumpet, and all the dead got up and brushed themselves off. Roy Klaplanahoo was with them, and the tall voitik corporal, Trosza, whose killing had laid heavily on his conscience. They all mingled, talking and laughing. Then one of them came up to him—Lord Quaie, still with the steaming hole in his belly. And he was not hostile. He was gesturing, his mouth working earnestly, but no words came out.

At that point Curtis wakened. It took awhile to get back to sleep.

He returned as undersheriff the next week, and enjoyed the work again. Loggers, many of them new to him, continued to flood the taverns and dance halls on Saturday evenings. But his reputation had preceded him. The Nehtaka *Weekly Sentinel* had given a brief summary of his military record—primarily assignments, actions, and military honors—provided by the Army's Office of Public Information. This inspired men who knew him from before to retell and exaggerate his prewar exploits in Nehtaka County, both as a law officer and a logger.

None of them knew of his exploits in Yuulith, of course.

Two years after Curtis's return, Fritzi had a stroke. In the hospital, slurring from one side of his mouth, he announced first his appointment of Curtis as acting sheriff, then his own retirement, to take effect at the end of June. In the hospital, and afterward at his home, Curtis sat daily by the bed, healing Fritzi by hand and gaze, sometimes with a silent Margaret looking on coldly. It was obvious to Curtis that she distrusted him.

Ten days later, Fritzi was up and walking, unimpaired. Doc Wesley told Curtis the recovery was a lot quicker and more complete than he'd expected. "I don't know what it is you do, young man," he said, "but I wish I could do it."

Afterward Macurdy imagined Wesley in Oz, apprenticing under Arbel, then returning to Oregon with his new skills. But even if the doctor could be talked into it, it wouldn't be possible. He might survive the transit through the gate—might even retain his sanity—but he'd never make it back.

4

Exposure

For the 1948 Memorial Day celebration in Nehtaka's Veterans' Park, Macurdy and a number of other wounded veterans, of two wars, were asked to participate in a "remembrance" ceremony. Curtis agreed to introduce the other Purple Heart recipients, and to read the list of those who'd died from enemy action.

He took the duty seriously, and practiced the names to avoid grossly mispronouncing any.

As master of ceremonies, Mayor Louie Severtson introduced Curtis: "Here," he said, "is a young man who really ain't so young. I've known him since '33—that's fifteen years ago!—when he was new around here. He was twenty-five then, and didn't hardly look it. He went to war in '42. In '43 he won the Distinguished Service Cross for exceptional heroism in combat, and later served as an OSS spy in Nazi Germany, earning a silver star for gallantry. And after all that, at age forty, he still looks like a twenty-five-year-old."

He turned to Curtis, grinning. "How do you do that, Macurdy?"

It seemed to Curtis his heart had stopped. "It runs in the family," he said. "And clean living helps."

He got through his own presentation, and sat down with a sense of foreboding.

He and Mary had been invited to supper at Fritzi's that evening. Margaret had little to say before and during the meal, but it was obvious she had something on her mind. After pie, they sat over coffee.

"You mentioned your family," Margaret said. "The sheriff says they farm, back in Indiana."

"They did. My dad's retired now."

"How old does *he* look?"

Curtis frowned, but his voice was casual. "About seventy-five, the last time I saw him. He was born in 1872, which makes him seventy-six now. Worked hard all his life."

"Who else in your family looked as young as you do at age forty?"

Curtis's lips had thinned at her question. "My double-great grampa, I'm told. And a great uncle. Actually I lied when I took the deputy job in '33. I was older. And I lied about my age in the army in '42, afraid they wouldn't put a man my actual age in a combat unit. I'm forty-four now."

Fritzi stared uncomfortably at his wife. "Margaret . . ." he began.

She cut him short with a gesture, and another question for Curtis. "I've also heard you were married before."

"Twice."

That stopped her, but only for a moment. "The sheriff told me something about you. About you and Mary, before you were married. When he overheard you talking on the front porch. It was almost like witchcraft, he said, the effect it had on Mary. After that she was changed. She'd always said she'd never marry. She hadn't even gone out with boys."

Curtis's face had turned stony, and his eyes smoldered. "I learned that from my first wife," he said. "She was a witch. From another world. Does that satisfy you?"

Margaret paled, more from his look than his words, but her eyes did not soften. "He is kidding you," Fritzi broke in. His mild accent had thickened, as usual when something upset him. "You had no right to ask him such questions, like a prosecutor. He was right to feel insulted. Now apologize to him!"

She stared pinch-lipped at her husband, then turned back to Macurdy. It was hatred he saw now, in her aura and eyes, and when she spoke, she bit the words out. "If I have wronged you, I apologize."

"You did wrong me," Curtis answered. "Frankly, none of it was your business. I've been part of this community for fifteen years, counting my service time, and I've never wronged anyone here. Not once! I risk my life as a lawman, and risked it a lot more as a soldier, for my country. I met Mary because I risked my life, killing the armed man who'd just shot Fritzi and two other men. I've always had better things to do than to pry in other peoples' private lives."

Abruptly he stood. "Fritzi, I apologize for the upset. You're a good man, one of the best I know. I lived nine happy years in this house with your mother and daughter. I helped heal your gunshot wound. Helped heal Klara after she got hit by that car. To me you're more like a second father than a father-in-law.

"I hope this—clash here tonight, doesn't hurt things between you and your wife. But I will not sit down in this house with her again."

He turned to Mary, who looked distressed. "We'd better go now."

She nodded and got up. "I'm sorry, Papa," she said. "I love you very much. You are welcome in our home any time." She turned to Margaret. "And so are you, if you care to come. But we will not come here. This was my home for more than twenty-five years. My happy home. You have made it dark for me."

Margaret did not get up, but her words and face were as hard as Curtis's had been. "It is not I who brought darkness to this home. I advise you to rid yourself of that person"—she pointed at Curtis—"before it is too late."

Curtis and Mary left, Curtis grimly pleased with himself, and at the same time sick with anger. He and Mary spoke almost not at all as they walked the mile to the small house they'd bought. He did, however, stop at a liquor store for a pint of bourbon. He wanted something to ease his agitation, and was out of practice at meditating. When they got home, he set the bottle on the living room table, where they often read in the evening.

"Curtis," Mary said, "I agree with you that Margaret was completely out of line. She showed me a side of herself I hadn't wanted to recognize before. Now it's in the open. But right now I don't want to talk about it, or about anything. I just want to have a drink of that whiskey, read awhile, then go to sleep. And wake up in the morning to a new day."

Curtis's eyebrows rose. He'd never known Mary to drink, and wondered if she had while he was overseas. He nodded without speaking. Opening the bottle, he poured about two ounces in a tumbler, and put it on the table in front of her. She raised her glass and took a swallow. Her eyes and mouth opened in shock, and she gasped. "So that's what it's like," she said blinking, and shuddered. Then she sat down at the table and opened the *Reader's Digest*. He poured half a glass for himself, took a sip, then sat down with the latest issue of *Blue Book*.

After a couple of pages and several sips, he looked at her glass. The level was down a bit; apparently she was determined. After reading a short story, he left the room, changed into his pajamas and brushed his teeth. By the time he'd returned to the dining room, Mary had finished the two ounces and poured another.

A few minutes later she got up and hurried to the bathroom, closing the door behind her. The next minute or so she spent vomiting and groaning. Curtis went into the kitchen, put the pint on the counter, lit a burner on the stove and put the tea kettle on it. Then he put bread in the toaster, and two tea bags into cups. Finally he spread butter on the toast.

While he waited for the water to get hot, he went into the hall and listened at the bathroom door. She was gargling; a good sign. He went back to the kitchen. While he was pouring water onto their tea bags, she came in looking weak and abashed.

"I made tea," he told her. "And buttered some toast; something easy to take."

"Thanks," she said huskily, and sank onto a chair. Cautiously she tasted the toast, then sipped some tea and took another bite. Curtis sat down and tasted his own, then examined her somewhat diminished aura. "How do you feel?"

She didn't answer at once, as if examining herself. "Actually not too bad," she said. "Weak. Embarrassed. Wiser. But not nauseous or anything. I'll be all right."

"No need to be embarrassed. It's happened to millions. Billions, probably."

She finished her bread. "I don't think I was cut out to drink liquor."

"Lots of people wish they could say that." He stood, and took the bottle off the counter. "Let me show you my magical trick," he said, and poured the contents into the sink. "There. It's gone."

He went to her, and bending, kissed her. She was about to tell him this was not a good night to get amorous, then changed her mind. *It is*, she told herself, *a very good night to get amorous*, and standing, kissed

him back passionately. In the way her Aunt Hilmi had
suggested for healing misunderstandings. It seemed to
her it might work for other traumas. After a moment
he began unbuttoning her blouse.

5

Sunday Service

In June 1948, Harvey Chellgren announced his candidacy for Nehtaka County Sheriff. A naturally social and political creature, he was a son of a large, considerably branched family, a member of the Swedish lodge (from his mother's side) and the Sons of Norway (from his father's). He was also a past master of the local Masonic Lodge, and treasurer of the Moose. Within a month, all four lodges declared their support for him. The local chapters of the American Legion and the Veterans of Foreign Wars, on the other hand, came out for Macurdy. The *Sentinel* published what it knew about both men, and forecast a close race.

The editorial closed with a personality summary. "Harvey," it said, "is bright, outgoing, and friendly. He always tries to handle things with a minimum of bad feelings, but is tough when he has to be. . . . Curtis is mild-mannered, but he has presence. Even if you don't know his military and police record, you tend to do what he tells you. Whichever of these two men is elected, we can expect to have a good sheriff."

❖ ❖ ❖

In earlier years, Fritzi had attended church irregularly, his attitude reflecting that of his mother. Basically, Klara had been somewhat religious, but as a young woman had become alienated by the state Lutheranism of Prussia. She was acutely skeptical of churches and preachers, and at any rate, in Nehtaka there were no services in German, the only language she knew. So she'd gone twice a year, at Christmas and Easter.

Now however, at Margaret's insistence, Fritzi attended church weekly.

Before the war, nudged by whatever unidentified impulse, Curtis had gone to church three or four times a year, and Mary with him. As a child, her Aunt Ruth had taken her regularly to the local Finnish church, where "her mother would have taken her, if she'd lived." Fritzi agreed, and enforced it. But when she'd reached her teens, Mary had resisted, and Klara had supported her. From that time on, she'd attended mainly with Klara, on the old woman's infrequent pilgrimages to Holy Redeemer.

Curtis, after his return, hadn't gone at all, had felt no need to. And the Lutheran liturgy at Holy Redeemer had always confused him; he'd gone too seldom to get the hang of it. At the only other church he'd attended—under duress as a child—the services had been much simpler. But now, Fritzi suggested, as a candidate for office it was well to be seen in church. "You don't have to go every week," he said. "After you're elected, once a month is plenty."

Curtis decided to take the advice, and the following Sunday, he and Mary were at Holy Redeemer Lutheran. In 1943, Pastor Huseby's wife had run off with an airman, and the pastor had moved elsewhere. Now Pastor Albin Koht presided. Mary did not look forward to it. Koht was arrogant and intolerant, she said, more suitable for a Missouri Synod church.

They walked the half mile through lovely summer

weather. The breeze off the Pacific was cool enough that climbing the slope of the final block, they hardly broke a sweat. Axel Severtson and his wife were the greeters. The old logger met them in the vestibule, and wrung Curtis's hand. Grinning he said, "The next time you wisit that Fountain of Youth, don't forget to bring me a bottle of that vater. But don't take too long. I'm coming up sixty-four this fall, you know. And after you hit sixty-five, it don't vork no more."

Curtis liked the organ prelude. Probably, he thought, it would be the high point of the morning. When Pastor Koht stepped to the altar, the pews were perhaps two-thirds full. Pastor Huseby had done better. Koht welcomed the congregation and made some announcements, while Curtis evaluated his aura. Christian love was not apparent there, but rejection and disapproval were evident. Perhaps, Curtis thought, they could try the Finnish church the next time, or the Swedish Covenant. They probably had English language services, and the Finnish church was nearer home.

Koht led the congregation in invoking God, then the sign of the cross, and then in confession. "If we say we have no sin," he intoned, "we deceive ourselves, and the truth is not in us. But if we confess our sins, God who is faithful and just will forgive us, and cleanse us from all unrighteousness." He paused. "We will now bow our heads in silence for reflection and self-examination."

Curtis bowed his head. He did, he thought, know his own sins well enough, had recognized and regretted them. And God, if he knew everything, didn't need Curtis Macurdy to point out either the commission or the remorse. But it was just as well, he supposed, to revisit them again.

"Most merciful God," Koht went on, and the congregation read the response: "Have mercy on us. We confess to you that we have sinned. . . ." Curtis found the place and joined them. Finally Koht intoned: "With joy, I proclaim to you that Almighty God, rich in mercy, abundant in love, forgives you all your sin, and grants you newness of life in Jesus Christ."

Curtis had detected no joy in the pastor. God's mercy and love, he thought, had a poor spokesman at Holy Redeemer. Then told himself wryly, *You're not exactly a fountain of joy and love either, this morning.*

Next they sang a hymn, the first in a series separated by prayers, pastoral readings, and congregational response. During the hymns, Curtis simply mouthed the words. He had a defeatist attitude toward singing. He couldn't read the music, didn't know the hymns, and couldn't manage the high and low parts.

At length, Koht announced the first Bible reading— Exodus 22, verses 18 through 20. His strong voice loudened as he began to read. " 'You shall not permit a witch to live. Whosoever lies with a beast shall be put to death. Whosoever sacrifices to any god, save to the LORD only, shall be utterly destroyed.' "

He paused and referred the congregation to Psalm 1 in the program. Accompanied by the organ, Koht read aloud verses 1, 3, and 5, the congregation interspersing 2, 4, and 6. Macurdy did not read. He told himself that this arrogant pastor would condemn Mary and himself just for being able to see auras.

"Therefore the wicked will not stand in the judgement," Koht finished, "nor sinners in the congregation of the righteous." The congregation wrapped it up with: "For the Lord knows the way of the righteous, but the way of the wicked shall perish."

Koht paused for a long moment. "The next reading," he said, "is Deuteronomy 18, verses 10 through 12." He paused, then read: " 'There shall not be found among you any one that maketh his son or his daughter to pass through the fire, or that useth divination, or an observer of times, or an enchanter or a witch.

Or a charmer, or a consultant with familiar spirits, or a wizard, or a necromancer. For all that do these things are an abomination unto the LORD: and because of these abominations the LORD thy God doth drive them out from before thee.'

"This is the word of the LORD," Koht finished.

"Thanks be to God," the congregation responded.

Again Koht paused, then bowed his head and prayed, asking that God strengthen the congregation in their will to resist and reject evil. While Koht prayed, Curtis thought of Varia. By biblical criteria, she no doubt did qualify as a witch, though she certainly didn't think of herself as one. To his knowledge, her magicks were neutral at worst. Usually they helped, though he couldn't guarantee the same for the rest of the Sisterhood. Certainly not Sarkia. But as far as he knew, none of them dealt with, or even believed in demons. They sought to learn and master potentials in the Web of the World.

Not that he'd explain any of that to the reverend. It would be a waste of time.

When Koht had finished praying, he scanned his audience. "The homily for today," he said, "is 'Sorcery, the Neglected Sin.'

"In reading Exodus 22, it is interesting to note the order in which God gave his admonitions to Moses. God's warning against witchcraft came ahead of his pronouncement against lying with beasts and worshiping false gods."

He paused, his gaze intent. "But what, exactly, is a witch? Must it be an old woman in a peaked hat, flying around on a broom? Regarding the verse in Exodus, today's biblical scholars, with older manuscripts to work from, and more accurate understanding of ancient Hebrew, translate the Hebrew word in Exodus as 'female sorcerer.' While in the verses in Deuteronomy, both 'witch' and 'wizard' are from the Hebrew for 'sorcerer.'

"So a witch is a sorcerer, someone who practices sorcery. And what exactly is sorcery? The examples I read from Deuteronomy can serve as at least a partial definition. Meanwhile my dictionary defines sorcery as: 'The use of power gained from the assistance or control of evil spirits.' "

He paused, looking over the silent congregation. "But this is 1948. Is it possible there are sorcerers around today? And evil spirits? In a place like Nehtaka County? If there are, how may we recognize them? In Matthew 7, verse 20, Jesus tells us: 'By their fruits shall ye know them.' In other words, by their results. He was talking about false prophets, but the same principle applies to any person."

Macurdy began to feel uncomfortable. Where was Koht leading with this bullshit?

"Consider the morality tale, *The Picture of Dorian Gray*, in which the principal character lives a life of utter evil, yet does not age. *Does not age! Does not deteriorate!* In that case due to sorcery woven into a picture."

Macurdy stared dumbfounded, his stomach sinking. Mary's hand squeezed his. Koht preached on.

"That is a novel, of course, a work of fiction. But it carries a powerful truth and lesson. If you believe that Evil cannot wear a pleasant visage, that Satan cannot give good fortune on Earth to those who worship him, you have not read, or have not heeded, your Bible. So. Is there a sorcerer in our community? I tell you that there is—and that you know him."

Curtis did not get up and walk out. To leave would draw attention, suggest a guilty conscience. How, he wondered, could this be happening in America in 1948?

The sermon was not long. Koht's faults did not include infatuation with his own voice. He ended with, "So then, if we find a sorcerer in our midst, or other evildoer as defined in the Bible, shall we run into the

fields and pick up stones, and stone him to death? Or
her? In the Book of John, chapter 8, verse 7, Jesus said,
'Him that is without sin among you, let him cast the
first stone.' And of course, no one was. Or is. While in
Deuteronomy 18:12 it is written, 'God doth drive them
out from before thee.' And how did God drive them
out? By the hand of the children of Israel! It comes
down to *people*, God-fearing *people*, like you and me!

"Yet Christ said we are to obey Caesar, that is, obey
the government. And the government does not allow
us to forcibly evict someone from our community except
by law. Which in fact does remove many evildoers from
among us. Removes them and sends them to the pen-
itentiary. But unfortunately, the laws do not recognize
sorcery as real, as genuine sin.

"So again, what can *we* do? While the sorcerer may
be free to move among us physically, we can shut him
out of our lives, have nothing to do with him. *Shun*
him."

He stopped abruptly, leaving people hanging, causing
their minds to reach. After a long moment he said simply,
"Let us pray," and bowed his head.

The rest of the service was a fog to Macurdy. When
it was over, the congregation filed slowly from the sanctuary. Again Axel and Sara Severtson stood at its door,
greeters in reverse, making friendly remarks, Axel shaking hands. When Curtis reached him, the old Swede
not only shook his hand, but gripped his shoulder, saying
something that didn't register. Instead of following the
crowd to the basement for coffee and cake, Curtis and
Mary left the building.

It was, he told himself, time to leave Nehtaka. But
he said nothing, because the place that came to his
mind wasn't a place he could take Mary. The transit
might kill her.

6

Fall-Out

Koht's allusion was not lost on his congregation, and he received considerable flack from members. A meeting of male parishioners was called to discuss the issue. Koht admitted that the sorcerer he had in mind was Undersheriff Curtis Macurdy. When questioned further, he said that Macurdy's failure to age was only part of the information he had against him, but he refused to elaborate, or name his source.

A vote was taken to remove him from the pulpit, but it fell short of a majority of the total male membership. At that, one of the members stated that he was resigning his membership, and walked out, followed by several others. On the following Sunday, attendance at Holy Redeemer was the lowest of memory. Some of the missing showed up at the Swedish Covenant Church, where Sunday morning services were already held in English, and the Finnish Lutheran Church, where English services were held in the evenings.

Three weeks later, Koht was rebuked by the synod, and resigned. Most of Holy Redeemer's missing members returned when he left, but the congregation had been factionalized. Now several Koht loyalists withdrew.

Meanwhile the story of his sermon circulated widely through Nehtaka County. Charges were made that Harvey Chellgren was behind it, and though most people didn't take them seriously, Harvey felt compelled to deny them. When questioned, Curtis said he'd known Harvey too long and too well to believe he'd do such a thing. Mary and he had Harvey and his family over to supper one evening, making sure the *Sentinel* learned of it, and a couple of weeks later, Chellgren returned the courtesy. The rumor died.

Fritzi had not walked out of the parishioners' meeting, but neither did he attend Koht's service the following Sunday. Instead he stayed home and listened to the Mormon Tabernacle Choir. At his firm insistence, Margaret stayed home too. He'd asked her point-blank if she had talked to Koht about Curtis's healings, and she admitted defiantly that she had.

He thought of telling Mary—his strong sense of honesty was pressing him—but when Koht resigned, he decided to leave well enough alone. The damage was done, and seemed less severe than he'd feared at first.

Two weeks later he had his first heart attack.

Three weeks before the election, a sawmill worker beat up his wife and threw her out of the house naked. The man had a history of arrests for violence, and had served time. Macurdy and a deputy went to arrest him. The man shot at them through a window, the bullet striking the police car, and yelled curses at Macurdy, whom he called "a creature of Satan."

From cover behind the police car's heavy engine block, Macurdy tried to talk the man into surrendering.

The man replied that Mary's barrenness was God's punishment. Then he fired another round and disappeared from sight. That bullet smashed through two patrol car windows.

Macurdy fired his .38-caliber revolver once, then rushed the house, covered by the deputy with a rifle. There was no return fire. He found the man dead in his living room. Macurdy's bullet had struck him in the throat.

The required hearing found Macurdy not at fault for the death. A minority opinion, though not recommending a reprimand, held that Macurdy should have continued talking with the culprit. The community in general rejected the criticism as bullshit, saying the man had gotten what he had coming.

Curtis, however, brooded over it. It seemed to him the minority opinion was correct.

Two weeks later, with Mary's blessing, he appointed Harvey Chellgren acting sheriff, then resigned, and withdrew from the sheriff's race. He and Mary would have left Nehtaka then, except for Fritzi's ill health.

The same day he resigned, Curtis went to Berglund's Logging Supplies and Equipment, and bought one of the new chainsaws—a 115-pound Disston. From Saari Ford he bought a pickup. Then he hired Paul Klaplanahoo, Roy's youngest brother, as a partner, and went logging for Lars Severtson. He told Mary it felt good to work in the woods again. He lost weight (he'd been getting fat), felt better physically, and insisted it was good to get away from law enforcement.

7

Fritzi's Cabin

In May '49, Fritzi had a coronary, and died. In his will he left the house to Margaret, along with his investments; he held mortgages on several properties. To Mary he left $10,000 cash—a lot of money!—and an abandoned homestead, one hundred sixty acres grown up to young Douglas-fir and hemlock. Rascal Creek ran through it. It was twenty-six miles from town, had a four-room log house with loft, a frame barn, a couple of log sheds and a privy. Fritzi had given the house a new roof and other essential repairs, and used it as a hunting cabin.

Curtis suggested they sell the land and leave. The word was, there were lots of logging jobs in Montana and northern Idaho. If they went there, he could call himself thirty; Mary could still pass for thirty. But she was pregnant. "I want to stay, to be near Dr. Wesley," she said, remembering her several miscarriages. And Curtis agreed.

With serious money in the bank, they decided he'd quit work for a while and fix up the cabin, make it suitable to live in. Drill a well so it wouldn't be necessary to haul water from the creek, put on a front porch, add a bathroom and laundry on the rear, install an electric generator . . . Using his saw, a hired 'dozer, and a rented truck, he could widen and gravel the one hundred fifty yards of dirt lane between the state road and the house. They could advertise the place in the Portland *Oregonian*. Well-to-do city people were paying good money for summer homes.

He worked on the cabin all summer and into the fall. Mostly he commuted from Nehtaka, over the hilly, winding state road, graveled but washboardy. But when he was pushing on some project, he sometimes batched in the cabin for two or three days, working by lamplight. His intention was to finish before the rainy season arrived.

Occasionally Mary went with him when he commuted, to do light tasks, being careful not to strain or tire herself. But mostly she stayed home. There she sewed curtains, and being handy with tools, built shelves, birdhouses, bird feeders . . .

By mid-September, they were in love with the house, and decided to live there themselves, after the baby came. The Severtsons would begin logging soon on a tract twenty miles beyond the cabin. Curtis would work there, commuting.

By mid-October the place was done. It had a hybrid wood-and-propane stove in the kitchen, a refrigerator, a small diesel generator and pump house, a shower in the bathroom . . . and for possible instances when the generator might break down, a new privy behind a screen of rhododendrons. At Mary's insistence, Curtis had converted a small shed into a sauna; everyone in her Finnish mother's clan had one in the backyard. The larger shed he'd rehabilitated for storage, to make up for the lack of a basement.

Fritzi's hunting cabin had become their dream home. It seemed to them they might not leave Oregon after

all, certainly not for years. People in Nehtaka were used
to the idea that Curtis didn't age, and while there were
those who felt as Pastor Koht had, and Margaret, the
couple could live with that.

Their daughter was born on November 2. She was
flawless, beautiful. They named her Hilmi, after Mary's
favorite aunt. On a late-November day, beneath sea-
sonal clouds with intervals of sunshine, Curtis moved
their household goods to their new home. He'd agreed
to start cutting for Lars Severtson on December 5. And
Mary had the Chevy. She could drive to town whenever she wanted.

Paul Klaplanahoo had gone to work on an uncle's
fishing trawler, so Curtis traded in his 115-pound Disston on a new, 65-pound McCullough, figuring to single-
hand it. Lars Severtson was skeptical. "I doubt even
you can do it by yourself," he said. "You're strong enough
the bucking will go okay, but some of those firs are
six, seven feet through. With those handlebars, cutting
the slant on the undercut will be a bear and a half."

Curtis said if he had to, he'd cut the slant with the ax.

Single-handing proved beastly hard, wearing a heavy,
waterproofed canvas jacket and pants against the rain
and the devil's-club. And while his spiked boots, for the
most part, kept him from slipping on fallen trees, they
didn't help a lot on steep slopes. The first couple of days
he seriously considered taking a day or two off, and finding
a partner after all. But that would complicate life, and
besides, single-handing was a challenge he'd come to
enjoy. By Christmas the work was going smoothly, and
he felt stronger than ever before in his life. The rain,
the cold, the slippery footing, the incredibly heavy work—
none of it bothered him. Between the job and his little
family, he was enjoying life immensely.

He was 45 years old.

❖　　　❖　　　❖

The rains had been frequent, sometimes persistent, and occasionally heavy. On February 17, a major storm blew in. The rain poured, and the wind made woodswork dangerous. At noon, Lars pulled everyone out of the woods who hadn't come out on their own. Macurdy loaded his gear in the back of his pickup and started home. Where the road crossed draws, the creeks were bankful, and in one place an overtaxed culvert threatened to wash out.

When he got home, the Chevy was gone, with Mary and the baby. Why they might go to town on that particular day, he couldn't imagine, short of injury or illness. Tight with apprehension, he stowed his gear in the shed, then got back in the pickup and started after them.

Three miles down the road, he found the Chevy. Another culvert had begun to wash out. The car had hit it, gone out of control, and smashed into a tree. Mary was dead, her chest crushed by the steering column. Little Hilmi was gone, her basket thrown out an open door.

Macurdy howled, grasped the tree with his big hands and beat his head on its trunk. Abruptly he stopped, and began thrashing around in the brush and devil's-club, looking for Hilmi. Not there. In the creek then. He broke into a trot, bulling through the brush along the stream bank, watching for the basket. Within a hundred yards he found it, bobbing upside-down, lodged against the limbs of a fir that had fallen across the stream. He plunged into the turbid rushing water, normally not knee-deep, now above his waist. Dropping to his knees in it, he groped among submerged branches, searching by feel.

After several minutes, blue with cold, he clambered dripping from the water, bellied over the fallen fir, and charged stumbling downstream again. He was too distraught to draw warmth from the Web of the World; it didn't occur to him.

An hour later, other loggers, who'd found his pickup and the wrecked car, found Macurdy. Like some huge beaver, he was groping beneath another blowdown, submerged. They saw him when he came up for air. He did not resist when they dragged him from the icy water.

They took him to town with them. He sat dumbly, shivering violently despite the heater blowing on him, whether from shock or cold they didn't know.

Wiiri and Ruth Saari took him in that night. They were as close to kin as he had in Nehtaka. They did almost all the talking, they and Pastor Ilvessalo from the Finnish church, whom they'd called in. Their guest sat slumped in a wingbacked chair, wearing flannel pajamas and a bathrobe belonging to their large son, off on a football scholarship at Oregon State. The wind whooshed around the house corners and porch posts, and the rain pelting the windows sounded almost as harsh as sleet. Macurdy's responses were mostly monosyllables. At length the pastor put his raincoat on to leave. Only then did Macurdy speak at any length. "Thank you, Pastor," he said. "Thank you, Wiiri. And Ruth. You've helped. You've all helped." Then he relapsed.

After the pastor left, Wiiri helped Macurdy to the guest room. "Sleep," he said from the door. "You won't feel good in the morning, but at least you'll feel alive."

Macurdy lay for some while in a sort of stupor. After a time, it seemed to him that Mary was there in the room. Mary and someone else, whom he could sense but not see. "Hello, darling," Mary said. "Do you know who's with me?"

He stared, unable to respond.

"It's Hilmi, dear. Our daughter. We're fine. We're both fine. And you will be. You'll be fine too. We love you very much."

Through brimming eyes he watched her fade, then sobbed himself quietly to sleep.

The funeral was on February 21, in the Finnish church. A double funeral. Little Hilmi's body had been found floating in the Nehtaka River, a remarkable distance downstream from where she'd died. Her casket was kept closed.

By that time Macurdy was functional, but seemed an automaton. A number of Severtson's loggers attended. Most were as uncomfortable in church as they were in suits. They'd have loved to carry him off to a tavern with them, get him drunk and hear him laugh. But it was, of course, out of the question.

He was more alert than he seemed. When Margaret Preuss came in with her new boyfriend, he wondered how long this one would last.

Wiiri gave the eulogy, breaking once despite his Finnish stoicism.

After the service, the attendees filed past, most murmuring condolences, the loggers shaking Macurdy's strong hand with their own. But afterward, the only one he remembered clearly was Margaret. She said nothing, but her eyes, her smile, bespoke satisfaction. Victory.

She had no idea how close she was to having her throat crushed in his hands. But he had places to go, and though he didn't consciously know it, things to do.

PART TWO
The Lion Returns

Kurqôsz stared down from his seven-foot-eight-inch height. His eyes seemed greener, his bristly hair more red, his skin more ivory than Macurdy remembered. His easy laugh was amiable and chilling.

"What then, you ask? Why, we will conquer, as our distant ancestors did in Hithmearc. And do what we please. First of all it will please us to punish the ylver for escaping us. Then we will domesticate the other peoples who dwell there, culling the intransigent. Cattle are invariably more profitable than their wild progenitors."

Crown Prince Kurqôsz
in a dream by Curtis Macurdy
while at Wolf Springs

8

Good-byes and Farewells

In a black mood, Macurdy sold the house in town to Wiiri, from whom he'd bought it. He was leaving Nehtaka County, he said, leaving at once. Wiiri bought the pickup, too, and the saw. As a small-town entrepreneur, he bought and sold a lot of different things.

Mary's Aunt Hilmi offered to broker the sale of the quarter section and its buildings for him. She had wealthy connections in Portland. He said he didn't want to wait, and didn't want anything further to do with the place. So she bought it herself, for what seemed to him a lot of money. She warned him she expected to make money on it. He told her good enough, and welcome to it.

Having converted almost everything he owned into cash, he deposited it in the Nehtaka Bank, in a savings account. The banker suggested more lucrative investments, but he refused them. He then willed it all to his parents, their heirs and assigns, with Frank as executor.

Wiiri had suggested he keep the pickup for transportation, but Macurdy said the railroads and Greyhound would provide all the transportation he needed. When Wiiri asked where he was going, he said to visit his parents. From there, he added, he expected to leave the States, and go to the country his first wife had come from.

He did not, of course, specify the country.

On the 2,400-mile train ride to Indiana, he had abundant uninterrupted time. To think, if he cared to. Some of it he spent watching the mountains slide by, and the Great Plains. Saw pronghorn and coyotes, cattle gathered around toadstool-shaped haystacks, and great expanses of snow. Some of it was spent brooding on the past, and on what might have been. And much he spent reading—a Max Brand novel and *Blue Book*—escapist adventures.

But he spent none of it planning his future. He already knew what he'd do for his parents. As for himself, he had only intentions of a general sort. He didn't know what conditions he'd find.

One thing though he'd surely do: learn whether Varia was still married. She probably was, and her ylvin lord was a hell of a good man, any way he looked at it.

He spent several days on the farm with his parents. They lived now in the house where Will had lived, and Varia. Frank Jr., his wife and children, lived in the larger house. Curtis told them of losing his wife and daughter, and that he was going to the country where Varia was. "Who knows?" he said. "Maybe she lost her husband. Maybe we can get back together." It was an explanation, something to ease them, and who could say it wouldn't happen.

Frank Sr. and Edith weren't surprised at his youth. After they'd seen Curtis in '42, Charley had told them the family secret, about its occasional men who didn't age. Now Frank and Edith, in turn, told Frank Jr. and his wife. Curtis transferred his account in the Nehtaka Bank to one in Salem, Indiana. He made Frank Sr. a signator, and told him to manage it however he saw fit, for their parents' benefit. The money spooked Frank—he wanted nothing to do with it. But when Curtis countered that his only alternatives were lawyers and bankers, Frank reluctantly agreed.

He also had a new will drawn up—the old one retailored to Indiana law. He then told Frank he didn't expect ever to be back.

It was easy to leave Indiana again. The only things he took with him were the knife given him by the Ozian shaman, Arbel, along with several silver teklota and a couple of gold imperials. He'd left them in a dresser drawer when he'd gone to Oregon in '33, and it seemed to him he should have them when he returned to Yuulith.

It was a Saturday when Macurdy got off the train in Columbia, Missouri. Charles Hauser was there to meet him. They gripped hands, then to Macurdy's surprise, Hauser threw his arms around him and hugged him.

"God but it's good to see you, Macurdy!" he said. He stood back with his hands on the larger man's arms, grinning at him. "You don't know how good! And you're hard! Hugging you is like hugging an oak!" He stepped back half a step. "And young-looking! It's those ylvin genes, sure as heck. It was never real to me before that you wouldn't age, but you look as if you'd skipped those seventeen years."

Curtis shook his head. "They weren't skipped."

Hauser waited for him to elaborate, and when he didn't, spoke to fill the vacuum. "I didn't realize, till you phoned, how much I needed someone to talk with about the years in Yuulith. It was like an itch with no one to help scratch. An itch I'd gotten used to, but I still feel it from time to time."

Hauser had long since given up on ever hearing from Macurdy. They'd said good-bye on a showery spring day in 1933, at the Greyhound depot in St. Louis. Macurdy had Hauser's family's address, and had promised to write when he got settled, but never had. Then, three days past, Hauser had gotten a phone call. Macurdy had found him through Hauser's brother, on the farm in Adair County.

"Have you eaten lunch?" Hauser asked.

"No, I haven't."

"Good. I know a place." He laughed. "Chinese. The food's not great, but the help doesn't understand much English, so we can talk freely. There are things you need to know before you meet my wife. Our stories need to gibe."

They sat over lunch for an hour and a half, getting refills on the tea. Macurdy said little, mostly monosyllables. It was Hauser who talked, his story beginning with their return from Yuulith. Before he could go back to the university and complete his graduate work, he'd realized, he'd have to account for the years he'd been gone. He and Professor Talbott. And if he'd told the real truth, the university would have dismissed him promptly as insane.

So before returning home to Adair County, he'd lived for several weeks in a flophouse in St. Louis. His days and evenings he'd spent in the downtown library, doing research for a fictional explanation that might be believed. The result was a story almost as bizarre as the truth, but far more acceptable.

The '30s were a period when stories by Melville, Stevenson, London, Conrad, Maugham—and films based on them—had made the little known reaches of Oceania seem both real and romantic to millions. Hauser laughed. "Before the war put it in a different light, and changed all that.

"I had more than ten years to account for, in a way that explained Talbott's absence, and why I hadn't notified anyone. What I came up with explained other disappearances around Injun Knob, as well.

"A number of banks had been robbed in the mid-South, in the years after the First World War. My story was that several bank robbers had holed up on an old farm near Neeley's Corners, and Talbott and I ran into them by accident. They didn't know how much we knew, so they tied us up. What they were doing, actually, was financing a gun-running operation for would-be rebels in Peru, the APRA."

Hauser had shifted into a delivery sounding like personal history instead of fiction. "From there they took us with them as captives and flunkies, on an auxiliary schooner headed for Peru. We went through the Panama Canal bound hand and foot in a storage locker. Once in the Pacific, the schooner's crew murdered the bank robbers and headed west for the Orient. Apparently the captain knew about the money, and decided he had better uses for it than to finance rebellion.

"And they took Talbott and me along, still as flunkies. We knew only that we were headed west. Neither of us spoke Spanish, but both of us heard the name Manila repeatedly. After a few weeks, we ran into a bad storm. The schooner lost her masts, the diesel broke down, and she was half-filled with water. Our captors abandoned her in the lifeboat, leaving us behind.

"That night the storm died down, and we were still afloat. The next day we got lucky—another small sailing ship picked us up. We had no idea what language they spoke to each other. To us they spoke pidgin, but no more than they needed for giving orders. We were still flunkies."

Hauser grunted musingly, as if remembering those

times. "Eventually we got to some godforsaken islands, their home. And Talbott's grave. I don't know what he died of. He seemed to just wear out. I was still pretty much a slave, not treated badly, but worked hard.

"Most of the people were fishermen and subsistence farmers, but some of their men were in interisland trade, hauling goods on their homemade sailing ships. And some I suspect were pirates. I still don't know where I was. The Malay Archipelago probably, or the Moluccas. Like the crew, the people spoke pidgin to me. Later I was taken as crew on another sailing vessel, and ended up on still another island, where I was put to work husking coconuts."

He made it sound as if it had really happened. "From there," Hauser continued, "I worked my way on different boats, figuring that sooner or later I'd get somewhere civilized. Eventually I wound up at Batangas, in the Philippines. It felt literally like a dream, seeing stores, carremetos, even motor vehicles—and actually being answered in English! You can't imagine what it was like. Except, of course, you can."

He grinned at Macurdy. "We can account for you as an orphaned kid I took under my wing, on a tramp steamer from Manila. You were eight years old."

Concocting the story had been the easy part, he went on. Learning enough to make it real and convincing had taken most of his time. Finally he'd left St. Louis, and hitchhiked to his family's farm, where he'd spent the summer working for his older brother. In September he went back to the university. After rehabbing and updating his science, he'd been hired as a teaching assistant, and completed his master's studies. Then he'd been hired as an instructor, and later promoted to assistant professor.

"It's been a good life, Macurdy," he finished. Serious now. "The bad times—the years of slavery in Oz—don't seem as bad in retrospect. 'Time heals' can be

more than a cliché." He paused, then added: "If you
let it."

He looked at his watch. "It's time to take you home
with me. Grace will wonder if something's happened
to us. Later we'll go somewhere and talk some more.
And I'll nag you till you open up to me."

Hauser's home was a pleasant bungalow near the
campus. His amiable, middle-aged wife made Macurdy
welcome, and did not ask intrusive questions. They sat
around and talked idly about current affairs—political, international, the approaching baseball season . . .

After supper, Hauser excused himself and Macurdy,
and they "went for a long walk." The evening was mild
for early March, but coats were welcome. Briefly they
walked around the campus, talking idly again, Hauser
nudging Curtis verbally, trying still unsuccessfully to
draw him out. Then they went to Hauser's office in
the Physics Building, hung up their coats and sat down.

"So," Hauser said bluntly. "What brought you here?
Obviously it wasn't any compulsion to tell me what you've
been doing. You haven't said 'peep' about your life."

Curtis sat silently for another long moment. "I'm
heading for Injun Knob," he said at last. "I'm going
back to Yuulith."

"Huh! What brought that on?"

Speaking slowly at first, and in a monotone, Macurdy
gave a synopsis of the past seventeen years. He didn't
cover everything—among other things, he left out passing through the Bavarian Gate, and his weeks in Hithmearc. But he provided a basic picture. By the time
he'd finished, he seemed to Hauser a little more like
the old Macurdy, as if looking back had put things in
perspective.

Hauser nodded. "I understand," he said. "C'mon.
Let's go home."

❖   ❖   ❖

On Sunday morning, Macurdy went to church with them, an Episcopal church. The sermon had nothing to do with witchcraft or shunning. After dinner, the two men walked to the campus, sat in Hauser's office again and talked, Macurdy participating somewhat.

Even as a slave, Hauser had pondered on how two parallel worlds, with their differences and their gates, could exist in an orderly cosmos. He was, after all, a professor of physics. But he'd come up with nothing very satisfying.

"Did you ever talk with Arbel about it?" Macurdy asked.

Hauser shook his head. "Arbel never showed a sign of thinking outside the traditional Yuulith cosmogony he'd grown up with. His was a wisdom of doing. He knew a lot of things intuitively, but not beyond those that were useful to what he did as an Ozian shaman.

"I'm sure he never wondered about the gate. To him it just was, a fact of life."

Macurdy nodded. "I guess I'm like Arbel in that. I'm not much for wondering."

Hauser chuckled. "You and most of the world."

"I remember you saying something about parallel universes."

Hauser nodded. "Even then I knew quite a bit of quantum theory. According to one notion, every time a decision is made, the universe splits. So theoretically there's an infinite number of universes. And theoretically, Yuulith could be one of them."

Macurdy frowned. "Sounds like an awful lot of universes. Where would they all fit?"

"They wouldn't have to *fit* anywhere. They'd be mutually exclusive. In any one universe, the others wouldn't exist."

Macurdy looked at the idea. "But Yuulith exists. You and I know that. And there's a gate between them, so in a way, they exist together."

Hauser shrugged. "Whatever is, is, whether we can explain it or not. And if something is, there's a true explanation for it, whether we've worked it out or not."

He paused. "D'you know what bothers me most? Our guns. They didn't work on the other side."

"Maybe they would have, if our cartridges had still had powder in them."

Hauser ignored the reply. "The rules of chemistry can't be different there. If they were, too many things would be changed: biochemistry, the metabolism of humans, other animals, plants . . . They'd be different, very different, all across the board." He shook his head. "Presumably our cartridges had powder in them on this side, and it was gone on the other. As if—as if God had emptied them in transit. My problem with that is, if there is a god, I can't believe he'd work that way. He'd set up the basic rules, and things would operate accordingly."

Macurdy shrugged. "It happened. That's enough for me. I pried the slugs out of three cartridges—two .44s and one .45-.70. None of them had any powder at all." He paused, remembering the TNT the Nazi SS had stockpiled for the voitar. Why hadn't the voitar accepted it? Probably because they'd taken some through, or tried to, and it hadn't worked. But it sure as hell did on this side. "Whatever happened," he finished, "it was probably in the gate. It has rules of its own."

Hauser shook his head. "There still has to be some physico-chemical reason," he said, and grinned without humor. "Every now and then I wallow around with that for an hour at a time. Then I pour myself a short glass of scotch, and read a mystery novel. Where everything's explained in the last chapter."

The next day, Hauser took his guest to the railroad depot, where he saw him off on a train to Poplar Bluff. He'd suggested that Macurdy wait till Thursday, a partly open day for him. Then he'd drive him to Injun Knob in his car. Macurdy had declined the offer. "I need to get on with it," he'd said.

On the platform beside the train, Hauser took a gold coin from his watch pocket, and held it out to him. "I still have one of those imperials you gave me—my lucky gold piece. Take it. You might need it."

Macurdy smiled, something he hadn't often done on this visit. "You keep it. I've got a couple of them too, and some silver teklota. And my luck is getting better on its own. I can feel it."

Hauser returned the coin to his pocket, and the two men shook hands. Hauser laughed. "I almost told you to write, and let me know how you're doing."

Macurdy added his own laugh, then the conductor called, "All aboard!" The two men shook hands, and Macurdy swung aboard the train. Hauser waited on the platform till the car began to pull away. They waved good-bye to each other through a window, then Hauser left.

9

Injun Knob

It was a considerable hike from Neeley's Corners to the conjure woman's tiny farmhouse at the foot of Injun Knob. The road was better than it had been in 1933. It was graveled and graded. Macurdy took no luggage, carrying nothing except the coins, and the sheath knife Arbel had given him. He wore jump boots, a set of army surplus fatigues, a surplus field jacket and fatigue cap. He needed none of it to keep him warm—he drew on the Web of the World—but he'd long preferred not to be too apparent about it.

It was twilight when he approached the cabin, the roof and walls of which were built of shakes. The only conspicuous change was a cross in the front yard, taller than Macurdy. He was still a couple hundred feet away when a large farm dog rushed raging and roaring from beneath the stoop, to dance around Macurdy not six feet distant, showing lots of teeth, forcing him to stop and pivot, and keep facing it. He'd about decided to shoot a plasma ball at it when a man stepped onto the stoop, shouting angrily. Reluctantly, the growling dog drew back, then trotted off behind the house.

Macurdy continued to the cabin. The waiting man appeared to be in his thirties, and looked gaunt but strong. "What can I do for yew?" he asked.

"I've walked from Neeley's Corners," Macurdy told him.

It wasn't an answer, but the man stepped back. "Well c'mon in. I expect yer hungry." Macurdy entered. "Flo," the man said, "we got us a visitor. A hungry one. Fry up some eggs and fat back."

Without a word, she put aside her mending and went into the kitchen. "Sit," the man told him, and gestured to a homemade cane chair. "What brings ya into these parts?"

Macurdy sat, realizing he hadn't concocted a covering story. "To see the old woman that used to live here," he said. "I knew her when I was a boy. Wondered if she was still alive."

"She's not," the man replied. Scowling now. "Dead a dozen years. She was a witch, and the Devil finally took her." He got up, turning to the kitchen. "Flo, hold up on those eggs and salt pork." Then he faced Macurdy again. "What sort of truck did yew have with her?"

Macurdy looked coolly up at him. "She introduced me to the mountain. Injun Knob." An impulse struck him. "The holy mountain."

The man flinched as if struck, and his answer was a startling near shout. "It was a curséd mountain, while she was here! The Devil come to it every month! Took living sacrifices, held orgies! When we first come here, we built the cross agin it in the front yard, and prayed morning and night! We still pray daily to God to keep it clean!" His eyes flared. "Holy mountain! If that's what yew think of it . . ."

Standing, Macurdy cut him off. "Mister," he said calmly, "that old conjure woman was twice the Christian you are." He paused, while the man stared bugeyed. "I'll tell you why I came here. I'm going up the

mountain and open it up again. I've been through it
before, and others like it. And I'll tell them on the other
side . . ."

The man roared with anger, then stepped toward
the fireplace, reaching for an old shotgun hanging
there.

Macurdy gestured, and instantly the shotgun's barrel and metal fittings were searing hot. When the man
took it from its pegs, he squealed with unexpected pain
and cast it from him. The shell in the chamber went
off spontaneously, pellets gouging a wall. Terrified, he
fell to his knees, his blistering hands cupped in front
of him.

"Bring water!" Macurdy said to the woman who
stared in from the kitchen door. Then he turned and
walked out. The dog didn't appear. As if it knew better.

Macurdy was in a state of self-disgust as he started
up the forested knob. *You're lucky that shotgun didn't
blow a hole in you,* he told himself. *Would have served
you right, after mocking and insulting that poor ignorant sonofabitch. He only did what he thought was right.
If you're not careful, you'll turn into another Margaret.*

It occurred to Macurdy then to wonder about the
efficacy of prayer. Did it actually work? *Sometimes,* he
decided. *When the cause is just.* But still—

What would he do if the gate didn't open anymore?
He himself had destroyed the Bavarian Gate, though
by nothing as mild as prayer. He wondered if Hithmearc, the land it had led to, was in the same universe
as Yuulith. There was, he decided, no way to know.
Meanwhile, if the man's prayers had shut off the Ozark
Gate, maybe he could find the Kentucky Gate.

At the very top of Injun Knob, another cross had
been raised. Midnight was hours away. He sat down
and leaned against it, feeling somehow soothed and
relaxed. There was a promise of hard frost in the air,

and he thought the formula that tapped the Web of the World for warmth.

He was, he told himself, wise to go back to Yuulith. He had friends there. And people were used to the idea of some folks not aging, because the ylver and the Sisters didn't age. Not till they'd lived close to a century. Then, of course, they went downhill like a runaway buggy with a stone wall at the bottom.

He closed his eyes, wondering if just possibly he could connect with Vulkan psychically from where he sat. But nothing happened, and his mind wandered. He thought of Omara. What might she think of marrying him? Would the Sisterhood allow it? Would she still feel the way she had about him? But first he'd look up Varia. Maybe Cyncaidh *had* died. Of course, if he had, Varia might have married someone else. She had no reason to expect *him* back.

He realized what he was thinking, and it struck him as disloyal to Mary, so recently buried. But the thought lacked teeth. He was on the doorstep to another world, another universe. Continuation of another life.

Then he slipped into sleep, and dreamed good dreams that he wouldn't remember.

10

Wolf Springs

There was a moment of startled nightmare as the gate sucked Macurdy in, then spit him out, to roll across last summer's wet grass and leaves.

The crossing had wakened him like a tomcat dropped into a pit of bulldogs. But the transit was familiar now, and the fear a momentary reaction to being jerked violently and unprepared from sleep. On the Oz side it was drizzling, and daylight, the noon nearest the full moon. (The phases of the moon were in synch with the phases on Injun Knob, but day and night were reversed.)

He got to his feet and looked around. Four Ozian warriors stood a little way off, watching him and speaking quiet Yuultal. They held their spears ready, for clearly this was no ordinary victim, sick in guts and limbs, or likelier comatose.

Macurdy folded thick arms across his chest. "I'm Macurdy, the Lion of Farside," he announced in their own dialect. "I've come back. Take me to the headman."

❖   ❖   ❖

It was actually Arbel whom Macurdy wanted to see, but it was politic to visit the headman first. His march to the village was unlike that first one. The corporal in charge walked beside him. It was clear from the man's aura that he was awed. The others followed, equally impressed. No one jabbed him from behind with their spear, harassing him, making blood run down the back of his legs. It was obvious his reputation still lived, perhaps exaggerated even more than before.

He'd half expected there'd be no warriors waiting to see what or who came through. If anything did. With the old conjure woman a dozen years gone, there'd be no sacrificial gifts put out, and perhaps no reckless rural adolescents, waiting on a dare for "the spirit to come a-hootin'." As for the Sisterhood—he had no idea whether they still used the gate.

The district headman's residence seemed unchanged, but the old headman had died. His replacement had been a soldier in what was now being called Quaie's War. "I saw you on the march," the man told him, "and at the Battle of Ternass. And when you came back to Wolf Springs afterward. You have the long youth." Then he offered Macurdy the hospitality of his home, and his choice of slave girls.

Macurdy answered that he'd come to Oz for a purpose. He'd soon be leaving for the east, and wanted to consult with Arbel, his old mentor.

The headman was relieved. How do you entertain a legend? It was easier to have them go away, and tell stories about them afterward.

Macurdy had arrived with no actual plan, only a few intentions and hopes. When he'd left seventeen years earlier, he'd intended to return someday—an intention forgotten, once he'd met Mary. Vulkan had said he'd know when Macurdy came back; that they had things to do together. Meanwhile Macurdy felt no urgency. Who knew how far Vulkan would have to come. Or whether, after so long, other things had come up.

Once Macurdy had finished his courtesy call on the headman, he walked to Arbel's house. It looked as he remembered it, except the whitewash was fresher. It was long and linear, its walls a kind of stucco—four large rooms plus storage rooms, with a full-length loft. Moss and grass grew on its steep roof. There were windows in every room, with translucent membrane—the abdominal lining of cattle—stretched across them in lieu of glass, to let in light. In summer, fine-meshed fabric would replace the membranes, admitting breezes but not mosquitoes. When storm threatened, the shutters would be closed. Just now, smoke rose sluggishly from two of the four chimneys, then settled and flowed down the roof.

Macurdy knocked, and a young man opened the door, frowning uncertainly at the formidable figure in peculiar clothes. "Who are you," he asked, "and what do you want?"

"I'm Macurdy. I've come to see my old teacher."

The young man's jaw fell, and for a moment he simply stared. "Macurdy? Just a minute! I'll tell my master!" Then turning, he hurried out of sight, leaving Macurdy smiling on the stoop.

Within a minute, Arbel himself was there. At sight of Macurdy, he grinned broadly, a facial expression he seldom indulged in. "Macurdy!" he said, stepping aside. "Come in! Come in!" Macurdy entered, and Arbel closed the door behind him. "I dreamed of you last night," the old man told him, "but it did not feel prophetic."

He ushered him through one room and into another that served as workshop and storeroom. A young woman was there, pestling dried herbs, and looked up as they entered. "Do you know who this is?" Arbel asked Macurdy.

It took only a moment to recognize her: dark

complexion, large dark eyes, thin curved nose and narrow mouth. And poised. At Macurdy's last visit, seventeen years earlier, she'd been Arbel's twelve-year-old apprentice. She was of average height, not tall as she'd promised to be, and wiry now instead of gangly. To a degree, her aura resembled Arbel's. Arbel's marked him as someone whose interest was in learning; healing provided a focus. Her central interest was in healing; learning provided a means. Both were patient and tolerant, she more than Arbel, Macurdy suspected. But her tolerance, like Arbel's, was underlain with firmness.

An interesting pair, he thought. She'd be twenty-nine, and Arbel near seventy. Maybe they knew an herb that kept him frisky.

"You're Kerin," Macurdy said, answering Arbel's question. "His assistant now, I suppose."

"And his wife," she answered. "He insisted you are one of the unaging. Obviously he was right. But you haven't gone untouched by life."

She reads auras too, he decided. "Untouched?" he said. "Beaten up by it, from time to time. No worse than lots of others, though."

No worse than lots of others. Having said it, he realized its truth, and wondered if she'd led him to it.

Macurdy spent several weeks at Wolf Springs. It was Arbel who dealt with the cases brought to his home. Kerin rode the rounds of the district, making house calls. Usually she was home for supper, but sometimes it was later. The cooking was done by the slave who'd met Macurdy at the door.

Arbel chuckled, talking about it. People expected prompt service when they brought the patient in, and expected it from the old master himself. With house calls they were less demanding. "Kerin has great gifts of insight and intuition," he said. "It's rare these days that I can do more for them than she can, and there are cases she handles better than I. But prejudice is hard to argue with."

He was interested in Macurdy's stories of healing in World War II, and invited him to sit in on his sessions. Macurdy accepted gladly. They would add to his own skills.

But his mornings he spent in physical activity. After an early breakfast, he'd saddle a horse to ride the country lanes and forest trails. His old war horse, Hog, was still alive and sound, though twenty-eight years old, and no longer much for running. Hog had belonged to Macurdy all those years, but been Arbel's to use. For some years, Arbel had used the big gelding on his rounds of the district. Then Kerin had taken over that duty, and Hog carried her. Now Arbel traded for him, became Hog's actual owner, in return for a splendid eight-year-old named Warrior.

In a fey mood, Macurdy renamed his new horse Piglet, though it was nearly as large as Hog. It was easy to laugh now, as if passage through the gate had finished healing the trauma of Mary's death, though the scar would remain.

He rode about swordless. Instead, in a saddle sheath, he carried a woodsman's ax, and on his belt, the heavy knife Arbel had given him so long ago. He'd stop awhile in a river woods, and practice throwing both knife and ax at sycamores, silver maples, gums and cottonwoods, renewing skills that had served him well in Yuulith. And in Oregon had led to his marriage.

For more vigorous exercise, he cut and split firewood for Arbel. And practiced with the Wolf Springs militia—two evenings a week with the youth class, and on Six-Day afternoons with the veterans. He would, he supposed, need his old warrior skills, which had rusted considerably. Fortunately they derusted quickly, for every eye was on him, and it seemed important that his reputation continue strong.

Meanwhile the redbud trees bloomed, then the dogwoods and basswoods. The elms and others burst buds, sheening the forest with thin and delicate green.

They were busy days, improving his healing and fighting skills, cutting wood, savoring the progress of spring . . . but all were secondary to reunion with Vulkan. Vulkan would know where to take him, or send him, and what to do next.

For the feeling had grown in Macurdy that he had a reason to be in Yuulith beyond making a new life for himself, with a woman who did not age.

At the end of the fourth week, he was visited by a strange dream. In it he found himself wearing an SS uniform. But not in Bavaria. This was on a coast, somewhere in Hithmearc, and he was visiting a shipyard with Crown Prince Kurqôsz. One minute the ships were square-rigged—barks. A moment later they'd be LCMs—World War II landing craft. Kurqôsz told him he was going to take an army across the Ocean Sea in them, to conquer a land called Vismearc. Which worried Macurdy, for it seemed to him that Vismearc was America.

Knowing the voitusotar, Macurdy wondered how any of them could make it across the ocean alive. Kurqôsz answered that he was taking an army of monsters across. "Monsters?" Macurdy asked. Then he remembered his dreams during the war, of huge monsters trampling GIs on the beach, and flailing them with anchor chains.

Now Kurqôsz was accompanied by a human woman. Macurdy asked why. The crown prince laughed. "I like their fuller curves," he said, "and their submissiveness. And when they are fertile with us, their boy children are rakutur. Very useful, the rakutur." Then the woman was Varia. She winked at him, and as if it was a signal, Macurdy woke up.

❖　　　　❖　　　　❖

That morning at breakfast, he told Arbel he was leaving before lunch. That he'd dreamt it was time to go. Arbel examined Macurdy's aura. "Yes," he said, "I see it is."

Well before midmorning, Macurdy had his saddle-bags and bedroll on Piglet. Along with the war gear he'd left with Arbel seventeen years earlier: helmet, saber, and a light-weight, dwarf-made byrnie, all still shimmering with Kittul Kendersson's protective spells.

Swinging into the saddle, he gave Arbel a good-bye salute, then rode off down the dirt track that in Wolf Springs constituted the main street. Quickly he was out in the countryside, headed for Oztown, the capital.

11

Zassfel

It was early dusk when Macurdy arrived at Oztown. By standards west of the Great Muddy River, Oztown was populous, with three or four thousand people. But it was rural nonetheless, with corn patches, chickens, cows, pigs, horses . . . Macurdy had a mile to ride down its principal "street" to reach the chief's residence.

Riding past a tavern, Macurdy thought he recognized a large man about to go inside. Though if he was right, the man had changed a lot. Guiding Piglet to the hitching rail, Macurdy dismounted and secured the reins. Then he cast a light concealment spell over the animal—enough to make him easily ignored—and went in.

The place reeked of pine torches. He looked the room over. The man he wanted was bellied up to the bar, and Macurdy walked over to stand beside him. "Hello, Zassfel," he said quietly.

The face that turned to him was fleshy, florid, and considerably scarred. For just a moment the eyes squinted suspiciously at Macurdy, then widened in recognition. "You!"

"Me. What are you drinking?"

It took a moment for Zassfel to answer. "Whiskey. What else?"

At that moment, the barkeeper set a glass of it in front of Zassfel. "Five coppers," he said.

"On me," Macurdy told him, "and I'll have one." He dug into a pocket and came up with a silver teklota. The barkeeper peered at it, then went to his scale and weighed it, returning with a smaller silver coin and several coppers.

Zassfel's look reverted to suspicion, underlain by hostility. "What are you buying me whiskey for?" he growled. "I'm no friend of yours."

"For old times' sake. I'm just back from Farside. Visiting old friends, and maybe curing old grudges."

Zassfel scowled. "This one'll take a lot of curing."

Macurdy deliberately misunderstood. "Not too much," he said. "Sure you had five guys jump me and beat me up. But that was a long time ago, and I evened the score the next day."

The old sergeant's mouth twisted, then he knocked back half his tumbler of whiskey. "You ruined my life," he said. "That damn Esoksson kicked me out of the Heroes, and I had less than a year to serve. One more year and I'd have had a big farm, livestock, and slaves to do most of the work."

"Huh? How did I make that happen? A slave like I was?"

"You took that dog-humping spear maiden with you, and that weasel Jeremid. Then people started saying it was my fault—that I'd 'abused my authority'—and Esoksson kicked me out."

Macurdy had started to react to the slanders against Melody and Jeremid, then let them pass. Zassfel took a smaller swallow and continued. "Then, after you got famous, and everyone was kissing your ass, they started throwing shit at me. 'Zassfel's a stupid horse turd,' they said. I had to start reminding them how I made platoon sergeant. Beat the shit out of three or four," he added with satisfaction. "After that they didn't say it where I could hear them."

"Ah," said Macurdy, nodding sympathetically. "Life can be like that."

Zassfel's scowl returned. "What ever happened to you, that you can say that? Everything fell in your lap."

"Not really. My first wife got stolen by the Sisters and ended up married to an ylf. And Melody drowned; broke through the ice." He didn't mention Mary and the baby. "And after I went back to Farside, there was a big war there. I got scars you wouldn't believe. Damn near bled to death." He laughed. "Not to mention your guys beating the shit out of me, just down the street from here. Didn't have a tooth left, except for my grinders."

Zassfel peered carefully at Macurdy's grin, then finished his whiskey. "I heard about you growing them all back. You're not even human. Part ylf on one side, part Sister on the other." Macurdy didn't trouble to correct him, but let him talk on. "Ylf, Sister, it's all the same thing, though. When I knew you before, we looked about the same age." He gestured. "Now look at me."

Macurdy signaled the barkeeper, then looked Zassfel up and down. "You don't look so bad, for someone that lives hard. I'll bet there's not many guys pick fights with you. What do you do these days?"

"Damn right they don't. One thing I've kept is my strength. I got a wagon and team. I haul stuff. Whatever anyone wants hauled, I load and haul it. And I'm not doing bad. I even got me a slave, a pretty good screw. She's home with the kids."

The two men stayed in the tavern till late, mostly trading off buying. Macurdy used the spell he'd concocted, based on one of Arbel's, to metabolize the alcohol as fast as he absorbed it. A spell he'd used in the army during World War II, to let him drink with his buddies without getting drunk.

Zassfel asked to see Macurdy's scars from the war on Farside, and Macurdy dropped his pants to show him. That got the attention of the tavern's patrons, who gathered around to see. The truth would have been incomprehensible to them, so Macurdy answered creatively. "You've got to watch out for those war dogs," he explained, and patted his scarred buttocks, torn by mortar shell fragments on Sicily. "You get busy with people in front of you, they'll hit you from behind."

It was the long surgical scars on his right leg that impressed the audience most, though. "Bhroig's balls, Macurdy!" Zassfel said. "I never seen scars like those before! What happened?"

Again Macurdy answered creatively. "I got knocked out of my saddle, and trampled by horses. A Farside shaman cut my leg open and put the bones together again."

Zassfel nodded thoughtfully, his eyes on Macurdy's groin. "And that's a real club you've got there. The party girls would have loved it." He paused, thinking, his lips pursed. "But you got the best of it. You got the spear maiden."

Zassfel had a large capacity for booze, but after a time he fell down on his way to the latrine out back. Macurdy helped him up, and Zassfel relieved his bladder in the weeds. He wasn't the first. It smelled of urine and vomit there.

"I'm drunk," he slurred. "Don' usually get this bad. Gotta get up early. Big job t'do, take all day." He laughed. "One thing 'bout me, never hung over." He patted his thick belly. "There's muscle behin' this. Drink all night, an' outwork anyone the nex' day."

Steadying himself, he thrust out a hand. "Shake, ol' buddy," he said. "Le's see how strong you are."

They gripped, Macurdy careful not to squeeze too hard. "That's a hell of a grip you've got, Zassfel," he said. "There's damn few I can't grip down."

Zassfel smirked. "Damn right. Same here." He paused, peering at Macurdy. "You know what?" he said.

"No. What?"

"You're all right, Macurdy. Damn if you aren't! I didn' give you credit before. 'Member that jaguar we treed . . . ?"

After another drink, they left the tavern together, Zassfel weaving along, singing bawdy songs off-key. It wasn't far to his house. When they got there, his wife had put the kids to bed. She'd been pretty once, Macurdy realized, probably one of the party girls brought to the House of Heroes on Six-Day evenings. She'd gotten somewhat hefty over the years, but bore no overt signs of abuse.

"Macurdy," Zassfel said, "this is Kleffi. She's a good woman and a good hump. You wanna try her, iss okay." He paused. "Or not. Thass okay too. I 'member how you never humped the party girls."

"You're right," Macurdy said, "I never did. That's an old custom among some people. They just hump their wives."

Zassfel nodded sagely. "Differn' people got differn' ways. Thass a fack." He paused. "You sure you don' wanna hump her?"

Macurdy nodded soberly. "I know she's good. I can tell those things. But for me, it wouldn't be all right to."

Zassfel peered at him, simultaneously earnest and vague, then reached for Macurdy's hand. This time it didn't turn into a gripdown. Instead the ex-sergeant stood silent, Macurdy's big paw grasped in his own. "You're all right, Macurdy," he repeated after a long moment, the words quiet. "You're all right . . . You're all right . . ." He paused, then gave the hand a weak squeeze, a slight shake, as if the evening had suddenly caught up with him. "You're all right," he said.

Then he let go. Macurdy clapped the Ozman's big shoulder and left.

He returned to the tavern for Piglet, then hired a bed in an inn. Afterward he took Piglet to a livery stable across the street, let him drink all he wanted, and saw that he had hay and oats. He brushed and rubbed him down himself. Then, in his room, he wove an insect repellent field about himself, and went to bed.

He did not sleep at once. Instead he reviewed his evening with Zassfel. And realized how good he felt about it. It had been healing for both of them, and it seemed to Macurdy that it marked a turning point in his life.

12

Vulkan

The next morning, Macurdy paid a courtesy call on the Chief of the Oz, and managed to be on his way again before midday. He wouldn't worry about Vulkan finding him. He'd found him before, without even knowing who, exactly, he was looking for. Presumably he'd find him again, if he was still interested. Meanwhile, Macurdy would cross the Great Muddy, ride southeast to the Green River Valley, and thence to the royal palace at Teklapori. Except for Arbel—and Varia, he hoped, and maybe Omara—his best human friends in Yuulith were in Tekalos. Pavo Wollerda was king there, or had been when Macurdy had left, and Jeremid had a farm in the Kullvordi Hills.

The route was familiar, and lovely in advanced spring. On the third day he rode a ferry raft across the Great Muddy into the kingdom of Miskmehr, rich in forested hills and valley farms, though not in money. The Miskmehri had provided two cohorts of tough, self-reliant infantry to fight the ylver in Quaie's War. Earlier, during Quaie's Incursion, only an unprotected border had separated them from the savage fate of Kormehr, and the memory had still been fresh.

Meanwhile, the weather had changed from showery to bright, cool at night, warm by day. Drawing on the Web of the World for nighttime warmth, Macurdy found it simpler and more pleasant to sleep beneath the forest canopy or open sky, than in an inn or some farmer's barn. Metabolic energy in general he could draw from the Web, thus even eating was less urgent than it would otherwise have been. Though his stomach complained when he didn't. For vitamins, minerals, proteins, he stopped at farms along the way, buying cheese, scrawny chickens, overwintered vegetables and wizened apples. And ate the mild forest leeks abundant in that season, until the smell of him could have repelled barn flies at twenty feet.

In time, the winding dirt road he'd been riding reached the wider, straighter dirt road known as the Valley Highway. At the junction, the brush-tangled forest blowdown where he'd earned the friendship of the dwarves, and the enmity of Slaney's brigands, was thick young forest now, fifty feet tall.

It was there he was halted by a voice he knew well, deep and resonating within his skull. «Aha! Macurdy! I knew I'd meet you soon.»

It was thought, not words that reached him. About forty yards ahead, a great boar trotted from the forest. In size, it suggested an Angus bull, though the large head and tusks, the high shoulders, the deep narrow body that tapered toward the hindquarters, all were strictly wild hog. Piglet began to prance skittishly, and Macurdy reined him in, while patting the arching neck. "Whoa, boy, easy now, easy . . ." Then a wordless calm washed over them both, intended for Piglet, who quickly settled down.

"Vulkan!" Macurdy called, "I figured you'd find me! When did you know I was back?"

The boar trotted casually toward them, stopping half

a dozen yards away when Piglet shifted restlessly again. There was black muck on the tusked snout, as if it had been rooting up skunk cabbages. And suddenly Macurdy was unsure whom he faced, for this creature had red eyes.

Then the boar answered. «I sensed a month ago that you were back. I was visiting the Scrub Coast, the ocean coast, reminding them of our existence. It is one of my duties. In this world, it is intended that humankind know a . . .» He paused, his mind tinged with amusement. «. . . know a larger reality than on Farside. And of course, I must maintain my myth; that is another duty.

«And on my way back to meet you, I stopped to visit the King in Silver Mountain.»

"The dwarf king? They let you inside the mountain? I thought everyone was scared of you."

«The dwarves do not fear us. A great boar befriended them in an earlier age. In the time of the high trolls, an experiment gone awry. You are not the only outsider they call dwarf friend.»

"When I knew you before, your eyes were black. Now . . ."

«Now they are red. They make me more impressive, which makes *you* more impressive.»

"Me?"

«You.»

Macurdy contemplated that a moment, then set it aside. "How are we going to travel together, with me riding Piglet?"

«He will be all right now. Though you may want to leave him at Teklapori.»

"Teklapori? How did you know I was going there?"

«Where else? When we leave there for the north—assuming you choose to—I can carry you. It will be a bigger public sensation if you ride on me.»

Macurdy laughed. "You got that right." He paused. "North together?"

«If you so choose.»

"Why do you want to create a public sensation?"

«A maximum of fame—suitable fame—will be useful to your task.»

"My task." Macurdy frowned. "What task?"

"I do not know yet. But it will be important. Critical. You are already a legend in Yuulith; you've been heard of even on the Scrub Coast. But to many it is a legend of the past. We must renew and enhance it.»

Vulkan's comments had introverted Macurdy. Now he shrugged them off. He'd think about them when he knew more, he told himself.

So I've been heard of even on the Scrub Coast. Huh! And I never heard of the Scrub Coast till just now.

Unlike the winding dirt roads through Miskmehr, the Valley Highway was much used; they met merchants several times a day, typically traveling in small parties, with pack animals. And farmers traveling to some village or market town several times an hour. Seen from a little distance, Macurdy was readily recognizable as a man on horseback. The creature trotting alongside could be a mule, or from closer up, a lean beef, polled and slab-sided. By the time they were close enough to identify it, they were too near to escape, should it be necessary. And after all, it was trotting alongside a man on horseback.

Thus as fearsome and alarming as Vulkan looked, and as his myth described him, almost none of the travelers they met actually fled. They did, however, get well off the road to let him pass. The degree of control exercised by the giant boar's human companion seemed uncertain, and the large curved tusks looked more fearsome than any sword. While the small, indomitable red eyes, fixed coldly on the passersby, showed neither loving kindness nor docility.

Judging by their auras, the shock was greater for

the traveler than for his horse or mule, if he had one. Probably, Macurdy thought, their animals didn't associate the smell of swine with danger. And despite Vulkan's size and fearsome appearance, his broadcast calm overrode their alarm.

Humans, on the other hand, had powerful imaginations. And folk tales—a whole gruesome mythology about the great boars. Nor did they fail to be awed by a man who kept company with such a monster.

There were villages along the road, and these were another matter. There, more often than not, people didn't see the great boar till he was close. Then doors were slammed and barred. Women shrieked, men cried out in alarm, children scurried howling out of sight. While dogs, seemingly less subject than horses to Vulkan's calming flow, scuttled off with their tails between their legs. As if they too had imaginations.

Neither Vulkan nor Macurdy qualified as chatty, but for the first few days they talked quite a lot. Macurdy related much of his recent seventeen years' experience on Farside, both civilian and military. Vulkan described Yuulith's geography, people and customs, particularly of regions unfamiliar to Macurdy.

One morning at a distance, Macurdy saw the inn at the crossroad near Gormin Town. He knew both inn and town; it was there he'd begun to seriously broaden his reputation, so many years past.

"You must be overdue for some actual food," he said to Vulkan. Even more than himself, the great boar had been relying on the Web of the World.

«Mmm, yes. Those cattail patches we've stopped at have been useful, but I could benefit from variety. And protein. Some animal source would be particularly appropriate.»

"Tell you what," Macurdy said, "suppose we stop at the inn. I'll eat there, and afterward they'll tell everyone traveling through about us, travelers on the north-south road as well as the east-west. After that we'll ride into Gormin Town," he gestured toward a palisaded town—its population several thousand—a half mile south of the crossroad. "There's a butcher's there, where I got offal for Blue Wing my first time through here. I suppose you eat offal?"

«Offal will be quite satisfactory, yes. I can, of course, take some farmer's calf or pig, but offal will do nicely.»

As Piglet carried Macurdy into the inn yard, the stableboy hurried out to meet them. At sight of Vulkan, he disappeared back into the stable. Macurdy trotted Piglet over to it, and dismounting, led him inside. "Stableboy!" he bellowed.

"Yessir?" came a voice from the hayloft.

"Feed and water my horse. At once! Then groom him."

A tousled head appeared, of a youth in his early teens. "Your—horse, sir?"

"What else? Come now! Get about it!"

"Sir, I'm afraid, sir. Of—that other."

"He won't hurt you. I've told him not to. I'm Macurdy, back from Farside, and he's my traveling companion. His name is Vulkan."

The lad stood now, staring down. "Would you, sir . . . General? Marshal Macurdy? Would . . . would you ask him to stay outside, sir? I'm afraid he might forget what you told him."

Macurdy grinned disarmingly. "As good as done. Now come down and mind your duties."

The youth eased worriedly down the ladder and took Piglet's reins. Then Macurdy left, walking to the inn with Vulkan beside him. They entered the taproom as nearly together as the doorway allowed, Macurdy stepping in first, Vulkan a step behind. There was a scream from a serving girl, a clatter of mugs from a dropped tray, shouts of male alarm, the crash of benches falling over. Men scrambled to get more tables between them and the newcomers.

"Helloo!" Macurdy called. "Who will feed a hungry man?"

A florid beefy face peered from the kitchen door. "Get him to hell out of here!" it shouted, more angry than fearful.

Grinning, Macurdy turned. "Vulkan," he said, loudly enough for everyone to hear, "wait outside for me."

As if obeying, Vulkan turned and went outside, the only sound his hooves on the puncheon floor. But the move had nothing of submissiveness about it. Red eyes fierce, the great tusked face had scanned the room as he'd crossed to the door.

The innkeeper eased in from the kitchen. "Mister," he said, "that was a dumb-ass thing to do, bringing that beast in here."

Macurdy raised his eyebrows. This innkeeper was no ordinary man. "He's not a beast," Macurdy said, "he's a wizard. A giant boar and a wizard. And curious. He'd never been in a taproom before."

The innkeeper frowned. "How did you get him?"

"Get him? I didn't *get* him. We met in the woods once, in Oz. There I was, and there he was. Next thing we knew, we were friends. That was seventeen years ago, just before I went back to Farside. Then I came back to Yuulith again, and riding southeast out of Miskmehr, there he was, Vulkan himself, waiting by the road. Now we're traveling together."

"Vulkan? Is that his name?"

"Yep."

"How do you know?"

"He told me."

"He talks?"

"Not with his mouth. With his mind. He talks directly into my head. I could be deaf as a stone, it wouldn't make any difference. I'd hear him."

For a moment the innkeeper stood silently, digesting what he'd heard. "You've been to Farside and back," he said. "Then you must be Macurdy, right?"

"Yep."

"An innkeeper hears a lot of stories, and learns not to believe most of them. Tell you the truth, I didn't believe half of what they say about you. Some of it, yes. I know damn well what you did in Gormin Town, and later with Wollerda, but . . ." He glanced toward the door. "Seeing you with him, a lot else starts looking believable." He paused. "Could he talk to me?"

"If he took a notion to. He doesn't make friends easily."

"Where are you going now?"

"To Teklapori, to see Wollerda. Vulkan sees the future a lot better than I do, though a lot of times it's foggy to him, too. He says it looks bad. Threatening. Wollerda needs to know."

The beefy face frowned with concern. "Huh! Another ylvin invasion?"

From outside the inn, Vulkan's mind spoke to Macurdy's. «Not ylvin,» it told him.

"Not ylvin," Macurdy said. "Beyond that we don't know yet. But we will."

"Huh! Well, if it's not ylvin, I'm not going to worry about it."

"Good idea. There are times for worrying, and there are times to eat. Your boiled cabbage smells pretty good. With a couple thick slabs of roast beef, and a mug of beer. And four inches of a loaf soaked with beef drippings. And for my friend, five teklotas worth of raw beef. That way he won't need to—ah, kill anything till we get away from here."

His money was shrinking, and he decided to skip Gormin Town. That way they'd reach Teklapori that evening, and Wollerda would fix him up.

❖   ❖   ❖

As Macurdy had expected, the innkeeper provided Vulkan with more like ten teklotas worth of beef. Probably "kill anything" had been the key phrase. Macurdy felt quite good about his performance. As they started east again down the Valley Highway, the two companions talked.

"I've got to admit, I enjoyed that little game back there," he said to Vulkan, and paused. "Tell me again why we need to make a big impression—make people think I'm more than I am."

He could sense the giant boar's mental frown. «My friend,» Vulkan said, «appropriate modesty is honesty about one's abilities and accomplishments, and the absence of swagger. As for 'making people think you're more than you are' . . .

«When you first arrived in Yuulith, you were made a slave. Then, by talent and force of character, you were accepted into the Wolf Springs militia, something nearly unheard of for a slave. As a trainee you excelled so remarkably, you were sent to Oztown, and accepted in the Heroes—which was quite unprecedented. There, again by talent and strength of character, you rendered your sergeant so jealous . . .»

"Wait a minute! I didn't tell you all that. Some of it, but . . ."

Vulkan cut him short. «You are not my only source of information. I overhear thoughts not even spoken. I have even eavesdropped on the Dynast; listened to the ravings of unhappy Keltorus; and conversed openly with a friend of yours named Blue Wing.» He paused, allowing Macurdy time to assimilate. «Who was it that freed Tekalos, my friend? Admittedly Wollerda deserves at least as much of the credit as you, but he started with a following. You started with two runaway Ozians, three dwarves, and a great raven.

«And when you'd freed Tekalos, you and Wollerda, you personally forged a league of allies who previously had seldom agreed on anything. Allies who even included Sarkia! You raised and led an army of contentious, sometimes truculent cohorts from throughout the Rude Lands and beyond. I am not sufficiently informed to evaluate your accomplishments in the great war on Farside, but I suspect they too were exceptional.

«So do not disparage yourself to me. 'More than you are'? Not at all!»

He paused. «Meanwhile I have not responded to your question: 'Why must we make a big impression?' First, over the years since your victories against the Ylvin Empire of the West, the bonds among the kingdoms and tribes of the Rude Lands have loosened again, despite increasing commerce and the influence of the Sisterhood. They have loosened because of rivalries old and new, and because they no longer perceive a common threat.»

Macurdy's wide mouth pursed in thought. "Before when we talked about this, you said we needed to beef up my reputation because of my task. But you didn't know what my task was."

«Only that you must meet a threat. A threat more serious than an ylvin army, even if the elder Quaie were still alive to lead it. I sense the vector, but lack the specifics.»

Macurdy looked at the creature beside him, its pace ill-matched with Piglet's. The big gelding's walk was faster than Vulkan's, who trotted to keep up. But so far Vulkan had seemed tireless. "Is there *anything*," Macurdy asked, "that you can tell me about this threat? Beyond it being big?"

«I suspect the cause, but with limited confidence. An infinite number of event vectors exist in the physical realm. Series of events having direction, force and duration. Some are driven by humans, others are influenced by humans, and some are beyond human influence. Some can be extended into the future with significant probabilities, others cannot. And while I have the gift of perceiving and predicting vectors to a degree well beyond the human, it is a gift with definite limitations. I am, after all, incarnate.

«Thus I cannot define the threat.» With his mind he peered intently at Macurdy. «However, I believe it was no accident that I visited the Scrub Lands when I did. For it was there I sensed the problem vector. It is focused on the coast. As if from the Ocean Sea, or across it.»

The statement struck Macurdy like a punch in the gut. *Across the Ocean Sea!* He remembered the dream he'd had, just before leaving Wolf Springs—a dream of Crown Prince Kurqôsz of the voitusotar, and "his army of monsters."

Vulkan allowed excitement to color his next thought-words. «That is it!» he said. «It verifies my suspicion. The voitusotar are the root and energy of the vector!»

"What are you talking about?"

«The dream you just remembered! It brought the vector into focus for me, and verified the cause, the sorcerers you told me of, who visited Farside. The voitusotar.» He examined Macurdy thoughtfully. «Your warrior muse is an excellent dream maker.»

Warrior muse? Dream maker? Macurdy examined the words warily, then set them aside. "Vulkan," he said, "I've got another question."

«Ask it.»

"You read my mind. You already know the question."

«Do I now?»

"Don't you?"

«Ask.»

Macurdy shrugged. "It seems you know my role in this. If it doesn't turn out to be a false alarm. But what's your role?"

Vulkan answered reflectively. «For a long time my broad role has been to observe Yuulith and its sentient beings—dwarves, humans, the great ravens, the tomttu, and the ylver. And to surround myself with a mystique. Eavesdropping while invisible is a specialty of mine. All in preparation for my new role—to support you in your efforts to save Yuulith from the voitusotar.»

"Why can't we switch roles? You save Yuulith, and I back you up. I could be your spokesman."

«Ah! But that is not what the Tao intends. Humankind is responsible for humankind, and the ylver for the ylver. And you are of both. It—the Tao, that is— may provide them with such as I, but our powers are limited. It is rare that the Tao intervenes directly, and then only to provide an autonomous agent. Or in this case two: you and me. The Tao does not part the waters of the sea, nor destroy the enemies of some chosen people.»

"Huh!" Macurdy had never been firmly sure there was a God, supposed he never would be. He'd suspected, even hoped there was, had even prayed occasionally, though he wasn't sure to whom. "What's this Tao like?"

«My comprehension of it is both imperfect and incomplete. It is easier for me to say what it is not.»

Macurdy frowned. "But if he talks to you . . ."

«Not he. It. Sex and gender do not apply.» Vulkan paused, his calm mind regarding Macurdy. «You misapprehend the Tao. It is not a sentient bull with magical powers, like Bhroig the Fertile, of the western tribes. Or the White Whale of the Ocean coast, who remarkably enough is thought to swim in the sky. Nor Brog'r of the Rude Lands, of whom it is claimed he visits from time to time in the form of a white stallion bringing gifts: corn in the ancient past, and more recently potatoes. Not even the All Soul of the ylver, who lives above the sky, dispassionately noting their acts, creditable and otherwise.» He paused. «Nor the concepts you're familiar with on Farside.»

Farside. Macurdy wondered if Vulkan had access to it, or if he knew of it only from him, and perhaps others who'd crossed over. He shook the matter off. "How far can you go in backing me up?" he asked.

«Your decisions are yours to make. I cannot make them for you. I can inform. I can educate. I can advise, suggest, and nudge. I can physically carry you on my back, but you must decide where to. For the decisions must be truly yours. I will not 'argue' you into something.»

Vulkan said nothing more then. After a minute, Macurdy asked, "That's it?"

«That's it.»

Macurdy frowned. He'd looked forward to Vulkan's muscular bulk and ugly tusks backing him up. Physically. Martially. "Suppose the voitusotar use sorcery?"

«They will. And I will not reply in kind. I am not, in fact, a sorcerer. I was incarnated with certain assets, most conspicuously a formidable body. I can draw on the Web of the World, as you have learned to do. When I wish, I can become unseeable; in fact imperceptible by any human senses. Within limits, I have power over gates. I can read auras in even greater detail than you, and I literally smell emotions. I can see into minds at the level of conscious thought, and below in the margin between the conscious and subconscious. Few sorceries can touch me. And obviously I can communicate with humans when I choose to. Although I have what might be termed emotions, they do not cloud my mind. And because I am immune to fear, I am immune to being mentally overwhelmed.

«But I do not kill ensouled beings, nor do I coerce, and my magicks are limited to the benign. I can do favors, as you learned at our first meeting, but they do not involve assaulting anyone.» He paused. «I believe I have answered your questions.»

After a bit, walking and trotting toward Teklapori, they conversed further. With Vulkan's prompting,

Macurdy described more of his observations of the voitusotar, including his training at Schloss Tannenberg, his experiences in Hithmearc, and his destruction of the Bavarian Gate. And the nightmares he'd had, during the war there, of monsters on the beach.

"But that was there," Macurdy said, "and a different war. I wasn't even sure that Hithmearc is in the same world as Yuulith."

«It is,» Vulkan said. «It is part of ylvin history, and another like myself has known them directly if not extensively. Apparently they have discovered a means of crossing the Ocean Sea.»

By that time they could see the town wall of Teklapori, a near-blackness in the gray of dusk.

«We shall soon see,» Vulkan said, «what the king of Tekalos thinks of this.»

Macurdy nodded grimly. He was not enthused at the prospect of confronting voitik sorceries.

13

Evening in a Palace

They traveled steadily the rest of the day, skipping Gormin Town. It was twilight when they reached Teklapori, whose gates had been closed at sunset. They bypassed it, too. Macurdy's business was a mile to the south, at the palace.

The last half mile was paved with flagstones, on which Piglet's shod hooves clopped loudly. Vulkan had cloaked himself, and could not be seen, heard, nor smelled. Macurdy, however, needed to be seen and heard to be let in. He recalled the difficulty he'd had the last time he'd arrived unexpected in the night.

Though the guards on the tower must have heard Piglet's shod hooves, no one called a challenge. And now Macurdy discovered something added since his last visit: a bronze bell resembling a large cowbell hung from a bracket beside the spy gate. Leaning in the saddle, he shook the bell noisily, at the same time bellowing: "Halloo! Let me in!"

Someone called back from the forty-foot tower: "Who is it?"

"Macurdy, come to see the king!"

Macurdy had expected disbelief, but after a long moment the voice answered, "Just a minute." It took more like four or five, but finally someone shone a target lantern through the "eye" in the narrow "spy's gate," its yellow beam finding Macurdy's face. In another half minute, the grinding of windlass and chain signaled the raising of the portcullis within the wall. Then the narrow gate opened and a guard stepped out, the lantern in his hand for a closer look. Another guard stood in the opening, crossbow wound and raised.

The guard with the lantern was middle-aged and thick-waisted, but gave an impression of tough competence. "Brog'r love me!" he swore. "It is! It's you! And you've not changed a whit! Not in all them years!" He turned, shouting more loudly than needed. "It's him! The marshal! He's come back!" Then he turned to Macurdy again. "Come in! Come in! I seen you when I was with Wollerda in the revolution. And later, in the Marches, I seen you different times, including at Ternass. So they rousted me out of my bunk, to be sure you weren't no impostor."

Gesticulating as he talked, the man led them through a ten-foot-long, tunnel-like passage through the wall. Vulkan followed closely, still unperceived.

When they'd emerged, the officer of the watch was waiting to check Macurdy personally, though he'd never seen him before. Cautiously semi-satisfied, he sent a mounted courier galloping ahead to announce the visitor, and with four mounted guardsmen, escorted Macurdy personally to the royal residence.

The king's houseguards had been alerted, and half a dozen waited respectfully at the entry. There Macurdy dismounted. Almost at once, Wollerda came out.

It took Macurdy a moment to recognize him—the

king had passed his sixtieth birthday and grown some-what heavier—but Wollerda recognized his visitor instantly. "Macurdy!" he said. They hugged, then Wollerda stepped back to arms' length. "You haven't changed a bit that I can see. God but it's good to have you here!" He hugged him again. "Well! Come in! Come in!"

So far Macurdy had merely grinned broadly. Now he spoke. "Just a minute. I've got a friend to introduce. He's wearing a concealment spell, otherwise folks might have got all upset." Macurdy stepped to one side. "Pavo, meet Vulkan."

With that, Pavo Wollerda, warrior-scholar, ex-revolutionary leader, king of Tekalos, found himself facing something he'd heard of all his life. A bug-bear he'd learned to fear as a child, had only half believed in since, and had never thought to see. The small fierce eyes were almost on a level with his own, gleaming red in the torchlight. The heavy yellow tusks were something out of nightmare. Reflexively the king stepped back, while his guardsmen's hands went to their swords.

"Vulkan and I are traveling together," Macurdy went on. "He's my friend and advisor. And smart as the sto-ries say, but not near as ferocious. Not normally. Mat-ter of fact, he's safer to be around than lots of dogs, unless someone gets crosswise of him, I suppose."

Wollerda stared, then thoughts entered his mind in the form of a pseudo voice, deep and resonant. «My function is not violence.»

The guards' nerves had eased a bit—their knees and backs had straightened—but their hands remained near their sword hilts. The king turned in awe to his old comrade-in-arms. "Macurdy, I've known for years you were a man of power. But to have a traveling compan-ion like that? No man in Yuulith is your match!"

Grinning, Macurdy shook his head. "I'm not much more of a magician now than when I left. Which isn't all that much. I'm older and more experienced, and smarter I hope. But whether I'm smart enough, time will tell.

"Ask us in and we'll tell you what we know. But I expect we'll learn more from you than you will from us."

Wollerda nodded toward Vulkan. "He goes in with us?"

"Unless you'd rather talk out here. I expect Liiset will want to meet him, too."

They went in then, the king leading, several guardsmen bringing up the rear. Briefly Wollerda wondered if Vulkan was housebroken. But intelligent as the giant boar seemed to be, and a wizard to boot, that seemed unlikely to be a problem.

The royal apartment was on the second floor. When they went in, Queen Liiset met them with no sign of shock, or even surprise, at Vulkan's presence. Macurdy decided she'd been watching out a window.

"Curtis!" she said smiling and took his hand for a moment. She was the first person to call him that since he'd left Farside. "Introduce me to your companion," she added, turning her gaze to Vulkan.

Vulkan introduced himself. «I am Vulkan. I have learned much about the Sisterhood in recent centuries, but you are the first of them whom I have addressed personally.»

When Wollerda learned that his visitors hadn't eaten, he ordered a meal sent for Macurdy. Vulkan said he'd wait till later, and that a lamb would be about right.

After eating, Macurdy described briefly his past seventeen years on Farside. He'd intended to mention the voitar in Bavaria, then didn't. He did mention Vulkan's premonition about a threat from across the Ocean Sea, but didn't elaborate. The time for that, it seemed to him, was if and when the threat materialized. Or perhaps if pushed to it by questions.

"What I'd like to hear about," he went on, "is how things are going in Tekalos, and with the Sisterhood."

Wollerda had been everything King Gurtho had not. He'd striven for justice, and taken care not to offend his subjects needlessly. There hadn't been a tax uprising since his coronation, partly because taxes were now set by fixed rates. And partly because, over time, a count, three reeves and five bailiffs had been found guilty of flagrant abuse of office, mostly for tax offenses. After a tour of the kingdom in chains, they'd made the acquaintance of the royal executioner, and their heads had decorated poles outside their official residences. This not only gratified the population at large. It was also an ever-present reminder to those who succeeded them in office, and a warning to officials elsewhere. For their heads were left on the poles till long after they were bleached skulls.

"Those are the only brutalities I've committed in office," Wollerda finished, "but I have no doubt Brog'r forgives me."

Early on he'd established militia training for all youth, somewhat after the Ozian system, and reduced the standing army. County forces too had been reduced, and put on a reserve basis to reduce taxes. Their annual field training now was done on a military reservation, to avoid trampling farmers' fields—a long-standing source of damage and resentment. Aside from the king, only counts retained military forces at all. Reeves and bailiffs replaced theirs with police, which were fewer in number, and regulated by law rather than whim.

Shamans had been legalized. "Most of them," Wollerda added, "aren't very effective. But the poorer of them soon find business sparse, and profit slight from the puny fees they can get. But even the completely bogus sometimes effect cures by belief."

Macurdy turned to Liiset, who looked as young and

beautiful as ever. She was a member of Varia's clone, and the resemblance was uncanny, even with their differences in aura. "And what's the state of the Sisterhood?" he asked.

Her eyes met his mildly. "Let me call Omara," she replied. "I get reports by courier, and make occasional trips to the Cloister, but she is Sarkia's executive officer."

"Omara is here?" Even as he spoke, Macurdy realized his response was giving away his feelings for the healer. But his aura would too, and Liiset wouldn't miss it.

"For a week," she answered. "She arrived this Three-Day, to initiate our children in the next stage of magicks and healing. She's considerably more advanced than I. And more fully informed of Sisterhood affairs. She'll be pleased to see you."

In minutes, Omara arrived from her quarters, smelling of fragrant soap. "My apologies," Liiset said, "if we interrupted you in your bath."

"I was done with it," Omara answered, with the calm that Macurdy remembered. "I was preparing to meditate." She turned, her gaze absorbing him. "Hello, Macurdy," she said, "it is very nice to see you again." He wondered how much she read in him. With her powerful talent and broad experience, surely she saw more deeply than Liiset or himself when she looked at an aura.

Only then did she give her attention to Vulkan. As hugely conspicuous and out of place as he was in the royal drawing room, she had not been distracted by him. "I was informed you were here," she continued. "I am Omara, as you have deduced, but I do not know your name."

«I—am Vulkan.»

Macurdy wondered if the others had caught how impressed the great boar was. "We're traveling together," Macurdy said. "I think of him as my tutor."

Liiset broke in. "Curtis asked how things stood in the Sisterhood. You may have information I lack."

Omara took a chair unbidden, as someone treated by the royal couple as a peer. "Why don't you begin," Omara said. "I can expand on it later, if appropriate."

Liiset nodded. "As I indicated, Sarkia still lives. Once decline sets in, it is rare for death to hold off as long as a dozen years. Nine or ten is typical. With Sarkia it's been eighteen, thanks to Omara's powers and her own strong will. She still has not chosen a successor, though she'd like to, and most of us feel serious concern over what might happen if she dies without naming one.

"In that case Idri would probably be the new dynast. She no longer hides her desire and intention, though she knows she's unpopular with the Sisterhood. She's spent most of her life making enemies. I'm one of the few she likes and treats with respect, and one of still fewer who feel affinity for her. But I recognize her unfitness to rule."

Frowning, Macurdy broke in. "Then who supports her? Even if Sarkia decreed her to be the new dynast . . ."

"The Tigers. The Tigers support her."

Macurdy frowned. "The Tigers?"

Liiset nodded. "Sarkia gave Idri authority over the breeding and training of Tigers. That was back when you were still here, on campaign in the Marches, actually. Before Sarkia began her decline. Idri had failed at every other command assignment she'd had. I suppose Sarkia hoped this might be one she could manage. At first it was a secondary responsibility, but Idri turned it into her principal one. She quickly began building their numbers as rapidly as she could, while seducing, politicking—conquering so to speak—key Tiger commanders. And saying the right things to make herself popular with the entire corps.

"Their numbers did not—could not—increase rapidly, of course. It takes the better part of twenty years to mature and train a Tiger, and fewer than one in three of us are suitable mother stock for them. Fewer than one in ten are prime mother stock. So from the very start, Idri used her influence to shorten the resting periods between litters by prime mothers. Which increased not only the number of Tiger births, but the number of potential prime mothers born. And of the other suitable mother stock, she convinced Sarkia to increase the number of Tiger breedings. Which wasn't popular with Sisters, of course, but very popular with Tigers.

"Today there are hardly any more fully trained Tigers than when she took command of them. "But there are far more Tiger youth in training. And this year will produce the largest number of completions ever, fully trained and ready. Next year, completions will be higher again. And so on."

Macurdy interrupted. "What does the King in Silver Mountain think of all these Tiger companies within the boundaries of his kingdom?" The king was Sarkia's landlord, the Cloister existing on land he'd leased to the Sisterhood. To Macurdy it had always seemed an odd arrangement, considering the reputation of the dwarves in general, and certainly of the King in Silver Mountain.

"Apparently it's not a problem," Liiset said. "In fact he doubled the lease holding about the time you went back to Farside.

"The increase in Tigers and Tiger young puts stress on the Sisterhood though. Our trade has to support them along with the rest of us. Fortunately Tigers are shorter lived. Which they resent of course. Not one has ever survived to a normal decline. Normally some vital organ, usually the heart, burns out after forty or fifty years, and they die more or less quickly.

"Idri wants us to hire out Tigers as mercenary units. But Sarkia is smart enough to see the temptations and problems that would lead to, so three years ago she drastically reduced the breeding intensity. Meanwhile we have to support the offspring of fifteen years of intensive breeding. And in eight years we'll have double the present number fully trained and ready."

Liiset looked knowingly at Macurdy. "You see what Idri has in mind, of course."

Macurdy nodded. Sarkia could hardly survive much longer. Any day could see her dead, naturally or otherwise. Then Idri would declare herself dynast, and intensify Tiger breeding again. She'd rent out Tiger companies, undertake alliances with ambitious kings, then try to take over the Rude Lands. And if she got away with that . . .

He looked at Omara. "What do you think of all this? What are her chances?"

As always, Omara replied calmly and concisely. "For becoming dynast? It approaches certainty. Unless Sarkia appoints someone else—someone formidable—to replace her, and then resigns. Overall, the Guards still outnumber the Tigers, and they too are excellent fighting men. Some Guard clones are equal to Tigers in most respects; your own two sons by Varia are examples. But all in all, Guards companies fall short of Tiger companies as fighting units. How short is not clear, but few guardsmen match Tigers in strength, speed, or endurance. The Tiger advantage in tactical and personal skills is less clear, but they do nothing but train. Guard units have numerous other duties."

"And," Liiset broke in, "our Guard units are dispersed. We have a platoon at every embassy in the Rude Lands, the Marches, and the ylvin empires. And a squad or more at each Outland craftworks, where there's not an embassy at hand."

Embassies even in the empires! Macurdy was

impressed. Probably, he thought, Cyncaidh had had a hand in that.

"That comes to nearly two cohorts," Liiset went on. "But only three companies are kept at the Cloister, not nearly enough to discourage a takeover by Idri.

"It's doubtful that Idri can go far with her ambitions, which I'm sure include conquests. But what she can do is create a shambles among the kingdoms and destroy the Sisterhood."

Macurdy nodded. Perhaps self-destruction was the destiny of the Sisterhood, but it would be a tragedy to see peace destroyed in the Rude Lands.

The Sisterhood, Liiset continued, had changed in other respects as well. Sarkia had married Sisters to every royal house in the Rude Lands—to the king or crown prince or both—with the single exception of Kormehr. Two had even married into royal families in the Marches. Those Sisters bore their children to foreign kings, children raised and trained at home. Thus the loyalty of the Outland queens to the Sisterhood was diluted.

The Sisters serving in Outland embassies and craftworks also came to look at the world and the Sisterhood with different eyes and minds than those remaining in the Cloister. To reduce this, for years Sarkia had rotated staff members every year or two. Only the ambassadors themselves had longer tenures. But she'd decided the returnees corrupted those who'd never been away, so now she mostly left them in place. She called them home mainly for breeding, and while in the Cloister, they lived apart.

"We've become a Sisterhood divided," Liiset finished. "There is now an Outland Sisterhood, and a larger Cloister Sisterhood. The latter tending to resent the former, but somewhat contaminated by them."

She gestured. "Omara is an exception. That Sarkia trusts her absolutely, I do not doubt. And despite Omara's role in keeping her alive, she sends her out for three or four weeks at a time, to investigate or handle Outland situations. Of the Outland queens, I seem to be the most trusted. Ironically enough, this is probably because Idri and I get along."

Liiset paused thoughtfully. "But of us all, Varia is Sarkia's favorite."

She caught Macurdy's surprise. "Decline has changed Sarkia greatly," she said, "in almost every respect. She has had to make many adjustments, and has made them well. When you knew her, she was strong willed and highly intelligent. But impulsive, sometimes destructively so, and slow to admit mistakes, even to herself. In decline she has grown honest with herself, and added wisdom to her virtues.

"Her great regret is having driven Varia into exile. She admires her above any of us. Varia the runaway, Varia the defiant. She truly grieves losing her. She has told me so, and her aura supports her words.

"As for Idri—" Liiset paused again. "Idri she neither admires nor trusts. She does, however, love her, and feels guilt for Idri's failures.

"Idri, on the other hand, hates Sarkia. Hates her, and in her way loves her, I think. And despairs of ever pleasing her. Emotionally they're thoroughly entangled." Liiset shook her head. "Don't ask me to explain it.

"But there is nothing ambivalent about her hatred of Varia. As girls, Idri and Varia were favorites of Sarkia. They'd vied for an executive apprenticeship in the dynast's office. Varia's virtues were talent, intelligence, and judgement. And good intentions. Idri's were energy and decisiveness. And ambition. Thus Sarkia chose Varia, and Idri never forgave either of them. Then, after a year in the apprenticeship—a successful year by all reports—Varia was sent to Farside to marry your uncle. Why her, I don't know. Bloodline perhaps."

She turned to Omara. "Do you have anything to add? About any of it?"

"Perhaps after further thought," Omara said, "but not now."

Throughout Liiset's exposition, Wollerda had said nothing. Now he spoke. "Then maybe it's time to end this conversation. We can take it up again in the morning. Our guests have had a long day; I suspect they'd like to rest. And Vulkan's supper has been delayed too long."

Vulkan voiced neither agreement nor disagreement, but Macurdy said that he'd already had more than enough to think about.

Earlier, Wollerda had sent a page with a royal order to have a sheep taken to a drill ground for Vulkan. Now Macurdy went with the giant boar, guided by a palace guardsman. They waited while Vulkan ate, not a pretty demolition. Then the boar was shown to a shed newly bedded with fresh clover hay, while a stableboy, looking ill, cleaned up the dinner mess.

Macurdy asked Vulkan if he'd prefer to be let out of the palace for the night. Vulkan said the shed would be fine. «I can wander widely enough in the spirit,» he added.

Macurdy wondered what that would be like.

After supper, Macurdy was invited to bathe with Wollerda and Liiset. The drill was a little different than it had been years before. Perhaps, Macurdy thought, because he hadn't bathed for several days, and then only briefly, in a river. Or maybe his bloodstream still held vestiges of the wild leeks of Miskmehr. At any rate, after being shown to his room, and offloading his personal gear there, he was taken to a small room off the royal bath, where there was a wash bench with basins, buckets of hot water, and a bowl of soap. There he and Wollerda soaped up and rinsed off.

Then they went into the bath together. It had the same large round tub he remembered, sunk half into the floor. Liiset already sat up to her shoulders in

steaming water. Macurdy pulled his glance away. Not
that he could see all that much, and what he saw was
distorted by the water. But he knew what she looked
like—incredibly lovely—because she was one of Varia's
clone-mates. Their auras were different, but physically
they were virtually identical. And eternally twenty, as
he was eternally twenty-five. Or if not eternally, close
enough by human standards.

He wondered what Pastor Koht would say about
that, or about this group bath.

After the two men got settled in the tub, Macurdy
asked Liiset what she'd heard about Varia lately. It
proved to be not very recent, but had probably not
changed. Gavriel was emperor, and Cyncaidh his chief
counselor. Though Liiset didn't say so, Macurdy suspected that Varia was Cyncaidh's close confidante,
sounding board, and unofficial advisor. They lived in
the capital most of the year. And they'd had a second
son, who Liiset said was a teenager now.

"Do they seem to be getting along?"

She looked knowingly at him. "Presumably. Selira
is Sarkia's ambassador there, and sees them from time
to time at official occasions. And Selira reads auras very
skillfully; all the ambassadors do. She'd be aware if
anything was substantially wrong. And being Varia's
clone-mate, I've asked to be kept on the information
line."

He nodded absently. It was what he'd expected, and
it seemed to him he should be glad. For Varia and
Cyncaidh. But he'd nurtured a hope, small, perverse,
and mostly suppressed, that Cyncaidh had reached
decline, and that Varia would soon be unattached.

He wondered, then, about his sons by Varia, sons
he'd never seen, who were claimed and held by the
Sisterhood. He would, he promised himself, meet them,
even if it required visiting the Cloister.

❖   ❖   ❖

After his bath with the royal couple, Macurdy was given a bathrobe, and went to his room. His grungy fatigues had been taken away for laundering. He was about to go to bed when someone rapped on his door. He knew who it had to be, and put his bathrobe back on. "Come in," he called.

It was Omara who entered, as on his last night at the palace, those long years before. Her gaze was unreadable and steady, as always. Besides a high level of the "ylvin talent," her aura showed intelligence, honesty, calm strength, and light sexuality. And an abundant sense of responsibility.

"Have a seat," he said, gesturing at a chair, then sat down facing her. "You came here to tell me something, or ask me something."

"I have come to ask when you intend to leave. And for where."

"Tomorrow after lunch, or possibly the day after. Depends on what comes up when we talk in the morning. As for plans—Vulkan and I will go north. To see Varia and her ylvin lord."

"Ah." Macurdy knew from the way she said it that she'd half expected that answer. She paused, then went on. "Sarkia tells me things she tells no one else. She trusts me not to repeat them, and I don't. This evening I will make an exception, because if she knew you were here, she would want me to. And it becomes urgent because you plan to visit Varia.

"Sarkia admires you, Macurdy, admires you greatly. Even knowing your dislike of her. And she believed, had faith, that you would someday return to Yuulith. She is very feeble now, weighs no more than a child, and sleeps sixteen hours of the twenty-four. Her only exercise is to shuffle around her room, leaning on a small chair with wheels, a nurse on either side. She receives three oil rubs each day, to stimulate circulation and prevent bed sores.

"She clings to life only because of her concern over who will succeed her as dynast. She has admitted to me that she erred in not deciding years ago. Now Idri is in a position to take the throne by force, once Sarkia dies, which may be next week or next year. Next week is the likelier."

Omara paused, looking long and inscrutably at Macurdy. Even her aura told him little. "The dynast considers you her last real hope," she finished.

"Me?"

"You and Varia. She hopes Varia will come back to succeed her, with you as her consort. Varia to rule, you to support her. Then Sarkia would resign, turning the dynast's throne over to Varia.

"She believes the Guards would support you. And that while she lives, the Tigers will not revolt, even if Varia exiles or imprisons Idri. Which she would, of necessity."

"What do you believe?" Macurdy asked. "About the Tigers. Is Sarkia right?"

"If she were not, Idri would already have deposed her. To the Tigers, Sarkia is their mother. Idri would murder her if she could, and hang someone else for it. And of course, Sarkia knows that very well. She keeps guards around her always, and has her own cooks."

Good lord, Macurdy thought, *what a mess.* "What about you?" he asked. "She trusts you, and you already run things for her. Wouldn't the Guards back you if she told them to? I'll bet the Sisters would—Cloister Sisters and Outland Sisters."

"Not against the Tigers. Conceivably they might, if I were charismatic, but I am not. Varia, on the other hand, is charismatic, and you are doubly so. You do not realize the respect the older Tigers have for you, from Quaie's War. They are not a breed much given to thought, but they are observant, and in their way, intelligent. And they admire charisma, something largely lacking in themselves."

She paused for a long silent moment. "Will you do it?" she asked.

Is this why I came back? Macurdy wondered. *Or part of the reason?* He wished Vulkan were there. "Omara," he said, "I can't answer you now. The most I can promise is that I'll tell Varia what Sarkia wants. But Varia loves Cyncaidh, of that I'm sure. She told me herself, and her aura backed her words. And they have children." *As we had. Have. Taken from her by Sarkia as nurslings, as property of the Sisterhood. Could she be influenced by them? And what would Cyncaidh say or do if she decided she did want to leave him?* From what he knew of the ylf, it was not inconceivable he might accept her decision.

"Tell Sarkia to hang on and hope," Macurdy said. "Maybe serendipity will help."

Omara actually frowned. "Serendipity?"

"It's a Farside word. I learned it from Varia. It means that sometimes something unexpected happens, and bails you out. It's nothing to depend on, but it's saved my ass more than once."

"Ah . . . Serendipity." She pronounced it carefully, tasting it. "I will remember that word. To my knowledge, we do not have one like it."

She got gracefully to her feet. Sisters, Macurdy told himself, are always graceful. "Now that we have discussed the Sisterhood's business," she said, "shall we discuss yours?"

"Mine?"

"I am a healer, Macurdy. The best. And an important part of my skill is seeing more in an aura than others do. In yours I see buried grief. Grief and loss." She stepped toward him till they were only a foot apart. His breath felt trapped in his chest, and testosterone flowed. "Shall I heal you?" she murmured.

Without waiting for an answer, she slipped her arms round him. He felt her body against his, lowered his face to hers, felt her lips . . .

Brief minutes later they lay beside one another, bare flanks touching. "I'm sorry," he murmured.

"Sorry? Why?"

"For being so rough. In such a hurry."

"Do not apologize. I remember what you were like before: thoughtful and skilled. But this time I did not intend or expect that. This was catharsis. It was to loosen the grief, put it in perspective." She chuckled. "A treatment I made up on the spur of the moment, and found highly agreeable.

"Now," she added, "tell me about that grief."

Omara already knew of the twofold loss of Varia: her abduction from Farside by Idri and Xader, then her marriage to Cyncaidh. And the loss of Melody, a loss that had driven him back to Farside. Now he told her of Mary. The settings and situations were strange to her, less than real, but her talent perceived both his love and Mary's. When he'd finished, Omara was very sober.

"Macurdy," she said, "you are a highly fortunate man, and your Mary was a highly fortunate woman. You had a love seldom known to either women or men, at least in Yuulith. And while you may not believe me, Mary still lives, in the spirit world, as Melody does. A clean, good, bright place. She is simply absent from your waking life."

Waking life. He remembered Mary visiting him, with their daughter. Remembered her words. Had it been more than a dream? And Melody's visit, that night in the surrey as he'd taken her body to Teklapori. He'd never known whether he'd been awake or sleeping, having a dream, or a visitation. Or maybe both. Either way it had helped.

"Sometimes I believe," he said. "For a little while anyway."

He raised himself on an elbow and looked down at Omara. "It's funny about you. It seems like you don't feel emotions, but at the same time you understand them better than just about anyone."

"Everyone has emotions, Macurdy. In some they are frozen—in some people who are ruled by fear. In others they are like quicksilver, in still others like flame. In some they are like a flood, leaving no footing for reason. Mine are quiet, and modulated by reason, but they are not cold."

Leaning over her, he kissed her lips. "You know what?" he murmured. "If you give me another chance, I'll do a better job as a lover."

14

Electric Luck

The next morning, Macurdy had breakfast with Wollerda and Liiset. His first question was directed to the queen. "Do you happen to know how wide the Ocean Sea is?" he asked.

"Actually I do. Thanks to you and Varia's ylf lord, we've developed substantial trade with the empires. And along with a change of attitude, one of the things we've gotten is books. We have a library at the Cloister now, something unthought of twenty years ago. One book I've read cites an ancient crossing from Hithmearc—which is the name of the other side. It supposedly took fifty-eight days."

Hithmearc! Macurdy thought. *That clinches it. The voitusotar are definitely the threat. And I bet she knows it.*

Liiset noticed his reaction. "What is it?" she asked.

He fudged. "It's hard to imagine danger coming so far. But it's hard to imagine Vulkan being wrong, too."

She gazed intently at him for another moment, aware that his answer had been less than candid. "True," she said nodding.

"Closer to home," Wollerda broke in, "how are you fixed for money, Macurdy?"

The question led to Wollerda buying Piglet. Ozian horses were prized throughout the Rude Lands, and Wollerda used this to replenish Macurdy's depleted cash. Meanwhile Liiset arranged for cash from the Sisterhood's embassy. If Macurdy was to take a message to the Western Empire, she said, he must be paid for his expenses, influence, and time.

Meanwhile the royal saddle maker was ordered to create a suitable saddle for Macurdy's new mount: Vulkan. The man was dismayed at the time requirement; he couldn't possibly form a saddle by midday to fit a giant boar. Macurdy assured him he planned no military or hunt riding, in fact little if anything beyond an easy road trot. "I just need something to ease the wear and tear on Vulkan's back and my butt," he said.

He settled for spending that day and night at the palace—or near it. That afternoon he rode tree-lined country lanes with Wollerda. Mostly they talked about the old times, the revolution. The threat from across the Ocean Sea came up only tangentially—Macurdy mentioned that on his way north, he planned to visit Jeremid. "If an army is needed," he said, "I want him as a commander."

That night Liiset invited Omara too to share the royal bath. And afterward the Sister shared Macurdy's bed again.

The saddle was delivered at breakfast. It fitted as far forward as proper movement would allow, to reduce the stress on Vulkan's more lightly constructed hindquarters and spinal column. Macurdy worried about how it would feel to the boar, until Vulkan told him: «My friend, it will be quite satisfactory. And should it turn out otherwise, you can buy a horse along the way, or ride bareback.»

An hour after breakfast, the travelers left. The king and queen waved good-bye from the broad, polished granite porch of the palace, then went back inside.

"He was not entirely honest with us," Liiset said.

"Macurdy?"

She nodded. "He knows more than he admitted about the threat Vulkan senses from the Ocean Sea. And I know what that threat is, what it has to be. It's all in a history of the ylver, the same book that told how wide the sea is. How Macurdy learned of it, I do not know, unless from Vulkan. And how would Vulkan know? But they do know, both of them."

Macurdy chose to ride through the town itself, escorted by a mounted squad of Wollerda's palace guard, to reassure the townsfolk and avoid disorders. Meanwhile rumor had circulated, the day before, that Macurdy was at the palace with a great boar. Many townsmen had already heard the story, spreading along the Valley Highway, of a tall, powerful warrior who rode with a great boar beside him. Part of Macurdy's legend had him riding a great boar—a fiction originating outside Tekalos, that had spread there after Quaie's War. It had derived from his riding the big warhorse he'd named Hog.

So the actual sight of him on an 1,100-pound boar was not the shock it might have been.

Still there were folktales of the great boars, their sorceries and savagery. Along with Vulkan's great-shouldered bulk, fierce red eyes, deadly tusks and sheer presence, Macurdy was given nearly the full width of the main street. Horsemen and carters pulled into alleys, or tried to. Bystanders stood with their backs against the flanking buildings.

And they did not applaud. On horseback and without Vulkan, a recognized Macurdy would have engendered enthusiasm. They'd have cheered their heads off for the hero of the revolution. But awe is not loud, and awe is what they felt.

Their ride through town had not been expected, so only a few hundred people actually saw them pass through. Afterward two or three thousand would tell of watching them in person. And Macurdy's long-standing mystique would be similarly multiplied. Imagine saddling and riding a creature who'd been feared for centuries! A monster whose rare tracks, let alone livestock kills, sent far worse chills down farmers' backs than the howls of any wolf pack. Not even trolls engendered greater fear.

When they reached the Valley Highway, the travelers turned west instead of east. From time to time they talked. Among other things, they discussed the situation in the Sisterhood, and Macurdy asked Vulkan what he thought of Sarkia's proposal. Vulkan replied that compared to the voitik threat, the future of the Sisterhood was unimportant. If Macurdy went with Varia to the Cloister, Vulkan said, it would be well to do it with the voitusotar in mind, and the defense of Yuulith.

The voitusotar. Macurdy couldn't imagine them actually invading Yuulith. They were too susceptible to seasickness. They died of it. They didn't even ride horses, let alone ships. Someone else might invade across the Ocean Sea, but not the voitusotar.

And then, having thought it, he remembered his dream.

But whoever invaded Yuulith, if anyone did, it seemed to him the Sisterhood's Tiger and Guards units could be useful in its defense. Vulkan agreed. Especially, he said, since the Sisterhood's predominantly ylvin ancestry should provide meaningful protection against voitik sorceries.

With few exceptions, the travelers they met had heard of the man traveling with a great boar. With, but not on. And they didn't know that the man was Macurdy. Certainly all had heard of Macurdy, but none recognized him. After so long, none had expected him to return to Yuulith.

At first none realized what approached them. A man on a small horse, they thought. When finally they realized, most were within eighty yards, with only time to get off the road. A man passing *on* a giant boar was even more awesome than someone simply accompanied by one.

Not till late was Macurdy recognized. Someone who'd seen them in the crossroads inn, he supposed, for the man pulled off the road and waved, greeting them by name as they passed.

They stopped again at the inn, for supper and the night. This time the stableboy ran not to the stable but into the inn itself, where he hid. For this time there was no horse, and he was terrified at the prospect of grooming the giant boar. Macurdy ordered supper, then sat outside on the broad low porch, to eat with Vulkan, who was having cabbages and potatoes. Bit by bit, the men inside came quietly out to watch. Before they were done, several had asked respectful questions, first of Macurdy, then of Vulkan. The giant boar answered as appropriate, letting them experience his mental voice within their minds.

At the break of dawn they left, northward on the North Fork Road, instead of continuing west. This was country Macurdy knew well, from the revolution.

By midday, Macurdy and Vulkan were well into the forested Kullvordi Hills, where they turned off on a narrower road, rockier but less rutted. Here Macurdy dismounted, and they continued, now only Macurdy visible. Reports of them might well not have penetrated this country lane, and he didn't want to panic the locals.

He recognized the place when they came to it. As was typical in these hills, the cropland and hayfields were in a valley, and the livestock grazed the adjacent forest and grassy glades. The large house was of pine logs squared and fitted, and there were numerous log outbuildings.

A female servant answered his knock, and when he identified himself, hurried off to "fetch the missus."

The missus. The other time Macurdy had been there, his old friend had had three servant mistresses, instead of a wife. After a minute, Macurdy heard a female voice seemingly giving orders in an undertone. Moments later, a strong handsome woman stepped onto the stoop. A mountain woman, he thought. Her face and aura told him she didn't believe he was who he'd said.

Jeremid wasn't home, she told him. A troll had raided in the neighborhood, and he was off with a party of men, hunting it with hounds. "If they find it by daylight," she said, "they can kill it."

"Is there anyone who can take me to them?"

"To the kill where they started from, I suppose. From there you'd have to track them."

"I'll give it a try."

She called a servant, a youth who arrived with a limp, and gave him instructions. Then she looked at Macurdy. "Where's your horse? You didn't walk here."

He made a quick decision. "It's no horse I ride," he said. "It's a four-legged wizard, a great boar. He's covered himself with a concealment spell. We didn't want to alarm folks up here, where you haven't heard of us."

She frowned. "Concealment spell?"

"Brace yourself and I'll give you a look."

She peered around, not knowing what to make of this.

"Vulkan," Macurdy said, "let her see you."

And there stood the giant boar, the midday sun shining on his back. She'd had no preparation beyond Macurdy's few sentences, which she hadn't believed. Abruptly she stepped backward, the blood leaving her face. But she didn't cry out, didn't faint, didn't turn and dart back through the door. It was the servant who fainted.

After a moment she found her tongue. "Holy Brog'r!" she said, then turned to Macurdy. "And he's got a saddle on him. I owe you an apology. I didn't believe you were the marshal." Stepping back through the doorway, she spoke to someone in the room. "Kurmo, hang up your crossbow. It really is the marshal, and you'd never guess what he rode up on."

She shook Macurdy's hand like a man would have, or Melody. "My name is Corla," she said. "I'll take you myself."

After saddling her mare, she led Macurdy and Vulkan to the next farm, a mile up the road. She had them wait in the woods a short distance from the house, and rode up to it. When she'd prepared the farmwife for what she was about to see, she waved them up. Then she introduced Macurdy and started home again.

A worried-looking hired boy led Macurdy and his mount to the edge of the woods behind the field. There they stopped, the boy pointing toward a spring that flowed into a wooden watering trough. Near it lay the remains of a plow ox. Macurdy rode up to it, and looked it over, impressed. The troll had been enormously strong to dismember it as it had.

The boy had remained at the edge of the woods, either he or his saddle mule unwilling to follow. "Can I go back now, Marshal Macurdy sir?" the boy called. His voice broke, partly from fear, partly from puberty.

"How many men are tracking it?" Macurdy asked.

"Six I think. That's what left the house. Please can I go back sir?"

"Sure, go on," Macurdy answered, and the boy, turning his mule, trotted it briskly homeward.

The ox's left foreleg was missing, with most of the shoulder, as if torn off and carried away. Macurdy wasn't much of a tracker himself, but the trail of five or six mounted men shouldn't be hard to follow. The problem was speed.

It was Vulkan who dealt with that. He started briskly up the ridge, Macurdy on his back. «My nose,» Vulkan said, «is more sensitive to smells than most dogs' are. The troll smell itself calls me, despite the hours and horses that have passed.»

At times the trail was steep enough that Macurdy, riding without reins, gripped the ridge of coarse hair on Vulkan's shoulders to stay aboard. Then they were over the crest, and started down the other side. Here Macurdy was especially grateful for the stirrups. Few horses would willingly tackle so steep a slope head-on. Probably, he thought, the men had walked, leading their mounts.

"How far do you think it'll be?" he asked.

«Trolls are more intelligent than given credit for,» Vulkan answered. «Some more than others. Normally they avoid the vicinity of farms. Big game is their staple. Those which succumb to the temptation of livestock are usually hunted down and killed, sooner or later. Occasionally one becomes clever at avoiding hunters. This is an exceptionally large male, which suggests age, experience, and intelligence.»

"But they can't tolerate daylight, right?"

«It varies with brightness. At night their eyesight is excellent. In full sunlight they are blind. Even in shade they see only dimly; otherwise they could not be hunted down and killed. In the forest, by dusk, they see decently,

and will travel in the evening. But at the first dawnlight, they know the sun will follow, so they find a place
to hide. Under the roots of a wind-tipped tree, or in
an old bear den, or under a dense copse. Or in a cane-
brake, if nothing better is available.»

Shortly they reached broken ground, with narrow
ravines, rock falls, and bluffs. Briefly Vulkan paused
for breath. «He has forced them to leave his trail,» he
thought to Macurdy. «Trolls have long, powerful arms.
They can clamber up slopes impossible for horses,
grasping trees to help themselves. The men have chosen
to go around, some in one direction, some in the other,
looking for easier terrain. The hounds will follow the
scent. Lay low and hold on. I will try to follow it
directly.»

The terrain was difficult even for Vulkan, who
repeatedly had to leave the trail. At times the troll followed the contour, more or less. *And it did all this last
night,* Macurdy thought, *when no one was tracking it.
It must have thought this through in advance, visual-
izing things that might happen.*

Vulkan replied to Macurdy's unspoken thought:
«They plan to a limited degree, varying with the individual.»

"How can it carry that foreleg here? Seems like it
would need both hands to climb."

«It has carried it in its jaws from the beginning. Trolls
walk easily on their two feet, but travel faster on all
four.»

After a bit the terrain eased, the trail continuing
more directly. "Are the hunters back on the trail?"
Macurdy asked.

«They are following the dogs. Do you hear them?»

"No. Do you?"

«For the last several minutes I've been guiding on
their baying. It is quicker.»

❖   ❖   ❖

They'd been following the troll for nearly two hours when Macurdy first heard the dogs, the sound growing louder as Vulkan gained on them. Thunder rumbled, and he realized the day had darkened. Shortly, beneath the forest roof, it became dark as dusk, and still. Sporadic rain spattered on treetops.

The dogs ceased their trail call, the sound changing to excited barking that said they'd caught up to their quarry. He heard a roar, the scream of a dog, furious barking and raging, more screams. More roars, in two voices overlapping; it hadn't occurred to Macurdy that trolls might travel in pairs. Men shouted. A horse screamed, then another. Vulkan had increased his speed, and with no free hand to fend off brush, Macurdy lay low on the heavy shoulders. Ahead a man screamed, the sound cutting off sharply.

Macurdy's attention was on the noise of combat. He'd totally missed the wind thrashing the treetops. Now a wall of rain marched across the forest canopy, with a sound he could not ignore—like an oncoming train. The fighting was less than a hundred yards away when the deluge struck—rain, hail, leaves and twigs. Lightning stabbed vividly, thunder crashed, branches and pieces of tree trunk thudded to the ground. A wild-eyed horse dashed past, an empty saddle on its back.

Then, in front of him, Macurdy saw two huge shaggy forms. The lesser, beset by a trio of furious hounds, was flailing at them with the broken remains of a man. The other stalked crouching toward two men a few yards distant, one man with a shortsword, the other with a knife. Three horses were down; the others had fled.

Vulkan stopped so abruptly, his rider almost lost his seat. A single thought slammed Macurdy's mind: «OFF!» He dismounted, drawing his sword.

Then Vulkan charged the troll who swung the battered corpse, and struck the creature head-on, driving it backward, his powerful neck and shoulders slamming great tusks deeply into the troll's belly. Squalling, spilling guts, the troll grabbed Vulkan even as it fell, taking him down with it.

Macurdy's attention was on the larger troll. Raising his sword, he shot a ball of plasma from its tip, a ball half as large as his fist. Then turning, he aimed at the troll wrestling with Vulkan, but afraid of hitting the boar, he turned back to the other.

His plasma ball had struck through the larger troll's guts. Yet the creature seemed unaffected, except that it had paused in its attack. Before Macurdy could fire again, lightning flashed, accompanied by a stupendous bang of thunder that drove him to his knees.

A minute or minutes later, his wits somewhat recovered, he lurched to his feet, pelted by cold rain and acorn-sized hail. Vulkan had shaken free of the troll he'd disemboweled. The other troll had disappeared, though examination would disclose scattered fragments. The two other men were on the ground. One was struggling to sit up. Macurdy wobbled over to him.

"Damn it, Jeremid," he said, "don't you know enough to get in out of the rain?"

The man stared up at Macurdy. "You!" he husked. "Bhroig's balls! Where in hell . . ." Then he looked at Vulkan, who was also coming toward him.

"He's my buddy," Macurdy said, gesturing with his head. "His name is Vulkan. He's bigger than me and he's smarter than me, and I think he calls lightning down from the clouds."

«Not I, Macurdy.» The "voice" resonated in their minds. «I am only a *bodhisattva* and great boar. You are the Lion of Farside.»

Jeremid had a broken arm. One of the trolls had jerked a spear from a man's hands and slammed Jeremid with its shaft, breaking his humerus. So it was Macurdy who loaded Jeremid's unconscious hunting partner across Vulkan's saddle, and lashed him securely in place with reins from dead horses.

Before they left, Macurdy took time to examine the troll Vulkan had killed. Eight feet from heels to crown, he judged, and five or six hundred pounds, with fangs to match. The hands were bigger than any he could have imagined, and bore claws. It was female, and had been pregnant. The other, the male they'd been following, might have stood ten feet, and weighed eight or ten hundred pounds.

They headed back toward the farm, Vulkan leading the way. Macurdy brought up the rear, whacking off saplings here and there with his sword, and blazing an occasional larger tree, so others could more easily find the bodies and bring them out.

By the time they got to the farm they'd started from, the sun was shining, low in the west. And Arnoth, the man who'd started out tied across the saddle, was sitting on it.

Of the four men who'd died, two were hired men on Jeremid's farm, one was the hired man from the farm the troll had raided, and one was a neighbor from farther down the road. Arnoth was not visibly injured, but was weak and dazed, seemingly from the lightning strike.

Arnoth's hired man had left a widow and orphan. The child—the lad who'd taken Macurdy to the dead ox—was sent to notify the dead neighbor's widow. Jeremid promised to get word to relatives of both women.

By that time the shock had worn off, and Jeremid had more than enough pain in his arm. Macurdy set and splinted it, then began the healing. Unlike Arbel, he used neither flute nor drum. Guided by Jeremid's aura, he simply manipulated the energy field around the break, and over the rest of the body. Finally they started down the road to Jeremid's farm, both men walking.

After supper, they sat on the side porch, in late spring twilight that smelled of moist soil, growing plants, and livestock. Jeremid had a jug beside him for painkilling. Vulkan rested on the ground a few feet away. Sundown had invigorated the mosquitoes, and Macurdy had woven a repellent spell.

He'd already given Jeremid a brief summary of his years back on Farside. Now he described his visit to Wollerda and Liiset, and what Vulkan had said about a threat from across the Ocean Sea. "So we're heading north to see Varia and her ylvin lord. The empires need to know." He didn't mention Sarkia's message.

"Hnh!" Jeremid peered intently at Macurdy. "And then what?"

Macurdy didn't answer at once. "I'll do whatever comes to mind," he said at last. "Something will. Some folks need a plan. But I seem to do best by doing whatever occurs to me. Sometimes it *is* a plan, and I follow it as long as it's working. But even then I do whatever seems best. There's no guarantees in life. I've learned that the hard way."

"I don't suppose you've got any attention on your ex-wife?"

"I haven't had much luck with marriages."

He'd answered without thinking, had been looking at his marriages as three tragedies: Varia kidnapped and lost to him, Melody drowned, Mary with her chest crushed. But his weeks with Varia had been remarkably happy, and he'd learned a lot from her. He couldn't imagine what he'd be like without having had those weeks. And Melody? Her open jaunty manner, her reckless fearlessness, her passion for him . . . And finally Mary; not counting his time away at war, they'd had more than a dozen years together. Sweet years, loving years. *Macurdy,* he thought, *instead of moping, you ought to congratulate yourself on how lucky you've been.*

Jeremid's thoughts had turned to what Macurdy had

told him about an invasion threat. "Looks like you might end up raising another army," he said. "You're probably the only one who can."

Macurdy nodded. "That's probably what Vulkan had in mind when he took up with me. Lord knows, life was easier for him before we got together."

Jeremid grinned, the same irreverent grin Macurdy remembered, but now it was to Vulkan he spoke. "Is that right? I thought you were the boss now."

«What Macurdy does is up to Macurdy,» Vulkan answered. «He makes his own decisions. My function is to support him. I inform as needed, and advise without insisting. I point things out.»

Jeremid laughed. "And on the side, gut an occasional troll." He cocked an eye. "I notice you left the bigger one for Macurdy though."

«I attacked the one I felt I could defeat. And Macurdy is the more formidable of us. I trust you noticed.»

Jeremid's expression changed. "Huh! I guess he is at that!" He turned to Macurdy. "You even call down lightning."

"Now don't say that! That's something I sure as hell didn't do."

"I leave it to Vulkan," Jeremid said, and looked at the giant boar, hulking in the dusk beside the porch. "Did he or didn't he?"

«I believe you witnessed his fireball. Had the lightning not struck, he'd have cast another, no doubt striking the troll in the chest or head. In which case it would have gone down. It was already dying, but they die hard. They have great vitality, and fight as long as they have life.»

Jeremid laughed again. "You didn't answer my question."

«Neither did I lie. Sometimes, however, I do not tell all I know.»

Jeremid grinned at the giant boar. "You sound smarter by the minute. Now I'll tell you two something. As a rule, I don't lie either. But when I tell the story of what happened today, I'm telling it that the Lion of Farside called down lightning from the sky to kill a troll. Obliterate a troll! And that's why I'm alive. Arnoth will back me up. He saw the fireball and experienced the lightning.

"And believe me about this: that story will spread all over Tekalos within ten days. In a month, six weeks, they'll know it in Oz, and in the Silver Mountain, and across the Big River in the Marches. By that time the trolls will be the biggest ever seen, all three of them. When it comes time to raise another army, that should help." He paused. "And if you need an experienced commander . . ."

Macurdy looked long at him, wondering how he deserved such friends. "Thank you, old pal," he said. "I intend to. I'd be a fool to reject your offer."

After Jeremid went to bed, Macurdy sat on the porch again and talked with Vulkan. "Seems like I don't treat you the way I ought to," he said, "but I don't know how to do any better. You do all the carrying. And when I'm lying on a feather bed, you're lying on the ground, or at best in hay. When I was with Omara, you were alone in a shed. While I eat a nice meal, you wait around to be given a sheep, or grub in the woods or a marsh, rooting up skunk cabbage or cattails. It doesn't seem right."

«My dear friend. First of all, I am used to being physically alone. It has been my way of life. Having a human companion is a new experience for me in this incarnation. As for the rest of it . . . I am a *bodhisattva*, incarnate in the body of a very large—most would say monstrous—wild pig. In fact, in important ways I *am* a wild pig, and have been one for centuries. Rooting up skunk cabbage, cattail, and various other tasties, or devouring entrails, is natural for me. I enjoy them. And wild swine are well adapted to sleeping on the ground. Sleeping on hay is a luxury, one I can both enjoy and do without. I appreciate your concern, but it is misplaced, I assure you.

«Now I suggest you go to bed. I am off to the forest. This rain should stimulate the emergence of certain mushrooms I find highly toothsome.»

15

Secrecy and Skullduggery

After three long days in the saddle from Teklapori, Omara had arrived at the Cloister well after dark. She'd slept till midmorning, then gone to her office long enough to check in with her aide. From there she went to Sarkia's apartment, on the same corridor as their offices.

Sarkia was awake, she was told, had been bathed and oiled and was having "breakfast." No doubt the usual beef broth and puréed vegetables or fruit, Omara thought. She chose to wait, rather than interrupt. Shortly the Dynast's attendant came out with a tray, two small cups, and a pair of spoons. Seeing Omara waiting, she stopped.

"There's been no apparent change in the Dynast's condition," she said.

"Good," Omara answered. There was never apparent change, on a day-to-day basis. Death was the only abrupt change that feeble body could accommodate. But looking back two or three months, one could see the deterioration.

She went into the Dynast's bedroom, which for three years had also served as office and audience chamber. "Good morning, Your Grace," Omara said, speaking loudly and clearly.

The bony, nearly bald head turned on the pillow, just enough that Sarkia could see her visitor. "Good morning, Omara." The voice, though weak, was surprisingly clear. "The embassy's courier reached me two days ago. What did Macurdy look like?"

"There can be no question now of the dominance of his ylvin inheritance, Your Grace. He is physically unchanged except for some interesting scars. Some years after you removed our post in Evansville, there was a major war—a worldwide war—on Farside. And he of course was in it, and survived."

"Hmm." The Dynast's eyes no longer saw clearly, but it was her psyche that studied Omara's aura. Her eyes merely helped focus her attention. "Where are the scars?" she asked.

Calm rational Omara blushed, and the old woman laughed softly. "I trust he remains fully functional. It would be a shame to lose him as potential breeding stock. One might hope he'd father as many litters as his uncle. On Varia if possible, or on you if she lacks the good judgement to have him again." Sarkia paused. "Or better yet on both of you."

From Sarkia that was a lot of words at once, Omara thought. "In a sense, that's what I've come to report. Macurdy planned to leave Teklapori a few hours after I did, bound for Duinarog, to see Varia. I took the liberty of telling him what you once said about Varia succeeding as Dynast here, with him beside her as her consort and deputy, and military commander. He promised to tell her."

"But he was not enthused?"

"Not enthused, but not antagonistic. He will tell her, but I doubt he will argue for it."

Then she told Sarkia about the giant boar, and summarized what Vulkan had said about a threat from across the Ocean Sea. While Omara spoke, the old Dynast lay silent, her eyes closed. Her aura, though, told Omara she was fully awake. It was a blessing she heard so well.

Not till Omara had finished did Sarkia speak again, her eyes still closed. She totally ignored what Omara had said about a great boar, and a threat from Hithmearc.

"To meet Varia," she mused. "We must ensure they decide in our favor. Did Liiset mention his sons to Macurdy? Of how, on my orders, she'd cultivated respect in them for Varia and himself?"

"I think not. He and I spent considerable time together, and I believe he would have mentioned it if she had."

The fragile old head turned slightly toward Omara again, and the lipless mouth smiled. "It is well that you have a relationship with him. It should improve us in his eyes. And I see it pleased you. I trust you pleased him as well." Omara colored again, slightly. "I see you did," Sarkia said.

"Well. Now what you must do is send their sons to Duinarog, as fast as they can get there. To meet their mother and father, and urge them to come here. That will make the difference. That will persuade them."

Sarkia no longer looked at Omara; it required too much effort. Her eyes were open, but directed toward the ceiling now, unseeingly. "They must leave early tomorrow," she said, "and travel fast. I want them there when their father arrives. Write them orders of what they're to do, not in detail, but in principle. And no one—especially Idri!—must learn of this. The mission must be concealed. Even the boys must not know, till after they have left."

Again she turned her head to look at Omara. The healer's aura told her nothing of consequence. "I'm tired now," Sarkia muttered, "dry husk that I am. And I must preserve my strength, my life, until they get here. Then I'll be free to die."

Idri's office door opened, and she looked up from her Tiger breeding schedule for the summer. "What is it, Jaloon?"

"Omara arrived last evening from Teklapori. She is with Sarkia."

Idri scowled. Without Omara, the old witch would be dead, and the waiting over. "So?" she said.

"Someone else arrived from Teklapori, early this morning: a courier from the embassy." Jaloon paused. "Macurdy was there, to see the king and queen. And Omara." She paused again. "A spy in the palace reports that Macurdy then left for Duinarog, to see Varia."

Idri's eyebrows raised sharply. She had long known, through an informer, that Sarkia favored Varia as the new dynast, had since early in her decline. To entice Varia, she'd planned to dangle Macurdy in front of her, as her consort and military commander, and probably her deputy. But Macurdy had returned to Farside instead. And when he didn't come back, it had seemed to Idri the danger was past. Now it was not only renewed, it was imminent.

She dismissed Jaloon and left her office. She routinely skipped breakfast, preferring to work for two or three hours, then go early to the executive dining room for brunch. As she reached the central gallery of the administration building, she saw two youths in Guards uniforms crossing it. The sight stopped her. She knew them at once—Varia's twin sons by Macurdy. What were they doing in *this* building? She watched as they entered the corridor which led to Sarkia's office and apartment, her nurses' quarters, and Omara's executive suite. And nowhere else.

Idri knew then, knew as if she'd been told: they'd

be sent to Duinarog, to influence Varia and Macurdy. They'd be rushed there, because Macurdy had a head start.

Idri, being Idri, found power and prestige a massive attraction, and assumed that everyone did. But she also knew that Macurdy had resisted it. And that Varia had prestige, if questionable power, as the wife of the Cyncaidh.

It seemed to Idri that Varia's response was the crux now, and Varia had learned peculiar ways and values on Farside. Would she prefer real power as Dynast, with her Farside husband and their two brats beside her? Or choose her ylvin husband and their children? And there was the matter of the ylf of course. Would he let her go if she wanted to? Offhand it seemed unlikely, but Idri had heard that though he was strong in some ways, in others he was afraid to impose his will.

At any rate, Varia was the problem and the solution. The rest were incidental.

Abruptly Idri turned and strode back to her office. Brunch could wait. She had things to arrange.

Omara's office door opened. "Varia's sons are here," her aide said quietly.

"Send them in, Posi."

Omara was on her feet when they entered. Entered respectfully, for she was the Dynast's deputy, and despite her youthful appearance, probably fifty years old or more. While they were nineteen, second-year ranks in the Guards.

Omara looked them over thoroughly. They were as tall as their father, and athletic looking. Within a few years they might approach him in muscle. Their hair was as red as their mother's, and their skin, from the drill field, the same unlikely tan. Their eyes were hazel green. "Sit," she said, indicating two chairs. They sat.

"You know your lineage," she told them. "Strong lineage, very strong. Able. The Dynast hopes for comparable qualities in you, and has decided you should have Outland experience. You are to leave at dawn tomorrow, and travel to Miskmehr for assignments in the embassy there."

The youths watched, their features controlled but their heart rates speeded. Omara took two sheets of paper from her desk, two lists, and gave them to the youths. "Here is the clothing and gear to take with you. Someday, not too distant, you may be carrying out missions for the Dynast herself. Some will be secret. Some will be urgent. So I am treating this trip as a trial and a drill, to see how you do. Do not disgrace yourselves.

"I want you there as quickly as possible without killing your horses. You will have remounts, and travel with an experienced sergeant who knows the route. He will meet you in the vestibule of your barracks no later than first dawn. First dawn. Be there, ready. Do not keep him waiting.

"On your way to your barracks, you will stop at supply and pick up two bundles containing clothing suitable to Rude Lands travelers.

"Say nothing of this to anyone. Not your platoon leader, not your sergeant, not anyone. I will be checking. If I discover you have broken secrecy, it will earn you a reprimand, and go into your records."

She paused, looking them up and down again. "If you have any questions or uncertainties, say so now . . . No? Good. You are dismissed."

When they had gone, Omara called in her page. "Lolana," she said, "go to the Guards duty office and tell them—*quietly!*—that I want to see Sergeant Veskabren Arva in the Rose Garden, at once. At once! But do not run. Do not draw attention to yourself. Do you understand?"

The girl nodded. "Yes ma'am," she said, then saluted and left.

In her office, Idri did not sit down. She paced. She needed to make decisions and necessary arrangements, and that required a plan. *Think!* she told herself. *How will Omara handle her part in this?* In the Sisterhood, males were little educated. And the twins would be—how old? Surely less than twenty years, and untraveled. Little traveled at best. Omara wouldn't send them galloping off by themselves. Who would she send with them? A Guardsman, of course, who'd been attached to the embassy in Duinarog, and was familiar with the route.

Her basic plan sprang full grown into her mind. A Guardsman attached to the embassy in Duinarog! *I have,* Idri told herself, *the perfect substitute.* It seemed a marvelous omen, and with Rillor she could terminate the risk irrevocably.

Abruptly she stepped to her door. "Jaloon," she said to her aide, "come in here. I want you to arrange something for me. Unobtrusively."

Idri looked over the information Jaloon had gotten for her. Omara had listed the twins in the travel book as going to the embassy in Miskmehr. So. They were indeed scheduled Outland. Miskmehr had to be a false destination, the cover story. A Guards senior sergeant named Veskabren Arva was also listed as going to Miskmehr; hardly a coincidence.

They would probably leave at dawn. That was customary for long trips. Now she had arrangements to make with Rillor and Skalvok.

Idri didn't have Koslovi Rillor come to her office. A Guards officer coming into this corridor might well be noticed. And would look odd, for she rarely had

official business with the Guards. Instead she met him
at the stable, where she was having her mare saddled.
She rode at least twice a week, to stay in shape for
travel, and because she liked to ride.

They did not speak, but rode separately out the
Cloister's open south gate, about a hundred yards apart.
The well-beaten bridle trail skirted the mountain stream
above the Cloister. Soon the trail entered the forest.
When she reached the junction with a side trail, she
stopped her mare, and waited till she saw Rillor again.
Then she rode out of sight up the side trail, and stop-
ping, dismounted.

A minute later he stood in front of her. He did not
reach, however. They were lovers, but on her terms,
not his.

Captain Koslovi Rillor was burly, hard-bodied, and
well endowed—the physical type that most stimulated
her.

"I have a vitally important mission for you," she said.
"If done properly, it will remove my single major rival
for the Dynast's throne. *Our* single major rival." She
didn't see auras, but she read faces. It was clear he
understood. "Do you know a Guards senior sergeant
named Arva?" she asked. "Veskabren Arva?"

"Right. We overlapped at the embassy in Duinarog
for a couple years. When he was there; he pulled courier duty a lot."

That explains why Omara chose him, Idri told herself. *It also gets rid of any doubt about where Varia's
brats are being sent.* "Ah!" she said. "Look, sweet pole,
this evening I'll leave my garden door unlatched. When
it's dark, come and see me. I'll have your mission instructions for you then; you'll be leaving the Cloister at dawn."

Rillor raised his eyebrows. "Mission instructions?
Is that all you'll have for me? It's been too long."

Idri chuckled. "It's never too long. The longer the
better."

He took a short step toward her, but she pressed him away. "This evening," she repeated. "Right now I need to get back. I have further arrangements to make."

They rode back separately, Rillor fantasizing the evening to come. Idri, however, was thinking about another captain—a Tiger captain. As far as she'd seen, Tigers had no scruples or reluctance about killing. They weren't even interested in the reasons. All they wanted was orders.

What they lacked was finesse, and not only in bed. Rillor was definitely the one for his role in this.

Before first dawn, Sergeant Arva quietly shut the door of his barracks behind him and looked eastward. He had an excellent mental clock, and much preferred being early to being late. There were no street lamps, nor any sign of dawn, only a slender crescent moon, still somewhat short of the meridian. Slinging his bag over a shoulder, he started toward the street.

Arva never heard the man step from behind an ornamental hedge, never heard the blackjack descend. He didn't even bleed, except slightly from ears and nose. His murderer dragged him behind some shrubbery, and quickly but systematically searched Arva's pockets, shirt front, and shoulder bag. Finding a large sealed envelope, he stuck it in his own shirt, then squatted beside his victim to wait.

Moments later a team and coach approached. Shouldering the corpse, the killer strode into the dark street. The coach slowed for him but did not stop. As it rolled by, he pulled its door open, heaved the body inside, then got in himself and pulled the door closed. The coach stopped a couple of hundred yards farther on, where tulip trees darkened the street even more. There the killer transferred the body to the coach's luggage boot, covering it with a tarp. That accomplished, he climbed to the driver's seat and showed him the envelope.

"Take me to Guards Barracks A, and hurry," he said. "I need to be waiting across the street before this Rillor gets there. And give him what I found on the carcass." He thumbed toward the back of the coach.

The driver grunted assent, and turned left at the next corner. *Deliver the envelope,* he rehearsed mentally, *then out the north gate and north a mile, across the line into Asmehr. Deliver the body to the guy waiting with a rubbish wagon. Then back here and return the coach before the stars have faded.*

He grinned. Nothing to it. He could develop an appetite for jobs like this. They'd keep life interesting.

16

Skin and Bones

In the design and construction of the Cloister, esthetics had been important but not primary. Cost, defensibility, and the efficient use of limited space set the constraints. Thus there was not much room between buildings—enough for narrow lawns, some flowerbeds and shrubs, and street trees. The residences—dormitories and barracks—mostly resembled each other. And of course, there were no street lights, nor any lights at this hour.

Captain Koslovi Rillor's barracks was adjacent to the Administration Building, at the center of the Cloister. Guards Barracks E, on the other hand, was on the East Wall Road. And like most of the Sisterhood, female or male, Rillor's night vision wasn't a lot better than human normal. But familiarity and the sickle moon told him exactly where he was.

Ahead, he recognized the building, and slowed to a walk, scanning about. The man he was watching for emerged from the shadow of a hedge, and stepped into the street to meet him. Rillor had never seen a Tiger out of uniform before, but he knew what he was by his demeanor—his sense of hardness and arrogance.

"Your name," the Tiger ordered.

"Rillor. Koslovi." He said it resentfully. He was, after all, a captain. The man before him might be, probably was noncommissioned. Arrogant!

The Tiger drew a large envelope from inside his shirt and handed it to the Guards officer, then loped off up the street.

Rillor tucked the envelope in his shoulder bag and angled toward the barracks' main entrance. He needed Omara's instructions to Arva, and the official offer to Varia and the Lion. Now, presumably, he had them. He wished he knew the *oral* instructions Omara had given Arva, and whether the two youths knew the identity of who was to pick them up. He couldn't pretend he was Arva. They might know the man.

You can't have everything, he told himself, stepping onto the stoop. Until he'd read the enclosures, he'd say no more than he had to.

Picking up the two young Guardsmen presented no problems. They were wide-awake and ready when he got there, and being well-trained, accepted his authority without questions. Together, the three had loped the half mile to the courier stable, where horses had been readied for them—three mounts, three remounts, and two packhorses.

Now they rode northward, the Cloister's defensive walls diminishing behind them in the faintly graying dawn. When it was light enough, Rillor intended to open the envelope and read the contents.

Ahead, a team and coach rolled toward the horsemen, and they guided their horses to one side, giving the rig abundant room to pass. Probably, Rillor thought, it carried some Outland trade representative.

❖   ❖   ❖

Ordinarily, in the Sisterhood, newborns were named
by their mother. That became their calling name. However, for routine records, breeding assignments and
performance ratings, the breeding stock or lineage
designation was used as a surname, and listed first.

But in conversation, the calling name was used
almost exclusively, except as necessary to clarify which
Rillor or Liiset or Jaloon was meant. Depending on
how common it was, one's calling name might be all
one's friends knew. In daily affairs, one's lineage was
usually not significant.

Thus Macurdy's twin sons were not known as
Macurdy. In the breeding record, their lineage was
listed as Jesarion 2x5—Jesarion for short. And because
of Varia's disgrace, she hadn't been allowed to provide their calling names. The only contact she'd had
with them was during the first weeks of their lives,
when she'd nursed them. She'd called them after her
two Macurdy husbands: the firstborn Will, the second
Curtis.

Sarkia had let Idri provide their official calling names.
The names she'd listed for them were obscenities, and
their nannies had objected to Sarkia in writing. Sarkia
had chastised Idri for it, and renamed them Ohns and
Dohns. In Old Ylvin, those meant first and second, but
in Yuultal they were meaningless. And in any case
unique.

Although Ohns and Dohns totally identified with
the Sisterhood and the Guards, they'd grown up feeling different from other children, simply by being a
two-member clone. Most clones numbered from four
to six.

Given the nature of small boys, they'd early been
made self-conscious of their peculiar calling names.
Ohns? Dohns? What had they done to deserve names
like those? Not surprisingly they were unusually close.

When they were ten years old, their clone aunt,

Liiset, had told them about their mother: her strengths, her character, and that she'd gotten into trouble and run away. Liiset had not elaborated on the reasons. No less a tracker than the famed Tomm had failed to bring her back.

She'd also told them what she knew of their father's family history. Most of it was anecdotal—stories of the Macurdies related by Varia during her marriage to Will. During those years, Varia had come through the gate to Ferny Cove every two or three years, to give birth. Back when the Cloister had been located in Kormehr, near the Ferny Cove gate.

More interesting to the boys, and much more exciting, had been Liiset's descriptions of their father's exploits during his three years in Yuulith. From slave, to revolutionary, to warlord, to victor over the ylver in only three years! Even knowing who their father was made them special, though they said nothing about it to others.

Afterward they'd imagined what their father was really like, and shared those imaginings with each other. To them, the Lion of Farside was larger than life, a mighty warrior and hero, admired and obeyed in all the Rude Lands, and feared in both ylvin empires.

The personality they imagined didn't resemble their father at all.

From Liiset's explanations of naming on Farside, they'd gathered that their surname there would be Macurdy, and they began privately to think of themselves as the Macurdy boys, each with a calling name of his own. Ohns, being the "eldest" and dominant of the two, claimed Curtis. After a brief argument and scuffle, he agreed that Dohns could be Curtis on Five-, Six- and Seven-Days. On the other four he'd have to settle for being Will. Dohns accepted the compromise.

All that, of course, had been nine years back. But

the feelings remained, albeit not much heeded in young manhood.

As the threesome rode westward through the Asmehri foothills, with the newly risen sun on their backs, Rillor read the instructions Omara had written to Arva. Then he told the young Guardsmen their true destination, and what their mission actually was. The boys rode on in stunned silence. They were to actually meet their parents! And hopefully bring them back to the Cloister, to be welcomed by Sarkia herself, and given important jobs.

Omara, in her instructions, had not included the posts Sarkia had in mind for Varia and Macurdy. That, presumably, was in the similar, enclosed envelope, addressed simply to Varia. It was sealed with wax, and stamped with the Dynast's signet, to be given to Varia when he met her.

To Rillor, the sealed envelope was unimportant. From what Idri had told him, he could guess the contents. But they were irrelevant, as Varia's sons ultimately were irrelevant. It was his job to ensure that, and he had no doubt he'd succeed.

It was on an early afternoon that Rillor and the twins reached the Crossroads Inn outside Gormin Town, and stopped to eat. Rillor arranged a feed of hay and oats for their eight horses.

In the taproom, it was the innkeeper himself who waited on the three travelers. As always he examined his guests without being obvious about it. There didn't seem to be much difference in their ages. A set of twins, and the other a few years older. He addressed the one who was senior. "Have you stopped here before?" he asked. "These lads look familiar."

"I've been here before, but my brothers haven't."

"Ah. I guess they look like someone I've seen,"

the innkeeper said thoughtfully, and left to fill their orders.

At almost the same time, another man came in. Seeing him enter, a guest called out to him. "Esler! What's the news up north?"

"Macurdy's back!" the man answered. "He arrived riding a great boar, if you can believe it! Just like in the stories."

"Tell us something we don't already know," someone else called. "He's been in here twice. First time he brought the boar right into the taproom. Ordered a beer for himself and a bucket of it for the boar."

"Yeah," another added. "Afterward he stayed at the palace with Wollerda. Rode his boar right down Central Street. Half the town saw them. Shit their pants, some of them."

The newcomer grunted. "That's nothing. He's staying at Jeremid's now, on his way up north. And that ain't but the start of it." He paused, scanning the room to make sure he had their full attention. "The night before he got there, a troll killed a plow ox on the neighboring place, belonged to a fellow named Arnoth. So Jeremid and him, and some others went hunting it. Figured to track it down before dark and kill it. Only it didn't work out that way."

He paused. "You remember that string of thunderstorms that came through, four, five days ago? Big old boomers? Well, when the dogs caught up to the trolls, turned out there were three of them! Trolls, that is. Two males and a female, one of the males a dozen feet tall. Jeremid said any troll that big had to be a sorcerer in troll form, and I expect he's right. Anyway, for there to be three together, there had to be sorcery connected to it. They were in thick woods where the light was weak, and one of them big boomers had just come over. It got almost dark as night, and instead of Jeremid and them jumping the trolls, 'twas the other way

around. Right away the trolls killed four men. Which
left only Jeremid, with a broken arm and nothing but
a skinning knife, and Arnoth with only a shortsword,
because a troll snatched his spear away. Might as well
have had blades of grass instead of steel. The horses
was all killed or run off, and most of the dogs were
dead. It looked like Jeremid and Arnoth were goners.

"Then up rides Macurdy on that pig. He jumps off,
and the pig goes for one of the trolls. Rip! He guts it
with his tusks! While Macurdy . . ." The man paused,
to tighten their attention. "Macurdy raises his sword
and points it at the clouds, and shouts something in
some Farside tongue—and two bolts of lightning come
down and fry the other two trolls.

"The next morning they went back in with packhorses and a litter, and brought out the female troll,
the one the pig killed. And those parts of the others
the lightning had left. She was eight feet four from heels
to crown. Jeremid skinned her. Figured to boil the meat
off her bones, hers and what little they brought out of
the others.

"When the hide is dry and the bones clean, he'll
take them around and show them, at Teklapori and all
the county seats. Charge folks to see them—a copper
for kids, five for grownups—and give the money to the
widows and orphans. Might be he'll show them here
at the inn."

Rillor had been listening from halfway across the
room, and looked at the twins; they were awed. When
Ohns spoke, it was in an undertone, almost a whisper.
"He's still there! On that farm! Can we go there?"

Rillor nodded. "Absolutely. Stay here. I'll go ask how
to find it."

He got up from the table and started over to the
man who'd told the story. Rillor had never imagined
such a break. It could simplify his job greatly.

✧   ✧   ✧

When they'd eaten, they left at once, riding north now, pushing their horses hard. It was night when they reached the side road leading to Jeremid's; Rillor almost missed it in the darkness. Half an hour later they saw the house, lamplight still showing from a window. The farm dogs began to bark.

The three rode in, their horses stamping and sidling, spooked by the circling dogs. The riders waited in the saddle, sabers drawn should the dogs overreach. A man with an arm in a sling came onto the porch, another man following. The first spoke sharply to the dogs, which backed away and sat down watchfully. "Who are you?" the man asked.

"My name's Rillor. Are you Jeremid?"

"That's me. What can I do for you this time of night?"

"These are my brothers." He gestured. "Ohns and Dohns. We've been visiting relatives in Asmehr. Now we're traveling back west to Miskmehr. We heard at the Crossroads Inn that Macurdy's visiting you, so we rode up here. We've been hearing about him all our lives. We hope to shake his hand."

"You're a few days too late. You eat yet?"

"At the Crossroads, and some dried beef in the saddle. We need to be back on our way again. We shouldn't have turned off up here in the first place, I suppose. We'll make up the time by riding at night." He paused. "Maybe we could see the troll skin while we're here."

"You're welcome to," Jeremid told them. "It won't take long. The bones are cleaned, too. Those jaws and teeth are something to see! Your horses can have a feed of hay while they wait. Cost you a teklota each."

"That's way more than we'd heard," Rillor said.

"For kids it's a lot cheaper," Jeremid answered. "Tell you what: two teklota for the three of you. These troll's made two widows and a double handful of orphans. The money goes to them."

"Well, all right. That'd be interesting." Rillor swung

down from his saddle, the twins following. Jeremid's servant took the horses' reins, and led them toward a shed.

Jeremid had heard more than enough to arouse suspicions. These people didn't sound like Miskmehri, or Asmehri for that matter. Their speech was refined, and lacked the nasality of Miskmehr, or the slight gutturality of Asmehr. And they'd given in way too soon on the price.

He didn't take his guests into the house proper, but to a built-on workshop in back. There, using splinters from a box, he lit two lamps from the lantern he carried. The troll skin had been removed like a mink skin—worked off the carcass like a glove. Then it had been stretched carefully on a frame made of saplings, to dry properly and minimize distortion. The hair side was in, to help the skin dry, but there was no question of what had worn it in life. And it was *big!* A large tear, carefully sewn shut, showed where the boar's tusks had ripped open groin and belly.

The bones were the most impressive though. Those of the hands had been reassembled, fastened together with copper wire. Of the rest, most lay on the floor, carefully arranged as in life, waiting. The skull and jawbone, with their large fighting teeth, had also been wired together, and lay on a workbench. Beside them lay an enormous thighbone, much larger than those on the floor. Odds and ends of large vertebrae, ribs and so on lay in a pile.

Jeremid held the lantern. The visitors were clearly impressed. He was as interested in them as they were in the skin and bones. As the three examined the skull, Jeremid groped through his memories. Who did the twins remind him of? And red hair . . .

The truth struck him all at once, unlikely as it seemed. It explained everything—speech, manners, everything.

"That was interesting," said the one in charge. "It makes the story we heard all the more real."

"Yep," said Jeremid. "A story like that can use a little proof."

"Macurdy went north, they said."

"That's right."

"Too bad. I wish we were." He turned to the twins. "Time to go, boys. Maybe we'll have another chance sometime."

Jeremid watched them ride off into the night. *Boys*. That clinched it. Not three brothers. A commander and his men—Macurdy's twin sons—sent off by Sarkia to follow Macurdy. He wished he had two good arms, and trained men at hand. He'd have disarmed the trio and questioned them. As it was . . .

For one of the few times in his life, Jeremid didn't know what to do. Gather some of his century maybe, and follow? North, for that was the way they'd go. But gathering men would take a couple of days. And the three had remounts and packhorses, so they were probably traveling hard, and camping where night found them. By the time his men could catch up, if they could, they'd be at least two days ride into Visdrossa, a dependency of Kormehr. And neither Visdrossans nor Kormehri would appreciate Kullvordi cavalry deep inside their country.

On the other hand, Jeremid told himself, *what harm might those three do? Odds are, Sarkia sent them to talk Varia into coming south with Macurdy. And if Sarkia's being straight about this . . . Hard to tell about her.*

And if she's not being straight, Macurdy and Vulkan can handle it. Be a shame, though, if anything happened to those twins. Break Macurdy's heart again.

17

On the Road to Duinarog

Macurdy and Vulkan crossed the border north into Visdrossa, turned east into Indrossa, then north again toward Inderstown and the Big River. The region was more prosperous than Macurdy remembered, and the roads and inns were better, especially as they neared the Big River. There were more travelers, and wagon traffic.

They traveled long days, now much of the time under Vulkan's invisibility spell, to avoid slows and complications. Vulkan drew most of his energy from the Web of the World—that was routine for him—pausing now and then to feed on roots and tubers along the road. Every three or four nights he'd nab a lamb or calf, or young pig.

Macurdy was surprised that Vulkan ate pig. «Numerous human tribes eat monkeys,» Vulkan replied mildly, «and humans are ensouled apes.» Leaving Macurdy to speculate on how he'd learned about monkeys, let alone the tribes that ate them. Vulkan had identified himself as a *bodhisattva*, but Macurdy had little idea of what a *bodhisattva* was, and less about the knowledge that might be part of it.

Macurdy too drew on the Web of the World, supplementing it daily with food purchased at some village, or a meal at an inn. His stomach complained when he went too long between meals, but it was adjusting. From time to time he got off and walked a mile or two to rest Vulkan—speed-marched, striding rapidly and trotting by spells to avoid slowing them excessively. Several times Vulkan stopped to swim briefly in a stream, Macurdy joining him, and when they stopped to sleep, Macurdy groomed him, to prevent saddle sores.

When Vulkan did drop his invisibility cloak, the result was much as it had been on their ride through Tekalos. But they outpaced reports of their moving north, and Vulkan avoided showing himself in villages and towns. When Macurdy needed to buy food, he'd slide from Vulkan's back as they approached a village or farm, and walk the last stretch.

Macurdy could afford inns, but he felt a certain urgency, and preferred to ride late. Only once did they encounter an inn when he was ready to stop. Usually they rode till after dark, and the days were long in that season. To Macurdy, Vulkan's endurance seemed magical. Often Macurdy bedded down in a barn or hay shed, for farms were numerous in the northern Rude Lands. Once, when soaked by rain, they'd traveled all night, letting the sun dry them in the morning.

Despite Vulkan's short legs and heavy burden, they made excellent progress.

Rillor and the twins pushed their horses hard. They did not, however, cover the miles they might have. Rillor's weaknesses included impatience and a love of comfort—not always compatible—and here there was no one to discipline him. The night after leaving Jeremid's, they hadn't yet cleared the forested Kullvordi Hills, so they slept in the woods. And as they'd ridden late, he decided not to trouble with setting up and breaking down camp. Instead they slept exposed beneath the trees.

Not long after midnight, a squall line passed through, and soaked them. Cold, bedraggled, disgusted, they rode the rest of the night. And to warm themselves from the Web of the World was beyond their training, and quite possibly their talents.

Camping had other drawbacks than weather. They'd have to hobble their horses instead of picketing them, so they could forage for food. And while foraging, even hobbled horses will scatter and be hard to find and catch. Also there was the matter of taking the tent down, folding it, and repacking the packsaddles.

Guardsmen drilled such things repeatedly in training, but still they took time.

So mostly they stopped at inns overnight, or occasionally a farm, sometimes well before dark. Then they rose at dawn and ate a quick breakfast. They'd be in trouble if they wore their horses out, Rillor said, and he was right, but on the road he pushed them hard.

They made excellent time, by normal standards, but they could have done better.

Macurdy and Vulkan crossed the Big River to Parnston, in the Outer Marches. Macurdy rode a ferry, while Vulkan swam, his body unseeable but his wake quite visible. If one looked. It was the odd sort of sight people tend to suppress, denying their senses.

Vulkan "talked" less than he had early on, but still from time to time he spoke at some length, usually in response to a comment or question by his rider. On the first morning north of Parnston, Macurdy was worrying about the powers they were up against in the voitusotar.[1] "The voitar I've known were all a lot more talented than me," he said.

«What of Corporal Trosza, of whom you told me?»

Macurdy frowned. "Trosza wasn't typical."

«In what respects was he not typical?»

Macurdy regarded the question for a moment. "Actually he probably was fairly typical. What I should have said was, my voitik instructors at Schloss Tannenberg and Voitazosz were a lot more talented than me. But people like them—masters and adepts—are what I'm worried about the most."

«Concern is appropriate, for they are indeed formidable. But in some respects less than you imagine.»

Macurdy didn't reply. He sensed there was more to come.

«Their psychic powers are narrow. As straightforward magicians, they are not exceptional. I doubt very much that any approach Sarkia in breadth and flexibility of magical response to situations. I speak, of course, of Sarkia as she was before her decline. And probably none of them approach you in psychic perception. Their great superiority is in major sorceries, sorceries requiring time and favorable circumstances to engineer, so to speak.» He paused. «I do not refer to arrangements or alliances with demons or the devil. Neither of which exist in the occult sense, though some voitar—and some humans and ylver—can behave quite satanically. What voitik adepts, and particularly masters have is an ability to manipulate astral matter, and susceptible forces of nature known as elementals. A talent largely absent among human beings and ylver.»

---

[1]*Voitusotar* is the collective noun referring to the species as a whole. (*The voitusotar are a tall people.*) *Voitu* refers to a single individual. (*The voitu twitched his long ears.*) *Voitar* refers to from two to many individuals, but not to the species as a whole. (*All the voitar in the city.*) *Voitik* is the adjective. (*Voitik cruelty is legendary.*)

"Wait a minute!" Macurdy said. "How do you know all that?"

«I have access to areas of general knowledge, with regard to sentient beings in this particular pair of universes. It is attributable in part to my status as a *bodhisattva*, and to those areas of knowledge I was given access to in preparation for my task. Knowledge now clarifying for me as my task clarifies.

«Beyond that it derives from my own observations of humans and ylver.» He turned his head, regarding Macurdy with one red eye. «But what I know of the voitusotar is partly from one of my own kind. He has paid no attention to them for some time now, and they were never his focus. But at one time he made a minor study of them. Through proxies. Your own observations fit his knowledge nicely.»

"You mean there are giant boars across the Ocean Sea?"

«Two of them. One in the west—west central, actually—and one in the east. We communicate from time to time, as the notion takes us.»

It was Macurdy's turn to be silent. He had things to ponder, and he wasn't much for pondering.

Several days later, at a village three miles south of Ternass, they encountered a half-starved child, seated on a bench outside a tavern. One leg was crudely splinted, and a crude crutch leaned beside him. He was, Macurdy thought, about ten years old. The boy's aura told him what the problem was—a crush fracture of the lower leg, both tibia and fibula. The pictures embedded in the aura showed Macurdy more than enough, and the event that broke the leg was not the worst.

Clearly the leg would mend crooked and short; the boy would be seriously crippled. Macurdy went over and squatted in front of him. "What happened?" he asked softly.

"I got run over by my dad's cart," the boy answered. His voice was a soft monotone.

"It must be a heavy cart."

The boy pointed at it, a dozen yards away. It held a dozen large burlap sacks of coal. A tall jaded mule stood harnessed to it, hitched to a rail.

"It was piled high with wheat sacks that day," the boy said.

"How did he happen to run over you?"

The answer was little more than whispered. "It was an accident."

"How come you're here, instead of at home?"

The boy said nothing.

"Is it all right if I heal it? I'm a healer."

The boy looked at him, but did not meet his eyes. "You better ask my dad."

"In there?" Macurdy gestured at the tavern.

The boy nodded.

"How will I know him?"

"He's big, and his clothes has got coal dust on them."

"Thank you," Macurdy said, "I'll ask him," and went inside.

The Marches were prosperous enough that glass was commonplace, and the tavern was decently lit, through windows less dirty than they might have been. There were only four customers at that hour. Macurdy spotted the carter and walked over to him. "What are you drinking?" he asked cordially.

Whatever it was, the man had had a few already. He scowled at Macurdy, who as usual had left his sword on a saddle ring. "I never seen you before," the carter said. "You got no business with me."

"I used to be well known around here, when you were young. Really well known at Ternass. You just don't recognize me."

"When I was young, you weren't hardly born."

"I'm a lot older than I look. My name's Macurdy."

The man glowered. The barkeeper and the other patrons had been more or less aware of the conversation; now the name Macurdy locked their attention. One of them in particular stared. His stubbly beard was gray, his hair getting that way. "God love me, it is him!" he murmured. "Or his double!"

Macurdy ignored them. "I saw your boy on the bench out front," he said to the carter. "He's going to be a cripple. Unless I heal him."

"He's none of your business, and neither am I."

Macurdy reached into his belt pouch and took out several silver teklota. "I thought I'd take him to Ternass with me, heal him, and leave him at the fort."

The man's voice raised. "Trying to buy him, are you! Healing's no part of what you got in mind! Get out of here before I call the constable!"

Macurdy grabbed the man's heavy wool shirt front and jerked him close. "Call the constable," he hissed, "and I'll tell him what you accused me of. In front of witnesses."

The carter's defiance took a shriller sound. "They heard nothing! They're friends of mine!"

He looked around. No one said a word. They weren't his friends; they knew him too well. Macurdy let the man go and turned to the tavernkeeper. "Drinks for everyone; whatever they're drinking." He gestured at the carter. "Him too. I'll have ale."

The middle-aged tavernkeeper had never set eyes on the Lion of Farside before, but it seemed to him this was the man. He began to draw drinks.

The carter had turned away from Macurdy, to sip from the mug he already had. Macurdy rested a heavy hand on his shoulder. "I'm a wizard, you know. I can look at the boy and see what's happened to him. All of it."

The man didn't speak, didn't look at him, only took another swallow of ale. His aura had darkened as if with smoke from the coal in his cart.

"You got a wife?"

The head shook no.

"Died, did she?"

The head nodded, the aura darkening further. Macurdy wondered what she'd died of. "Ah," he said. "It's got to be hard, bringing up a boy without a woman in the house. Working all day to buy food. Hardly anything left for a drink after a hard day of loading, unloading, carrying . . . I bet you had it tough when you were a boy, too, eh?"

A remarkable tear swelled and overflowed, running down a grimy cheek to lose itself in stubble. Lightly, Macurdy clapped the man's shoulder. "Tell you what," he said. "I'll give you this gold imperial to close the deal. In front of these witnesses. I'll take him off your hands—" he paused "—and off your conscience. I'll take him to the fort, to their infirmary, heal him body and soul, and leave him with the commandant. They'll see he's taken care of, and you'll never see him again." Again he paused. "Never trouble him again."

Once more the man faced him, somehow deflated now, defeated. He put out a hand for the coin.

"You've got to say it out loud," Macurdy told him, "so we can all hear it. Say 'The deal is closed. I'll never trouble him again.' "

"The deal is closed." The man paused, then continued. "I'll never trouble him again." Said it just loudly enough to be heard by the patrons and tavernkeeper.

Macurdy shook the hand, then put the gold coin in it. "Good. We've made a deal. Thank God for it. If you break it . . ."

The man turned away. Macurdy saluted the others and left, his own ale untouched. He knew what the man would do with the imperial: stay drunk till he was broke. A gold imperial would buy gallons of cheap booze. Then, when he'd recovered, he might or might not go to Fort Ternass and look for the boy. But probably he wouldn't. That would take energy and initiative.

Outside, Macurdy stepped in front of the boy and spoke to him again. "What's your name?" he asked.

"Delvi."

"Delvi, I talked to your dad. He's not your dad any longer, unless you want to come back to him. That's up to you. For now you're my boy. I'll take you to Fort Ternass and heal your leg. Then we'll see about a new home for you. One where they'll feed you better, and won't—do what that one did to you. All right?"

"It's up to him," the boy murmured.

"No, no it's not. Not any longer. He sold you to me for a gold imperial."

Despite himself, that widened the child's eyes. "A gold imperial?!"

Macurdy nodded solemnly. "You're worth a lot more than that, but he didn't know it. Someday you'll be a man of pride and reputation." He paused. "That's the truth. I wouldn't lie to you." And to Macurdy it felt like truth.

A well-grown youth had been passing by, and had slowed, then stopped, to listen. Macurdy asked his help, and together they got Delvi onto Macurdy's back, arms around his neck. Then Macurdy hiked out of town with his rider, Vulkan invisible beside them. Delvi smelled bad, of old sweat, pain, and fear. His splints dug Macurdy's ribs, and Macurdy's shoulders got cramped from walking with his arms behind his back, supporting Delvi's small, awkward weight. But it was nothing compared to lugging a machine gun on his shoulder thirty miles through 'dobe clay mud in Algeria.

Ternass was a major town, claiming 4,800 people. Not having a defensive palisade, it was more spread out and cleaner than such towns in the Rude Lands.

The kingdoms of the Marches had their own regular

armies now, and the ylvin garrison had long since turned the fort over to two companies of home-grown cavalry. So Macurdy, unsure of his welcome there, hiked to the nearby commons school. Hermiss, Varia's one-time traveling companion, was now the school's administrator, and she recognized Macurdy at once. She'd married, her father had retired, and her husband had replaced him as headmaster.

Privately, Macurdy described the situation to her. She didn't hesitate, but came around the desk. "I'll introduce you at the fort," she said, "and keep track of Delvi when you've left."

To his surprise, the commandant remembered him more for his humanity and generalship than as an invader. Partly because he'd killed Lord Quaie, and partly because, through the treaty he'd negotiated, the March kingdoms had become self-ruling, though owing nominal allegiance and token fees to the emperor.

Macurdy was given a room in the officers' quarters, and stayed there for four days, treating the boy. The leg improved with astonishing speed. Over the years, Macurdy had learned a bit about healing the psyche too, mainly from Arbel. And had had success with it, notably with Mary, and Shorty Lyle. So he exercised that, as well. Meanwhile both the fort's commandant and its surgeon had become interested in the boy, and promised Macurdy the father would not get him back. Beyond that, the mess sergeant had taken an interest in Delvi, and his thin features were already showing some flesh.

Hermiss visited daily—on the second and third days with her husband. It seemed to Macurdy the boy might get foster parents and foster siblings out of this as well.

Meanwhile Vulkan had disappeared. After breakfast of the fourth day, however, he spoke to Macurdy's mind. He'd just arrived outside the fort's defensive wall.

Macurdy had him let inside, then packed his saddle-
bags, saddled the boar, and climbed aboard. On their
way to the highway, they passed the great burial mounds
of the battlefield, brightly spangled with meadow flow-
ers. Macurdy wondered what Sicily looked like now,
where he and so many others had bled. And Belgium,
and Bloody Hürtgen, where what was left of the 509th
had received its final wounds. He'd been spared that.

He wondered if he could confront another war.

On Macurdy's last day at the fort, three other men
had arrived at Ternass, well mounted, with remounts
and packhorses trailing behind. Two of the saddle horses
needed reshoeing, and Rillor had decided he couldn't
delay it any longer. They'd lodge the horses at a stable, see to their shoeing, enjoy a bath house and inn,
and leave the next day.

For the past several days, no one seemed to have
seen a man with a giant boar, but Macurdy was probably
still ahead. He was known as a wizard, and according
to legend, the great boars were sorcerers. Belonging
to the Sisterhood, concealment spells were entirely real
to Rillor, even though he lacked the power to cast them.

Meanwhile, three days of steady riding would bring
them to Duinarog. There, Rillor told himself, he'd learn
how the situation stood, and how best to complete his
mission. He felt confident of his ability to carry it out.

18

Supper with the Cyncaidhs

Rillor and the twins learned how near they were to Macurdy from conversations overheard while steaming in the Ternass bathhouse. What they did not learn was when he planned to leave. Rillor thought briefly of riding to the fort and looking him up, but decided not to complicate matters. As it stood, they'd arrive in Duinarog either ahead of him or on the same day.

The twins were confused by what they heard. Their father had carried a crippled boy three miles on his back? To heal his leg? Who'd been in charge of the child? Why hadn't the community corrected the situation? Had they no healers?

They didn't ask Rillor those questions. He was their commanding officer; they were lance corporals.

They left in midmorning, after picking up their horses at the farrier's. Within an hour they came to the Great Marsh. They'd spent their lives closed in by mountains, and most of what they'd seen on this trip had seemed at least somewhat strange. But the great marsh, and the highway that crossed it, were the strangest. The highway was built on a raised bed of rock, packed with dirt, topped with gravel, and flanked by large, water-filled ditches. Straight as a die it ran, through the marsh to the horizon and no doubt beyond, wide enough for wagons to pass on. It seemed to them that only a marvelously rich and able people could build such a road.

The marsh itself stretched out of sight ahead and to both sides, a vast expanse of cattails, and black pools sheened with limonite. Scattered here and there were patches of ten-foot reeds, or brush and scrubby trees. Blackwater creeks passed with imperceptible currents beneath small stone bridges, and along their low shores, muskrat lodges humped like miniature beaver dens. Redwinged blackbirds provided the nearest approximation of birdsong—a monotonic but pleasant trill. To the twins, it was intriguing. Dohns, the more imaginative, wondered what lived in its water, and if it extended all the way to Duinarog. Ohns wondered how one might take an army over it, if the road were defended.

To Rillor it was desolate, and he gave his attention to his mission.

Poison was the logical means of assassinating Varia and Macurdy—and the twins if convenient. Idri had supplied him with an envelope each of two potent poisons. One was to be ingested in drink or food. Very little was required, and supposedly it had almost no taste. (He wondered how anyone alive could know that.) Also, Idri had assured him, it had a delayed action, allowing several people time to take it before the first showed any effects.

The other poison could be sprinkled on the surface of lamp oil. When the lamp was lit, heat caused the tiny crystals to dissolve. The contaminated oil then rose up the wick to the flame, where it produced extremely toxic fumes. By the time the telltale pungency could be detected, it was too late. The victim collapsed and died.

He wondered where Idri had gotten them. Perhaps from Farside, he thought, back when she'd run the outpost there. He didn't have to wonder why she'd gotten them. She'd no doubt wanted the dynast's throne half her life ago, or more.

At any rate, his job was to apply them. In his mind he rehearsed a scenario set in the Cyncaidh's residence, as he imagined it. He'd present Varia and Macurdy with their sons, then with the sealed envelope from the dynast's office. At the same time presenting himself as the dynast's courier. They would, of course, invite him to supper. Almost invariably, ylvin nobility were courteous to embassy personnel.

The food poison would be his primary weapon. It was the most target-specific. If he used the lamp poison at all, it would be before dark. Then he'd make an excuse and leave.

He'd be the prime suspect, of course, so he'd planned his escape carefully. Too bad, he thought, that he didn't have a concealment spell, but wits would serve. During his years at the embassy, he'd become familiar with the city. There'd been several boat rental businesses on the Imperial River, below the Great Rapids. Embassy personnel sometimes rented boats from them to fish for the huge pike there. He'd rent one, ride it downstream to the Imperial Sea, land on its south shore, then make his way back to the Cloister.

It was, he told himself, all quite simple.

On the second night out of Ternass, Macurdy stayed at an inn, while Vulkan prowled the countryside. The inn's standard of cleanliness was quite good, and it had a bathhouse and laundry. The innkeeper's wife even cut hair. In the bathhouse, Macurdy was propositioned by an attractive ylvin "lass," whose aura suggested she

might be on the verge of decline. She didn't seem to
be a professional. A widow perhaps, burning her can-
dles. He was not tempted.

The next day he came to a crossroad, with a sign
that said DUINAROG 15 MILES. Just beyond it was a police
post. No one was near, so Macurdy dismounted, and
walked out of Vulkan's concealment cloak. Vulkan, still
unseen, then followed him to the post, where Macurdy
stepped onto the porch and went inside. A constable
got to his feet and asked what he wanted.

"My name's Macurdy. I'd like to speak to your commander."

Rumors had reached there of Macurdy's appearance
at Ternass, so while the trooper wasn't entirely convinced, he wasn't surprised at the claim. The traveler's
clothing and boots were peculiar enough to be from
Farside, that was a fact. "The commander?" he said.
"Just a minute. I'll tell him you want to see him."

The commander too had heard the rumor and, like
the constable, felt dubious. "You're Macurdy?" he said.
"What can I do for you?"

"I'm riding to Duinarog to see Lord and Lady
Cyncaidh, and I'd like an escort. I have an unusual
mount, and without an escort we might cause disturbances in the city."

"Disturbances?"

"Come out on the porch. You'll see what I mean."

Frowning, the commander followed him. Stepping
out the door, he looked around, and opened his mouth
to speak. Macurdy anticipated him. "Vulkan," he called,
"let the commander see you."

And there he stood, more than half a ton of wild
boar. Seemingly half of it head and shoulders, ten percent tusks. Gawping, the commander turned to Macurdy.
"Good God!" he said. "I never quite believed in them.
And saddled! Is he sapient, as the tales claim?"

Macurdy didn't know the word, but guessed its

meaning. "He's smarter than me, and a lot better magician."

«Macurdy, do not undervalue yourself,» the deep voice said, allowing the ylf to perceive it. «Accomplishment is incontrovertible evidence of intellect and character, and you have accomplished marvels, both in Yuulith and on Farside.»

Macurdy grinned at the ylf. "On Farside there's a saying: a man's best friend is his dog. I've got a hog. Or he's got me. Actually, it's a free and open friendship; neither of us owns the other one. But I get more good out of it than he does." He laughed. "If he ever finds out how one-sided this is . . ."

Fifteen minutes later, Vulkan was jogging up the highway with Macurdy on his back and a trooper on each side. A courier had galloped off ahead, to inform Lord Cyncaidh of Macurdy's coming, and his estimated time of arrival.

Chief Counselor Raien Cyncaidh had a splendidly appointed office in the imperial palace. The palace was a complex of buildings, only one of them the imperial residence. The others housed the empire's central administrative and judicial functions, and the assemblies of the three estates. Five or six mornings a week, eight months a year, Lord Cyncaidh arrived there by 8 A.M. But his personal residence was less than a mile away, and more often than not he returned there at midday, for lunch with his wife. Bringing a pile of reports to read and annotate in the afternoon, relatively free of the interruptions that beset him at his office.

Relatively free. The police courier, after going first to Lord Cyncaidh's palace office, arrived at his residence shortly before 1 P.M. The courier was a genuinely young ylf—of mixed blood, actually. Pink-cheeked, brown-eyed, with raven hair and no sign of beard, only his rounded ears showed the extent of his partly human ancestry.

He delivered his message, not omitting Vulkan, then added: "If your lordship approves, he'll be brought here as soon as he arrives at the palace."

"Of course. What time might we expect him?"

"I'd guess sometime about two, your lordship."

"Hmm. I take it the boar is, um, well-behaved?"

"Seems to be, your lordship. If he really is a boar. He might be a wizard wearing a spell; in his way, he speaks as well as anyone. Seems to be physical though, flesh and blood. At any rate he carries Marshal Macurdy easily enough, and the marshal is a large man."

The courier left his lordship with that informational lump, and Cyncaidh called his butler. "Talrie," he said, "we'll have guests for supper, and probably for the night. A man riding on a giant boar. A boar who speaks, I might add." He gave Talrie a moment to grasp and accept the statement. "Prepare a stall for it in the coach house, with clean straw and, um, whatever you think such a creature might like to eat. They may be here as soon as two o'clock."

"Very well, your lordship. Do you anticipate the horses being upset by him?"

"I think not. They're being escorted by mounted police. Apparently the creature is compatible with horses."

Talrie left, to give appropriate orders to the housekeeper, cook, and stableboy. Cyncaidh strode upstairs to inform Varia. Opening her study door, he paused. She sat in her wicker reading chair, facing away from him, no doubt with a book in her hands. *What*, he wondered to himself, *has Macurdy come here for? His business is surely with her, not me.*

She'd heard the door, and after marking her place, got to her feet, turning. *Graceful, always graceful*, he told himself. She was dressed for summer, in sheer green over a gauzy white underdress, setting off her vividly red hair. Her feet were bare—a private quirk of hers. Like her arms and face, they were lightly tanned and perfectly formed. Physically she was more beautiful even than Mariil, he thought. And mentally, spiritually? Equally beautiful, but different. *Cyncaidh,* he told himself, *you've been blessed all your life.* And hoped that blessing wasn't in danger.

"Hello, love," she said smiling. "What brings you to my lair?"

It was difficult to hide his feelings from her. She was exceptionally perceptive of auras, when she paid attention. "Guess who's coming to supper," he said.

Her eyebrows rose. "I have no idea." She eyed him quizzically, then grinned despite the discomfort revealed by his aura. "Someone you feel uncomfortable with," she suggested. "Not Quaie the younger. Not that uncomfortable. Someone you—like but feel uncomfortable with." She grinned again. Her fists were on her hips now, challenging. "Who?"

In spite of himself he smiled. "Curtis Macurdy," he answered. "The Lion of Farside, if you'd rather."

Her smile disappeared. She stepped to a chair that faced him, and sat down. "Curtis? Really?"

"And his saddle mount. I'm sure you recall the name of his warhorse."

She frowned, puzzled. "Hog. He named it after a horse of Will's. Why?"

"Now he's riding a different sort of hog."

"Different?"

"He stopped at the police post south of the city. At the Riverton Road crossing." He paused. "Riding a giant boar. An actual giant boar, with a saddle."

She stared, then laughter bubbled out of her. "Curtis? Good God! Whatever became of my quiet, homespun farmboy with literal hayseeds in his hair?" Her husband's solemn, even lugubrious expression stilled her mirth. Getting up, she stepped over to him and took his hands. "It's been nearly twenty years since we saw him last. My decision hasn't changed, and it will not." *I wept all that out of my system after he left,* she added inwardly, *out of my system and out of your sight. I chose you because of the love we had—we have—and for little Ceonigh. And now there's Rorie as well.*

There was more to it that she wasn't looking at. With Raien she had security and stability. After her ordeal at the Cloister, security was important. And Curtis had changed, even eighteen years ago. Anyone changed over time, but to become the Lion of Farside . . . ? And perhaps hardest to confront, she could not go back to life on the farm, even if he could. Not farm life as she remembered it.

She would, she knew, love Curtis Macurdy till the day she died. And Cyncaidh for just as long. But Cyncaidh she knew, from nineteen years of familiarity and sharing, from love and admiration. She couldn't imagine leaving him and their sons.

Macurdy and Vulkan arrived shortly after two. Vulkan's bulk and hooves were ill-suited to the carpets and hardwood floors of the Cyncaidh residence. (At the palace at Teklapori, the floor's were mainly of granite, with rugs largely restricted to the royal apartment and guest rooms.) So Talrie ensconced him in the carriage house, with a peck of corn and some cabbages. "A fat turkey has been obtained and is being plucked for you," Talrie added. "It will be brought out directly, unless you'd prefer it roasted. That would take quite some time."

Vulkan told him he preferred it raw. And that meanwhile a brief wallow in the fish pool would be welcome.

In the residence, Macurdy met with the Cyncaidhs for only a few minutes. The last time he'd met Varia, the circumstances had been utterly different than he'd expected. He'd been thrown completely off-stride, his reaction unsure and tentative. This time he knew her circumstances. What he somehow wasn't prepared for was how beautiful she would seem to him; she took his breath away. Liiset was beautiful, and they were clone sisters, but Varia's loveliness put her somehow in a class of her own.

Varia's greeting, while warm and fond, set enough distance between them to cool whatever hope he'd arrived with. She'd changed, of course. Her speech sounded ylvin now, both in accent and syntax, and her aura reflected a matured serenity that told him her life was happy and complete.

When the Cyncaidhs excused themselves, Talrie took Macurdy to a guest room. Adjacent was a bath with a deep tub, freshly filled with hot water. Macurdy bathed, then lay down in borrowed pajamas for a nap that was slow in coming. He'd been highly skeptical that Varia would accept Sarkia's invitation, but now he realized how much hope it had kindled in his subconscious.

And now having seen her, spoken with her, read her aura, it seemed to him there was no chance at all that she'd agree. Still he'd deliver Sarkia's message. Because he'd said he would, and because he would not waste whatever hope there might be.

Chief Counselor Cyncaidh had not missed Macurdy's reaction to Varia—the Farsider had been shaken by the sight of her—but her reaction had not matched his. She'd spoken graciously and fondly to him, and her aura had matched her words, but she'd shown little male-female response.

Meanwhile, Cyncaidh was a disciplined man, and returned to his reports with full concentration. After a bit someone knocked again. "Your lordship," said Talrie's familiar voice, "a diplomatic courier has arrived from the ylvin embassy, with two guardsmen. And an envelope. They wish to see you personally—yourself and Lady Cyncaidh. He did not divulge his mission."

Cyncaidh arose tight-lipped, and followed Talrie downstairs. It seemed to him he wasn't going to like this. Three minutes later he came back upstairs, going first to the guest room where Macurdy was napping. He'd known at a glance who the two youths were, had known before the captain said a word.

He shook Macurdy's shoulder. "Curtis," he said, "wake up. Some men have arrived. They wish to see you."

Macurdy sat up abruptly. "Who are they?"

"I'll let you hear it from them. I have to notify Varia."

Frowning, Macurdy got up and began to dress, while Cyncaidh went to Varia's study. He told her no more than he had Macurdy, and she didn't press him.

Talrie had already conducted Rillor and the two young guardsmen to the first-floor parlor. They wore dress uniforms now. Varia knew at first sight who the red-haired youths were, though they'd been only four months old when she'd seen them last. Sons seldom looked so much like their fathers as these did, though part of it was Curtis's lasting youth. Standing beside her, Cyncaidh put a reassuring hand on her arm.

They both knew the one reason Sarkia would have sent them. She wanted Varia back.

Macurdy was the only one who had to be told. Having no need to shave, he'd never looked much in mirrors. Cyncaidh introduced them. "Varia, Curtis, this gentleman is Captain Rillor, a courier from the dynast. And these two young men are your sons, Ohns and Dohns. They've come to meet their parents."

Macurdy was thunderstruck. He knew instantly what this was about. And if Sarkia had asked, he might conceivably have agreed to it. But to have it imposed on Varia like this . . . Anger surged in him, shocking even himself. If he'd had his saber, he might have cut the courier down. And Rillor felt it. His knees threatened to fold.

Cyncaidh felt it too, and saw it surge through Macurdy's aura. It made his skin crawl. He even sensed the cause. The twins also felt it, and saw it in their father's aura, but lacking the background knowledge, they had no notion what was wrong.

Varia missed all of it, though normally she was more perceptive than any of them. She was dealing with her own emotions. Mariil, in her healing sessions, had greatly unburdened Varia of her griefs and losses. But this confrontation brought down upon her what remained of them.

"Thank you for bringing them, Captain Rillor," she said quietly. Gently. "Ohns, Dohns, I am glad you've been allowed to visit."

Ylvin had become a fossil language, taught to children but not used in day-to-day life. As Lady Cyncaidh, she'd learned a bit of it in connection with ceremony and tradition, and realized the significance of her sons' calling names. "Ohns," she added, "when you were newly born, I named you Will. And Dohns, I named you Curtis. If you will indulge me, I will call you by those names."

As alike as they looked physically, she had no difficulty distinguishing them. Aspects of their auras told her that Ohns was born a warrior, and Dohns a would-be scholar.

"Mother," Ohns said, "you may call me whatever you like. I will be happy to hear it." Dohns nodded firmly. "And I," he said.

Rillor reached inside his dress jacket and drew out the envelope from Sarkia. "My lady," he said, bowing slightly, "I have the honor of giving you this envelope from the Dynast."

She accepted it. "Thank you, Captain," she said, but did not open it. Her glance included all three Guardsmen. "I trust you'll stay for dinner."

Cyncaidh wished she hadn't included Rillor; he'd disliked the man on sight. But it was, he told himself, the proper and necessary thing to do.

They went to the ground-floor parlor together, where Varia put the envelope on the mantle. Then they sat talking of trivialities. Not wishing to draw needless attention, Rillor hardly participated. Some of these people—Varia surely—would see auras in dangerous detail, if she focused on them. He wished she'd open the envelope. It would engage their attentions enough to make his job easier. Meanwhile he cased the room, careful not to be obvious. There were handsome, cut-glass lamps scattered about. One, with a stem for carrying, stood on a lamp table by the door. *That one*, he thought. *It's the one they'll light first.*

A servant brought in a tray with glasses and a wine bottle, and placed it on a small buffet not far from the door. *Ah*, thought Rillor, *there's my chance.*

And with that realized he'd overlooked a crucial step. He could hardly take an envelope from his jacket, open it, and pour poison into their wine glasses in front of everyone. His failure shook him.

"Thank you, Jahns," Varia said to the servant, and glanced around. "It's a light appetizer wine, dry and semisweet. You may wish to try it."

With the others, Rillor went to the buffet, poured himself a drink, and returned with it to his chair. Soon afterward Talrie came in. Dinner, he said, would be served in fifteen minutes. Cyncaidh suggested that anyone in need use one of the four water closets off the hall.

As shocked as he'd been minutes earlier, Rillor was resilient. He excused himself at once, and locked himself into one of the water closets, where he poured some of the food poison into a palm, then transferred it into his right-hand pants pocket. Next he put some of the other into his left-hand pocket. After that he washed possible traces of the powder from his hands, urinated, and left.

Back in the parlor, he found himself alone. Quickly he took some powder from his right-hand pocket and sprinkled a pinch in the glass where Macurdy had sat, then another in the glass where Varia had sat. He was tight, jumpy, sure that if any of them looked at him now, really looked, they'd *know*. After brushing off his hands, he took his own glass and started back toward the buffet. Dohns came in but paid no attention. Rillor fished a pinch of powder from his left-hand pocket and paused by the lamp table before going to the tray and topping off his wine glass.

One by one, all the others returned except Varia. When Talrie announced that dinner was served, Macurdy had not sipped his poisoned wine. As they left, Rillor saw Talrie, with the tray in one hand, picking up the glasses.

The dinner was simple, not lavish as Rillor had expected, but he was impressed with the quality. It included a dinner wine, and a brandy custard for dessert. Meanwhile Cyncaidh had favored Rillor with more than one meaningful glance, as if inviting him to leave.

Afterward they returned to the parlor. The previous glasses and wine bottle were gone, replaced on the buffet by an after-dinner wine and clean glasses. Meanwhile the sun was low enough that the room had begun to dim.

It seemed to Rillor he had only one more chance. He got to his feet. "Excuse me, my lord, my lady. But sometimes rich food troubles my stomach. May I try just a swallow of that wine? Then I really must return to the embassy and write my report."

"Of course," Cyncaidh said. "We quite understand. If the message you brought requires a reply, we'll send for you. Meanwhile we'd appreciate your allowing these two young men to spend the night, if they'd care to."

"Thank you, my lord. They're free to if they wish." The twins accepted the invitation, definitely but warily.

Not daring to look back, Rillor walked to the buffet while the others conversed, dipping into his right-hand pocket as he went. He moved casually enough, but anxiety clutched his gut. If Varia, and perhaps Cyncaidh or even Macurdy focused on his aura, surely they'd know something was wrong, and not just with his stomach.

As before, the glasses were on a tray. The same move that picked up the bottle dropped powder into every glass but one. He poured a splash of wine in it, drank, then left quietly. In the hall, his knees nearly buckled with relief.

He fidgeted in the waiting room while a servant got his horse. The stableboy had to saddle it, of course, and Rillor expected at any moment to hear a commotion upstairs. If only one of them died, he hoped it was Macurdy. The man's anger had frozen his blood, and he feared being hunted by him.

It seemed to him his horse would never arrive. Actually he'd waited barely five minutes before Talrie handed him his cap and jacket, and wished him good night.

Once in the saddle, Rillor fought the impulse to gallop away. There were traffic laws in Duinarog, and it could be fatal, on that evening, to be detained by the police.

No one else went to the wine tray. They were all more or less sated from supper, and the twins were ill at ease, not knowing the protocol there. Varia began to question them, first about the Cloister, then about themselves. Their answers were mostly short, and she decided they weren't ready to open up.

"Well," she said, "I should see what Captain Ril-lor's envelope holds." She took it from the mantle, opened it, and silently scanned the enclosure. The hand-writing was clear and firm, definitely not Sarkia's, but she might well have dictated it. When Varia had fin-ished, she looked at the others.

"The dynast," she said, "would like me to return. With Marshal Macurdy. I to serve as dynast, he as my deputy, and commander of the Sisterhood's military forces. This would reunite us with our sons—mine and Curtis's." Varia looked at her small audience. "She totally ignores my present marriage, of course," she added drily, "as she did my first one, years ago."

Her eyes moved to Cyncaidh, then to the twins, finally settling on Macurdy. "I have no doubt Sarkia meant well by this, but she has given me a cruel choice: my sons—or my sons. But I cannot abandon my hus-band. Or my children by him, whom I nursed and cud-dled, cleaned up, fed, taught, scolded, and on occa-sion disciplined."

Her focus turned to the twins. "Imperial law allows exiles from foreign lands to apply for residence here. If you wish to stay, we welcome you abundantly."

She paused, looking at Cyncaidh. "Raien?" she said.

He nodded and stood, his eyes too on the twins. "If you wish, you can live with us," he said, "as part of our family. Normally, at the beginning of Seven-Month we go to Aaerodh Manor, our home on the Northern Sea. Our . . . other sons left for there when the spring lectures ended here at the university. At Aaerodh you can begin learning our ways, and a profession. Perhaps train as officers in my own ducal cohort, with the option of transfer to the emperor's army, where there are greater opportunities for advancement. With the training you've already had, it should go quickly and well for you."

He paused. The twins stared soberly, saying noth-ing. "Or perhaps you'd rather not," he went on. "We may seem too foreign to you. At any rate you will doubt-less want to discuss it between yourselves. And per-haps with your parents."

He turned to Macurdy. "Curtis," he said, "I'm afraid we've rather left you out of this. No slight was intended. If you . . ."

Talrie entered without knocking. "Lord Cyncaidh," he said, "something urgent has come up. Zednis, in the kitchen, has taken severely ill." His eyes turned to Varia. "If your ladyship can come . . ."

Scowling, Cyncaidh interrupted. "Have you any idea what it might be?"

"My lord, I think she's poisoned. I'm told she'd drunk from one of the untouched wine glasses. They know they're not supposed to, but . . ."

"Go then!"

Talrie and Varia hurried away. Macurdy and the twins watched Cyncaidh walk to the buffet and look in the glasses there. Raising one, he tipped it. A tiny pinch of powder fell to the polished walnut buffet top. One by one he did the same with the others, with the same result.

"Apparently," he said, "Captain Rillor has tried to poison us. I must ask you to leave this room. I'll send for His Majesty's investigators, to see what manner of powder we have here."

Two investigators arrived within an hour. The first thing one of them did was light the lamp by the door. He then lit a long match from it, and went around the room lighting the others. His partner swept the sus-pect powder from the buffet, then holding the lamp, was checking the floor when the poison reached the lamp flame.

Apparently he realized instantly what he smelled. Lurching toward the open patio doors, he cast the lamp outside, where it shattered on the flagstones, the oil forming a thin puddle on the ground, flames spreading quickly over it. Then he crumpled on the floor. The other investigator staggered outside. There the fresh evening breeze dissipated the fumes, but even so, he too collapsed.

The Sisterhood's embassy was enclosed by a wall. It was not militarily effectual, of course, but it kept out thieves and vandals. And with occasional attention by the resident magician and her assistant, it discouraged would-be assassins. For if Quaie the Elder was long dead, and his Expansion Party badly shrunken, there were still fanatics dedicated to his memory and his hatreds.

Rillor had paused at the embassy just long enough to change back into the civilian clothes in which he'd traveled, and to get a loaf of bread and block of cheese from the pantry. He departed on horseback, then left the horse at a livery stable on River Street, saying he'd pick it up the next day. When he didn't, they'd wait a few days, then claim it for nonpayment. Next, packroll on his back and saddle on his shoulder, he walked a block to a boat rental.

By that time it was not much short of night. Occasional dedicated sport fishermen were still rowing in, returning their boats and picking up their deposits. Using a false name, Rillor rented a trolling rig, a landing net, and a boat with skeg, spar, and sail. He planned, he said, to row downstream, trolling, and spend the rest of the night at his cousin's in Riverton. He'd spend a day sailing on Mirror Lake, then hire a tow back up the river behind a freight barge. It was a common procedure. He left his saddle and a gold imperial for security.

Before he left, he stepped his spar, then rowed out into the river and unfurled the small sail. The current and the northwest breeze, would take him to the Imperial

Sea by next afternoon. Supper at the latest. He could stop at some riverside inn for a meal. Then he'd cross the so-called sea by skirting the wild marshy west shore, camping in his boat in the mouth of inflowing creeks. If weather developed, he could shelter in one of them. With favorable winds, the crossing wouldn't take more than a day and a half. Two or three if he had to row; five at worst.

With luck, he assured himself, it would be a pleasant excursion, at worst a survivable ordeal.

PART THREE

A Murmur Of Trumpets, A Mutter Of Drums

Looking aft, the old man spoke more to himself than to his grandson. "What the devil is he doing?"

Within his field of vision, more than a score of ships lay to seaward, ships unlike any he'd seen before, tall, with square sails. A light, schooner-rigged vessel had separated from them and was closing astern, bearing down on him. In an effort to get out of the way, he steered too closely into the wind, and his small sail luffed, flapping.

His thirteen-year-old grandson sat numb, hands motionless on the sheet. The schooner veered past, missing them by perhaps two fathoms. At the foredeck rail, a man had a crossbow pointed at them. The boy heard a snap, then a "thuk." His grandfather grunted, pitched forward across a coiled trawl line, and lay unmoving.

The schooner sent a work boat to pick the boy up. Leaning, one of its men took an ax to the fishing boat, and it settled to the gunnels.

The boy was taken to one of the large ships, where he was questioned by the tallest, most frightening man he'd ever seen. The giant's accented Yuultal and his own Scrub Lands dialect were not entirely compatible, but the lad did his best. When his interrogator had the information he wanted, the boy was sent to join his grandfather.

Occurrence off the Scrub Coast

19

Follow-up

The small household staff huddled waiting on the front lawn. The breeze thinned the aroma of rosebushes, replacing it in the esthetics mix with the rustle of leaves. Staff wasn't paying much attention. Their normally stable lives had been severely shaken, first by the convulsions and death of Zednis, the kitchen girl, then by the murder of a policeman, and finally by being ordered from their quarters into the night. They talked quietly, casting occasional glances at the two large young men in foreign uniforms. According to Jahns, these were their lady's sons by Marshal Macurdy, but they'd arrived with the man who was said to be the poisoner.

The twins stood somewhat apart, stoic in the face of the evening's events. They'd concluded on their own that the murderer was Rillor. They'd known him far better than the others had, and had paid more attention to him. He hadn't been himself since they'd arrived at this house.

While they waited, men came with an ambulance, and getting out of it, disappeared through the garden gate. Minutes later, two of them reappeared with a litter.

171

The sheet had been folded back, and a face could be seen. On the second and third trips, the faces were covered. When the last litter had been secured, the driver climbed onto the seat and spoke to the horses. With a clop of hooves on brick pavement, the ambulance left.

Soon afterward, Talrie came out the front entrance and told staff the house was safe again. It had been opened to the breeze—first the doors, and after an interval the windows, downstairs and up. He, with his lordship himself, had emptied all the lamps on the first floor, refilling them with fresh oil. The hall lamps had been relit, and staff should return to their rooms.

They filed along the walk that took them to the rear of the house, to the servants' entrance. Then Talrie walked over to the twins. "If you will follow me," he said, "I'll take you to Lord Cyncaidh. The Chief Inspector of His Majesty's Police is expected momentarily, and he will want to question you and his lordship about Captain Rillor."

They didn't have long to wait, and the inspector's questioning was brief. Then the twins went to their room. They were getting ready for bed when someone knocked at their door.

"Who is it?" asked Ohns.

"It's Macurdy. Your father. Are you still dressed?"

"Partly."

"Get dressed enough to come with me to the garden. Someone else has questions for you."

It was Vulkan who awaited them. «So you are Macurdy's sons,» he said. «You resemble him. My questions are about Captain Rillor. It is quite apparent that he is responsible for the deaths here tonight. That he intended the deaths of your parents, and everyone else in the room where the lamp was poisoned.» He paused, examining their conscious minds, and the surface zone of the subconscious. «Did he say anything, give any clue, as to where he might go?»

When they came up with nothing, Vulkan asked a few more questions, garnering no specific information, nor sign of anything withheld. But he did gain a certain psychic sense of Rillor. He also knew the scent of Rillor's horse, and by eliminating other known scents, that of Rillor himself. That might well suffice.

After thanking the twins, he dismissed them. They went back to their room, and minutes later were in bed.

But not asleep. There was too much to talk about. They agreed their mother was even more beautiful than her clone sisters. And although they did not perceive auras in much detail, it was clear that few Sisters were as talented psychically. They wished she'd return to the Cloister, but there seemed no chance of it.

Their father had awed them. He too was psychically talented, and to have so awesome a companion as Vulkan . . . Also they'd felt his surge of anger at Rillor, even if they hadn't understood it. Such power! And at the same time control. Ohns said their father should be king somewhere, or even emperor, and Dohns agreed unreservedly.

Cyncaidh too had impressed them. His talent and integrity were obvious, and he'd invited them into his family. Dohns was tempted to accept the offer. Ohns was not, though he wasn't ready to dismiss it. He would, he said, rather follow their father, if he'd have him.

It was not the first time Vulkan had roamed the streets of Duinarog invisibly, but it was the first in many years. He followed the scent of Rillor's horse to the embassy, which he then circled, and picked up the horse's trail again. It led southeastward, ending on the riverfront, at a livery stable.

From there, Vulkan followed Rillor's scent to the dock where the man had set out in a rental boat. His strategy was obvious.

To inform Cyncaidh would probably result in the man's capture, but Vulkan decided not to. At most it would provide revenge. And meanwhile . . . Vulkan couldn't complete the thought. The vector spray was too unclear. But he trusted his *bodhisattva* intuition in all things, even recognizing that the results might not be what he hoped.

20

Old News, Bad News

Cyncaidh had had a long night. He'd ridden with the chief inspector to the Sisterhood's embassy, told the ambassador of the evening's events, and shown her the letter from the dynast. The letter had been the key to her cooperation. She'd recognized the handwriting—that of the dynast's deputy, a Sister named Omara. Whom, she insisted, would never involve herself in assassination.

Though he didn't voice it, Cyncaidh was skeptical. Given what had happened to Varia at the Cloister, it seemed to him that Sarkia would hardly have an ethical deputy. Macurdy, however, would support the ambassador's claim when he heard of it after breakfast.

After seeing the letter, the ambassador had her guardsmen search the embassy for Rillor. When they didn't find him, her master at arms had brought the dress uniform Rillor had worn. The ambassador had given it to the Chief Inspector, who, back in his office, cut the pockets out. In the trouser pockets he found remnants of powder. It would be tested on rodents, but neither he nor Cyncaidh doubted what the result would be.

At breakfast, Cyncaidh summarized for Macurdy and the twins what he'd learned the night before. Rillor's flight, before he could have heard of the poisonings, was damning in itself. They'd finished eating, and were sipping hot sassafras tea with honey, when Talrie entered, to inform his lordship that Cadet Corleigh had arrived. The young man was waiting in the first-floor parlor. Cyncaidh then told the twins the cadet was to give them a tour of the imperial palace. They realized they were being dismissed. Perhaps, they thought, their elders wanted to discuss Sarkia's proposal further. They'd have preferred to stay and listen, but a tour of the palace sounded better than waiting in their room.

Afterward, Cyncaidh and Varia led Macurdy to the garden. Obviously they wanted to talk with him privately, and he wondered if Varia had had second thoughts about Sarkia's proposal. In spite of himself, the thought quickened his pulse.

In the garden, three large wicker chairs had been arranged in a semicircle. They'd hardly seated themselves when Talrie arrived, leading Vulkan, who lay down facing the others. Then Talrie left.

Cyncaidh looked at Macurdy. "Varia and I," he said, "have been wondering why you returned."

What he wanted to know was what brought Macurdy back from Farside, but Macurdy misunderstood. "A dream," he answered.

"A dream?"

"A dream I had in Wolf Springs."

"And where is Wolf Springs?"

"It's the village at the Ozian Gate. What the Ozians call the Wizard Gate."

Cyncaidh frowned. This wasn't what he'd had in mind.

"I'd arrived back through the gate in Three-Month," Macurdy continued, "and spent a while there with Arbel, my old teacher in healing. Ordinarily I don't think about healing. I'll see a need, but it doesn't often occur to me that, hey! I can do something about that. And Arbel'd decided I wasn't intended to be a healer.

"Still, I find myself wanting to improve my healing skills. Ever since a guy stabbed Melody nearly to death on our wedding night, leaving me to do what I could for her. Incidentally, it was Omara who saved her life."

Cyncaidh nodded soberly. Some of the story was part of the Macurdy legend.

"What about the dream?" Varia asked.

"I'd planned to tell you about that, then with all the stuff that happened last night, I didn't get around to it. After I got back from Farside, I spent a few weeks with Arbel at Wolf Springs, getting more lessons and experience in healing, while I waited for Vulkan to show up. Vulkan and I got to know one another before I went back to Farside, all those years ago. He'd said that when I came back, he'd know. Anyway I was getting lessons from Arbel, and then one night I had this dream. And the next morning I knew it was time to head east. The dream had made that clear."

He paused, sorting out how to continue the story, then looked around at the others. "Actually," he said, "the story starts on Farside. In Nine-Month, seven years ago, in a great war that killed more people than you can imagine, soldiers and civilians. And I was in it, along with maybe fifty million other men. I won't even try to describe how it was fought." He looked at Varia. "It was way bigger than the first World War. And had airplanes with a hundred-foot wing span, flying more than a thousand miles on a flight, at two, three hundred miles an hour. Dropping bombs weighing a ton. There were tanks as heavy as locomotives, going twenty, thirty miles an hour . . ."

He looked at Cyncaidh and shook his head. "I'm going to leave out most of the story. It would take too long, and wouldn't make any sense to you. But anyway, I was a spy, in a country called Germany. At a place where the Germans were trying to have people trained as . . ." He pursed his lips thoughtfully. "As magicians, I guess you could say. And the people they had teaching us were from a place called . . ." His eyes locked on Cyncaidh's. "Hithmearc."

Cyncaidh jerked at the name. "Hithmearc!" he echoed. The name had jarred Varia, too.

"I see that means something to you." Macurdy looked at Varia again. "Some voitar had crossed to Farside through a gate in the Bavarian mountains. And I was their most promising student, so they took me through it into Hithmearc. To see if I'd survive the gate, and if I did, to train me there." He didn't elaborate, and didn't give them time to ask.

"The voitu in charge was their crown prince," he went on. "Named Kurqôsz. They'd done some sorcery to make the gate open every day. I managed to close it later. Permanently, I think."

A thunderstruck Cyncaidh was staring at Macurdy, who ignored him now, and told about his dream. "It didn't feel like an ordinary dream," he finished. "It seemed to me, when I woke up, that it was a warning. A message that the voitusotar plan to invade Yuulith. And that people—you people, Wollerda, the dwarves, everyone in Yuulith—needed to be warned.

"After a few hours I didn't feel so sure anymore. It got to feeling pretty unreal, even to me, so I couldn't see myself convincing anyone else. But I left anyway, and headed east. Then Vulkan found me, like he'd said he would, and told me something that made me sure again."

He paused, gesturing toward the boar. "Because he

wears a saddle, and doesn't tear people up and eat them like the stories tell, it's easy for people to look at me as if I'd conquered and tamed him. But no one can conquer him, and he never needed taming, or changing, or anything else. He is what he is. And between him and me, he's number one. I make the decisions because he tells me I'm supposed to. And he stays with me because . . . because we were intended to do this together. He's the one with real power, but he has to operate through a human. And that's me."

He paused, frowning. "Where was I?"

"Vulkan told you something that made you sure again," Varia said.

"Oh yeah." He turned to Vulkan. "Why don't you tell them?"

Vulkan did, his "voice" speaking in their minds, describing what he'd felt while visiting the Scrub Coast. «And while I have your attention,» he said, «I will add this: Macurdy has more power than he admits, even to himself. I suspect his excessive modesty is not entirely curable. It is partly the result of a Farside culture in which assertiveness and self pride are frowned on, and overcompensation praised.» He turned his massive head, to fix his red eyes on Macurdy. «And because his is a family with secrets, and discourages the drawing of attention. And finally because on Farside, powers like Macurdy's are severely disapproved of—as he has learned to his distress.

«Fortunately his self-deprecation, though sincere, is superficial. He invariably exercises his powers as the need arises. And the need *will* arise, at levels beyond anything he has faced before.»

Vulkan turned his gaze to Cyncaidh. «As yet I perceive the vector only vaguely, but it is heavy with power and danger, both sorcerous and military. And the controlling power is highly mercurial, which makes it unpredictable.»

Their stories had sobered Cyncaidh. Now he nodded. "I have something to add to your accounts," he said. "Something that makes the threat seem more real than it otherwise might.

"As Varia can attest, there are two principal books on ylvin history, copied, recopied, and extended over the centuries. One is on the Western Empire, the other on the Eastern, and they agree on our origins. We once dwelt in Hithmearc, and on Ilroin, a large island some sixty miles off the Hithik Coast. Then the voitusotar came, and over a period of time conquered Hithmearc. We were their most difficult adversary, because we were not susceptible to their sorceries. In those times we had not interbred as much with humans, and our powers were greater than they are now. Or so say the histories.

"At one point we stalled the voitik conquest for years, and for this they hated us.

"Like ourselves, they are not a prolific species, and though they live long, they were not so numerous as the Hithik humans. They age throughout their lives, much as humans do, but more slowly. And usually they die while still able-bodied, when their heart fails.

"But they made up for their lack of numbers with their talents. And they were much more than sorcerers. They were superb warriors, very tall and fleet of foot. Also, they supposedly share a hive mind, by which they coordinate their actions. And while they could not tolerate riding on horseback . . ." He paused. "This part is rather difficult to credit, but supposedly their speed and endurance while running is such that their infantry was equivalent to light cavalry."

He looked his audience over. He had their full attention.

"Eventually they destroyed our army on Hithmearc, and many of our people fled across the straits to Ilroin, which was our ancient homeland. Of the rest, the voitusotar killed brutally almost all the men and boys. The women and girls they kept for themselves, as slaves. Or gave to their human allies, for public brutalization." He grimaced ruefully. "Brutalities as extreme as Quaie's at Ferny Cove, and on a much greater scale."

"We—our ancestors, that is—felt safe on Ilroin, for on the water, the voitusotar get so seasick, they die. But after one hundred twelve years they sent a human army against us, on human ships. At great cost of lives we fought them off, and destroyed many of their ships. But as soon as they'd withdrawn, we began to plan our exile. Because we knew—*knew* that the voitusotar would try again with a larger army.

"A tale had been recorded by the ancients, of sea-farers who supposedly had traveled far to the west, and encountered land. A land they named Vismearc. The descriptions were grotesque, extreme enough to seem imaginary, which of course caused doubt that the trip had ever been made.

"But the globe had been measured, so to speak, by our astronomers, so clearly there was a shore out there somewhere. And it seemed we were doomed unless we put much more than sixty miles between us and our enemies. We cut whole forests to build ships. Hemp became a major crop, for sails and cordage, and the tapping of pine for pitch and tar was greatly increased."

He spread his hands, which surprised Varia. Her husband seldom gestured when talking.

"In short," he said, "the whole population of Ilroin left the island, and . . . here we are."

Cyncaidh sat back, his jaw set. "That, of course, is history. And now we come to the point of this tale. Fifteen or so years ago, a ship of peculiar design took refuge from a storm, in a fishing port on the Ylvin Coast. Her crew did not answer hails, as if they didn't understand Yuultal. Their only response was to threaten with cross-bows and swords.

"When the storm blew over, she left.

"Afterward, coast guard sloops landed at several harbors along the Scrub Coast, to see if it had landed there—small places, where fishing and smuggling are a way of life. Far to the south, they learned of a vessel which had taken refuge there from a storm. Its crew too had been hostile, firing crossbows at the local men who approached. So the locals assumed they were pirates exploring northward from the Southern Sea. Which they may have been, though they left without attacking the village.

"At any rate, the eastern empire built a flotilla of rams, and added additional sloops and light schooners to their coast guard. In case the strangers had in fact been scouts for some ambitious pirate fleet. But after four or five years without further intrusions, the rams were decommissioned and their crews let go, to save the expense."

Cyncaidh stopped again, examining his strong, long-fingered soldier hands. "In a recent packet of reports from Aaerodh, my ducal manor, there was a letter from my senior healer, A'duaill. He'd dreamt of a voitik invasion, and thought I should know of it.

"I told Gavriel of A'duaill's dream—A'duaill is a splendid healer, but has never claimed to be a seer—and His Majesty's reaction was much like my own: dreams are dreams. Neither of us connected it with the strange ships on the coast."

Cyncaidh's patrician chin jutted forward, lips pressed briefly tight. "And now I have these reports of yours, which I find quite troubling. I'll tell Gavriel of them, but even combined they're a thin basis on which to recommend mobilization or other readiness actions. As the Council will surely tell us, should we propose any. And they hold the purse strings.

"But I'll recommend to the emperor that we pass your story on to Colroi, the capital of the Eastern Empire, and leak your reports here at home. Gavriel will approve, and Duinarog has a considerable pamphlet press which will love it. Then, if there is an invasion, our people will not be caught so unprepared mentally. And if there isn't, the story will blow over in time, and be forgotten."

Macurdy nodded. When you bit down on the evidence, it wasn't very meaty, just suggestive as hell. "Well then," he said, "we'll wait till the invasion fleet arrives. And hope that's not too late."

But thin as the evidence was, after what Cyncaidh had told them, he had no doubt at all there'd be an invasion fleet. The only question was when.

Until then, the kings of the Rude Lands would be even less ready than the ylver to do anything. But he'd visit each of them, he told himself, and describe the threat as he saw it. Call it the *possible* threat. And tell them if it should happen—if it should—another joint army might be needed. Make it sound theoretical, speculative, and ask no one to do anything. Then, when it happened, they'd be used to the idea, prepared for it, and they'd look to him.

Sound the alarm, he told himself, *but softly. Otherwise they'll resist the idea, and resent me for it.*

Minutes later, Cyncaidh was on his way to the palace. Varia went inside to look after domestic matters, particularly the morale of staff after the poisoning death of Zednis. And Vulkan—Vulkan disappeared. To snoop, Macurdy supposed, perhaps eavesdrop around. He wondered what some unprepared ylver would think, to suddenly see Vulkan's great formidable bulk listening to their conversation with great bristly ears.

Macurdy went to the room his sons had slept in, and knocked. They were, he discovered, wrapping up a discussion they'd begun the night before, on what to do next. Dohns had decided to return to the Cloister with his brother.

"Maybe we'll see you there, sir," he said. Hope tinged his voice.

"Maybe you will. I expect to be there by Ten-Month at the latest. I'll make a point of looking you up." He paused. "I don't plan to leave till morning. Maybe we can go somewhere today."

Ohns looked at him, surprised. "I—we would like that, sir."

"Good. I'll talk to Varia, and see if she can go with us. The last time I saw her, eighteen years ago, she told me about the animal park here. They have wild animals from all parts of Yuulith, from the Southern Sea to the far north."

Ohns looked pleased, and Dohns enthusiastic.

Macurdy went to find Varia, and an hour later, the Macurdy family rode to the zoo together in an open carriage. And Curtis got to see the 800-pound *Panthera atrox*, the boreal lion. Varia teased that it was the animal he'd been named for, though on Farside, *Panthera atrox* had been extinct for millennia. "It was Raien," she said, "who named you 'The Lion of Farside.' "

She wants us to like him, Macurdy thought. He gave the animal a final look. Its summer coat was tan with a tinge of pink, and it had more of a ruff than a mane. But it was a lion for sure. One hell of a lion. It seemed to him twice as big as the African lion he'd seen as a boy, at the Louisville zoo. He'd been nine or ten years old. It had been Varia who'd taken him there, too; Varia and Will.

When they left the zoo, they had lunch at an expensive restaurant, then took a carriage ride along the Imperial River, stopped to admire the surging water of the Great Rapids, then walked through Gorge Park. As they rode home, Macurdy felt both good and bad about their outing. It seemed plain they'd never have another day together as a family. But they'd had this one, and they'd all carry the memory.

❖   ❖   ❖

Cyncaidh hadn't gotten home till midafternoon, and as usual, busied himself with reports. Varia entered his office, kissed his temple, and told him she had some final things to talk about with Curtis. He smiled up at her. "I'll see you at dinner," he said.

She and Macurdy went into the garden again, and sat on a cushioned marble bench. "You know what?" he said. "There's something you used to do that I miss here: the way you used to wear your hair."

"My hair?"

"Tied in two bunches, with yellow ribbons. Like ponies' tails out to the sides."

She laughed. "At the Cloister we wore them like that a lot. It was simple and quick. So when I went over to Farside . . ." She looked at Macurdy fondly, and felt the old attraction—sexual and spiritual—tugging at her. "How did Melody wear hers?" she asked, "when she wasn't at war?"

"Bobbed off," he said, "the same as when you met her at Ternass. Only not quite so short."

Then she guided him to the subject of Melody's death, on his estate in Tekalos. He told her how it happened, and how he'd tried to revive her. They'd both been soaked with icy water, and the day had been freezing and windy. "I cried like a baby," he said, and to his dismay, choked up in the telling. After recovering himself, he looked at Varia thoughtfully. "When you were stolen from the farm, I never cried at all. Cursed and swore, but didn't cry, because I was sure I'd get you back. And when I found you married, and you told me you were going to stick with Cyncaidh—well, I cried some that night, but I could see you'd outgrown me." He paused. "You know, I never actually said that to myself, but inside I knew it. You outgrew me. I wasn't in the same class with Cyncaidh. If you'd have come with me, I'd have done it in a minute, even though I was in love with Melody. I hadn't been at first, but she

was in love with me from the get-go, and finally I found
myself in love with her."

Then he told her about Mary, and how she'd died.
"I went crazy after that," he said, "didn't know what I
was doing. Some guys came along—loggers I worked
with—and they dragged me dripping out of the creek
and hauled me to town. But I couldn't stay there any
longer. My dreams were dead." He almost added, "for
the third time," but stopped himself. "After the funeral,"
he went on, "I sold everything and went back to
Indiana."

Then he told her about Charley and Edna and Frank
and Edith . . . people she'd known as family for twenty
years.

"And now I'm here again, and can't imagine going
back."

"What will you do next?" Varia asked quietly.

Unexpectedly he grinned at her. It wasn't quite the
boyish grin she'd known back in Washington County;
it held a touch of ruefulness. But it made him very attractive. "I'm going to sit here," he said, "and listen to you
tell me about your life since I saw you eighteen years
ago."

She laughed. "It will have to be after dinner. I've a
few things to do before then."

As always, Cyncaidh was considerate. After supper
he left them to themselves, and they talked in the garden for more than an hour. When they said good night,
Macurdy felt a powerful urge to take Varia in his arms.
Not to kiss her, he told himself, only to . . . what? It
couldn't work. They'd both regret it, lightly if nothing
happened, and heavily if they ended up in bed. In this
universe she was Cyncaidh's wife, not his.

When the twins returned to their room after supper, sunlight still angled through the windows. Jahns

arrived with mugs of mulled cider, and the two of them sat sipping.

"You know," Ohns said thoughtfully, "I'm not sure I could get used to this Outland system of living with parents. But it might be pleasant to be near them—us in the barracks, Curtis and Varia in the palace."

Dohns looked at his brother. "But apparently the only real options we have are to return to the Cloister, and probably never see Varia again, or else stay here with her and Cyncaidh. It's tempting to stay, to see what it would be like, but I'm not likely to unless you do. It seems to me we're supposed to stick together, you and I."

Ohns nodded. They'd been born to be together. And being in the Guards, there was a good chance they'd continue to be. "What would you say," he asked, "if the Lion let us travel with him? We could ask to, you know. Volunteer."

Dohns frowned. "Do you think we should?"

"I'm . . . not sure. I'd like to apprentice under him, but . . . For one thing, there'd be no breeding assignments. Mainly, though, I don't think he'd go for it. And in the Guards, we're the top in our year. Given time, we're almost sure to be ranking officers."

Dohns nodded, though their career prospects meant less to him than to Ohns. Ordinarily he was more interested in new things than his brother was. Actually, the idea of staying with their mother and Cyncaidh on the Northern Sea was more attractive than following the Lion around the Rude Lands. But if they chose that option, then didn't like it, the dynast would never accept them back, except as culls. And Ohns was right: He'd miss the girls.

"Anyway," Ohns said, "by Ten-Month, the Lion will visit us at the Cloister. We'll have time to ask him then, if we decide to."

❖   ❖   ❖

Before he went to sleep that night, Macurdy examined something he'd said to Varia—that if she'd wanted to come back to him, that evening eighteen years past, he'd have done it in a minute. Would he, really? Just the evening before that, Melody had proposed—not for the first time—and he'd told her yes, sealing it with a kiss. Wondering at the time how he could possibly be saying it.

He looked at that. And it seemed to him now that he must have known, from some deeper wisdom, that he'd never have Varia back. That it wasn't to be. That if it had been, he wouldn't have said yes to Melody.

The next morning after breakfast, Macurdy and Vulkan set off for the Rude Lands again, this time with a small pouch of gold imperials, from the emperor via Cyncaidh. To cover expenses, because they would, after all, be acting in the interests of the empire, preparing the rulers and people of the Rude Lands for a possible voitik invasion. The twins went to the embassy, and a few days later, headed back to the Cloister, as guards for a courier.

Within a week, Cyncaidh and Varia were on a packet rowed by a dozen brawny oarsmen, traveling up the Imperial River to the Middle Sea. There they'd embark on the *Sea Eagle,* a graceful forty-four-foot schooner built for speed. Within three weeks, perhaps less than two, they'd be at Aaerodh Manor, on the Northern Sea. Cyncaidh would stay only briefly—a month—then return to the capital. Varia would stay on till Nine-Month, unless he sent for her. Stay with their sons. She'd look at them from a slightly different perspective since she'd met Ohns and Dohns, but she'd love them as much as ever. They were truly hers, unshared with the Sisterhood.

21

Tussle in the Grass

Macurdy didn't linger in the Marches. He wasn't widely familiar with them, and they lay in Gavriel's and Cyncaidh's realm of influence. His responsibility was the Rude Lands, and he and Vulkan would spend much of the summer traveling them.

There, for the most part, Vulkan didn't use his concealment spell. Though the Rude Lands lacked a formal postal system, word traveled far and reasonably fast, if it was interesting enough. And an accepted legend riding a great boar remained interesting in spades, even after people got used to the idea.

Stories spread, interest heightened, and inevitably, rumors and exaggerations were accepted as reality. Macurdy ate regularly in inns now, and told of speaking with the Imperial Chief Counselor. There was, he said ominously, evidence of a possible invasion from across the Ocean Sea.

And what Macurdy said tended to be credited.

His first royal visit was in Indervars, the throne home

189

of Indrossa. Next he paused to visit Jeremid again, before continuing on to Tekalos to see Wollerda and Liiset. Wollerda was by far his closest royal ally, and he greatly respected the old Kullvordi revolutionary. Who'd had weeks to get used to the idea of a possible voitik invasion.

Macurdy had hopes that Wollerda would have worthwhile thoughts to share. He didn't. But he was impressed by Cyncaidh's story of the two strange ships, fifteen years earlier, and the letter the ylf lord had received from his healer and magician.

Then Macurdy and Vulkan turned west for further royal visits. Their most agreeable discovery was Kormehr's new king. The late Keltorus had been a whiskey-sodden lunatic, who for years had abused his power. Finally he'd been deposed and murdered—"executed"— by his own guardsmen. The new king was someone Macurdy knew and respected. He'd promoted the man to captain after the battle of Ternass. Arliss hadn't forgotten, nor had his warriors, and the Kormehri were exceptional fighting men, comparable to the Ozmen.

Macurdy was received courteously everywhere. And by carefully telling no one what they should do, or that they should do anything, he'd left on good terms.

In the Rude Lands, the palaces were more richly furnished than when he'd known them in the past. Sisterhood products were prominent, not only in palaces but in the better inns, and presumably in the homes of the prosperous. Floor and wall tiles, statuary, jewelry, lamps . . . Especially lamps. The more fragile glass products were almost surely from Outland operations, transported mainly by river barge.

Macurdy realized he'd played an important, if indirect, role in the growth of the Sisterhood's Outland operations. His invasion of the Marches had shown his Rude Lands soldiers wealth, amenities and roads beyond anything they'd known. And the peace terms he'd worked out with Cyncaidh had greatly expanded markets and trade between the Empire and Marches on the one hand, and the Rude Lands and Sisterhood on the other.

But Cyncaidh deserved most of the credit, it seemed to him. The treaty they'd hammered out had provided the foundation. The ylf lord's knowledge, authority, diplomatic skills and commercial connections had built on it. Cyncaidh. He could have hated the ylf. Instead he admired him. Even liked him.

Finally it was time to pay his first visit to the Cloister. En route he stopped again at Teklapori, and shared his further impressions with Wollerda. There was interesting news from the Cloister, too. Omara, Liiset told him, was no longer Sarkia's deputy. Idri had demanded her ouster, probably as much to test her new power as to deprive Omara of the position.

"New power?" Macurdy asked.

Liiset explained. For years, Idri's single most powerful supporter had been the commander of the Tigers. But she'd been unable to seduce his executive officer, the second in command. The XO had had exceptional respect among the Tigers, and in a showdown would have backed the dynast. But the XO had recently died, apparently of natural causes, and Idri had the new XO in her pocket.

Initially she'd demanded that Omara be assigned Outland; she wanted Sarkia deprived of her services as a healer. But Sarkia had refused, and Idri, backing down, had accepted the compromise.

It had to be tough for Idri, Macurdy supposed, after waiting so long, and wanting so badly to be dynast. For clearly she was impatient by nature. But to risk a showdown . . . According to Liiset, Sarkia might die tomorrow—she'd almost surely die within the year—leaving the Sisterhood in Idri's hands risk-free.

Then Sarkia had filled Omara's administrative

position by promoting Omara's assistant, Amnevi, who
might well be Omara's equal, or nearly so, in executive skills. Meanwhile Omara continued as Sarkia's
healer.

From Teklapori, Macurdy headed for the Cloister.
He'd never been there before, had considered it dangerous to him because he distrusted Sarkia. Now, he
told himself, the danger lay in Idri's new power, and
her hatred of him. She was genuinely crazy, he told
himself, a bomb waiting to go off.

But he needed to visit there. The Tigers, and probably the Guards, were significant military forces already
well trained. And if what Cyncaidh had said was true,
about the ylver not being susceptible to voitik sorceries, then the Tigers and Guards shouldn't be either.
Some or most of them, at least.

On the way, he stopped to meet the King of Asrik.
All Macurdy had seen of Asrik before was the wilderness of the Granite Range, many miles to the north.
Where the Valley Highway passed through Asrik, the
landscape was of high rugged hills, rich in rock and
heavily forested. A wilder, stonier version of the Kullvordi Hills. The road, however, was as good as any he'd
seen in the Rude Lands, including the River Kingdoms.
Mud holes had been drained and filled, and streams
were crossed on well-made stone bridges. Through gaps
ahead he glimpsed much higher crests, the Great Eastern Mountains. This far south, Vulkan told him, they
were at their highest.

By reputation, Asrik was a sort of democracy. Its
king wasn't even a king; that was simply what the other
Rude Landers called him. He was elected every five
years by voice votes at local meetings. The Asriki called
him *wofnemst*, which Vulkan said was an ancient word
meaning "principal."

Now Macurdy spent an evening with him. The man

managed to be affable without being hospitable, and avoided saying anything that might encourage Macurdy's coming back to him for help.

Macurdy had been prepared for that by Jeremid and Wollerda. The Asriki, they'd told him, were an ingrown people, and very resistive to change. Family feuds were a serious part of its culture, and one of the wofnemst's two major roles was to control their excesses by levying reparations—blood money—and decreeing outlawry against the worst offenders. His other major role was to maintain good relations with their powerful neighbors, the dwarves. A wofnemst whose rulings sufficiently offended the local councils, or the population at large, was turned out of office early. Or exiled or hung, if he'd sufficiently insulted Asriki principles.

The road, Macurdy supposed, had been built by the dwarves, to facilitate their commerce with the outside world.

Some thirty minutes after leaving the "royal" residence, Macurdy and Vulkan topped a pass that gave the best view he'd had of the Great Eastern Mountains. They reminded him of the Northern Cascades, in Washington, with snow fields and jagged peaks. These, Vulkan told him, were the heart, but by no means the extent, of the dwarvish kingdom.

The Cloister was within the Kingdom of the Dwarves in Silver Mountain, and only a mile or so from its border with Asrik. Macurdy reached it the same morning he left the Asriki royal residence.

The name "Cloister" had three applications. It was a sort of synonym for the Sisterhood; it referred to the twelve-square-mile territory housing their nation; and it was what they called their walled town, which covered more than two square miles. It was a sovereignty within a sovereignty, leased to the Sisterhood by the King in Silver Mountain. According to Liiset, the lease

was for one hundred years, and renewable, and couldn't
be broken except for specific, extreme causes. The King
in Silver Mountain, of course, could evict them any
time he wanted, agreement or not. He had an army
far more powerful than Sarkia's. But breaking his lease
would damage his reputation, his and his kingdom's,
and the dwarves treasured reputation almost as much
as wealth.

Macurdy was stopped at the town's north gate. Mounted on Vulkan as he was, the Guardsmen could hardly
fail to recognize him, and according to Liiset, would
expect him. Nonetheless, the sergeant in charge required
him to identify himself and state his business. Then they
assigned a cadet to guide him to the dynast's palace.

Riding through the town, Macurdy was impressed.
It was attractive, orderly and clean. Most of the buildings seemed to be dormitories. It was midday, lunch-
time, he supposed. There were not a lot of people on
the streets. Most were female, all of them attractive
and seemingly young. Most wore their hair as Varia
had, back in Indiana—twin ponytails, one on each side.
They wore a semi-fitted coverall tucked into low-cut
boots. As he'd seen in the photos he'd found in Varia's
attic, on that weird morning twenty years earlier.

At the palace, it was obvious he was expected. A
Guards officer led him to a receptionist, who called
Omara, who took him to the dynast with no wait at all.
Sarkia would speak in little more than a whisper, Omara
warned him. For she had much to tell him, and was
very weak.

Even so, he was shocked at her appearance. The
woman he'd negotiated with in Tekalos, eighteen years
earlier, had been strong, beautiful, radiating unusual
energy. Now she was shrunken—tiny and fragile—and
nearly bald. She did not sit up to speak, not even
propped. Her body aura was alarmingly weak, and her
spirit aura showed tenacity more than strength.

She listened to his story, of his dream and A'duaill's, of Vulkan's sense of danger from the voitusotar, and Cyncaidh's story of the two strange ships. She heard him out, but scarcely reacted. Her focus was totally on the succession, and on surviving till it was worked out. Macurdy understood that. The Sisterhood had been her life and focus for more than two centuries, and now she had no energy for other issues.

She confessed to him a day of discouragement, a sense of defeat, when her ambassador to Duinarog had forwarded Varia's unwillingness to serve. But she'd rallied. "To persist is my only choice," she said.

Macurdy told her that Rillor had destroyed whatever chance there'd been of Varia coming south. She agreed, adding that Rillor had been flogged, demoted, and assigned to the embassy in Miskmehr.

Astonished, Macurdy asked why she'd left him alive.

"You are aware of the infertility problem we've inherited from the ylver," she answered. "Rillor is a proven sire, more fertile than most, and his offspring have some superior qualities. Mostly physical," she added wryly. "But more to the point, Idri insisted on his being spared." The old dynast chuckled, a sad soft sound. "It is," she said wryly, "the first instance of honest loyalty I've ever seen in her. She is pregnant by him. In her sixty-six years she has had sexual intercourse with innumerable men, but this is her first pregnancy."

The old eyes turned thoughtful, focusing inward, and she rested a minute before continuing. "Given the situation, I have found it necessary to reevaluate the importances of almost everything. Thus I give way on many issues. But from time to time, with Omara's help, I have forced Idri to her knees on some issue or other. To remind her that she is not the dynast." Sarkia paused thoughtfully. "Backing down is far more painful for her than for me. Twenty years ago I could not have said that. I was strong willed to a fault."

She turned her head enough to meet Macurdy's eyes. "Varia knows that as well as anyone. When you see her next, tell her I deeply regret what happened. That I love her and wish her well, as unbelievable as she may find it."

Then her head rolled back and her eyes closed. "I am tired now," she murmured. It was barely audible. "Go. With my good wishes."

Except for her aura, she looked like an embalmed corpse. Macurdy left, far more impressed with her than he'd been when she was strong and beautiful.

Amnevi's office was a door away, and he went to it. To his surprise and momentary shock, she was physically a duplicate of Idri, a clone sister. But her aura reflected a very different personality, and strong talent. He asked for a meeting with Idri, partly to read Amnevi's aura when he asked it.

Idri, she replied, was away from the Cloister. Where, she didn't know. "She comes and goes as she pleases," Amnevi told him, "asking no one. And telling no one, except perhaps the commander of her Tigers."

He thanked her and left the building. When he'd arrived, he'd left Vulkan on the lawn. Now he couldn't see him anywhere. «Here, Macurdy,» said the familiar voice. «In the shade of the building. Cloaked. I drew undesired attention from a platoon of Tigers marching past.»

Macurdy frowned. "Can they harm you?"

«They cannot harm *me*. But in their numbers they could deprive me—and you—of this highly useful body.»

"So you cloaked yourself."

«Precisely. Cloaked and displaced myself.»

"Displaced? You mean walked?"

«It is the only means of transportation I have.»

While they talked, three Sisters left the building, looking oddly at Macurdy, who seemed to be carrying on a conversation with himself. So having no confidence in his own cloak, against persons of talent, Macurdy stepped over to Vulkan, disappearing within his. Vulkan's had the further advantage of concealing sound, and Macurdy preferred to voice his words. To simply think them felt unsatisfying and incomplete to him.

"Tell me about that attention they gave you," he said.

«It was not overt. They simply contemplated action. They regarded me as a challenge.»

"Were they in ranks?"

«At the time, yes. They did and said nothing, nor was their attention coordinated. But several of them wondered independently how many it would take to make pork of me. There was also the explicit thought of bringing up the matter to others, with the possibility of action. They were not aware of my connection to you.»

"Hmm." Vulkan's addendum relaxed Macurdy somewhat. "How many would it take, do you suppose?"

«If the situation precluded flight, and I did not cloak myself, half a dozen should suffice. Certainly with spears, but they would be highly dangerous with swords as well. By the standards of your species, Tigers are more than extremely strong and athletic. They are also highly skilled, and do not fear death. Danger is a spur to them. They accept that death is not the end; that they will reincarnate. Where they err is in believing they'll return as Tigers. Given their perspective from the other side, that is extremely unlikely.»

"Other side?"

«The off-stage side.»

"Huh! What did they think when you disappeared?"

«They were reminded of my reputation as a wizard.»

Macurdy frowned thoughtfully. "I wonder how good they are at hand-to-hand combat."

«I do not know. I watched them drill just once, when the Cloister was at Ferny Cove. They drilled with practice swords, appearing to be very quick and highly skilled.»

Macurdy considered what he'd planned for the evening, and how it would affect Vulkan. The boar had eaten a whole lamb the night before in Asrik. "Do you want to wait around here?" he asked. "Or slip out through the gate? Or what?"

Vulkan heaved himself to his feet. «I will accompany you,» he said. «Cloaked. This environment is not without hazards for you, too, particularly considering what you are contemplating.»

Macurdy went to his sons' company orderly room. Their company, he learned, was outside the wall, training. The desk sergeant notified the company commander, who sent an orderly to take Macurdy to watch them. Afterward, the captain added, the marshal was welcome to eat supper with his sons' squad, or with himself.

After arranging with his sons to spend part of the evening with them, Macurdy ate supper with the captain, questioning him about Guards training, and what he knew of Tiger training.

After eating, he was taken to his sons' barracks. Together they went outside, and began a leisurely walk along the grassy margin of the street. Grinning, they told him they both had breeding duty that evening at nine.

"You like that, do you?" he asked.

"Oh yes," said Ohns. "It's our favorite."

"What do the women think of breeding duty?"

"They like it too, except for Tiger breeding. Tigers are rough, they say, and show no respect. Often they hurt them."

"Do you breed the same ones all the time?"

"It varies," said Dohns. "So far we've been assigned to breed members of three clones. I'll bet anything that if you asked, they'd schedule you in, too."

Nonplused by the suggestion, Macurdy didn't respond. Instead he broached his real interest. "Are Guardsmen trained in hand-to-hand combat? Without weapons?"

"We train in both wrestling and blows," Ohns said.

"Are you good?"

"Very good." Ohns grinned again. "Would you like to test me? We've both wondered how good you are."

Macurdy accepted the challenge, and they stepped onto a lawn, where he took off his belt pack. Ohns fronted off with him, and began to feel him out. Macurdy was more direct. He feinted, drew a countering move, and slammed the young man to the ground with a simple hip throw. Afterward he had them demonstrate Guards wrestling techniques on each other, stopping them now and then with questions. He soon had a sense of the overall style.

"What about the techniques for blows?" he asked. "Could you demonstrate those? Not on each other. Show me the drills you do."

After a few minutes, and more questions, he knew as much as he felt he needed. "What about Tiger training?" he asked. "Does theirs go beyond yours?"

"They don't train much in hand to hand," Dohns answered. "Guardsmen can be assigned to embassies and craftworks, and to protect property and personnel, we have to be able to control people without killing them. Tigers fight only to kill, and train endlessly with weapons. Though they do wrestle each other for fun and exercise; we've seen them."

Afterward they demonstrated their wrestling techniques on each other. And again on their father, who played the role of an untrained antagonist.

When he'd left, the youths walked together to the

breeding dorm, in the pleasant Eight-Month evening. "Blessed Sarulin!" said Dohns. "Did you feel his strength? His hands are so strong, I thought he was going to crush my arm with his fingers. I must be black and blue where he gripped me! I wonder if he has any idea how strong he is."

Ohns nodded thoughtfully. "And quick. I'd never have believed it."

Macurdy ate a light breakfast the next morning in the Guards command dining room. There he sat beside General Grimval, answering questions about the Ozian system of training. Afterward he returned to what was commonly referred to as the Dynast's Palace, though its official name was Executive Hall. There he sat briefly in the shelter of Vulkan's cloak, and talked with the boar about his plan. It was not explicit; he'd have to play things by ear. But he had a definite idea of what he hoped to accomplish.

It seemed reckless to Vulkan, but he didn't say so. Macurdy would have many decisions to make, and no doubt some would have to be bold in the extreme. To argue now could weaken his confidence and resolve. And at any rate Macurdy had done what he could to prepare.

Half an hour after lunch, they walked together to Tiger headquarters. At the stoop he was stopped by a scowling sentry, who demanded to know his business.

"My business is with your commanding officer," Macurdy answered, and stepped onto the stoop as if to walk past the man.

The Tiger flushed at the insolence, and stepped between Macurdy and the open door. There was not twelve inches between the two men. "He is away from the Cloister," the sentry said.

Macurdy's tone was casual but absolute. "Someone's in charge here," he said. "I'll speak with him."

"Private!" called a voice.

Inside, the sergeant major had overheard them, and from his desk could see a situation developing. During Quaie's War, he'd been in the Tiger platoon guarding Omara's healing coven, and recognized Macurdy. The sentry too should have known him. Word of his arrival had spread throughout the Cloister. But the sentry was young.

"Yes, Sergeant Major!" the sentry called back. It was difficult talking to someone behind him while this foreign pile of shit was pushing his face at him.

"Let him in. I'll speak with him."

Reluctantly the sentry stood aside, and Macurdy entered. "Thank you, Sergeant Major," he said. "I appreciate your help; I don't know your regulations." He gestured toward the stoop and its sentry. "If I bent them, my apologies."

The sergeant major ignored both thanks and apology. "In Colonel Bolzar's absence," he said, "Subcolonel Sojass is in charge. Before I interrupt him, it is necessary that I know why you want to speak with him."

Macurdy nodded. "Yuulith is in danger of invasion from across the Ocean Sea. I've been traveling through the Rude Lands, looking at their armed forces, and their effectiveness. The Tigers have a reputation which I presume is well deserved. But I need to see for myself."

The sergeant major's jaw set. "Be seated," he said. "I will inform him." He got to his feet and disappeared into an adjacent room. Macurdy could hear voices through the closed door, but couldn't make out the words. A well-knit, pre-adolescent boy sat near a corner of the room, watching and listening. A Tiger cadet pulling orderly duty, Macurdy supposed, and wondered what the boy made of an outsider coming here. After a long minute, the sergeant major reappeared, again closing the door behind him.

"Subcolonel Sojass is busy," he said. "I can have you taken to a company drill field."

He stood waiting for Macurdy's response.

"Thank you, Sergeant Major. I'd appreciate that."

The sergeant major sat down, and jotted a note. "Thessmak!" he said as he wrote. The boy got sharply to his feet and stepped to the desk. The sergeant major finished writing and handed him the note. "Take Marshal Macurdy to Captain Skortov's company. Give the note to the captain."

"Yes, Sergeant Major!" the boy snapped, then turned to Macurdy, who got to his feet. They left at a brisk walk. Macurdy got the impression the boy would have preferred running.

Twenty minutes later they were outside the wall, at a drill field divided into squares of perhaps forty yards on a side. Four platoons were there, drilling with short spears in a thin haze of dust. Their swift forceful movements seemed choreographed. An officer paced by each platoon, circling it, watching. Barking brief orders at intervals of a few seconds, the platoon responding without pause.

Macurdy was impressed. Their drill was faster and sharper than the spear drill of Ozian Heroes, if less exuberant. Whether they'd be more formidable in battle, he didn't know. Stronger, certainly, and no doubt more tightly disciplined.

It occurred to him that he hadn't fought for years. He hoped he wasn't biting off more than he could chew.

The cadet took Macurdy to the company commander, a chiseled-faced captain who watched the drill from a flat-topped mound, a grassy command platform. After speaking to the captain, the boy handed him the note. Frowning, the captain read it, then green eyes unreadable, looked at Macurdy. His aura, however, showed no hostility. "I am Captain Skortov," he said. "What do you want to see?"

"I'm seeing some of it now. I'd also like to see how strong these Tigers are. Feel their strength in personal combat."

Something flashed behind Skortov's eyes, and the Tiger smiled. Without a second's hesitation he shouted an order, a booming, effortless bellow. The whirl of activity stopped at once, each man turning toward Skortov, spear butt by his right foot in what Macurdy would have called "order arms."

"We have a visitor," Skortov bellowed, "come to watch you train. He is the Lion of Farside. He led the army that defeated the ylver in the Battle of Ternass, and destroyed the evil and treacherous Quaie in single combat." He turned to Macurdy, but spoke so the company would hear. "What do you think of their drill?" he asked.

Macurdy was caught unprepared by Skortov's praise, and hoped he wouldn't blow it. Looking at the Tigers, he matched the captain's bellow. "I am impressed. They are very good, as I expected."

Skortov spoke to his Tigers again. "He asked to see how strong you are. He wants to feel your strength in personal combat. Corporal Corgan! Come up here and show him!"

The Tiger who strode toward the mound was taller and huskier than most of them. "Do not use magic," Skortov murmured to Macurdy. "It would offend the men, and hurt your reputation."

Macurdy heard, but did not respond. No magic. What would these men make of the jujitsu Fritzi had sent him off to learn? Technique or magic? If he didn't use the skills he knew, this might backfire on him. He watched Corgan climb the low mound, the Tiger's aura reflecting anticipation and utter confidence. And a smoldering hostility that surprised Macurdy. Meanwhile the interest of the company was so strong, Macurdy's aura vibrated to it, a feeling new to him. Corgan stopped not four feet from him, glowering in his face as if to intimidate.

"You will wrestle," Skortov instructed them. "There will be no blows struck, no choking, no gouging of eyes, no attempt to break or dislocate bones. The purpose of this is for each of you to discover the strength of the other." He stared meaningfully at Corgan. "Is that understood, Corporal?"

"Understood," Corgan growled.

Skortov turned to Macurdy. "Agreed?" he asked.

"Agreed."

Belatedly, Macurdy wished he knew if there was a standard opening to bouts like these. Skortov waved them back till they stood ten feet apart. Macurdy didn't focus on Corgan's eyes or feet. He had the knack of taking in the entire opponent. Then Skortov's callused hands clapped loudly, and the two men closed.

Corgan was direct. He grabbed at Macurdy, who grasped the Tiger's sleeve and shirt front, and threw him with a basic leg throw. He heard Corgan's loud grunt and stepped back. *That'll give him something to think about,* he thought.

Corgan was on his feet quickly, his hostility transformed to hatred. However, though his intention was no less, his confidence was bruised. He closed again. This time Macurdy used none of the judo throws he'd learned. For a moment they grappled, feet wide and braced—and Macurdy discovered he was the stronger. He raised Corgan off his feet, and as he did, the Tiger drove a fist into his ribs. Macurdy slammed him down, landing on top, and for a wild minute they struggled on the ground. Then Skortov's voice shouted "Up!" and Macurdy felt Corgan's grasp relax. He relaxed his own, and both of them got to their feet. Skortov waved them apart again, then stared meaningfully at Corgan.

"This match is wrestling, not blows!" he bellowed. "Do not forget again! You will disgrace us!"

Then he waved them together. This time Macurdy didn't meet Corgan's embrace. Instead he feinted another leg throw, converting Corgan's reaction into a hip throw that ended with the Tiger's arm behind his back. Held there by Macurdy, who applied enough pressure to let him know he could dislocate his elbow if he wished. He expected some kind of cry from Corgan, but when there was none, he let him go and backed away.

Now the hatred in the Tiger's aura showed wildness as well. When Skortov waved them together, Corgan loosed a straight left that struck Macurdy in the face, sending him staggering backwards. Then the Tiger was on him with lefts and rights, and suddenly it was over. Macurdy stood bleeding from cheek, nose, and mouth. Corgan had rolled down the grassy mound, coming to rest in the trampled dust of the drill field. After a moment the Tiger rolled over and tried to get up. He made it to his hands and knees, but no further.

Skortov bellowed another order. Two grim Tigers strode to Corgan, jerked him roughly to his feet, and manhandled him away. Then the captain turned to Macurdy, took his wrist, and raised his arm in victory. There was no cheering, and for a moment Macurdy thought they disapproved. Then he shook off his fog and looked out at the company. There were no grins, but neither were there scowls. Their auras reflected approval.

"Company," Skortov bellowed, "continue your drill!"

They did, less smoothly than before, as if thrown off stride by the distraction. Pleased but rueful, Skortov looked at Macurdy. "Corgan has no particular reputation as a skilled brawler," he said. "I chose him because of his reputation for strength. And because he feels he has a grudge against you."

"Grudge?"

"The story is that the runaway, Varia, had been your

wife on Farside. And that she ran away to return to you. Corgan had sentry watch when she escaped from the barracks. He was put on punishment for months, and blamed you for it."

Now Skortov grinned. "I presumed you would win," he said. "I was along in Quaie's War."

Still bleeding, Macurdy left the mound and, at the road, called Vulkan to him. Invisibly they walked together to the river, where Macurdy washed his damaged face in water that not long before had been snow on some high slope. Then he stripped, and washed the blood from his U.S. Army fatigues. After spreading them on a bush, he and Vulkan lay beside it in the sun. It took a minute to get the proper mental focus, then Macurdy used his healing skills on his face. When he'd finished, they napped.

That evening they ate with Amnevi. The swelling in Macurdy's face was gone, and the lacerations and abrasions almost entirely healed, but some discoloration remained. His explanation was brief. He had, he said, told a Tiger officer he'd like to test himself against a Tiger.

Amnevi's brows rose. "What was the outcome?" she asked.

"I'm surprised you haven't heard by now. I won. Decisively." He told her then of Corgan's hatred, and its roots.

"Hmm," she mused. "I find myself not surprised at your victory, though why you should want such a test is beyond my imagining. Well. Your legend is not unknown here. This will add a page to it." She paused. "And to Varia's."

It was then he told her why he was there—of the threat of invasion from across the Ocean Sea. Of his dream and A'duaill's, of Vulkan's premonition, and his own experience in Hithmearc. And Cyncaidh's story of the two strange ships. He expected, he said, to raise an army when the time came.

He put it more strongly than he had to most of the Rude Lands rulers. As he supposed, she'd heard much of it before, from Liiset, via courier. She wished him well but promised nothing; he supposed it was as far as her authority allowed.

Besides, Sarkia could easily die tomorrow—today for that matter—and who knew what Idri would do when she took over? Not cooperate with him, that was certain.

The next morning, Vulkan, fully visible, trotted out the Cloister's main gate with Macurdy on his back. They were on their way to see the King in Silver Mountain, the last royalty Macurdy would visit on that round.

22

The King in
Silver Mountain

Macurdy had never heard a description of the royal residence in the Silver Mountain. He'd assumed most dwarves worked underground, and probably lived underground, but the palace?

The road, being paved with bricks of stone, was even better than the road through Asrik. It was cut into a forested slope above a rowdy mountain stream, and ditched on the uphill side. Numerous brooklets, springs and seeps fed water into the ditch, to pass at intervals beneath small stone bridges. It seemed to Macurdy the prettiest road he'd seen in two universes.

After an hour or so, he came to a stone post with 2 MILES carved into it, without saying to where.

The last half mile was the floor of an upper valley. Here the road was magnificent, paved with squared and fitted flagstones, and flanked on both sides with a row of monster white pines taller than tulip trees. The most slender of them was nearly five feet through, their mighty trunks rising like columns eighty feet or more to the lowest branches. Macurdy's practiced eye made them well over two hundred feet tall; they'd have looked at home in Nehtaka County.

Then he topped a rise, and the avenue through the trees widened, funnel-like, still flanked by great pines. This provided a broader view of the "where," a hundred yards ahead: an entrance into the mountain itself, and beyond a doubt the royal residence. It was surely the grandest entrance in Yuulith. So grand, the landscaping—mossy lawns, sculpted yews, beds of rhododendron, arbors overgrown with roses—went nearly unnoticed.

A section of precipitous mountainside had been carved away, leaving a polished—polished!—vertical face a hundred feet wide and a hundred high. The entrance itself had been cut into that, and fitted with massive double doors, each ten feet wide and fifteen high. As Macurdy drew nearer, he found the massive doorway fittings faced with gold, and magnificently detailed with intertwined serpents and leafy vines. From among the leaves peered carven tomttu, birds, and small animals, as if they lived among them. The doors themselves were plated with polished silver and gold, intricately and imaginatively ornamented. It would be easy, Macurdy told himself, to spend a day sorting out the patterns, and finding things one had missed.

The guards were large and powerful dwarves in their prime. Even bare-headed (which they weren't) and barefoot (which they were), they stood five feet tall, or close to it. Stripped they might have weighed one hundred sixty pounds of muscle. Their splendid silver helms reached higher than Macurdy's shoulders. Their knee-length hauberks and seven-foot spears shimmered with dwarven magic, and no doubt their swords as well, when unsheathed.

He was expected. Amnevi had sent a courier ahead for him. He was detained just long enough to dismount and formally identify himself. Vulkan was escorted down a side path to a stable out of sight in the forest, escorted with the respect due a dwarf friend. Then one of the great doors opened smoothly and silently, and an attendant emerged to lead Macurdy inside.

There they walked down a high narrow colonnade, its polished granite columns carved from the mountain itself. Flames danced and swayed in open oil lamps wrought of silver, but Macurdy smelled no smoke. The place seemed ventilated, with circulation driven by some mechanical system. Or possibly magic. And the lamps were not the only source of light. At intervals, white light flooded from apertures overhead, leaving Macurdy to speculate about systems of mirrors relaying daylight from somewhere above.

The colonnade led to a large waiting room, where an usher took custody of him. From there Macurdy was taken down corridors less grand, to a guest room not large but well furnished. All it lacked was windows. The bed was more than large enough, large though he was. On a heavy oak table stood a bowl of grapes and two platters, one with apples and pears, the other with a loaf of dark and pungent rye bread, a knife, and a wheel of cheese. A pitcher of cool water stood beside them, and a bottle of red wine, with glasses. On another table was soap, a towel, a silver wash basin, and a pitcher of warm water.

"His Majesty's aide will be here shortly," the usher said. "Ye may want to refresh yerself." Then he bowed and left.

Before Macurdy had left the Cloister, Amnevi had told him his appointment with the king would probably be on his third day there. Even royalty couldn't expect a first-day audience. Half an hour later, however, His Majesty's aide knocked on the door. His Majesty, he said, would see him later that afternoon. "Meanwhile yew've time for a nap," he added. "I'll have ye wakened for your appointment." Then, seeing the surprise on Macurdy's face, he explained: "Yew've been named dwarf friend, for rescuing a trade embassy from highwaymen. Perhaps ye'd forgotten. It carries with it certain privileges."

Macurdy remembered well enough. But when Kittul Kendersson Great Lode had dubbed him dwarf friend, he'd thought it was between himself and Kendersson's party, from the Diamond Flues, the better part of a thousand miles west. Seemingly Kittul had spread the word. And apparently a dwarf friend was deemed a friend to all dwarves, regardless of where.

"Meanwhile," the aide continued, "there are things ye should know. About the king himself, and the protocol of his court." Finn Greatsword, he said, was very ancient, even for a dwarf: he'd already lived 337 years, and ruled for the last 179 of them. During his reign, the dwarves in Silver Mountain had much increased their wealth, and without increasing the precious metals they dug. What Greatsword had done was increase the base metals taken from the mountain and refined— copper, tin, antimony, and others in varying quantities. But especially iron.

All the better grades of pewter were spun in Silver Mountain, and the better weapon-grade steel was forged there. The very finest swords were dwarf made. They were expensive, of course. When enhanced with spells by dwarven masters, they were especially expensive, and the dwarves were particular about to whom they sold enchanted blades.

Macurdy showed the aide his saber. "It's not dwarf made," he said, "but it carries a dwarven spell."

The aide peered intently at it, then passed a hand along its blade, not quite touching it. "Indeed," he said. "The spell's not one of ours, but excellent nonetheless." He concentrated. "From the Diamond Flues. Yes."

"Kittul Kendersson Great Lode spelled it."

"Kendersson! Excellent! A pity, though, to waste a Kendersson spell on a blade not dwarf made."

Macurdy felt a twinge of resentment at the aide's arrogance, and it showed in his voice. "It happened on the road, and it's all the blade I had. It served me well in more than one fight."

"Of course, of course. I have no doubt. With old Kittul's spell on it, it would. But on a dwarven blade, and applied during the forging . . ." The aide's gesture finished the thought. Before he left, he asked Macurdy for custody of the saber. " 'Tis in need of polishing," he said, "and yew'll not need it here."

"My thanks," Macurdy told him, his voice still tinged with annoyance. "But my purse is too thin."

The aide shook his head. "For yew there'll be no cost, dwarf friend. Courtesy of the Mountain and His Majesty."

Macurdy realized the value of the offer. Anyone with a little coaching and the proper tools could put an edge on a sword. But few swordsmen could produce the edge a professional polisher could, and a professional greatly improved a blade's appearance. Reputedly even its temper, though Macurdy was skeptical. Professionals with a reputation, however, charged more than many swordsmen could pay. And dwarven masters of almost any craft were said to be the best.

The lesser audience chamber was small, perhaps twelve by twenty feet. Near the far end, Finn Greatsword, the King in Silver Mountain, sat on a throne not merely golden, but of actual gold. The twenty-inch dais on which it stood was clothed with furs. As were the walls; a king's ransom in furs. As instructed, Macurdy approached to a short line, eight feet in front of His Majesty, and stopped.

Finn Greatsword had always been bulky, and his years had not shrunk him. He still looked formidable, though his large hands were gnarly with arthritis. His once-golden beard was white, shot with pale yellow and parted in the middle, the halves braided, and resting on his thick thighs. His spadelike teeth were almost brown with age, but they seemed all to be there.

"So yew are the Lion of Farside." The deep guttural voice issued from a barrel chest, to rumble out a wide mouth.

"I didn't give myself the name," Macurdy answered.

"Of course not. T'was the ylver gave it to ye. I've heard the tales, including those of the Diamond Flue clans. And I'm told of yer reason for coming here. However, we do not divulge our strength at arms, even to dwarf friends."

He examined Macurdy, then seemed to make a decision. It was, Macurdy realized, done for effect; the dwarf king already knew what he was going to say. "But to yew," Greatsword rumbled, "to yew I'll tell more than I would most others. Every dwarf lad is trained for years, in sword, crossbow, spear and poleax, and in tactics above- and below-ground. As well as in the skilled trades by which we earn our way in the world. We start as boys. The use of both weapons and tools are as natural to us as breathing.

"But I keep no army. Guards, yes, but no army. If I need an army, I send the war torch through the mountain, or such part of the mountain as I choose, and all who see it rush to arms, and to the proper mustering hall."

He paused, eyeing Macurdy with interest. "And now I'd like to hear the tale you bear, from yer own mouth."

Macurdy repeated the story, his delivery well practiced by now, and the dwarf king seemed to absorb it all. Macurdy finished with the usual comment: "Nothing may come of it. Dreams are most often just that: dreams. A great boar's premonitions are more worrisome, but it's possible they foreshadow nothing more

than the grandfather of storms, sweeping in to ravage
the coast and the lands behind." He gestured. "As for
the strange ships— Who knows where they came from?
Still, considering everything together, they're food for
thought, and worth our attention."

The king's large head nodded. "When I was a lad,
and books still were copied by hand, King Harlof the
Fearless bargained with the eastern ylver over a particular ruby their emperor coveted. Part of the exchange
was books, ylvin books, and one of the books told of
the voitusotar. And the terrible sickness that grips them
on the sea."

He paused, his old eyes glinting. "Of course, who
knows what herbs they may have learned to brew since
then, or what sorceries. Eh? For that was twenty centuries past, or more.

"But the same book described the perils found here,
in what they called Vismearc." He leaned forward
intently. "And suppose—suppose they do invade, rich
as they are, and powerful. They know about us, here
in the Mountain—know about us and are warned. 'Tis
in the book! 'Most terrible of all,' it calls us. 'Short of
leg but long of arm . . . bodies of stone . . . the strength
of giants . . . no concept of mercy.' "

He shook his head. "If they come, they'll avoid trouble with us. And we are an ancient lineage. Even as
individuals, our lives are far longer than the ylver's and
the Sisters', and yer own. We watch dynasties come
and go; they sprout like mushrooms after rain. Allies
become enemies, and enemies allies. Tyrants are thrown
down. Unlikely princes become statesmen, and are
succeeded by handsome fools."

He paused, leaning forward again, eyeing Macurdy
intently. "And we trade with them all. If the voitusotar
come, they will not trouble us. They will trade with
us. If they come."

He sat back. "Is there aught else you'd care to say?"

Macurdy shook his head. Nowhere else had he arrived with greater hopes, and no one else had brushed him off like that. *They will trade with us!* He left more than disappointed. He left with a bad taste in his mouth.

The next day he was given a tour of diggings, great screening rooms, forging rooms. He inspected jewels being cut and polished, beautiful vessels being made of silver and gold. Heavy dwarven jewelry. And began to appreciate why some people—human, ylver, dwarves—put such value on them.

But some things he was not shown, and he missed them. Things that made the Mountain livable—the ventilation and drainage systems in particular.

On the third day, Macurdy ate breakfast with the aide who'd briefed him. From a fur, the dwarf drew a well-worn scabbard—Macurdy's—and laid it on the table. Macurdy picked it up, and from it drew his old Ozian saber, now beautifully polished, looking better than new. Then the dwarf brought forth another, in a splendid silver scabbard set with gemstones, and held out the hilt to Macurdy. "Draw it, dwarf friend," he said. "It's yers. Draw it and tell me what ye think."

Macurdy drew it. It shimmered awesomely with magic, and felt like an extension of his arm. "Blessed God," he whispered. "I never knew there were weapons like this."

"Spells were laid on it at every stage of its forging. It's the best we could do in two days. We could have done little better in any case. His Majesty wishes ye well. If the voitusotar do arrive, he says, he sees in yew the best hope of the tallfolk. Yew and yer great boar."

Half an hour later, Macurdy was on Vulkan again, riding down the avenue of pines, reciting what he'd seen and learned. He'd decided the King in Silver Mountain was not as bad as he'd thought.

«He's not,» Vulkan agreed. «He sees things from his own viewpoint. And there was wisdom in those words that annoyed you.» He paused reflectively. «But he does not appreciate what Yuulith would be like, ruled by the voitusotar. I am not sure that you and I do, fully.»

PART FOUR
War: Bloody Beginnings

Among the voitusotar, succession to the throne is not subject to dispute. A crown prince is selected by what they term the "Soul of the Voitusotar," most often from the family of the existing Crystal Lord.

The nature of the Soul of the Voitusotar is not clear. It appears to be an aspect of the voitik hive mind, acting upon the total knowledge of the species, but having its own volition. . . .

Talent in sorcery is not held by the voitusotar to be the supreme virtue. It shares that honor with intelligence. Knowledge, on the other hand, is taken for granted. The hive mind is the receptacle of everything known to them, and what one knows is available to all. But understanding presents problems, as does accessing specific knowledge only vaguely identified by the seeker. And while the content of that vast repository includes decisions, it does not hold wisdom. . . .

From: *The Voitusotar*
by Admiral Rister Vellinghuus
(translated from the Hithmearcisc
by Magister Dohns Macurdy).

23

The Language Instructor

Of the three ships sent exploring westward, fifteen years earlier, only one returned to Hithmearc. That voyage had predated voitik knowledge of sextants, and navigation had been by the sun, the pole star, and dead reckoning. But after sixty-one days and nights at sea, with winds from various quarters, and having twice been driven far off course by storms, dead reckoning had left a lot of slack.

The surviving ship had been the smallest of the three, and the one given the most northerly course. The first land she'd raised had been a high rocky coast, dark with coniferous forest, and showing no sign of habitation. She'd replenished her water supply but not her food, then explored southward. After a week, a fishing boat was sighted, then more of them, along with villages, small towns, and several cargo ships of modest size, schooner-rigged for coastal travel. Her own square sails made the Hithik vessel conspicuous, and her human skipper nervous.

219

Meanwhile his food supply continued to shrink, and he'd already learned that Vismearc was inhabited and civilized. All he really needed besides that were captives to take home with him, from whom Vismearcisc could be learned.

Thus he anchored one night and sent out an armed party, which captured two youths just back from tending lobster traps. With this modest but important booty, the Hithik skipper set sail for home.

Before he got there, he became involved with autumn storms, and reached home late and hungry, his vessel severely battered. One of his captives had died of a bleeding flux.

The captain had early assigned his eleven-year-old cabin boy to be the captives' tutor, and the boy showed a talent for language. By the time they'd reached Hithmearc, both tutor and captive had made major progress in speaking and understanding the other's language. And in the process, the cabin boy learned that the ylver had indeed arrived in Vismearc, and prospered. The Ylvin Coast began a day south of the captive's village.

At the voitik crown prince's order, the cabin boy remained the captive's companion. A year later, the captive died of a plague. The cabin boy then became the crown prince's personal language instructor, and indirect resource for the hive mind.

24

An Ill Wind

On the horizon, the admiral of the voitik armada could see a low coast that could only be Vismearc. But where in Vismearc? The Ylvin Coast? South of it? North of it?

The armada had clocks; clocks had long been familiar in Hithmearc. It also had sextants, courtesy of the Occult Bureau of the Nazi SS, via the Bavarian Gate. So the admiral knew rather closely where on the globe they were. But as he pointed out to the crown prince, what he didn't know was where on the globe they needed to be.

The crown prince was not, of course, surprised, but the admiral felt uncomfortable with it. He was, after all, merely human, as were all the armada's officers and crew, and one preferred not to disappoint one's voitik masters.

Minutes later, the lookout reported a small sailboat to windward, and the crown prince ordered a captive taken. The admiral had signal flags run up, and for miles astern, the vast fleet hove to. A courier schooner was sent in to pick up the boat's occupant. From him, the crown prince learned that the ylver land was "off north some'rs"—far enough, he knew no more about it. Off north was adequate.

The armada had experienced no major storm, but constant strong westerlies had seriously slowed it. The crossing had taken sixty-four days, and supplies of drinking water were seriously depleted. So instead of turning north at once, the crown prince decided to land and refill the water casks. Meanwhile the troops could go ashore. The voitar were desperate to stand on stable ground, and stop taking the antiseasickness potion provided by voitik herbalists. Prolonged use had caused chronic bowel disorders.

The flat, sandy Scrub Coast had no harbors to accommodate 304 ships. By Hithik standards it had no harbors at all. Its fishing boats and smugglers' sloops sheltered in the lee of offshore islands and sand spits. And in the tidewaters of streams, few of them large, though some could accommodate ships in their lower reaches.

Thus the armada was scattered along some ten miles of coast. Ships carrying the wasted, ramshackle cavalry horses took turns at such wharves as could accommodate a bark. Others lay in crowded anchorages, many of them aground at low tide, for there were no deep water anchorages inshore. Many lay at anchor in the open sea. Lifeboats shuttled to the beaches and back, landing troops.

The local population had fled into the sparse forest before the first anchor dropped. Only elders and the disabled remained, and they were questioned. There was, they insisted, no land route northward to the ylvin land—"the empire," they called it. A great swamp intervened.

Cavalry patrols were sent out on the more serviceable saddle mounts, seeking fodder and grain for the horses, and women for the officers. They found the country sandy, and the forage coarse. Here and there were boggy areas, mostly small, with lusty mosquito populations. Scattered along the streams were hard-scrabble farms, on silty or sandy bottomlands, growing corn, squash, melons and groundnuts. But not fodder. Few owned a horse, and their cows and pigs foraged for themselves, tended by boys and young girls in no better flesh than the livestock.

The ships' crews were hard at work. Lifeboats made trip after trip up streams, carrying casks to be filled with dark and dubious water, then were rowed back to their ships. The crown prince was impatient, and soldiers were assigned to help with the rowing, which went on around the clock. The weather was hot and humid, and the oarsmen, and the men on the tackle raising the casks, sweated copiously. The breeze gave scant relief.

The next morning dawned to stronger breezes, and high thin clouds that thickened through the day. The ships' officers began to look nervously over their shoulders. Orders were shouted to hurry the work, but after a brief response, the pace slowed again. Before supper, signal flags ordered all ships secured for a storm. Spare anchors were lowered.

By dawn, a gale had the sea in its teeth. By midday the armada was gripped and shaken by a category three hurricane. The low offshore islands and sand spits reduced the seas but gave no protection against the wind itself. Anchors had not settled into the firm sand bottoms of the anchorages. Wind combined with the storm surge drove many onto the beach, or up shallow streams.

Ashore, the troops had sheltered in any buildings available, and in tents. But before the winds ever peaked, few buildings still stood, almost none with a roof.

When it was over, 112 ships had foundered or broken

up. Most of the rest were aground, a few of them high
and dry at low tide. Few had a standing mast, and most
had deck or hull damage. Grim and bedraggled, Crown
Prince Kurqôsz counseled with his staff and the admiral, and began to plan the recovery. Gangs were put to
work salvaging what they could from broken ships—
tools, cordage, spars, hatch covers, canvas, barrels of
pitch and tar, unbreached water casks, anchors—anything useable. Ashore, troops were sent into the sparse,
brushy woodlands to find where their tents had blown
to, and salvage what they could of them.

Over subsequent days, the horses recovered slowly.
There was little grain on the Scrub Coast, and the forage was poor. Searching for food and fodder was systematized and intensified.

Two mounted reconnaissance patrols were sent to
explore to the west. They found that the sandy plain,
with its open scrub forest, extended sixty miles or so
inland. Beyond that lay a band of hills and heavier forest which the patrols did not explore. Beyond the hills
a mountain range could be seen, not particularly high,
but rugged looking.

Neither patrol had seen so much as a village.

A cavalry platoon had been sent off northward, to
check the claim that there was no land route to the
ylvin empire. It was gone for nine days. Two days' ride
northward, it had come to a vast uncrossable swamp
of black water, with great flare-bottomed trees, and
mosquitoes beyond belief. The patrol had turned westward then, looking for a way around it. It ended at a
steep and forested ridge, difficult for men and worse
for horses.

And at any rate a river, the source of the swamp,
was in the way. It flowed out of the mountains, par-
alleled by a good wagon road. There was a stone wharf
at its outlet into the swamp, but no sign of recent

activity. Brief exploration up the road found the valley quickly narrowing to a gorge, with rapids unsuited to boating.

After getting the platoon's report, the crown prince brooded all one night. The hive mind provided no help. When morning came, he gave new orders.

Four weeks later—four weeks of beautiful weather—repair crews had 147 ships serviceable. Patched, jury-rigged, with stubby masts of local pine, but serviceable. They were adequate to transport seventeen regiments of infantry and five of cavalry—more than half the army—northward up the coast to attack the ylvin empire. They'd be badly crowded, but the voyage was expected to take a few days at most. Over a period of several days, the ragged fleet assembled at sea off the mouth of the river that drained the great swamp.

Then it set off northward, pushed by light southwesterly winds, and carrying with it far less than half the available food: it would conquer or starve. Crown Prince Kurqôsz felt no misgivings. In his mind, to attack was to conquer.

The fleet left not because the crown prince was impatient, though he was, but because the rations wouldn't last till enough ships were ready to take the entire army.

Kurqôsz had left his younger brother, Prince Chithqôsz, on the Scrub Coast with seventeen regiments—fifteen of infantry and two of cavalry—and one circle of sorcerers. Kurqôsz, his twenty-two regiments and two circles of sorcerers, would find a major port town, capture the district or region there, and send back ships to get the regiments left behind.

Meanwhile ship repair would continue on the Scrub Coast. And the troops left there would continue to forage, to supplement their shrinking food supply.

❖   ❖   ❖

Unknown to the crown prince, on the same day he left (night, actually, for it was on the other side of the world), a large, seagirt mountain exploded. Cubic miles of rock were pulverized and blown high into the sky; the sound was audible two thousand miles away. Effects more significant than sound would be felt much farther.

25

Attack on
Balralligh

No word of anything worrisome reached the East
Ylvin Coast Guard for weeks after the armada landed.
The hurricane had run up the coast, weakening a bit,
but damaging harbors and vessels extensively. A week
afterward, a refitted Coast Guard flotilla—a schooner
and three sloops—had run south on a routine smug-
gler patrol. It kept the low coast in sight, but saw no
craft at sea, not even a fishing boat. Which in itself
might have inspired investigation, but didn't.

Its pass back northward, two weeks later, was a bit
closer inshore. This time, on the Scrub Coast, eight
hulks were spotted on offshore islands, dismasted and
no doubt derelict. The commodore entered them on
his log, but did not investigate.

Three days later, the log was turned in at the Coast
Guard office in Balralligh, and interest was finally
sparked. Two seers had recently reported dreams of a
voitik fleet, but no one had informed the Coast Guard.
It learned of it quite incidentally, well after the patrol

flotilla had sailed off southward, and then didn't take it seriously.

Now the admiral sent a message to Emperor Morguil. Who had just received a dispatch describing Gavriel's and Cyncaidh's concern, after their meeting with Macurdy and the great boar.

All military leaves were canceled. Level One mobilization orders were issued, carried by the best postal service in Yuulith. Command staffs down to cohort level were ordered to report. All other officers and men were to make themselves ready and available should further mobilization become necessary. And the rams were to be refitted and recrewed as quickly as possible.

Meanwhile, a light flotilla—four fast sloops—was sent to investigate the hulks. In the face of southerly winds, they sailed southward till they spotted the first armada ships close offshore. Ugly with their stubby replacement masts, about forty of them rode the hook in the assembly area, awaiting the others. The Coast Guard sloops made about and headed for home.

Within an hour of their arrival, the great bell at Balralligh Fortress banged its alarm across the city, continuing for ten head-rattling minutes. Couriers galloped out, headed for every other city in the eastern empire, particularly Colroi, the imperial capital. And as dusk thickened into night, a great beacon, newly piled on Balralligh Hill, was fired. It could be seen for thirty miles. Within sight of it were other beacons waiting for the torch, and within their range, still others.

The ylvin admiral was sticking his neck way out. There'd been no identification of the ships seen, and no consultation with the imperial palace. But forty strange ships? If they weren't voitik, then they were some other potent threat. And in his talented bones, he felt those ships were what his people had first feared, then largely forgotten about over the generations.

From his palace in Colroi, Emperor Morguil ordered full mobilization.

The Balralligh Legion was more human than ylvin—four cohorts of ylvin cavalry and six of human infantry. For even with long-youth mixed bloods registered as ylver by the census, humans outnumbered ylver in the eastern empire.

The legion's officers and men were all from the Balralligh and Lower Ralligh River Districts, and within three days they were almost fully mobilized. They were decently trained, though inevitably they lost some of their edge and physical conditioning between the annual exercises. But given the nature of the alarm, all were in a state of repressed excitement. If it came to a fight, they felt ready.

The Coast Guard had sent picket sloops south to watch, and on the fourth day the armada was seen approaching as briskly as it could, given its jury-rigged masts. As it approached, the pickets turned home one by one. Balralligh's great alarm bell banged again, this time at intervals all day. And again couriers galloped off with brief but fearsome reports and orders. The newly rebuilt Balralligh beacon was doused with oil in preparation for nightfall.

General Kethin, Lord Felstroin, stood atop the wall of Balralligh Fortress. It no longer provided the security it had fifteen centuries earlier, when it had still enclosed all there was of the mile-square town. Since then, Balralligh had greatly outgrown its enclosure, spreading over an unwalled area eight times as large.

Still the fortress, and the mangonels atop its walls, commanded the harbor and its wharves. And fifteen years earlier, during the "pirate" scare, a lesser fortress had been built on the promontory commanding the harbor entrance. Now, to intercept the invaders, the

imperial battle fleet had put to sea—twenty rams,
biremes with rows of muscular human oarsmen, and
cargos of ylvin marines.

Landsman though he was, General Kethin knew the
basics of naval warfare, and had seen the picket reports.
None of the enemy ships appeared to be rams. Troop-
ships then. But surely the voitusotar wouldn't send ships
that couldn't be defended. They might, he supposed,
land men down the coast a day's march or so, at effectively unfortified harbors: two ships at one, three at
another, four somewhere else. Even here at Balralligh,
not more than twenty could dock at once, though many
more could lay at anchor to await their turn.

He wished he could see better. The moon was well
into the third quarter, and had not yet risen. And though
he had a fair degree of ylvin night vision . . .

From the promontory above the harbor entrance,
he saw a streak of fire arc across the water, then others in quick succession, fireballs cast by the mangonels
positioned there. Before the first hit the water and was
extinguished, nearly a dozen were in the air. Two struck
ships, and within a minute, flames could be seen spreading through their freshly-tarred rigging. Cheers arose
from the fortress wall. But neither ship took fire generally. General Kethin imagined teams aboard them
manning pumps and hoses, attacking any burning
material that fell to the deck.

He hoped it was merely pumps and hoses. Voitik
sorcery was his greatest concern. His ylver should be
resistive to it, but hardly his human troops.

Fireballs continued arcing across the water, less
concentrated than the opening volley. The intervals
varied with the loading speed of the crews, and the
need to turn the heavy track-mounted carriages for aiming. The crew chiefs in charge were ylver of strong talent,
but their powers were in aiming and igniting. They
couldn't control the flight of their pitch-soaked missiles.

The invading ships continued to pass through the entrance. Now several more had fires aboard, but seemingly under control. Within minutes, the crews on the fortress walls would be operating their own mangonels.

Now the general became aware of light from the sky, and looked up. A weakly glowing cloud was building overhead, roiling and ruddy, and somehow obscene. It drew every eye on the fortress wall, every eye of the troops waiting on the docks, or sitting their horses in the streets. As it grew, it became the color of smoky blood, and despite its light, the night seemed darker. *Sorcery!* The air reeked of it. The cloud pulsed, once, twice, a dozen times, sending lightning bolts crackling onto the city, the docks, the fortress. One struck the wall, and a section of balustrade rumbled into the street.

Yet there were no cries; the shock was too great.

Then a great throbbing began, like some monstrous drum—or heartbeat!—growing nearer. It filled the air, and the cloud in the sky dimmed to its earlier ruddy glow. Before the general's eyes, monsters took gradual shape among the ships, as if coalescing from some other reality. Like the cloud of light, they were the color of embers, and they exuded evil. They stood taller by half than the masts . . . and began striding upright over the water, reaching the docks through a cloud of arrows. In their hands they held great chains, like whips, and swung them crashing down among the soldiers.

Lord Felstroin stared transfixed. There were screams, a ragged chorus of them from the wall and the docks. To his eyes, the monsters were foul, but they were also ethereal. And their chains appeared no more solid than the abominations that wielded them. Yet when they struck among the foot troops on the docks, the carnage was horrific, with men transformed to bloody pulp.

He became aware that the mangonel crews on the walls had broken, scrambling for the stairs while their ylvin crew chiefs shouted curses at them. In their panic, some fell or were pushed from the wall or the steps, plunging into the stone-paved bailey. Before the wall a monster loomed. Its chain swung up, then down, and despite himself, his lordship flinched. It slammed the wall beside him, smashing men to paste, rose again, struck down again, coated with blood and mashed flesh.

Yet it had no effect on wall or floor!

Felstroin's fear flashed off as he realized: while the human mangonel crews were being killed, their ylvin chiefs were not. Unlike the lightnings, he realized, the monsters were not physical in any earthly sense. They were effective only on those who couldn't see through them.

Meanwhile the walls were nearly unmanned now, cleared of mangonel crews by the apparitions.

From where he stood, on the fortress wall above the harbor, Kethin couldn't see into the broader city. But he saw the torsos and heads of monsters passing the fortress on both sides, flogging with their chains.

Compassionate All Soul, he thought, *save us from this evil.*

He hadn't prayed for years.

The very tall, slender, red-haired officer saluted sharply. "Your Highness, the enemy's commanding general has been brought here as ordered. He is in the bailey."

"Thank you, Captain. Bring him up."

It was near midday, and Crown Prince Kurqôsz stood on the fortress wall. Not on the harbor side, but over-looking what had been the city. He hadn't slept yet; he was too exhilarated. He'd removed his helmet; his fine-haired, six-inch-long ears stood out conspicuously. A fresh breeze cooled his sweaty, red-haired scalp.

The breeze reeked of smoke and char. After intensive, systematic looting, he'd torched the city outside the fortress walls, as an object lesson. Little remained but smoking rubble. Perhaps a third of the population, mostly women, had survived the initial massacre and fire. Of those, most were enclosed in rope corrals outside the city margins, guarded by his human troops. Some had escaped, of course. That was inevitable and desirable; he'd ordered his commanders not to hunt them down. They would spread word that an ylvin army had been crushed by sorcery and arms, and the city destroyed. He'd also ordered that the ten most attractive ylvin female prisoners be held unmolested, for his inspection. He'd been without unconscionably long, and he'd never seen, let alone had, an ylf woman.

A scuffing of boot soles on stone steps turned his head. It was Captain Jorvits and an enlisted man, with the prisoner.

Again Jorvits saluted. "Your Highness," he said, "here is their general."

From his seven-foot-eight-inch height, the crown prince gazed coldly down at an ylvin lord, who stood disheveled and proud, his hands tied behind him. Kurqôsz spoke in accented Vismearcisc. "You have a name, I suppose."

"I am General Kethin, Lord Felstroin."

"Ah. That is an abundance of names. If I decide to keep you, you will be called simply Dog. To reflect your status."

"In Yuulith," the general said stiffly, "we have civilized rules for the treatment of prisoners."

Kurqôsz turned his face to the captain, who spoke to the soldier in words foreign to Felstroin. The soldier, a heavy-shouldered human, struck Felstroin hard in the belly. Whoofing, the general doubled over and sank to his knees.

"This land is no longer Yuulith," Kurqôsz said mildly. "It is now Vismearc, a province of the Voitik Empire. And *we* have civilized rules for addressing one's betters. I am Crown Prince Kurqôsz; I am your better.

Captain Jorvits is your better." He gestured. "This human, this common soldier, is your better."

He paused. "But you were not brought to me for training in courtesy. I am considering you as a possible—carrier? Courier! A courier to the ylf dog who claims to rule this land." He paused. "Tell me how you were captured."

Felstroin got slowly to his feet, and spoke with difficulty through his pain. "I was captured while trying to leave the fortress."

"Ah! Then what?"

"My hands were tied. I was taken from the city before it was torched, and put in a rope pen with other captured soldiers. Then, my rank being recognized, I was removed." He stopped, lips tight, eyes on the voitu's aura, gathering what insights he could.

"Yes?"

"Then my comrades in arms, all with their hands tied, were lined up by your soldiers and used for spear practice. Mostly not killed outright. They were played with, stabbed, struck with spear shafts. Many were mutilated."

The voitu's eyebrows rose mockingly. "Really! Then what?"

"I was held separately until someone decided to put me with the civilians."

"Civilians? I thought I'd ordered them killed too. Ah! They must have put you with the captive women."

His lordship's face worked, but he did not speak.

"That must have been enlightening. Well." The crown prince turned to his aide. "Trilosz, write a safe conduct for our friend Dog. Using his former name. And give him the sealed message I signed earlier, for the person who no doubt still claims to be emperor here. Then put Dog on a good horse. Have him escorted beyond our outposts, and released with his hands freed."

He turned back to Felstroin. "Take good care of

my message. In it I tell your emperor what he must do if he wants to prevent the kind of things you witnessed after your capture."

With that, he turned his back in dismissal, and the general was taken away.

Kurqôsz made no firm decision on his next actions till he'd received a review and recommendation from his high admiral. He had more confidence in Vellinghuus than in any other human.

Nine of his ships had been rammed and sunk, though some of their men had been fished from the water. Eleven others needed rerigging and other repairs, due to fire damage. Of the remainder, the hasty storm-damage repairs on thirty-eight had proven inadequate, and they'd taken water faster than their pumps could deal with. It had been necessary to transfer additional pumps to them, from other ships.

All told, only eighty-nine ships were deemed still serviceable, and they were more or less marginal.

There were three shipyards on the Ralligh River, close upstream of the city, with ship materials of all sorts including tall, white pine masts. The high admiral wanted to make use of them, to refit his fleet as rapidly as possible.

The crown prince decided to send the best seventy ships south, to bring as many of Chithqôsz's troops north as they could carry. It would relieve the pressure on the dwindling food supplies of the Scrub Coast. The rest of the ships were to begin refitting at once. Meanwhile he'd give his staff seven days to gather further provisions from the countryside and prepare to march. Then he'd leave an infantry brigade at Balralligh to protect his base, and some engineer companies to assist in refitting ships. The rest of his army he'd march to Colroi, sixty-eight miles northwest, and capture the imperial palace.

❖   ❖   ❖

Two mornings later, the seventy serviceable ships left the harbor and started south. They carried no sorcerers. On the second day, a storm struck, with strong winds and heavy seas. A number of ships lost spars, canvas, even makeshift masts. Three foundered. Nine others went aground while the fleet attempted to take shelter in the mouth of a large river. Of those driven aground, five were broken up by storm waves.

There was a minor town, a port, a short distance up the river, and an enemy garrison nearby. On the first night, the garrison sent some twenty fire boats down the river into the voitik ships at anchor. Fortunately for the fleet, the fire boats were mostly ineffective. They tended to deflect off the ships they struck, without setting them afire. Also, the layer of sand put in the bottoms of the fire boats hadn't prevented some of them from burning and sinking before they reached the fleet. Still, the storm wind whipped the fires that were started, and several ships took significant damage.

The vice admiral in charge of the expedition felt seriously at risk there. Surely the ylver would try other ploys. The patrols of marines he sent to reconnoiter and harass were attacked, and routed with casualties. But not before one of them had watched large rafts being built, and firewood piled. And there were barrels on the river bank, presumably of tar, and butchers' cauldrons for melting it. The admiral could imagine a string of fire rafts chained or roped together, floating down to hang up on his ships. That would be catastrophe.

So when the storm abated the next day, he took his whole fleet out of the river, and labored back northward through still heavy seas toward Balralligh.

When they arrived, Kurqôsz had already left with his army, to capture Colroi.

26

The Willing and the Unwilling

The late summer evening was cool, hazy, and autumnal, and Macurdy was on foot, giving Vulkan a half-hour break, more or less. Something he did several times a day. He'd decided to get in better shape, and had taken to trotting instead of walking during the breaks.

This was good farmland, somewhat more cleared than wooded. And as much improved as roads had been in the river kingdoms, in the Marches they were better. Certainly the Imperial Highway was. It even had reliable and fairly frequent mileage signs. The last had read BLACK GUM 2, and Macurdy and Vulkan had decided to spend the night there.

To the west, across a pasture, was a sunset that reminded Macurdy of murky red sunsets he'd seen in Oregon, in the '30s. There'd been a series of them lately. He slowed to a walk. "That's quite a sky," he said. "I'd think it was forest fires somewhere, but if it was, we'd smell smoke." He laughed. "There are people who'd take skies like that for an omen."

«As it may be.»

"People will make it out one, that's for sure. And afterward choose something that happened, and say that proves it."

«True.»

"Got a candidate?"

«The cause of these vivid sunsets is a natural event that will affect many vectors more or less importantly.»

Vulkan's bland certainty took Macurdy's interest. "Really? What else do you know about it?"

Vulkan gazed westward, and he didn't answer for half a minute. «Weather will be the mechanism,» he said at last. «Definitely the weather. Over an extended period.»

Macurdy looked at that without responding. Floods, he wondered? Blizzards? Heat waves? He'd know in good time, he supposed.

They arrived at the village of Black Gum, and stopped at its crossroads inn. Word had already arrived that they were on the highway headed north, and the stableman wasn't spooked in the least to see a man ride up on a great boar. He was, though, ill at ease about being left alone with it. "I'll send out a roast for him," Macurdy told the man. "He outeats me twenty to one."

«An exaggeration,» Vulkan replied, making the thought perceptible to the stableman. «Ten to one would be more accurate.» The man blinked in surprise.

Macurdy went into the inn and ordered supper— roast beef, a large roast potato, boiled cabbage, a quarter-loaf of dark bread with butter and honey, and a mug of buttermilk. And an uncooked pork shoulder for Vulkan, which a pot boy took warily out to him.

Only after he'd ordered did Macurdy pay any attention to the conversation in the taproom. It involved some half dozen men—all who were there except for himself and the innkeeper. One man had the information; the others provided questions and interest.

The sentence that snagged Macurdy's attention was: "What do they look like, these voita somethings?"

"Too tall to go through doors without ducking. Red hair, great long ears like a goat . . . And they're sorcerers. That's the main thing."

My God! Macurdy thought. *It's happened!*

"Ears like a goat? Not likely," another man said. "Someone's put you on."

"Ears like a goat," Macurdy interjected. "I guarantee it." Then he turned to the message bearer. "How did you hear of them?"

"I stopped at the post station at Venderton. An express rider had just stopped for a remount and a bite to eat. He'd given the station keeper a bulletin on it, to post there. The keeper asked him questions while he ate, and I listened. Before I left, I read the bulletin. You can too, if you stop there."

Quickly Macurdy got the principal points: A voitik army had captured first the Eastern Empire's main seaport, then its capital. Messengers had been sent hurrying west to Duinarog.

He restrained the impulse to run out, jump on Vulkan, and gallop off northward. Instead he finished his meal, then went outside and told Vulkan. Five minutes later they were on the road again, invisible now. They'd go till midnight or so, then sleep by the road and be off again at dawn. If they pushed it, they could be in Duinarog in four days.

They arrived at the imperial palace early on the fifth. The gate guards didn't hesitate to let them inside. In fact, the stableboy who took charge of Vulkan told them, "They're expecting you in there. Word came yesterday that you were in the Marches on your way north."

Macurdy had scarcely left the stable when a page came pelting across the courtyard and took him to His Majesty's audience chamber. Cyncaidh was there with

the emperor. Both ylver were on their feet, and shook
Macurdy's hand. "I knew you'd come," Cyncaidh said.
"As soon as you heard the voitusotar had arrived."

"I didn't hear about it till I got to Black Gum. A
little place in—Broglium, I think it is."

Gavriel nodded. "Broglium. Correct. How much do
you know about what happened?"

Macurdy summarized the little he'd heard and read.

Gavriel nodded. "The best thing to do next," he said,
"is have you hear Lord Felstroin, who commanded the
Balralligh Legion, and Lord Naerrasil, Morguil's military advisor."

"Morguil?"

"The eastern emperor. Naerrasil is here seeking an
alliance against the voitusotar." Gavriel gestured toward
Cyncaidh. "Raien's job is to bring in the Marches. We
hope you can bring in the Rude Lands. And mine—is
more basic. I must convince the Council."

Macurdy frowned. "Convince the Council?"

"Quaie's infamous incursion into Kormehr, and your
own armed . . . retaliation, resulted in new law. Which
requires approval by the Council to send the Throne
Army outside the empire. I need eight of the twelve
votes."

"Eight votes? Will that be hard?"

"I have discussed it with them already, without
requesting a vote; their formal rejection would block
reconsideration for a month. The members have serious questions about the wisdom of it. Their feeling is,
the Eastern Empire is already lost."

Macurdy pursed his lips. "If your council won't agree
to send an army," he said, "what do you suppose the
kings of the Rude Lands will say when I ask them to?"

"That is precisely what I will ask my council before
it votes. But their reluctance is not without grounds.
Hold your judgement until you've heard the battles
described, and the current tactical situation. I've sent

for Lord Naerrasil and his aide, and Lord Felstroin, to brief you. Brief you and my war minister, Lord Gaerimor, who like yourself has just arrived. And an old friend of yours who was there."

"A friend of mine? At the battle?"

"The chief of a dwarvish trade mission from the Diamond Flues: Tossi Pellersson Rich Lode. He was at Colroi when it was captured. The voitik leader, Crown Prince Kurqôsz, took one look at the dwarves, then had them courteously escorted clear of the voitik lines, and released." Gavriel chuckled mirthlessly. "I suppose the crown prince has read the mythical description of Vismearc's terrors, and decided to take no chances with dwarves."

At Cyncaidh's suggestion, they met after lunch. In one of His Majesty's gardens, in order that Vulkan could attend. Naerrasil had brought more than an aide and Lord Felstroin with him. He came with half a dozen other east ylvin officers. There, against the quiet background of wind chimes and splashing fountains, Macurdy was briefed. Felstroin led off with his observations of both battles, and as a prisoner at Balralligh. And described his experience with the voitik crown prince. Lord Naerrasil described the tactical situation as it had been when he'd left, and his estimate of the voitik resources.

"Apparently their enlisted personnel are all humans," he said. "Voitar make up the command levels above some undetermined grade." He paused, then added glumly, "We do not know how many troops we faced. But judging from an estimate of the ships that brought them, they numbered between thirty and fifty thousand.

"Which actually is only half their army, though half was quite enough. And their losses were minor."

"Half their army?"

"The other half sits stranded on the Scrub Coast. A great storm destroyed or crippled many of their ships."

"How did you find that out?"

"Of the ships that brought them to Balralligh, most were then sent back to bring the rest of the army north, or as many as they had room for. But on their way south, they were struck by another storm, which destroyed some of them and drove the rest to shelter in the river Seorroch. We had a garrison there, which then attacked the fleet with fire boats—unfortunately to little avail. Meanwhile the voitik fleet sent marine patrols out. There was fighting. Three wounded marines were captured, and questioned separately.

"They were human, of course, and assumed they'd be tortured if they were not forthcoming. So they spoke earnestly and, from their auras, honestly. And their stories matched quite well. Our commander in Port Seorroch reported it to us by messenger pigeons. The messages were numbered, and all but two arrived."

Macurdy sat examining his fingernails. They needed cleaning. His whole body needed a bath. "So what happened when the storm ended?" he asked. "I suppose the fleet continued south?"

"Seemingly not. Message number twelve said it turned north when it left. The storm had driven nine aground that we know of, and it's probable that others foundered. Those that anchored in the river had taken considerable damage. Our assumption is, they returned to Balralligh harbor, probably to the shipyards on the river, for repairs."

What interested Macurdy more than anything else was the description of voitik sorceries at Balralligh and Colroi. Most were not directly effective on ylver, though some sorcerous lightnings had been. Tossi Pellersson added that to the dwarves, the monsters were little more than wisps. " 'Tis rock that's real," he said. "Rock's what we see best."

Naerrasil summarized the situation as he saw it. "Our

primary problem," he said, "is our strong dependence on our human infantry. But given the size of the voitik army, along with our lack of allies, we have no choice. And as long as we stand alone, no chance. What we need—" he paused to look grimly at Gavriel "—what we need is an all-out effort by every trained ylf in the two empires. In the face of voitik sorceries, human troops are useless to us." He looked at Tossi Pellersson. "And even then the odds look bleak. But if the dwarves joined us, and if they're as good as they claim to be, our prospects would be much improved."

Tossi's eyes were hard. "It does ye no good to tell me about it. I'm a trade representative, not a king. I'll take word to the Diamond Flues, but it will be weeks before I arrive there. And on my way, I'll send a messenger to Finn Greatsword, in Silver Mountain. His people are far more involved with the Eastern Empire, and far more numerous to boot. But if ye know anything at all about him, ye can guess what he'll say."

Macurdy then told of his audience with the King in Silver Mountain. The dwarf king's attitude of "wait and trade" brought a bitter twist to Naerrasil's aristocratic face. Then Macurdy summarized briefly his own experience with the voitusotar, on Farside and in Hithmearc. Including the sorcery he'd witnessed, that had caused the Bavarian Gate to open daily instead of monthly.

"The thing is," he said, "it took a circle of them to do it, a team working together under the right conditions, directed by a leader. Major sorceries aren't something done on the spur of the moment. They take time and preparation."

He paused, wondering if he was right, if that was true. It had better be. He continued.

"Suppose you had small units of human troops well trained and daring. Operating behind enemy lines, moving in the woods or at night, striking where the

enemy didn't expect them. What could sorcerers do
about them? By the time they knew where the raiders
were, they wouldn't be there anymore. It would be up
to the voitar's human troops to deal with them. And
what've they done so far? Mop up, after the defense
had been panicked and broken by sorcery. That and
kill, rape, torture and burn."

Lord Naerrasil had been shaking his head while
Macurdy spoke. "Behind enemy lines, you say." His
voice was bitter, tinged with scorn. "When we left, he
was lined up along the Merrawin River, rich farmlands
with few woods. His engineers were making pontoons
and bridge sections. When he's ready and it suits him,
he will send his monsters across, and follow them with
all the troops he cares to. If he hasn't already. We'll
try to stop them with what ylvin units we have. And be
overrun."

Sneering, he finished: "And you tell me we need
human raiding parties fighting in the woods!"

Everyone's attention was on Macurdy now. All but
Naerrasil's; his was befogged by emotion. When he'd
delivered his closing jab, it had seemed to Cyncaidh
that Macurdy would explode, with a sound that would
buckle Naerrasil's knees.

Cyncaidh misjudged. The Lion did not roar. He
looked Naerrasil over thoughtfully, then surprised everyone by bowing slightly. When he spoke it was quietly,
softly, making them reach to hear him.

"Your lordship," he said, "what wars have you fought
in?"

Naerrasil sensed what Macurdy was implying, and
flushed. "This is my first," he said. "But I have an excellent military education and training."

"Your first." Macurdy's voice remained soft. "We
might hope a man could live his life without any at
all, but that's not how things are. Not now." Macurdy's
eyes didn't let the ylf go. "In your position, you damn

well need to be good, very good. And you need to be willing to learn, not spout off a bunch of . . . half-understood generalities." Macurdy had stumbled on the edge of saying bullshit. "A military education and training aren't worth much, if they don't lead to good military judgement."

Naerrasil's fair face was deep red now.

"I suggested a strategy," Macurdy went on. "Not an entire plan of war, but a strategy for part of it. You rejected it without examining it. As if you'd rather have your empire destroyed than consider possibilities. Rather leave your people to the mercy of an enemy that doesn't have any, than deviate from what they spooned into you at military school."

He paused, glancing at Cyncaidh to see how he was taking all this. Cyncaidh's face was frozen, and Macurdy turned to Naerrasil again. "I have no more suggestions for you. I'd be wasting my time. But I trust that others of your people are willing to exercise will and intelligence. If they ask, I'll tell them what they need to know to get started."

Still speaking quietly, he turned to Naerrasil's entourage. "I have yet to see country in Yuulith that doesn't have wooded areas. And winter is coming, with its long nights. Armies travel mostly on roads. Their supplies are hauled on roads, and voitik supply columns will get longer as they move farther west. Daring men, ylver or human, can attack them there. And the raiders don't need to win victories. They only need to strike quickly, kill men and horses, loot if there's time, then disappear into the forest or the night.

"With raiders rampant, the voitar will have to send strong cavalry escorts with their supply trains, cavalry that won't be at the front, fighting you."

He turned back to Naerrasil. "The men who fight such wars aren't like you. They don't have comfortable quarters, orderlies to shine their boots, and cooks to prepare meals on order. They are often hungry, often cold, often exhausted. They sleep on the ground. In the rain. They forget what it is to be clean, to be comfortable. They see comrades die. They may end up lying in the mud or snow, staring at their own entrails." He paused. "But they will punish the invader. They may even break him. Because the invader is no hero. He's a rapist and a butcher, who doesn't have much taste for anything that puts his life in danger."

Macurdy looked around at the assemblage. A single pair of hands clapped, slowly but loudly: Tossi Pellersson's. "If anyone wants to talk with me about this," Macurdy finished, "I'll be lying in the sun, on the lawn outside the main entrance." He turned to Vulkan. "Shall we go, good friend?"

Vulkan got to his hooves. «I believe it is time. You have said what was necessary.»

They left then. Macurdy's mood was beginning to sag from the rough brutality of his own words. The message had been needed, he told himself, but he wished he'd spoken less cruelly.

He'd begun to wonder if anyone was going to take him up on his offer, when Cyncaidh appeared, and sat down beside him on the lawn. "Lord Gaerimor," Cyncaidh said, "is busily rubbing oil on Lord Naerrasil's wounded pride. While discussing possible modifications of standard military philosophy. I believe he'll make more progress than one might expect.

"Meanwhile, Gavriel and I discussed our own situation. My emperor's strengths do not include matters military, and he tends to accept my advice on them. He is, of course, imperializing and mobilizing the twenty-eight ducal armies, most of them numbering two companies. They and the Throne Army will move at least to the border, and if the Council approves, to wherever the front is.

"My own dukedom is the largest, and my army consists of five companies, though normally I have only one on active duty. The rest are reserves, meeting in each season for a week of training. And all are mounted—human as well as ylver—trained to fight both on foot and horseback.

"Some grew up townsmen, some farmers, some woodcutters or fishers or trappers, but most are woodsmen when they can be. In the north, even townsmen grow up to hunt.

"As required by law and tradition, my ylver and my humans are in separate companies, the humans with human officers. But they are all very good. And in the northland, many humans show the talent—lighting fires with a gesture, and some of them even weaving repellent fields against insects. There's been cross-breeding through the centuries, you see. Not abundant, but enough. And it seems to me that some of my humans, perhaps many, will see through the monsters the voitar create. Especially when prepared in advance."

He looked at Macurdy's typically human features. "I'm sure you understand that."

Macurdy looked wryly back at Cyncaidh. "You're not telling me all this to pass the time," he said.

"Of course not. You see, Gavriel has given me dispensation to keep my cohort independent. To train and lead them as raiders in the manner you described. And within the Throne Army, men will be offered an opportunity to volunteer for another such cohort."

Macurdy realized he was frowning, and why: He doubted these people could do it successfully, and the doubt irritated him. Why couldn't they? In the 1930s, the U.S. Army had been painfully conservative. And ignorant. Yet a few years later it had the world's best air force, a number of armored divisions, and five airborne divisions plus ranger battalions. Decision was the beginning, and the decision had been made. There, and now here.

"You'll need advice," he said. "Principles. Some guidelines. I don't have time to train your people, not even a cadre. I'll tell you things, you and any others who want to listen. Then you ask questions and I'll answer them. You can take it from there yourself."

Cyncaidh didn't grin, but his aura, and his slight smile, told Macurdy how confident he was. "As a youth," the ylf said, "my greatest pleasure was to track wildlife. I seldom hunted to kill; at Aaerodh Manor we had no need of wild meat. I tracked simply to learn more of how they lived, and to glimpse them from time to time. To run through the forest in moccasins in summer and autumn, and on skis and snowshoes in winter. My father used to tell me I spent too much time at it."

Macurdy smiled back at him, a smile that took life of its own and became a grin. "How about this evening? Can you get people together by then?"

"This evening after dinner. At my home. Varia hasn't returned from Aaerodh yet, but Talrie will see that we're properly fed and have clean bed linens. You will stay with me, of course."

Of the fifteen who met that evening at Cyncaidh's residence, three had come west with Lord Naerrasil, each of them making a point of shaking Macurdy's hand before they sat down. That raised Macurdy's eyebrows. He'd done more good than he'd realized, that afternoon.

He didn't get to bed that night till after two.

The next morning, Cyncaidh went to the palace at his usual hour, leaving Macurdy still asleep. After a bit, Talrie woke him. "Marshal Macurdy," he said quietly, "there is a gentleman in the foyer, waiting to see you.

A Mr. Pellersson. Shall I invite him to breakfast with you?"

Macurdy sat up, gathering his wits. "Tossi Pellersson? Sure. And tell the cook that dwarves like big breakfasts." He swung his legs out of bed, hurried through his morning preliminaries, and pulled his clothes on. When he reached the breakfast room, Tossi was waiting there for him, drinking the usual ylvin sassafras with honey. He and his trade mission, Tossi said, were leaving that morning for the Diamond Flues—a four-week ride on dwarf ponies.

The two ate leisurely, food secondary to talk. Tossi had been up to see the sun rise. It had been as red and murky as the sunset. "It's of the Earth," Tossi said.

"What do you mean?"

"The sky has the smell of rock."

"Rock?"

"Aye. My people know the smell of rock. And not just with the nose. Something like this happens every few decades. Though rarely this strong, I think."

Macurdy let it pass. Mostly they talked of the old days, when Tossi and two younger cousins had mixed into tallfolk affairs to the shocking extent of taking part in the Kullvordi revolt. Then Macurdy told briefly of the evening meeting that had gone on till well after midnight.

Tossi grinned ruefully. "I wish I could help," he said. "But in the Diamond Flues we're far removed from the ylver and their troubles. My people will say the invaders will never come so far west, and they may well be right."

His eyes peered at Macurdy from beneath heavy brow ridges, crowned with thatches of coarse hair. "As for the folk in Silver Mountain—they're far more numerous than we are. The last I heard, they could call seven thousand to the surface, armed and ready. If they felt the need. But in Silver Mountain, their focus is on wealth

even more than ours is. Ye'd have to convince them
the invader is a threat, and I doubt even yew could do
that."

Macurdy had already come to that conclusion. When
they'd finished eating, Tossi got to his feet and thrust
out a hand. "I hope our paths will cross again, Macurdy,"
Tossi said. "Yer more than a dwarf friend, ye know. Yer
a brother to me."

Then he left for the inn where the others of his
party had been staying.

Macurdy gathered his own things, then he and Vulkan took to the highway. Southward, to see what he
could accomplish with the kings of the Rude Lands.

27

The Younger Brother

Prince Chithqôsz was as tall as his elder brother, and to voitik eyes as handsome. What he did not have was Kurqôsz's power and certainty, his ambition and focus.

Nor was he jealous. It was much easier to be the younger, lesser brother, occupied with his concubines and sketch pads, his blocks of marble, granite, and limestone; walnut, cherry, and linden. With his drills, chisels, knives, saws, files, and charcoal. He considered his sculptures superior, both in stone and wood, and in important respects they were. They were not inspired, but his craftsmanship was superb, and his eye for form and nuance excellent.

As a youth he'd wanted to be like Kurqôsz, so he'd studied sorcery. Psionically he proved talented—the one indispensable requirement—and advanced with remarkable quickness through the levels. Until the work became demanding and exhausting. Then his interest sagged.

He was certainly not all his imperial father would have liked. But His Supreme Majesty, the Crystal Lord, might have settled for a sculptor in the family, had it not been for Kurqôsz's dream—to someday reach Vismearc, conquer it for the voitusotar, and punish the ylver. And when the exploration ship returned from Vismearc, the project changed from visionary and speculative to firm and dedicated. The Crystal Lord himself contracted research on a remedy for seasickness, while Kurqôsz launched serious if somewhat dangerous research into new levels of sorcery.

To Kurqôsz, his younger brother seemed the perfect collaborator; he had psionic skills, and was compliant. So he asked Chithqôsz to be his assistant. And Chithqôsz, who'd have preferred not to be, said yes. The younger genuinely and greatly admired the elder, who in turn was considerate, avoiding needless or arbitrary demands. In fact, Chithqôsz's new duties did not greatly reduce his sculpting. Mainly they reduced his loafing.

Meanwhile their research was productive. First the time-honored use of "circles" was rationalized and systematized. Then they expanded their reach. New and more powerful effects became possible, admittedly with greater demands and stress, but now with less danger for the sorcerers. Chithqôsz was proud of his role in it, and in his performance, which his elder brother praised.

It was the invasion itself that drastically changed Chithqôsz's life. For their father ordered him to go along. Kurqôsz himself would command the circle of masters, tapping energies and elementals too powerful to control with adepts. Meanwhile the two circles of higher adepts would manipulate lesser energies, to produce monsters and panics—the basic weapons of the new sorcery.

It could be necessary, from time to time, that one

of the circles of adepts link with the circle of masters, to anchor it and stabilize its power. Which required a master to lead it, one who harmonized well with Kurqôsz. The Crystal Lord assigned Chithqôsz to the job.

For the first time in his life, Chithqôsz seriously resisted. He was sure, he said, that at sea he would die. (The truth was, he had a low tolerance for contemplated discomfort.) His father pointed out that the years of herbal testing had provided a palliative which worked for almost all voitar, and insisted Chithqôsz try it on a 130-mile, round-trip test voyage across the Ilroin Strait. To Chithqôsz's dismay, though he felt queasy, he never once threw up. His father declared him perfectly suited, and ordered him to complain no further.

Actually Kurqôsz had suggested to their father two other masters of suitable age who might be substituted. But the Crystal Lord had decided. Chithqôsz, he said, needed to get out of the palace, take responsibility, and act like a prince. And of course Kurqôsz gave way, as Chithqôsz did.

As it developed, Chithqôsz survived the sixty-four-day crossing of the Ocean Sea better than most of the voitar on the voyage. In fact, he was one of the handful who outlasted most of the symptoms. All but the medication's principal side effect, an enervating chronic diarrhea for which no useful medication had been found. Thus he ended the voyage proud of himself on the one hand, and on the other, determined that once back in Hithmearc, he would never, ever, set foot on a ship again.

After ordering seventy ships back to the Scrub Coast, Kurqôsz assumed he'd taken care of matters there, and marched off to Colroi unworried. While ravaging the capital, he learned that the ships, those which hadn't been destroyed, had returned with their mission aborted.

He had instantaneous communication with the force left at Balralligh. Every headquarters, from battalion on up, had a voitu communication specialist, whose skills enabled him to quickly locate specific information in the hive mind. Thus Kurqôsz was quickly informed when the fleet returned. Twelve ships had been lost, and others newly damaged by storm or fire.

There'd been no voitu with the mission, so the events were not recorded in the hive mind. Neither the communications specialist nor Kurqôsz had any way to view the events directly. Therefore the crown prince's first response was to order the vice admiral flogged. His second was a query to the high admiral, asking how seaworthy were the ships that had returned.

The answer was, not very, particularly given the continuing bad weather. If a new expedition was sent, he'd recommend that it comprise not more than the best thirty ships.

So Kurqôsz contacted Chithqôsz directly through their personal subchannel of the hive mind. The younger prince was in excellent spirits. How had the fighting gone? he asked. Chithqôsz was delighted with the answer. Briefly they exchanged thoughts and images, including the matter of the aborted rescue.

Chithqôsz insisted things were going well on the Scrub Coast, and that the problem of provisions had been handled for the near future. He'd learned that to the people of the Scrub Lands, their cattle were their wealth, their pride, and their reputation. And when word came of the invaders, they'd driven most of their livestock deep into the back country. Now his cavalry had a swarm of platoons out hunting them. Already they'd begun bringing in cattle in quantities. The men might tire of eating mainly beef, especially tough stringy beef, but they would not go seriously hungry.

✧   ✧   ✧

It had been a reassuring exchange, Kurqôsz told himself. Chithqôsz was handling his command adequately, and was in good spirits. Nor had it hurt that his younger brother had found an attractive woman for his bed, a woman stupid but passionate.

Next he contacted the chief communicator at Balralligh again, and gave him a message for the high admiral. Push hard on refitting ships. As soon as eighty were in thoroughly sound condition, send them south to pick up the remainder of the army.

Meanwhile he'd send patrols west to the Merrawin River. When he had adequate information, he'd march his army there, and with that he'd control a third of the Eastern Empire. The rich and fertile third. Autumn, it seemed, came early there, winter would follow, and provisions were necessary in fertile lands as well as poor. He needed to collect, store, and safeguard food for his troops. And fodder for his cavalry, and for the thousands of draft horses he'd appropriated.

"I am told you claim to have been over the road that goes through the mountains," Chithqôsz said. He spoke Yuultal—"Vismearcisc"—as well as any of the voitar, and for the most part understood what was said to him in the Scrub Lands dialect.

"Yes, your lordship. Twicet each way."

"For what purpose?"

"Trade, your lordship."

Chithqôsz frowned. "Trade?" he asked. Surely these people had nothing to trade.

"Of salt fish, your lordship."

"I've seen no salt fish here. And why would anyone trade for salt fish?"

"There's some prosperous kingdoms acrosst the mountains, your lordship. A market for delicacies."

"Salt fish is a delicacy?"

"A partic'lar kind is. Calls 'em smelt. Mighty tasty.

They runs up the cricks in the spring of the year, to spawn. Some years folks takes 'em in great muchness, and salts 'em down in barls. And if they's enought, I hauls 'em crosst the mountains soon's they's salted down. They's best if they don't lay in the salt too long. It renches outen 'em better."

Chithqôsz didn't ask many more questions. His attention was stuck on two pieces of information. *Prosperous kingdoms across the mountains,* and *twelve or fifteen days by wagon.* He had the human given a gold morat for his information.

Fortunately for the trader, the voitusotar do not see auras.

Chithqôsz might not have decided as he had, were it not for the weather and the living conditions. During the nearly two weeks since he'd painted a rosy word-picture for Kurqôsz, the wind had blown almost constantly. Cold wind. And rained enough—cold drizzles, mainly—that things had gotten wet and not really dried out. Especially in the shelter tents occupied by his troops.

However, after he'd talked to the "fish merchant," the day before, the sun had come out. A good omen. He'd run for an hour on the beach, in the sunshine, and thought about prosperous kingdoms across the mountains.

The next night he dreamed of them. And woke up chilled despite his down quilt and the fire his orderly kept in the fireplace. A newly risen sun shone through the membrane—the lining of a cow's abdomen—that covered his window. But when Chithqôsz went outside, he found the surface of the ground frozen. It was then he made his mind up. As soon as he'd eaten, he contacted Kurqôsz and made his proposal. The crown prince asked some questions, then exchanged thoughts with General Klugnak, Chithqôsz's chief of staff.

Finally he touched minds with his younger brother again, and approved his proposal. However, Chithqôsz was to let his chief of staff make the operational decisions. Klugnak was a good and experienced senior officer.

Meanwhile, Kurqôsz's own campaign had proceeded without a hitch. And according to his intelligence officers, the kingdoms outside the ylvin empires were human. Except for the rare dwarvish enclave, and the dwarves were interested only in trade.

28

Triple Whammy

A brigade—some six thousand officers and men—were left behind, distributed at various points along the ten miles of coast. They would safeguard the ships, and the crews and engineers refitting them.

The rest marched away, in a column ten miles long—soldiers, cattle, packhorses, and wagons. The cattle—mobile rations—had been distributed to the individual battalions, each battalion responsible for its own. Wagons were relatively few—from two to eight for each battalion, depending on whether the battalion was infantry or cavalry. They carried the equipment of the battalion's engineer platoon, and corn and minimal hay for the horses. The troops carried their own gear and cornmeal.

The voitar themselves walked. They'd have run much of the time, but were slowed by the pace of their human infantry. Voitar, of course, carried almost nothing except their swords and daggers. Officers' baggage was carried by packhorses.

It took five days for the lead unit to reach the point where the river left the mountains and entered the swamp. Chithqôsz was impressed with the stone wharf there, and the road, what he could see of it. Obviously neither had been built for commerce in salted fish. Meanwhile the weather had held good—cool, but with hazy sunshine. General Klugnak ordered the army to make camp. He'd rest the men and horses a day before starting them up the road.

He did, however, send scouts up the road on horseback. They returned an hour later. The valley, they said, narrowed to a rocky gorge, little more than wide enough to accommodate the river—the Copper River, according to the fish merchant. The road had continued westward, in places carved into the gorge wall. At the mouth of the gorge they'd found a small building of neatly cut and fitted rock, but no one had been there. A toll road, Klugnak guessed aloud to the prince, manned in season by whoever had built the road, but this was not the season.

The next morning at dawn, the army started up the river.

The heart of the Great Eastern Mountains—the part that had inspired the "Great" in the name—lay some sixty miles south of the Copper River Gorge, and farther from the sea. The head of the Copper River Pass was only 3,100 feet above sea level, and the shoulders above the pass only 600 feet higher. That far north, the mountain range is particularly broad, an extensive series of north-south ridges, from whose drainages, small mountain streams empty into the Copper River. Mostly from hanging ravines, via falls and cascades.

The army's progress was less than swift. Here and there were rock falls, the source of the innumerable tumbled blocks of stone over and around which the Copper River rushed and romped. When the lead unit encountered a rock fall partly blocking the road, trumpets echoed through the gorge, stopping the column.

Then men and horses went to work clearing the rock. Even so, at late dusk of the first day, the hindmost battalion had entered the gorge.

There wasn't a hint of rain, which was fortunate, because there was no place to pitch tents. Men and junior officers slept on or beside the road itself, on rock or rubble. Senior officers slept on pallets laid on hay. There was no forage along the road; the horses were skimpily fed from the fodder on the wagons. Klugnak hoped these mountains did not outlast the fodder supply.

At midmorning of the second day, the lead battalion—the command battalion—reached a remarkable bridge. Two massive stone piers arose from each side of the river, anchoring ropes made of steel wire. Ropes the like of which Chithqôsz had never seen before. Suspended from them by similar but smaller ropes hung a bridge floored with thick, white-oak planks. The planks, like the cables, were ancient, made immune to decay by dwarven spells. Chithqôsz sensed the spells as he crossed, and found them neutral, without threat.

A few hours later, scouts came back to report another suspension bridge, with a manned guard station at its far end. They'd seen it from a little distance, and believed the guards had seen them in turn. It seemed to Klugnak the scouts were uneasy about it, no doubt at the possibility they might be ordered to cross the narrow span in the teeth of crossbow fire.

"Continue the march," the general ordered. Thirty minutes later, the prince and the general could see the bridge ahead, and the guard station at its far end. The building was small, built of stone against a sheer rock face. A wooden barricade arm had been lowered, blocking the road. Even seen from a hundred yards away, the guards were short and broad, with disproportionately long arms. Lines in a book came to the minds of both voitar: ". . . savage warriors no higher in stature than the nipples of a man." A human man. "Short of leg but long of arm . . . and no concept of mercy."

A chill bristled Klugnak's hair, but he rejected it. The warnings of sea dragons and serpents, bees the size of sparrows, great birds that killed and ate men— all had been fantasy. He turned to his aide. "I want the place captured and the guards taken prisoner. Kill them only if they resist."

The voitik major saluted sharply. "As you order, sir."

A squad of the prince's personal guard company— rakutur, voitik halfbloods—approached the guard station. Their sergeant ordered the two guards to put down their weapons. One of the guards skewered the sergeant with his spear. Within half a minute, both guards lay dead. But on the ground before them lay four rakutur—four rakutur!—two dead, one dying, and another whose next shirt would need only one sleeve.

Klugnak himself examined the building's interior. Despite the dwarves' short stature, the door was more than high enough to accommodate the towering voitu nicely, and two human soldiers could pass through it side by side if they chose. He wondered why. Actually it was to permit dwarves to hurry out with their weapons, including spears and poleaxes.

In back, the door leading into the mountain was little more than five feet high. To pass through it, a human would have to bend or crouch, a serious problem if it was defended from the other side. It opened into a large chamber with two rear entrances. One was an upward-slanting tunnel, polished slippery smooth, and too low for even a dwarf to stand in. The other was about six feet high, at the foot of steep stairs that climbed into darkness. All of which should have told Klugnak several things, as should the faint lingering odor of lamp smoke in the room. But his arrogance got in the way, and at any rate the die had been cast.

Outside the guard station, the rakutur destroyed the wooden bar that blocked the road, and the column moved on.

An hour later, a short stocky figure emerged from a tunnel eight hundred feet higher, and half a mile south of the gorge. The dwarf carried a trumpet as long as himself, and raising it, blew a single long piercing blast. Then he sat down to wait.

A short while later, a vulture-sized black bird arrived, resembling a large-headed raven with a crimson cap. It settled on a nearby pine.

"Everheart?" the dwarf called.

"Himself," the bird answered.

"How are yer nestlings?"

"Grown, flown, and on their own, I'm grateful to report. I am ready for another twenty-year vacation from parenting." The bird cocked his red-crowned head. "Why have you called on the great ravens?"

Like the dwarves, the great ravens were disinclined to involve themselves in politics. They didn't need enemies. But they had an agreement with the dwarves. The surface of the Silver Mountain kingdom was almost entirely wilderness. And there all the great ravens in that half of the continent built their nests and raised their young, untroubled by human predators.

"I've a report for the King in Silver Mountain," the dwarf said, then described the skirmish at the bridge.

Everheart didn't need to fly it to the king; the great ravens had their own hive mind. He simply needed to get the attention of others. Another of his kind, located near the palace, could deliver it much more quickly than he.

By late on the second afternoon, the river, though still boisterous, was smaller than it had been. From that, Klugnak judged that the lead battalion would reach the head of the pass late the next day, and start down the other side. After days of unbroken hazy sunshine, there now were tall clouds in the sky. He hoped it wouldn't rain. He felt a vague anxiety, and wanted to get out of the mountains as soon as possible. Again he did not halt for the day until dusk had thickened nearly into night.

Again they slept in the road, and again it did not rain.

A great raven had given the report to the King in Silver Mountain. The king had given him one in return, which the bird relayed to the entrance of the Great Northern Copper Lode. Production there was not what it had been a century earlier. But still there were more than three hundred adult male dwarves within a five-hour speed march of the head of the pass, and as many more within nine hours. The speech of message gongs sounded throughout the networks of drifts, dwelling areas, and utility and connecting tunnels, inspiring swift but organized activity.

Shortly after noon the next day, the lead battalion approached a third suspension bridge. There the river was a relatively modest stream. The road was cut into the south side, forty or fifty feet above the river, and the gorge walls, though still precipitous, were not so high as before. Clearly they were near the head of the pass.

The scouts had already crossed the bridge when their trumpeter blew a warning peal: danger!

It was a signal to more than the army's commanders. Within seconds, a swarm of crossbow darts hissed down from the opposite rim. Soldiers fell, along with voitar, horses, cattle. Nor did it seriously abate after the first volley. The dwarf physique is ideal for stirrup-cocked crossbows, providing a rate of fire not so inferior to that of an ordinary bow skillfully used. And their accuracy was excellent. Soldiers and animals panicked, filling the air with screaming, whinnying, bawling, and shouted curses. And trumpet blasts, which stopped the rearward battalions where they were. The panicked cattle were especially dangerous because of their horns. A number of men and horses were crowded off the edge of the road, to fall to the broken rocks along the river's edge.

Until the whole army could stop and turn around, there was no place to go except ahead. The first unit of the command battalion was the prince's company of mounted rakutur. Without conferring with Chithqôsz, General Klugnak ordered them to charge, to take and hold the bridge. They charged.

As if the charge were another signal, a barrel-sized stone started down from the gorge top, rolling and bounding to the road, where it killed two men, squashing one of them. It hadn't yet landed when others started down, then still others.

All remaining order dissolved. The men who could, crowded against the gorge wall, hoping the stones would land farther out, as most did. For two or three minutes the bombardment continued on the lead battalion. Then it stopped, only to begin farther down the column a few minutes later.

Between the assault of boulders and crossbow darts, the only voitik eyes that had followed the charging rakutur were Klugnak's. He watched the lead squads make it across the bridge without drawing fire. Then a swarm of darts slammed into them, and on those jammed up on the bridge behind them. The bridge span began to sway from side to side, as wounded and panicked animals reared, trying to escape. Some got their forelegs over the hand line, and overbalancing, fell to the rocks and water below. On the far side a block of stone— half a ton or more—struck the top of a bridge pier.

The upper part of the pier shattered, releasing the great ringbolt that held a suspension cable. The bridge span fell sideways, dumping horses and men into the gorge. A few rakutur held on, dangling from the hand lines and targeted by sharpshooters.

That was the last that Klugnak saw. A block somewhat smaller than most, perhaps a hundredweight, struck and killed him, instantly and messily. Chithqôsz stood five feet away, flattened against the cliff, his eyes pinched shut. He saw none of it. Then his communicator gripped his arm and pulled him back down the road.

The lead battalion was a shambles. Although many were dead, a large majority had survived, but their morale had been demolished. More by the crashing rocks than by crossbow bolts, though the latter had caused most of the casualties. And the way ahead was destroyed. The army's only option was to get back downstream, out of the gorge. They'd taken something more than two and a half days to get where they'd gotten. If asked, they'd have said a day and a half would get them back out.

The entire dwarf attack had been concentrated on the first two battalions in the column, but word passed swiftly backward. Within two hours, the final battalion in the ten-mile-long column had heard what had befallen the first, a report enriched with exaggerations. By then, all of them had seen the two dead dwarves lying by the gatepost of their barricade, their beards plaited in war braids.

Now the legend felt real.

Meanwhile the command lines had begun to function. The rear battalion became the lead battalion, and its voitik commander sent mounted scouts out "ahead," back the way they'd come. It was downhill, and the scouts rode briskly. At length they rounded a bend from which they could see the guard station—and the second suspension bridge. They stopped, staring. Its oaken span had been burned; its cables hanging loosely in sagging arcs. Feeling ill, they rode down to it and looked long, then started back to report.

The voitik colonel commanding the 4th Infantry Regiment had crowded and intimidated his way past the twenty-two hundred officers and men of his command, to the new "head of the column." Any voitu was intimidating to hithar, and the colonel more than most. He was nearly as tall as the crown prince, and for a voitu burly, 320 pounds. And a magnificent runner, where there was room to run.

When he saw the ruined bridge, he didn't waste time swearing. First he ordered his trumpeter to call the army to a halt, and his communicator to send back the reason. Then he examined the situation more closely, and gave other orders. Not far upstream, a brawling tributary entered the gorge from a hanging ravine, tumbling fifty feet down a stairstep falls. The colonel sent a team of engineering troops, equipped with axes, struggling up the difficult slope. They were to cut trees—pines so far as possible—fifteen inches or so in diameter. Drag and slide them down to the stream, and float them over the falls. Squads below the falls were detailed to intercept them, and pull them onto the bank. Horses would drag them to the road, and down it to a relatively quiet stretch of river, not far upstream of the bridge piers. There, rope from the engineer wagons would be used to tie some of them together, end to end, in a string along the riverbank. They were to build a small raft at the upstream end. When securely tied together, and the downstream end anchored to the shore, the raft would be launched into the current, ridden by men. The colonel didn't volunteer to be one of them. The current should swing the chain of logs out to lodge on the far bank, where the men were to anchor it.

The whole process was to be repeated, and the two chains of logs fastened together side by side, with wagon planks spiked to the logs. The army would then have a narrow bridge. Unstable, wet and slippery, perhaps, but a bridge.

That was the theory. The colonel's engineers, all of them human, were not as confident. But they kept their mouths shut. After his log cutters had disappeared upslope into the forest, the colonel sent word of the situation to Chithqôsz, via his communicator. Chithqôsz started back at once along the stalled ten-mile column.

The first object to come down the falls was a dead soldier, soon to be followed by others. Grim and angry, the colonel sent up another team of log cutters, this time preceded by a company of infantry to protect them. Soon logs began coming down the falls. The colonel decided there'd only been a few of the enemy, probably those sent to destroy the original bridge. And they'd slipped away when they saw the infantrymen with their crossbows and swords.

On the other hand, they may have heard what the colonel had not: distant thunder over the western slope of the mountains.

The storm first struck what had been the lead battalion. They'd seen the storm clouds, and over the river noise had heard their rumbling, so they were not taken totally by surprise. An onslaught of hail and icy rain swept them, with swirling wind, blinding flashes, crashes of undelayed thunder. The troops were soaked in the first seconds. Hail fell for only four or five minutes, but the extreme rainfall did not slacken for thirty. And when it did, it was only to a heavy, steady downpour.

It seemed to Chithqôsz he'd never seen it rain so hard. With his orderly and his bodyguard, he picked his way among the miserable soldiers huddled and shivering in the road. Hundreds of new rivulets poured

down the side of the gorge in miniature waterfalls.
Within half a mile he came to one of the tributaries,
previously small. It was already storm-swollen, surging from its ravine.

Below it he saw no further casualties, and wondered
if the storm had driven their assailants to cover. If so,
it might prove a life saver. At about five miles he wasn't
so sure. A new squall line had passed over them, and
he'd never realized that water could be so deafening,
short of a major cataract. The side streams had swollen beyond recognition, and the river itself was a raging torrent. Close ahead it had flooded a stretch of road
that before had been six or eight feet above the water.
It was impossible to go farther downstream.

Then, loud as the river was, it took on a new tone—
a booming and rumbling that was *not* thunder.

Here and there were trees along the margins of the
road, mainly on the uphill side. Abruptly his bodyguard
grabbed the prince, manhandled him to a large hemlock, and shouted unheard words in his face. Then grab-
bing him, turned him to face the tree, and boosted him.
Chithqôsz realized the rakutu wanted him to climb.

It was a thick-boled tree, but well equipped with
dead branches, and gripping them, Chithqôsz began
to climb. When he paused, ten feet up, his bodyguard
shoved him, and he climbed again; the rakutu would
not let him stop. The booming grew louder, more alarming, and he no longer needed urging.

At twenty feet he saw it: a wall of water ten feet
high, carrying at its front a crest of fallen trees, like
battering rams. Men were swept off the road and disappeared. Chithqôsz realized now what the booming
was—great boulders carried rolling and bounding downstream by the torrent. One struck his tree a heavy blow,
the shock almost dislodging him, and for a moment
he feared the hemlock would be torn from its roothold.
Swiftly the water climbed the trunk, and panicking,

Chithqôsz began to scramble upward again, into green branches, pursued by the water.

He spent the evening and night there, the rain never stopping, though gradually it slowed. Exhaustion and hypothermia weakened the prince, and long before midnight he'd have dropped into the river, had it not been for his bodyguard. The rakutu somehow got out of his own breeches and used them to tie the prince to the tree. Then, clinging to the trunk with powerful arms and hands, the half-breed jammed a broad shoulder under the prince's rear, for support.

Numb with cold, Chithqôsz slipped into a sort of sleep, dreaming, but always aware of the rain. Were he not tied to the tree, he'd have fallen. At some point he became aware that his bodyguard was no longer there.

Eventually the rain nearly stopped, and although he couldn't see it, the water level had dropped somewhat. It seemed to him he was alone in the gorge, his whole army drowned, carried away. He was sure he would die.

He was wrong on both counts. Dawn thinned the darkness. The river was less loud, and he heard shouts! Then the sun came up! The sun! Sections of the road had remained above the flood. Men had retreated to them. Others, where the slope allowed, had scrambled up out of the gorge. The base of his tree became visible, then the road surface beside it. With his dagger he cut the breeches that held him in place. Then, with exaggerated care, he climbed unsteadily down from the tree.

He was shivering with cold and shock. Other voitar found and fed him, and together they worked their way down the gorge. In places the road was still under water, and they waded, or waited. Late in the day they came to the ruined bridge. Some soldiers had crossed on the deck cables, holding on to the hand lines. Others had butchered horses and cows, and lacking dry wood, were eating the meat raw. Many were coughing, harsh hacking coughs rooted in shock and hypothermia.

Using his communications aide, a colonel had reached the hive mind, and reported the catastrophe to the crown prince's headquarters, then to the brigadier left in command on the Scrub Coast.

Meanwhile they ate, stashed raw meat in their packs, and took their turns crossing on the cables.

Two days later, coughing, wheezing, wobbling, sweating with fever, Prince Chithqôsz emerged from the gorge. A remarkable percentage of the troops who emerged were similarly ill. Someone had ordered camp set up near the stone dock, with fires and crude lean-tos. The weather was clear, the nights cold, even frosty. They ran out of the meat they'd brought with them. Many died of pneumonia.

A relief column arrived from the coast. Ships from Balralligh came up the river channel through the great swamp, and loaded men at the dock.

The magnitude of the losses in the gorge would not be sorted out for another week. Nearly six thousand men were missing or known dead.

And of course, the army had a new enemy, though it occurred to no one that their significance would go beyond this one encounter.

Many of the bodies snatched away by the flood were swept out to sea by the current. There, some were taken by sharks and other marine scavengers. Many were carried along the coast by offshore currents, then deposited by waves on the beach, to be scavenged by an assortment of beach fauna, from gulls to vultures, crabs to possums.

One very long corpse, face down in the sand, was examined curiously by a fish crow. Earlier scavengers had reduced the clothing to shreds, the body to bones and cartilage. Lying beneath the ribcage was a shiny stone—a blue crystal, round and polished, about the size of a hickory nut with the husk on. The fish crow walked around the ribcage, looking for a way to get at the stone.

Circling above, a great raven watched, large as a vulture but incomparably more intelligent. Deciding to investigate, it swooped down. Complaining, the fish crow flew off a few yards and waited.

The great raven grasped the rib cage with its large powerful beak and tugged, tugged, and tugged again. Then reaching, it picked up the stone and flew away with it.

PART FIVE
An Early Winter

Charisma is spiritual, but at the same time it is an artifact of being incarnate.

In the case of Curtis Macurdy, nearly all the variables, including an imposing body, predisposed him to strong charisma. Before his first transit of the Oz Gate, it was not conspicuous. Afterward, almost every experience strengthened it, culminating with his victory at the Battle of Ternass, the defeat of the elder Quaie, and the negotiation of peace. All within a few days.

Afterward he retreated somewhat from that charisma, particularly during his return to Farside. But when he exercises it, he is difficult to resist.

This guarantees neither his success nor his survival. Certainly not in conflict with Crown Prince Kurqôsz, who apparently is also charismatic, and has far greater resources. But it will enable our friend to forge alliances, and to contend.

From a brief conversation between
Vulkan and Lord Raien Cyncaidh,
before Macurdy's departure from Duinarog

29

Reunion

A great raven receives its first name when fresh from the egg. After leaving the nest, it commonly renames itself or is renamed by others, a process sometimes repeated over the decades. The ancient bird with whom the King in Silver Mountain wished to speak, had come to be called Old One. The great ravens of the east admired Old One more than any other, and though he had no formal authority, they deferred to him.

When a dwarf king wanted to communicate with the species as a whole—perhaps twice a century—he did so through the most respected of them. And Finn Greatsword wanted very much to communicate with them. Enough that he came out into daylight because Old One wouldn't go into the mountain.

The great ravens flew widely and saw much, and they had the hive mind. Thus Old One knew things about what had happened in the gorge that Finn Greatsword did not. Nonetheless the bird listened patiently and with interest to the king's description. And when the dwarf had finished, added for him what the great ravens knew, but not the dwarves. "There was carrion

275

enough to fatten us all," he finished, "right down to the sand crabs. To the gulls it was paradise.

"But all that is in the past." He stopped then, waiting for the dwarf king to tell what he wanted without being asked. Unlike many great ravens, Old One was always courteous. Even when being blunt, he put things respectfully.

"Aye. Now it's time to look to the future. Ye know, of course, of the human called the Lion of Farside. And what he accomplished in Tekalos and the north."

"We do. Including what he did to become 'dwarf friend.' It is in our hive mind. One of us was his companion then."

The king nodded. "He has returned, riding about on a great boar now. I'm sure ye know that too. It's even told he fought a duel with a troll, and called down lightning from the sky to win it. He's visited the kings of all the Rude Lands, and the emperor in Duinarog. And myself, in the Mountain."

He paused, to give Old One a chance to comment. "Indeed!" the bird said. He'd heard a bit about the travels, but not their purpose. The king went on. "He told of a dream he'd had, that warlike sorcerers would come across the Ocean Sea with a great army. And that if it came to pass, he might call on the kingdoms to drive them out.

"And it has. It has. With two invader armies, including the one we drove from the gorge. But the larger one's captured much of the Eastern Empire. I suppose ye know that, too."

"Indeed I do."

"When the Lion talked with me, none of that had happened, and I did not encourage him. If invaders actually came to Yuulith, it seemed unlikely they'd commit offenses against us. But now they've trespassed on my kingdom and murdered two guards. Then yesterday I received a message from a dwarf of the Diamond

Flues, Tossi Pellersson Rich Lode. He'd been in Colroi when the sorcerers captured it. Captured it and committed unspeakable acts against the people there, humans and ylver. Afterward Tossi went out of his way to visit Duinarog, to tell the western emperor what he'd seen.

"The Lion was in Duinarog too. He advised the emperor, and the delegates from the east who were there. Then he left to rouse the Rude Lands if he can. I want yer people to find him for me, and tell him he'll have our help. And that of the Diamond Flues, I have no doubt. For an offense against one is an offense against all."

The king withdrew his gaze from the bird, reexamining his thoughts. "The army that entered the gorge walked into a fool's trap, where we had every advantage. We cannot expect them to repeat such stupidity. Then the Storm Lord added the flood, but the Storm Lord is neutral, favoring no one. It's the people of Yuulith who must drive the invaders into the sea. And to do that, they must join, and the Lion must lead us. No one else can."

He paused, lips drawn tight across spadelike teeth. "We must know what he wants us to do. And then— then I need yer people to serve all of us, tallfolk and small." He raised a hand in restraint. "I know ye don't mix yerselves into the affairs of men—ylver, humans, or for the most part ourselves. And we respect that. But these invaders must be beaten—driven out or killed. And yew—yer people will be our messengers, using yer wings, yer mindspeak, and yer tongues." He paused. "If ye will."

Old One peered at the dwarf king with eyes like black marbles. The dwarf hadn't threatened, or even hinted at cancellation of sanctuary. Before the Old One opened his beak to reply, Finn Greatsword added something else. "I dreamed last night that the invader held

us all in the palm of his hand. Actually in his hand! It
was the most terrible dream I've ever had. He'd brought
down sorceries upon Yuulith that even we could not
withstand. Nor were yer own people spared."

Old One harrumphed. Though his people easily
made the sounds of speech, a good harrumph was an
accomplishment. "Your Majesty," he said, "I will have
the Lion found and notified. As for your larger request—
it is in our hive mind now. I will call attention to it,
and my people will decide together. What you ask goes
far beyond anything we have ever contemplated. And
no one of us can decide for all. We must decide together.
For if even a few do what you ask, we will all be held
accountable, I have no doubt."

In the Rude Lands, many could not read and write,
and those who could, seldom had paper or pen at hand.
People learned to listen and remember. And some, by
nature and long experience, remembered and repeated
quite accurately.

From Duinarog, Macurdy had gone first to the royal
palace at Indervars, the throne-home of Indrossa. Which
was the easternmost of the River Kingdoms, the nearest to the Eastern Empire and invasion. The king, he
learned, already knew of the war, of the destruction of
Balralligh and the occupation of Colroi. And the massacres of their people—human as well as ylvin.

Macurdy did not ask him to promise troops for an
allied operation. He simply said he planned one. Given
the horror stories the king had heard—apparently not
far from the truth—he might well hesitate. The queen
would work on him. She'd sat in on their talk, and she
was a Sister. So all Macurdy suggested was that the
king order the reserves to train evenings and Six-Days,
in case they were needed to defend the kingdom.

He also spoke with the king's lord general and his
staff, discussing the principles of hit-and-run attacks

by small mounted units. Units trained to fight on foot and on horseback, attacking escorted supply columns, especially in forest and at night.

With his reputation as a war leader, they paid attention. But Macurdy left with the impression that any forces they mustered would be defensive.

He moved on. The Sisterhood Embassy at Indervars had agreed to courier a message for Macurdy, to Wollerda in Teklapori. Wollerda would know what to do, and Jeremid could carry a copy to Asmehr, for whatever good that might accomplish. He himself mounted Vulkan and headed west for Visdrossa, and on to Kormehr, Miskmehr, and Oz.

Old One had quickly gotten the attention of the raven he had in mind: a venturesome male known as Blue Wing, still in his prime. Blue Wing had been the Lion's companion during much of the human's earlier years in Yuulith. Remarkably enough, Blue Wing was even then in the Great Eastern Mountains, newly returned from wandering. He'd been away since early spring, visiting first the Southern Sea. Had explored its coastal districts, then worked his way back north via the shore of the Ocean Sea. He'd seen the scavenged corpses washed up on the Scrub Coast beaches, and learned from the hive mind of the debacle in the Copper River Gorge.

But he'd not put his attention on the long-departed Macurdy, and hadn't been aware of his return.

The Lion, said Old One, had been reported traveling on a great boar, headed west through Visdrossa. "If you would," Old One said, "I hope you will find him and stay with him. Communicate to him and for him, be his mind-ears and far-tongue. He may be at Ferny Cove by the time you can catch him. If any of our people see him, they'll tell him you're looking for him."

❖   ❖   ❖

Blue Wing agreed, but he didn't set out at once. He had a nest, so to speak. Not the pile of sticks in which he'd help raise a brood. That had long since been claimed and enlarged by a pair of young eagles. What he now thought of as home was a small ledge, little more than a niche beneath an overhang on Silver Mountain itself, a niche large enough to perch on comfortably. His people sometimes cached things they thought pretty, or interesting, or that had a personal meaning. And in that nest, covered with sand and pebbles, he'd hidden something he realized now he wanted Macurdy to have.

He flew there at once. And in the morning, after breakfasting on the remains of a cougar kill (its owner was sleeping off his own breakfast), Blue Wing got his polished blue stone. Then he flew with it to the entrance of the king's palace, where he laid it down and asked to speak with Finn Greatsword.

The guards had been instructed to inform the king if Old One came around, but this wasn't Old One. "What's yer business?" asked the senior guard.

"I am carrying out an errand for your king, and I need his assistance."

They let him in then, and with the stone in his beak, the bird rode on the arm of a page to the royal apartment. There he laid the stone on the table in front of His Majesty. "I am Blue Wing," he said, "Macurdy's companion when he was in Yuulith previously. Old One wants me to go to him, to be his mind-ears and far-tongue. And I want to take this stone to him, but I need something in which to carry it. It's awkward and burdensome to carry in my beak; it slows me. And there's always the danger of dropping and losing it."

The king stared at the polished blue gem.

"My people," Blue Wing went on, "have little of what yours call 'talent.' But when I saw this, I felt sure it was enchanted."

He cocked his head, his obsidian eyes on the dwarf. "I took it from a tallfolk skeleton on the Scrub Coast beach, a skeleton so long, I suspect now it was one of the invaders'."

Cautiously the king picked it up, and examined it by lamplight. "Yer right," he said, "it is enchanted. It's far the most powerful stone I've ever touched or seen. And it never formed in the earth, I'll tell ye that. Like the best swords, it was created by wizardry, with a spell added at every step." He looked up at Blue Wing. "Not protection spells, or curses. Something . . . neutral. But very powerful." He put it down again. "Myself, I wouldn't keep it around, rare though it is. The Lion, though—he's said to have killed Lord Quaie in a contest of magicks. And to have killed a troll this very Six-Month by calling down lightning from the sky. So you may be right. It may be something he can use."

Turning, he called toward the door, and a servant came in. "Send Glinnuth to me. Have her bring sewing things, and some light, tough cloth. Spider silk would be right. I need a sack made, big enough for this." He gestured at the stone. "With a drawstring," he added.

The dwarf lad scurried off. "This could," the king said, "prove good or ill. We'll let the Lion decide for himself. To me he seems a lot more lucky than unlucky."

The comment did not reassure Blue Wing. Among his people it was a truism that those whose luck ran heavily to the good would pay for it eventually.

In the Rude Lands, Macurdy had been eating routinely at inns along the highway, often going unrecognized. For when he wished, he used his concealment spell lightly, leaving him visible, but easy to overlook. Meanwhile Vulkan waited or foraged invisibly outside. This allowed Macurdy to listen, instead of answering questions. Reports of the invaders had penetrated the

Rude Lands, news worrisome but sparse. And in the River Kingdoms, like the Rude Lands in general, farming and herding remained the heart and backbone of their economy.

So while the war was often talked about, the main topic of conversation was the peculiar weather. Ten-Month had arrived, and in most years, in northern Kormehr, the first freeze was still a few weeks in the future. But this year there'd been frost almost every night since before the equinox, with some hard freezes. Even the gaffers couldn't remember such a year.

Nonetheless, tapping the Web of the World for warmth, Macurdy and Vulkan often slept out on clear nights, in a haystack, or beneath some hedge-apple row beside the road. They traveled till it was getting dark, or sometimes after, and let dawnlight waken them. Macurdy would eat breakfast at the first inn they came to—sometimes deep into morning—and a second meal toward evening, or later.

Reason told him it would be colder, probably quite a bit colder, in the empires than in the River Kingdoms. The voitar would need to secure provisions for winter, and shelter for their army. When the ylver moved out of an area, did they burn the villages as he'd instructed them? Herd the livestock with them? Take all the food they could carry, then burn the granaries and haysheds? It could make the difference between winning and losing.

Could the voitar draw on the Web of the World? It seemed to him such powerful sorcerers would have learned to do that, yet in their homeland they'd bundled up warmly when they went out on winter days. At least Rillissa and her father had, and their retainers. That could, of course, be a matter of form. Regardless, their human soldiers would need shelter and heat. So if the retreating ylver burned their towns, villages and farms, the invaders would have to halt their campaign soon enough to build shelters: squad huts with fireplaces, if it got as cold as seemed likely this year.

He was depending on it, to give him time. To give the Rude Lands time. At best they'd have none too much. He'd thought seriously of buying a good horse. But Vulkan needed less care, and if he couldn't cover distance like a horse, he could nonetheless trot almost endlessly.

On the previous evening, they'd seen a sign that said FERNY COVE 18. An hour later they'd bedded down by a haystack near the road. When the sun came up, Macurdy rose, stretched, scratched, relieved himself, then gave Vulkan a good scratch around the base of the ears. Some cattle stood off a bit, watching warily.

«Macurdy,» Vulkan said, «carrying you around would almost be worth it for the grooming and ear scratching.»

"With the rivers getting so cold, maybe I should buy you a warm bath from time to time. If the innkeepers will allow it."

«Hmm. There is a saying on Farside: 'When pigs fly . . .'»

"How did you know that?"

«Most of my human incarnations were on Farside. Including one in rural England, centuries ago, where the expression was current in the Middle English vernacular. And the memories, of course, are accessible to me. As I have told you, I am a *bodhisattva*.»

Macurdy remembered the conversation when Vulkan had explained the term. *Bodhisattva* still didn't seem very real. As Vulkan had described it, being a *bodhisattva* meant he'd completed the "necessary lessons" as an incarnate human being, gotten all his karma cleaned up, and no longer had to be reborn. But he'd volunteered to come back anyway, to deal with something in Yuulith. Something they were both committed to.

"Well—does that mean I'm a *bodhisattva* too?" Macurdy had asked. "I don't remember any earlier lives."

«If you were,» Vulkan had answered, «you wouldn't need to ask. What you seem very definitely to be is the major action factor, and a *bodhisattva* is not eligible for that role.»

Macurdy had felt relieved at that. He thought of himself as a human being, albeit with a strong ylvin strain through his Sisterhood ancestry. Since then he'd learned a lot, done a lot, and obviously had a lot more to do. If he lived.

They started down the highway, Macurdy trotting to "warm up his system." That particular stretch of road had an open field on both sides, and the early sun made them easy to see from above. Certainly by great ravens, carrion birds with little sense of smell, who need to spot dead animals, usually small, and often more or less concealed by vegetation.

"Macurdy!"

The call was faint—from some two hundred yards behind them, and as far above. A great raven's throaty "Grrrok!" can be heard much farther, but speech with beak and tongue is less loud. Macurdy stopped in his tracks, dumbfounded. He knew that voice; knew who it had to be. Turning, he shaded his eyes with a hand.

"Macurdy!" the voice repeated.

"Blue Wing!"

Watching the great black bird swoop down, Macurdy felt almost like a boy again. He put his arm out, and Blue Wing landed on it. Large though he appeared, so much of the great raven was feathers and slender hollow bones that he weighed barely seven pounds.

"It's good to see you again, my friend," the bird said. "You look unchanged." He turned his gaze to Vulkan. "You said he would probably come back. But when I heard nothing more of him over the years . . ." He shrugged his feathered shoulders.

«I see you carry sorcery on your shank,» Vulkan remarked.

"Indeed. It is something I brought for Macurdy. A gift. I also bring other things, services." He turned to the human. "Offered at the suggestion of Finn Greatsword, and approved by my people."

They proceeded down the road, Macurdy riding now, Blue Wing perched in front of him on Vulkan's massive neck. The bird began by describing Finn Greatsword's request. "Then," he said, "before I left, my people held a conclave in the hive mind. And agreed almost unanimously that we may serve as communicators—your mind-ears and far-tongues." He paused. "It is, of course, out of character for us, but we know what the invaders are like. It's recorded. Not the capture of the ylvin cities. None of us observed their fall; we rarely visit them. But one of my people witnessed atrocities committed on farmfolk, and another the torture and butchery of a band of refugees that was overtaken. A dwarvish trade mission witnessed the savaging of Colroi. The deeds were carried out largely by humans, but their commanders were the aliens."

"The voitusotar," Macurdy said. "That's what they call themselves."

"We are aware of that," Blue Wing said, "as the dwarves are. It was a dead voitu who unwittingly provided the gift I've brought. The gift whose ensorcelment friend Vulkan noted despite the bag." He touched the object tied to his leg. "I'll be glad to be free of it. It's a nuisance to carry." His bright black eyes fixed Macurdy's. "If you would remove it . . ."

Carefully Macurdy cut the knot, removed the bag and took out the stone. "My gawd," he breathed, "it's beautiful."

Vulkan didn't even try to look back. He'd seen what

was most important about it when it was still in the
bag on Blue Wing's leg. «Beautiful?» he said. «What
else do you see about it?»

Macurdy blinked. Looking again, he saw what he'd
somehow missed at first glance. "Huh! It's got an aura!"

«I'm not sure the term *aura* applies in this case. It
does, however, have a complex energy field. I suspect a
different spell was laid on it at every stage of its creation.»

Blue Wing blinked. "Remarkable! That's what Finn
Greatsword said when he saw it. Also that it wasn't a
protective spell, or a curse. Neutral, he called it, and
very powerful. He also said he wouldn't want to have
it around."

Macurdy frowned. "Is it all right for me to carry
then?"

It was Vulkan who answered. «I doubt it will harm
you. In fact, I suspect when you have carried it awhile,
it will—become quiescent, 'get used to you,' let us say.
More quickly, I believe, if you carry it in your shirt
pocket, near the heart chakra.»

"Maybe you should carry it," Macurdy suggested.

«In a manner of speaking, I am.»

"I mean . . ." Macurdy paused. *What do I mean?*
he wondered. "What good will it do us?"

«I do not know. But I suspect it will prove useful.
Importantly so. Certainly it did not arrive in your care
by sheer chance. If one of us detects anything amiss
with it, anything threatening, that will be the time to
consider—consider disposing of it.»

As if by agreement, they dropped the subject.
Macurdy asked Blue Wing how he'd gotten the stone.
Blue Wing then described the events at Copper River,
as told by Finn Greatsword on the one hand, and on
the other, recorded in the hive mind of the great ravens.
It relieved Macurdy to hear it; it made the voitik threat
seem less severe. And when Blue Wing had finished
telling it, Macurdy said as much.

«Less severe perhaps,» said Vulkan, «but still extremely dangerous.»

Macurdy spent three days at Ferny Cove. Along with the Ozmen, the Kormehri had been his most effective troops in the Quaie War, and they'd been more numerous. They'd be good again, he had no doubt.

The first day he spent with King Arliss, describing what he knew of the voitusotar, and of the war so far. On the other two days, and evenings, he spent most of the time in a hall with Arliss, his ranking officers, and Arliss's entire elite guard company. There they discussed the principles of guerrilla raids, even imagining possible circumstances, and what might be appropriate in them.

From time to time, Macurdy took questions from the ranks. He warned them not to take their imaginary scripts as more than mental exercises—against scripting an action in advance, when one didn't know the actual on-site circumstances. Let alone the choices and events that might occur within them. "Stay light on your feet," he said. "Ready to adjust, and take advantage of opportunities that come up. And always keep the goals in mind: to disrupt their supplies, kill their men and horses, and wreck their morale."

Vulkan and Blue Wing sat in on those sessions, which made an impression on both the troops and the officers. The troops and officers in turn impressed the three visitors.

Macurdy told them about the monsters and the panic waves. He also told them he doubted they'd have to face any. If they did, he said, they could break off contact, ride for the woods and reassemble.

They were not afraid, only grim. It seemed to him their fearlessness grew mainly from a sense of tribal superiority.

If voitik sorcery was sufficiently adaptive to use

against raiders, it seemed to him that fearlessness would not survive. And that breaking contact, and riding for the woods, would fail as a tactic. He worried that the monsters would prove intelligent. Clearly they knew enough to flail their chain whips. Felstroin had said they hadn't begun to flail till they reached the docks. Then they'd seemed to strike at targets.

Macurdy didn't voice those thoughts though. It would attach too much of their attention, to no good purpose.

Nor did he mention the ravens as Yuulith's version of radio communication between forces. He hadn't had time to give it much thought. He did, however, set Arliss up for it. He told him to be ready in case another great raven came to see him. "He may stay with you for a while," Macurdy added. "We can consult with each other through them."

Arliss whistled silently, as if seeing the potential.

When his officers and men had gone to their quarters for the night, the king left the building with his guests. "There's more to the three of you traveling together than meets the eye," he said thoughtfully.

It was Vulkan who replied. «The three of us constitute a team. Each has powers the others do not, or has certain powers more strongly. The combination makes us far more able than any of us could be singly. But the Lion is the center, the keystone. The decisions must be his.»

Then Macurdy walked Vulkan and Blue Wing to the stable. Blue Wing flew to the top of a large spreading white oak for the night. Macurdy groomed Vulkan for a quarter of an hour, drawing an occasional *aaah* of pleasure.

"About me as the keystone," Macurdy said. "Each of us is the keystone. We're like a three-legged stool: no leg more important than the others."

«A flawed analogy,» Vulkan replied. «Your task would

be much more difficult without us, and the odds of success much poorer. But still you would have a chance. A small chance. And you are the only one who would. As I said previously, my role cannot be as warrior. Nor can Blue Wing's. Only you can destroy the enemy's heart and brain. Which I believe is what it will take.

«But do not be overawed by the size and difficulty of the task. Remember Schloss Tannenberg and the Bavarian Gate. You carried that off. It is reasonable to hope you might carry this one off as well.»

Reasonable to hope. Might. Not all that reassuring, Macurdy told himself, *but maybe it'll keep my feet on the ground and my head out of my butt.*

Vulkan knew Macurdy's thoughts, but kept his own private. *Indeed, my friend. By your own telling, you are given to episodes of total disheartenment. Perhaps a little inoculation in advance, along with the medicine of honest praise, will strengthen you against them.*

30

Sisters!
Guardsmen!
Tigers!

"My name's Macurdy. I've come to see Sergeant Koslovi Rillor." Macurdy handed the young red-haired woman the letter from Queen Raev of Miskmehr, another Sister. "But the ambassadress," he added, "needs to see this first."

This Sister really was young; he could tell by her aura. She glanced at the letter, sealed with wax and marked with the queen's signet. Then she looked again at Macurdy, got to her feet, gracefully of course, and disappeared into a hallway.

Macurdy looked the room over. By Rude Lands standards its furnishings were rich but not extravagant. Anything more would have been undiplomatic in Miskmehr, which was picturesque but poor. Even the building was small for an embassy, as was its staff—four Sisters and a single squad of Guardsmen. With no more foreign trade and connections than Miskmehr had, even that was only marginally economical.

Or so the queen had said. A small Outland crafthouse was the largest export manufactory in the kingdom, weaving handsome carpets from Miskmehri wool. The Cloister planned to build another crafthouse there the next year, to make stoves. Reportedly, the royal residence and the embassy had the only stoves in the kingdom. Everything else had fireplaces. And the Great Muddy was only a dozen miles west down the Maple River, a highway for export.

The receptionist returned. The ambassadress, she said, was at breakfast; she'd be out shortly. Actually it was only two or three minutes. Physically she looked as young as her receptionist. Her aura suggested a few decades older. "What do you want to see Sergeant Rillor about?" she asked.

"In Duinarog last Six-Month, he tried to poison Varia and me, and Varia's husband, the emperor's deputy. I want to congratulate him on his failure. Success would have scuttled diplomatic relations with the empire, and threatened your Outland operations. Then even Idri couldn't have saved him."

A frown darkened the pretty face. "What possible good," she asked, "would it do either of you, or the Sisterhood, to tell him that? It could provoke a fight."

Macurdy's smile was relaxed and easy. "I don't actually know what good. Maybe I just want to see his expression. But I don't have a fight in mind. If you want, I'll let you hold my saber." He almost offered her his knife, too, then thought better of it. It was his life insurance.

"Keep your saber," she said drily. "Sergeant Rillor has a reputation for volatility." She turned to the receptionist. "Find the sergeant. Have him come here and talk with Marshal Macurdy. And give them a few minutes of privacy." She watched the younger Sister leave the room, then turned to Macurdy again. "The privacy will save the sergeant some face; otherwise he might well do something foolish. He still hasn't recovered from the humiliation of his demotion and flogging."

With that she left. Macurdy was impressed with her.

It took Rillor several minutes to show up. His face was flushed, his expression surly. His aura reflected hatred and fear. *The sonofabitch blames us for his troubles,* Macurdy realized. "Hello, Rillor," he said mildly. "Your aura doesn't look too good, but the rest of you looks recovered. I wonder if you know how lucky you are. If Varia had died, or Cyncaidh, even Idri couldn't have saved you."

Rillor stood stony-faced, his mouth clamped shut.

"That's all right," Macurdy added. "No need to talk. I can understand that. But there's something else you should know. Vulkan tracked you. Tracked your horse to the livery stable, then tracked you to the boat dock. And said nothing about it when he got back. Otherwise you'd have been caught at Riverton for sure, and been tried for murder. Of a kitchen girl who drank the wine, and the policeman that lit the lamp.

"And if I'd died, Vulkan would have shoved one of those big tusks up your sorry ass and turned you inside out."

Macurdy didn't suppose that Vulkan would have done any such thing, but it sounded good. Meanwhile his face had lost none of its mildness. "You still don't admit you were lucky. I can read it in your aura. But think about it. And think about how easily Idri sent you into a situation where, if you'd been caught, they'd have hung you. I suppose she's a good screw, but she's not worth it."

He paused. "Anything you want to say?"

Rillor's expression didn't change.

"Well then, better luck with the rest of your life." Macurdy turned and left. The man hadn't learned

a damn thing, he told himself. He still thought he was
a victim.

From Miskmehr, Macurdy and Vulkan crossed the
Great Muddy River into Oz, where they spent two weeks
including travel time. Macurdy talked with the chief
and his council, and watched the Heroes demonstrate
their fighting and riding skills. *God but they're good!*
he told himself. *Better than the Kormehri!* He wished
there were more of them.

The Heroes were at least as delighted with Vulkan
as with Macurdy. And Vulkan, of course, added to
Macurdy's already considerable legend there.

They also went to Wolf Springs, Macurdy riding a
warhorse borrowed from the Heroes, to give Vulkan a
vacation. There they spent two evenings with Arbel and
Kerin. On the Six-Day in between, they watched the
local militia train on horseback. The chief had heeded
his earlier urging, and the militias were preparing to
fight as both cavalry and mounted infantry. He galloped
with them on a wild, headlong race through forest, riding
almost as recklessly as Heroes. Their fighting skills
wouldn't match the Heroes', but they were good, and
had a lot of the same attitude.

Back at Oztown, the chief told Macurdy to keep
the warhorse, then asked what the empires would pay
for troops. So far from the war, and having little commerce with the east, he wasn't interested in simply a
share in hypothetical spoils. He wanted a guaranteed
minimum. Acting as agent for the West Ylvin government, Macurdy retained three companies of Heroes—
the active company and two of reservists—along with
a cohort of Ozian militia. He stressed that winters in
the empire were much colder than in Oz. They'd need
heavy woolens and sheepskin coats.

The Heroes were to leave for the Teklan military
reservation in ten days. The militia would follow as soon

as they could muster with suitable gear, supplies, and packhorses. They'd be assembled from ten different districts, sixty men from each. Their commanders would be appointed by the chief, from Heroes who'd completed their service. They'd get to know each other on the road. That had worked passably during Quaie's War; it ought to for this one.

Free passage had already been arranged through Miskmehr and Tekalos. Kings Norkoth and Wollerda expected the Ozians. They were to arrange for supplies.

The Ozians were to behave themselves in transit. With Ozmen one could only hope, but Macurdy left a firm policy with them: thieves, rapists and murderers were to be summarily executed.

Riding eastward beside Vulkan, Macurdy considered the sort of army he was assembling: a lot of small forces that would operate as individual companies, or pairs of companies. Operate independently. Where coordination was needed, they'd have to work it out for themselves, through the great ravens. But guerrillas had operated effectively in similar circumstances during World War II. Often not smoothly, but effectively.

Provisions were a more worrisome uncertainty. Behind voitik lines they'd depend on captured supplies. He had no idea how that would go. They'd have to wait and see.

He hated to think what might happen if he'd misjudged voitik sorcery. If the monsters had human-level intelligence, this could turn into a catastrophe.

Or if Kurqôsz had major sorceries of sorts he hadn't shown before. Now that *was* a worrisome thought.

Jeremid was at Wollerda's palace when Macurdy arrived. The three of them reviewed together the Teklan forces to be sent. The Royal Cavalry Cohort had been reequipped as light, instead of heavy, cavalry. The chief remaining question was how to insert them behind voitik lines.

Macurdy rode north into the Kullvordi Hills to watch the Royal Cavalry train with the Kullvordi 2nd. Companies took turns being escorts and raiders and road patrols, chasing and fleeing pell-mell down roads and through forest, replete with ambushes. They looked damned good, in make-believe.

The next day, through Blue Wing, Macurdy described the training to every kingdom he'd stopped at.

When saying good-bye, Jeremid told him "don't pass through Asrik without stopping to see the king." He refused to elaborate. Simply grinned.

En route from Teklapori to the Cloister, Macurdy would have stopped at Asrik's royal residence anyway. To his surprise, Wofnemst Birgar received him with something like enthusiasm. Finn Greatsword had invited the wofnemst into the Mountain, and there laid out for him the dangers of the voitik invasion. He'd urged him to contribute troops, and after taking it up with the People's Council, Birgar had agreed. General Jeremid, during his visit, had suggested he send two companies of scouts: mountain men, fur hunters who could travel quietly and quickly, and had an instinct for finding their way. They would, Jeremid had said, be good for reconnaissance and as guides.

Acting in character, Birgar agreed to send one company instead of two. He already had a great raven staying in the hayloft of the royal stable. The dwarf king had arranged it.

Macurdy left wondering what leverage Greatsword had applied to the Asriki. Or had he simply convinced them of the danger? He asked Blue Wing what he thought.

The bird focused his attention, scanning. "I find no definite answer in the hive mind," he replied. "Until these last few weeks, we had rather little political information. However, the Silver Mountain dwarves are rich and powerful neighbors to the Asriki. And a few hundred years ago, according to a tomttu storyteller, Indrossa coveted the Granite Range for silver deposits believed to exist there.

"We generally treat information from tomttur as gossip. But you are well aware, I know, of their invisibility spell, which is adequate for most situations. Along with their native curiosity, it results in eavesdropping from time to time.

"So one might speculate that the dwarves, preferring a stable and acquiescent Asrik as a neighbor, discouraged an Indrossan takeover. And if all that gossip and speculation is correct, Finn Greatsword may have chosen this time to call in an old favor."

Macurdy was impressed with Blue Wing's reasoning. He wouldn't be surprised if it was a lot like the truth.

Weeks earlier, via the ravens, Macurdy had messaged Amnevi that he wanted to train and lead the Tigers as raiders behind voitik lines. Amnevi had messaged him back that Sarkia had approved. He'd assumed that Idri would block the move, but hadn't heard anything back on it.

When he arrived at the Cloister, he learned he'd been right. "When Idri was informed," Amnevi told him, "she said if Sarkia forced the issue, she'd take over the Administration Building with them."

"Why didn't you let me know sooner?"

Amnevi smiled slightly. "Because Sarkia hasn't given up on it. She has a plan to bypass Idri, and take her power from her. We've had to keep it secret, of course. If Idri found out, she'd block it, and follow through on her threat. She'll try to anyway, but she's less likely to succeed then." Amnevi gestured toward the door of Sarkia's sickroom. "I'm to explain it to you in the dynast's presence, so she can elaborate, or answer questions. I must ask, though, that you do not stress her. She is very weak, and on Five-Day she'll need all the strength she can muster."

Macurdy frowned. Five-Day, he thought, must be the day when Sarkia would make her move.

The dynast seemed asleep when they went in. Her body aura was even weaker than when he'd seen her in the spring, but her spirit aura was steady, and . . . serene was the word that came to him, a word and concept he seldom thought of.

Omara sat beside her. "How is she?" Macurdy murmured.

"She is persisting," Omara replied. "And awake, incidentally. With her it is not always easy to tell." She looked at Amnevi. "You've prepared him, I believe."

Amnevi nodded, then described the plan to Macurdy. Sarkia never stirred, never even opened her eyes while her deputy spoke. Macurdy didn't notice. His attention was on Amnevi's words: In a public ceremony on Five-Day, he'd be named the Cloister's new military commandant, over both the Guards and Tigers. "Are you willing?" Amnevi asked.

"Yes," he said, nodding slowly. He hadn't foreseen the proposal, but it didn't surprise him. The dynast had taken a lot for granted, he told himself, but she'd had little choice. And it was simple. It could even work; it felt right. "On Five-Day," he said. "Good. That gives me two days to take care of other business."

He left the room with a sense of empowerment he would never have expected. On Five-Day he'd be ready. Then—who knew?

After supper he visited his sons. Before leaving them, he hugged them. It hadn't occurred to them that a father might hug his sons. Then he went to the Guards' stable and curried Vulkan. "Tomorrow," Macurdy said, "we'll visit the King in Silver Mountain."

«No complications have arisen then?»

"Actually something has, something good. I'll tell you tomorrow on the road. I'd like to ride you again, if that's all right."

«Of course.»

After hanging up the curry comb and brush, Macurdy walked to the Administration Building, where he was lodged in a guest room.

He was preoccupied, but it wasn't Five-Day or the dwarf king he had on his mind. Ever since he'd left Indiana, little more than six months earlier, a thought had lodged in the back of his mind, only occasionally looked at: that something might have happened, and Varia would come back to him. Now he told himself he'd been dreaming. It wasn't going to happen, and it seemed to him he needed a wife. Wanted one anyway, or would when this war was over. And when he thought about it, he thought of Omara.

But somehow he felt uncomfortable with the idea, as if he'd be taking advantage of her. Partly because it was himself he was thinking of, not Omara. But mainly because what he felt for her was not what he'd felt for Varia, or Melody, or Mary. What he did feel was respect and admiration—which was good as far as it went, but less than the complete package.

On the other hand, it had been Omara who'd initiated their sexual relationship, nearly eighteen years back, and so he'd assumed she'd like to be his wife. But politics had been part of that, and . . .

It occurred to him he really didn't know much about women, other than his wives. And somehow all three of them had proposed to him. He'd never really thought about that before. It was simply the way it had happened.

If you're ever going to do anything about this, he told himself, *you need to talk these things over with Omara.* He examined the thought. *But not now,* he decided. *After Five-Day maybe, or after the war. If I'm still alive.*

In the Mountain, Macurdy met with both the king and Aldrik Egilsson Strongarm. Strongarm, a stony-looking dwarf, was to lead the dwarven army north. A whole legion! Lads and gaffers would stay behind for home defense, and to keep things running in the Mountain.

Strongarm's surname sparked Macurdy's curiosity. Just how strong were these people? He was tempted to invite Strongarm to arm wrestle, and find out, but it seemed unwise. He knew too little about dwarven pride and customs. If he beat the dwarf, it might cause resentment, while if the dwarf won, it might lessen his own status and respect.

The king had received Macurdy's messages to the Rude Lands kings on tactics and training, and now made it clear that his army would follow their own strategy and tactics. "Yours are fine for tallfolk," he said, "with their great long legs and long-legged horses. But my folk will fight as an army. We've far less need than tallfolk for food. Ye've no idea what we can subsist on, if it comes down to it. Nor do we need fires or fuel. The All-Power keeps us warm."

The All-Power. *The Web of the World,* Macurdy realized. "All of you?" he asked. "Or just the more talented?"

The old king sized him up shrewdly. "Ye know what I'm talking about, don't ye? Yes, all of us. It's a gift given us by the All-Power itself, in the time of sorting, when we agreed to live in the Earth and delve for things of beauty."

They could, he went on, travel all day at better than

two miles an hour, and sleep anywhere. Or travel at night, for dwarven eyes made use of the least light. "Even rock gives off light," the king said, "for those who can see it. And trees as well. Weakly 'tis true, but we'll not crash into them in the darkness. And yer aware that voitik monsters have no effect on us.

"We'll march north when winter comes. Cross the Pomatik River behind the invader's lines, and strike his encampments as we find them."

"The Pomatik River?" Macurdy interrupted. He'd never heard of it before.

"Our trade missions and embassies travel everywhere," Greatsword said, "and our youth are schooled in geography. I recommend it to ye." He chuckled, a deep throaty rumble. "And I've made good use of Old One's feathered folk. We know where the invader's lines are, and the encampments he's begun building against the winter." His old eyes gleamed into Macurdy's. " 'Twill be a grand war. Between the two of us, we'll grind them to dust."

It would, Macurdy thought, take more than the two of them.

It also occurred to him how little he knew of Yuulith's geography. He knew the Rude Lands, the eastern third of Oz, a small part of the Marches, and a little corner of the Western Empire, but not much more. All he knew of the Eastern Empire was, it was east of the Western. He'd correct that ignorance, he told himself. After Five-Day.

If there was an after for him. Somehow he'd never worried about dying; it was, after all, inevitable. His fears had been of failure, not death. Failure, and mistakes that could cost others their lives.

The last thing he did before leaving the mountain was accept the uniforms and gear of several rakutur: the half-voitar of the elite company that had charged onto the footbridge to their death, near the head of Copper River Pass. Rakutur who'd made it across before dying.

It was Finn Greatsword who brought the matter up. His people had been puzzled by the dead rakutur. At first they'd thought them Tigers, odd as it seemed. So they'd preserved the bodies with a spell, and sent them to the king. The king had recognized the difference, or thought he did, and brought it up to Macurdy. Macurdy examined the corpses. The reddish to red hair, the green to green-hazel eyes, the strong build—all resembled a Tiger's. But the ears were wrong. A Tiger's ears were ylvin in size and shape. A rakutu's were furry, conspicuously longer, and lay less close to the head. To a degree they could even be directed forward like a voitu's, though not aft.

But it seemed to Macurdy that Tigers, dressed in facsimiles of rakutik uniforms, could get to places, and carry out missions they otherwise could not.

Assuming they did, in fact, become his Tigers. Presumably Five-Day would settle that.

On Five-Day, Vulkan stood on the ridge across the stream from the Cloister's parade ground. From there he had an overview. The body he wore differed from the normal porcine in more than size, brain, and eye color: his distance vision—both in magnification and resolution—was equivalent to an eagle's. And of course, he processed information exceedingly well.

The review stand was new and freshly painted white, forty inches high and without railings. Its purpose was not to provide an elevated vantage for officers reviewing a parade, but to give people on the ground a view of the dynast.

The afternoon was sunny and warm compared to recent days. The Cloister's personnel pretty much filled the parade ground, facing the stand, which was on the

west side. The twelve Tiger companies and nine Guards
companies stood in ranks on the other sides, forming
a box. Within that three-sided box was everyone else,
except those with a role in the ceremony.

The review stand was flanked by honor guards.
Immediately in front of it stood Sisters of high rank.
To one side of them stood the Guards band.

When the spectators were in place, the band began
playing, sounding vaguely oriental. A short line of people
entered the square, Macurdy one of them, and strode
down an aisle through the crowd, more or less in time
with the music. The other twelve were the highest-
ranking people in the Sisterhood, administrative and
military. When they reached the stand, they climbed
the five steps to the top.

Vulkan watched them form a shallow backswept vee,
so the crowd at the sides could see the dynast when
she took her place. Then the band changed tempo and
volume, the trumpets leading a fanfare. Litter bearers
entered the square, carrying the dynast on a litter. Leading and flanking them were Guardsmen in dress uniforms—bright blue trimmed with white and red. Drawn
sabers glinted silver at their shoulders, competing with
the polished gold of plumed ceremonial helmets.

Even at a distance, Vulkan could *feel* the crowd's
reverence. The dynast was far older than anyone else
of ylvin lineage had ever been. She was a granddaughter
of the Sisterhood's founder, and had led it herself for
more than two centuries. Against all odds, through
magicks and strength of will, she'd brought it—*driven*
it—through the bloodbath and terrors of the Quaie
Incursion, escaping both ylver and Kormehri. Had
engineered the agreement with the Silver Mountain
dwarves. Had made an unlikely alliance with the Lion
of Farside, contributing to the punishment of the ylver,
and indirectly to the death of the elder Quaie.

Starting with a camp of tents and crude shelters, at

first without even a palisade, she'd created the present Cloister. And even suffering decline, had formed and driven a whole new foreign policy and economy. The Sisters were still somewhat less numerous than during their final century at Ferny Cove, but they were secure and increasing.

Or feel more secure, Vulkan told himself watching. The rank and file knew little about the voitik invasion, which at any rate was hundreds of miles away.

The litter bearers had practiced by carrying a large bowl of water on the litter, until they'd done it without spilling, even while negotiating the stairs. He did not doubt they'd perform as smoothly now.

While the crowd expected an announcement of the succession, Macurdy and Amnevi knew better. After all, Amnevi had planned this ceremony, which was to name Macurdy as the Sisterhood's military high commander. On the stand, he stood one position left of the vee's point, beside Amnevi. To his own left was General Grimval, commandant of the Guards. On Amnevi's right, stood Idri, her pregnancy beginning to show, and on Idri's right, Colonel Bolzar, the Tiger commandant. The vee was completed by executive Sisters whom Macurdy didn't know.

With minimal head movement, he examined everything. Sarkia and Amnevi believed it was here, at this ceremony, that Idri would make her move, but Macurdy gave Idri no particular attention. Her first move, he suspected, would be to have Sarkia killed, but someone else would do it for her.

The question was who. It seemed unlikely to be someone in the crowd, before the dynast reached the stand. Her escort took their duty seriously—two of them were his sons—and they had their sabers in their hands. It seemed to him it would be after her pronouncement.

As the litter reached the stand, the fanfare bridged

into a quieter movement. The litter and its retinue turned, and started around the stand to the steps. As the litter passed by the band, Macurdy spotted Koslovi Rillor playing an end-blown flute. Rillor! Macurdy almost jumped.

Smoothly and carefully, the litter bearers mounted the steps. There was a small rack near the front of the stand. They engaged the litter on an elevated crosspiece, then lowered the foot to a piece sixteen inches lower. Macurdy was aware of them, but his attention was on Rillor. With the litter secured on the rack, the bearers stepped sharply back, moving to the ends of the vee, where they waited at attention. At that point the music ended, and the musicians lowered their instruments to a sort of present arms.

A single attendant, Omara, remained by Sarkia, standing behind her and to the left. Now General Grimval stepped forward, to stand just behind the litter on the right.

"Sisters! Guardsmen! Tigers!" Grimval's big voice boomed, a voice trained to bellow commands. "The dynast will now address you. Because she is frail, she will say a sentence and pause, while I repeat it for the more distant of you."

The more distant, Macurdy thought. *As weak as she is, that means anyone farther than the front row.* Turning his head a few degrees, he watched Rillor from the corner of his eyes. His ears, however, were tuned to the dynast.

"Sisters, Guardsmen, Tigers," she said. Her voice was weaker than it had been that spring, but it carried a sense of authority and rationality. *What will!* Macurdy thought.

Unobtrusively, Rillor tucked his flute in its case, freeing his hands of it. The dynast continued.

"I have few days more of life . . . It is time to turn over the dynast's throne to someone else . . . I have pondered long on who it should be."

She spoke without notes, Grimval repeating each sentence or phrase verbatim. "It must be someone strong-willed and fearless . . . Someone who can deal effectively with the factions in our Sisterhood . . . Someone respected by other rulers . . ."

Rillor had undone a single button on his tunic, reaching inside. Macurdy's body vibrated with readiness.

"Someone powerfully charismatic . . . Someone who can make war but is not truculent . . ."

"My God!" The whisper came from Amnevi, just off Macurdy's shoulder. "That's not . . ." She cut off, as if realizing she was thinking out loud.

Macurdy knew who Sarkia was about to name as dynast. His scalp crawled.

"Someone who does not want the job . . . but will do it wisely, forcefully, successfully . . . Someone with the strength to turn it over to someone else, when the time of trial is past."

Every mind, it seemed, was intent on the dynast's words. Every mind but Rillor's, and half of Macurdy's.

Rillor drew from his tunic what might have been a flute, fumbled with it, raised it to his lips. At the same moment, Macurdy realized it was no flute. Beside Rillor, another flutist had become aware of Rillor's actions, and had turned toward him, mouth opening as if to ask what in hell he was doing. In a flash, Macurdy's right hand reached across his body for his heavy belt knife—

"As our new dynast, I name Macurdy, the Lion . . ."

Macurdy's arm flashed back, then forward, as Rillor's chest and cheeks inflated. The heavy blade slammed into and through his breastbone as he forcibly exhaled. There was a scream, and in two strides Macurdy was off the platform, leaping to the ground, hitting it in a forward landing roll. His momentum and two long strides brought him to the fallen Rillor, over whom the other flutist was kneeling. The head of the heavy knife

told Macurdy where he'd hit Rillor, and that the man
was dead.

Macurdy turned to the stunned band director. "Play!"
he barked. The word broke the director's paralysis, and
calling an order of his own, he began to direct. Several instruments responded at once, raggedly, others picking it up. Then Macurdy bounded back onto the platform.

The dart had struck Idri, of all people, its shaft sticking out of her shoulder. She'd sunk at once to the platform, more the result of realization and shock than of
the poison. Colonel Bolzar knelt over her, pulled the
dart free, and stared at it.

"Put it down, Colonel," Macurdy snapped. Bolzar
turned to stare at him. "Down!" Macurdy repeated.
Slowly the colonel began to straighten, holding the
dart like a small knife now, between thumb and fore-
finger. Macurdy slammed him between the eyes with
the heel of his hand, and the colonel fell backward
like a tree.

From his distant viewpoint, not even Vulkan's eyes
had taken in all of it. Macurdy seemed in charge for
the moment, but . . . Turning, the great boar set off at
an angle down the ridgeside, picking his way at an irreg-
ular trot among the trees.

He needn't have worried. There was no Tiger
uprising. Nor was the assembled throng ordered immediately back to work. While Omara spoke with the dynast,
Macurdy and Amnevi conferred briefly with Grimval.
It was Grimval who summarized for the crowd what
had happened. Koslovi Rillor was the assassin. His target
had been Sarkia. Macurdy's knife had struck as the dart
was being launched, spoiling Rillor's aim.

Actually, Macurdy had no doubt that Rillor's target
had been himself, though initially—who knew? The

blowgun had been pointed at him when Macurdy had thrown his knife. But he let it go at that.

Nothing was said about Colonel Bolzar. That, Macurdy had decided, would wait till certain steps had been taken.

After Grimval's brief talk, Macurdy addressed the crowd. He accepted, he said, the appointment as Sarkia's successor. Amnevi would continue as deputy. When he'd finished, he bent over Sarkia and spoke quietly. "You tricked me," he said. "Were you that sure of my answer?"

She opened her eyes and chuckled faintly. "You are a person who takes responsibility," she murmured. "I had no doubt you'd accept."

He nodded. *And,* he added to himself, *you reminded me it could be temporary.* In fact, he was glad she'd named him dynast, instead of simply military overlord. The realization felt strange to him.

The musicians had recovered their poise. Now they played again, an almost sprightly march, and accompanied by her retinue, Sarkia was borne from the parade ground. When they were well away, and the band had stopped, Amnevi dismissed the assembly. The Tigers marched to their barracks, and the Guards to theirs, without tension. Talking quietly, the Sisters walked in clusters to their jobs or their quarters.

Colonel Bolzar had been taken to the infirmary with a severe concussion. Macurdy wrote an order relieving him of command, and arresting him, on charges of conspiracy to depose the dynast by force. Idri had threatened Sarkia repeatedly with a Tiger takeover, to force concessions. That was widely known.

But Macurdy delayed having the arrest order posted. Instead he sent for the Tiger Captain Skortov, and afterward for the Tiger sergeant major. He asked each of them what prominent Tiger officer had been most free of Idri's influence. Each named the same man, a Captain Horgent. Horgent had been the commander of Omara's Tiger guard platoon in the Quaie War. And though he'd been regarded as an excellent officer, Idri had bypassed him repeatedly for promotion above captain.

Macurdy then wrote an order promoting Horgent two grades, to subcolonel, and named him commandant, bypassing Subcolonel Sojass for command.

And before having that posted, he had Sojass sent to him. The Tiger XO stood rigidly at attention, while Macurdy, also standing, examined his aura thoroughly, without a word. When the subcolonel had waited long enough, Macurdy spoke.

"Do you know why I asked you here, Sojass?"

"No."

"No what?"

"No, Your Highness."

"I asked you here because you were Idri's lover, or one of them. As Bolzar was." He paused, then added, "As Rillor was."

The mention of Rillor took Sojass visibly by surprise.

"He'd been her favorite for years," Macurdy went on. "She sent him to Duinarog last summer, to kill Varia and me, and Varia's ylvin lord. Even in failing, he endangered our trade and diplomatic relations with the Western Empire. Our bread and butter, Sojass. *Your* bread and butter."

He peered questioningly at the man. "Do you realize what the Sisterhood and the empires are up against, with this invasion?"

Sojass seemed puzzled by the question. "No, Your Highness," he said.

"I'll have some reading assigned to you when we're done. You'll wait in reception while it's brought to you. Then you'll read it there, and I'll question you to see what you've learned. Understood?"

"Yes, Your Highness."

"Good. What do you think of Captain Horgent?"

Sojass frowned at the change of subject. "Horgent is a good officer, Your Highness."

"Why did Idri bypass him repeatedly for promotion? He was a captain when you were a sublieutenant."

"I do not know, Your Highness."

"Because, Sojass, he was with my army, with Omara's coven, in the Quaie War."

The light dawned.

"Bolzar will be executed on One-Day, for conspiracy against Sarkia."

Sojass stood stunned.

"I am trusting that you were not seriously corrupted by either Idri or Bolzar. I'm leaving you as executive officer, promoting Horgent to subcolonel, and making him your new commandant. Do you have anything to say to me about that?"

"No, Your Highness."

"Good." He surprised Sojass then by stepping around his desk and extending his hand. Flummoxed, Sojass met it, and they shook. Macurdy didn't try to grip him down, but he satisfied both of them that he could. It was the sort of action the Tiger could understand.

From that point, whenever he encountered Sojass, Macurdy made a point of casual friendliness.

The next morning Macurdy met with Horgent and Grimval, and they worked on plans for raider training. Only Tigers would be sent to the empire. Grimval's Guards companies would remain as defense forces, at least for the time being. In training they'd play the role of escorts and road patrols.

Macurdy began his own training in the geography of Yuulith. From a book, with guidance from Blue Wing, Vulkan, and Omara. Later he'd get a geography session from Finn Greatsword and his trade minister.

And he read more than geography. Amnevi, having seen the sorcerer's stone that Blue Wing had given him, showed Macurdy a translation of an ancient book on sorcery and circles and stones. He wasn't sure what good it might do him, but it was interesting.

On Six-Day, Idri's corpse was placed atop her funeral pyre, and the oil-splashed wood ignited. Only a few attended, including her surviving clone sister, Amnevi. And Macurdy, who afterward, via the great ravens, notified Varia of Idri's death, and how it happened.

Despite Idri's long enmity and cruelties, Varia quietly wept without knowing why.

Bolzar was throttled on the following One-Day, as Macurdy had promised. The execution was formal and private, carried out by the Tiger provost, a captain. The official witnesses were Macurdy as dynast-to-be, the dynast's deputy, and Subcolonel Horgent. As usual after executions, Bolzar's body too was burned, with the basic courtesies but without public attendance. Macurdy, Horgent, Sojass, and the sergeant major stood together, watching the smoke rise and thinking their own thoughts.

On the second day after Bolzar's pyre, Sarkia died quietly in her sleep. Her pyre was attended by the entire Cloister, and by the King in the Mountain and the wofnemst of the Commonwealth of Asrik.

Macurdy messaged Varia of this, too, and again she wept.

31

Winter
Wonderland

Kurqôsz slowed to a walk, his face damp with a mixture of sweat and melted snowflakes. It had been snowing since midday, large wet flakes drifting vertically down, so thickly he couldn't see two hundred feet. At breakfast the ground had been tan. Now snow lay on it halfway to his knees, which were very high knees.

At home he'd liked snow, liked to run in it. The hive mind showed the forefathers running *on* it, on broad skis split from birch and strapped to their feet, with furs laced on for traction. Their ancient homeland had been rich in snow, and the forefathers had run on skis to herd reindeer.

He himself had never had time to learn the skill. Few did. The lands they'd migrated to seldom had prolonged snow cover except in the higher mountains. In winter it rained a lot and snowed only occasionally.

Here in Vismearc he'd slighted running, as he had in Bavaria. He'd been too busy. Even on the march he'd slighted it, slowed by the pace of his human infantry.

Then, after establishing their forward line on the Deep
River, they'd begun setting up their winter base at the
west side of the Merrawin Valley. And he'd begun running an hour each evening.

That had been late Ten-Month, barely a week past.
Even allowing for the cold autumn, there should have
been time to build hutments for the troops before
weather like this. As it was, most of the huts consisted
only of survey stakes set by the engineers. Stakes now
buried. The huts completed were for voitar and the
higher ranking humans. Even most of them were without
real roofs—log walls with a tarpaulin over a roof frame,
their doors and windows mere holes in the walls, with
curtains, blankets actually, that one could hook shut,
more or less.

A truly wretched base camp! His father would not
approve.

As it was, his father didn't know, for the hive mind
had proven to have distance limits. Well before his army
reached Vismearc, the rest of the species had faded
out of touch. The historical hive mind it carried, but
as for current events—they knew only those of the army's
own seventeen hundred voitar.

They'd adjusted to the sense of disconnection, but
it could still be disconcerting on occasion.

His run hadn't taken him through the hutment area
and the vast bedraggled tent camp. That would simply have aggravated him. Instead he'd run in the quiet
forest, on a narrow woods road, then followed his tracks
back. Already they were little more than a shallow groove
in the snow. Now he could make out his quarters
ahead—a forester's cabin at the forest's edge, simple
but comfortable. The ylvin torch had missed it.

He'd already decided to move his headquarters to
a large manorial farmhouse he'd been told of. Not only
the house, but the barns and other outbuildings had
all escaped burning. It was much nearer the Deep River,

where the 1st and 4th Divisions were on line. And where winter quarters were no more ready than they were in the Merrawin Valley base camp.

Major General Hohs Gruismak stood in the vacant doorway of his cabin, watching it snow. He'd never seen so much fall so early, or so fast.

Gruismak was not a commander. He was a human, General Orovisz's hithik aide, and his job was dealing with "administrative" problems. Mostly problems that could have been avoided if he'd been allowed advance input.

Troop morale had been low since Prince Chithqôsz's army had been brought north. Their stories of the small-folk—of their ferocity and devilish ingenuity—had spread like a grassfire through the rest of the army. Stories enriched by the notion that dwarven sorcerers had called down the storm and the flood.

And now this damned snowstorm. The men had been busy much of the day trying to prevent the wet snow from collapsing their tents.

The army, he told himself, should never have left the Merrawin River, only twenty-five miles east. True the locals had torched the towns and villages, but many walls remained, needing mainly roofs and doors. And to the north, patrols had found pine woods. Thus it hadn't been necessary to move west to the edge of forest. Poles for roofs, and logs for hutments, could have been floated down the Merrawin. While here the forest was mostly of hardwoods, harder to cut, heavier to haul and raise, and requiring far more time-consuming dressing with axes to fit together halfway decently. Nor were hithik soldiers skilled at such work.

But none of that meant anything to Orovisz or the crown prince. They didn't have to solve problems. They just created them, and ordered others to solve them.

He turned to his orderly. "Corporal," he said, "make

damn sure your men don't let the tarp come down on us. Otherwise the provost will have a busy day tomorrow with his strap."

"Yessir, General, sir!"

Gruismak walked to his bedroll near the fireplace. The chimney wasn't drawing properly, and the hut was smoky. He sat on his pallet to pull off his boots. *Not even a damned stool to sit on,* he thought. He wished devoutly he'd never heard of Vismearc.

At about midnight the snow had ended. The sky had cleared and the temperature plummeted. Now the newly risen sun glistened off miles and miles of white. Men moved like lines of ants to the firewood piles, or huddled around the thousands of warming fires whose smoke settled and spread among the tents. It was cold enough, the moisture from their breath formed frost on their collars.

Then officers appeared, human and voitik. Sergeants shouted orders. Reluctantly, heavily, the soldiers left their fires, or dropped the wood they carried, and formed ranks. Within minutes they were trudging through the knee-deep snow to their work details. The smarter of them saw the value of it. They needed to get their huts built, so they'd have effective shelter before winter arrived.

Before winter arrived!

The great raven soared high above the Pomatik River, more than a hundred miles south of the invader's base camp. It was the twelfth of Eleven-Month. The past few days had been bitter cold, and he'd spent the night in the dense crown of a hemlock, sheltering from radiative heat loss. Now, circling in the hazy morning sunlight, he could see a broad ice shelf along each shore of the river, formed since the day before. Between the shelves, the channel was filled with ice that had broken away in the current. Unless it warmed considerably during the day, the bird knew, the river would probably freeze over by nightfall. If not, another such night would do it.

It was something to call to Old One's attention.

32

On the Move

Winter had come with a vengeance to the country north of Duinarog, around the southern end of that great sweetwater lake called the Middle Sea. Cyncaidh's cohort had reached Southport on four three-masted schooners, two days after the season's first big snowstorm. There the snow had come on a cold wind, and drifting had been severe.

Two days later, Gavriel's war minister, Lord Gaerimor, had arrived in a sleigh, a large cutter drawn by two strong horses. With him he brought five east ylvin refugees to serve the cohort as guides. A great raven had arrived on its own, to be Cyncaidh's communicator. The drifts had delayed arrival of their supplies three days longer, and a bureaucratic foul-up delayed arrival of their horses from the military remount reservation longer still. Meanwhile there was no additional snow, and temperatures much colder than seasonable gripped the land.

On the day after the cohort's arrival, Varia had arrived in a light cutter pulled by a single horse. Through the several days till the cohort was ready to ride east, she stayed with Cyncaidh in the Southport Inn. Both of them recognized the extreme dangers in his mission, and on their last night, their lovemaking had been exceptionally passionate.

Afterward Varia had laid awake thinking. If Raien was killed, what would she feel? What would she *do*? They'd been together for nearly two decades, two good decades. She would miss him in her bed, miss him around the house, and across the table from her at meals. Miss him in her life.

She shook the thoughts off. He was remarkably good in the forest, a fine swordsman and skilled soldier. He'd come home if anyone did. But if he didn't—she was the mistress of Aaerodh Manor, and the mother of their sons. She'd return north, and adjust as necessary.

By hindsight it seemed she'd begun loving Raien Cyncaidh even when she still hated him. Hated him for not leaving her free to find her way to the Ferny Cove Gate, which she'd imagined would take her back to Curtis.

He had, of course, rescued her from Tomm the tracker, and the Sisterhood, but that hadn't been important in her feelings. She'd been attracted to him physically, perhaps from the start, but surely by the day they'd crossed the Big River. What had been most important, though, had been his considerate treatment, his decency and patience, and his love for her.

She did not allow herself to dwell on the possibilities with Curtis. That would be treasonous. Raien lay beside her still breathing, still strong, still her husband and beloved. She had long since chosen to remain with him, and their love had grown and matured.

The next morning she said good-bye to her ylf lord, and to their firstborn, Ceonigh, a corporal in his father's cohort. It was saying good-bye to Ceonigh that caused her tears to spill. Ceonigh, whose life was just well under way.

Wearing sheepskin greatcoats, the companies formed a column of twos on the road. A trumpeter blew "Ride!" and they trotted away, clattering over a heavy plank bridge across the Imperial River. The ice wasn't safe yet for horses.

It was Blue Wing who told the new dynast that the Great Swamp had frozen over. Macurdy planned to start north the next day, with both Tiger cohorts and a train of packhorses. They'd follow the route of the dwarves, who'd left ten days earlier.

"So?" he said.

"The shortest way to the enemy is over the Copper River Road and across the swamp."

He frowned. "Not a lot shorter."

"But shorter. And after the dwarves have crossed the Pomatik from the East Dales, the voitar may be alert to further crossings there. Something you pointed out yourself. But they'll hardly expect something from the Scrub Lands."

"What about the Copper River bridges? I know the dwarves planned to replace the spans, but as short as they are on manpower now . . ."

"They are already rebuilt."

"Will the ice be thick enough to cross the swamp with horses?"

It was Vulkan who replied. «Water which is shallow and quiet freezes more quickly than deep water, or water with a strong current. And for the first four days, the two routes are the same. If the weather continues cold till then, the ice should hold you.»

Should hold, Macurdy thought. *Should's not the word I want.* "If we take that route," he asked, "will we be able to muster enough boats to cross the Pomatik?"

"I'll find out," Blue Wing said.

"You have trouble with numbers," Macurdy reminded him.

"You need many boats. Many is not a number."

«The North Fork of the Pomatik is frozen,» Vulkan pointed out.

"That's the North Fork. What about lower reaches?"

Blue Wing didn't answer at once. Instead he sought briefly, and found the memory stem of a great raven who'd seen it that morning. "Not frozen yet," he said, "but the backwaters are. If this cold continues . . ."

First should. Now if. "All right. We'll start in the morning, and see how the weather's held when we reach the Copper River Road. Then I'll decide."

Finn Greatsword gave Macurdy and his Tigers free passage should they decide to take the Copper River Road. He also confirmed that the bridges were ready, and that the river level was low. Where it passed through the swamp, the current should be negligible.

The next morning they left the Cloister. For four days the temperature never rose to the freezing point, and fell well below it at night. So on the fifth day, the two Tiger cohorts turned east on the Copper River Road. Being mounted, they reached the swamp in three days. For the first mile below the dock, the river was open, though the swamp was frozen. Below that, ice covered the river, too. After another mile, Macurdy took an ax from a packhorse, and walking a little way out on the river ice, tested it. Four inches. Which was probably enough, but he remembered Melody, and backed away. A couple of miles farther he tried again. Five, maybe six inches. Getting on his warhorse, he started across, testing it. It held all the way, without a creak.

Looking back, he shouted orders. The cohorts spread out downstream and crossed in files by platoon. In every file, no man started across till the man ahead had made it.

When all were across, they started north again.

✧   ✧   ✧

With Raien gone, Varia was nearly alone. Even Rorie, their youngest, was gone. A private learning the military profession, he'd left with the 1st Royal Cavalry Cohort. It had marched south from Duinarog in mid Ten-Month, then turned east on the South Shore Highway, along the Imperial Sea.

She'd arranged other employment for all the household staff but three: Talrie, who now took care of all maintenance work, and tended the furnace and water heater; Talrie's wife Meg, who'd been cook, now handled all the kitchen work; and Correen, who'd become Varia's all-purpose housegirl. If additional help was needed from time to time, she'd hire temporary workers.

Most of the house was closed off and the furniture covered. The doors were ajar, however, so the house's cats could patrol for the mice which might otherwise damage the furniture. All the horses were boarded out except Chessy, Varia's own. Chessy she cared for herself, feeding and brushing her, bedding her down, and cleaning up behind her. Meanwhile she'd begun work at the Royal Archives, as a volunteer historian's assistant, and had already become quite knowledgeable about the job.

At home, after supper on Solstice Eve, she sat down to read. It was a book she'd brought with her from Farside, thirty years earlier on maternity leave: *The Complete Works of William Shakespeare*. Amazingly it had survived Ferny Cove—which was better than her children by Will had done—and Raien had gotten it back for her through diplomatic lines after the war.

But reading by oil lamp tired her eyes. After two or three hours, she took a hot bath and went to bed.

After a time she awoke with a start, to the covers being jerked away. Hands grabbed her arms, and before she could resist or even scream, she was flopped onto her stomach, her face pressed into the featherbed. Other hands gripped her ankles, and quickly she was tied, then gagged. Someone stood her up, and a cloak was draped over her.

"Excuse us, Your Ladyship." The tone was sardonic. "Your life is threatened here. We're taking you away. To safety, you understand."

"Shut up," said another. Then someone slung Varia over a shoulder and carried her out into the winter night.

A carriage sleigh stood waiting in the street. Two people sat in back, but even with snowlight it was too dark inside to distinguish features. One, by his aura, was an enforcer type, perhaps a bodyguard. The other she classified as marginally psychotic.

They waited while her abductors returned to the house and went inside. "Here," the enforcer said to her. "I'm going to take out your gag and open your mouth. One screech and I hurt you. Badly."

She sat carefully still, and felt fingers loosen the gag.

"Now open," he said. "His lordship will give you a draft of something. Drink it!"

She felt a flask at her lips, and accepted it. It tilted slightly. The taste was of brandy, good brandy, and she swallowed its warmth. There was, she thought, something in it. There had to be.

In a minute the front entrance opened again. Before her abductors closed it behind them, she saw flames inside. "There are people in there," she whispered muzzily; the drug was taking effect.

"No, my dear," the second man said. "There is no one. Not a living soul."

Of course not, she realized. All three would have been killed. Meanwhile she'd recognized the voice. Not one she knew well, but she recognized it. It seemed to her she wouldn't come through this alive.

PART SIX
Expansion And Intensification

Macurdy awoke to dread, and sat up slowly, not breathing, trying to hold the darkness to him. But it lightened, became a murky, smoky red. There was a smell of burning flesh and hair.

"So! There you are, Herr Montag! You cannot hide from me, not even in your dreams."

It was Kronprinz Kurqôsz. *His ears had become horns. With a table fork, he raised the cube of raspberry jello that encased Macurdy, and peered closely, his eye enormous. "You thought I did not know who to blame." His low laugh rumbled. "It was you who inconvenienced me in Bavaria, and who burned down my gatehouse. Now you annoy me with your foolish little armies."*

His smile was not pleasant. "You will waken soon, and discover this was only a dream. But do not feel relieved. You think you have seen sorcery? When my lightning strikes, I will have your soul in a bottle! With all the others."

From a dream by Curtis Macurdy
in the forest behind voitik lines

33

The Alliance
Makes Itself Felt

Kurqôsz met daily with his staff and their aides, to review and plan. This morning, the emphasis was on enemy raids on supply trains.

There were three suitable east-west roads through the central forest region. Initially the trains had been sent by whatever route was shortest to the reception point. After the first raids, that policy had been dropped. Everything had been routed on one road, which was patrolled by strong cavalry forces.

Almost at once the raiders had taken to felling numerous trees across the road, in places where turning was difficult, and the nearest detour well behind the train. Sometimes the detour was blocked too. And clearing the road was slower than felling the trees had been, for typically the felled trees lay atop each other, making access cumbersome and slow for the axmen clearing them.

So numerous small patrols were sent out to interrupt, pursue, and kill the axmen. But the axmen had pickets posted, and horses at hand to flee on. Pursuers had been led into ambushes. Patrols had been waylaid on the road.

It seemed to the crown prince that the raiders were little bothered by his counterefforts. They adjusted simply and quickly, and whatever they did was troublesome.

Now all three east-west roads were being used again, with larger escorts. Hithik cavalry drew escort duty. Rakutik companies were assigned patrol and counterstrike duties.

But roadblocks were still made. And raids continued, causing losses of men, draft horses, wagons and supplies. And time.

Even so, hithik troops along the Deep River Line were undoubtedly more comfortable and better fed than the raiders. The raiders' horses in particular must be suffering from hunger. At any rate, on several occasions the raiders had waited by hay wagons till the last possible minute, to let their horses feed. And if they made off with nothing else, they took sacks of corn and other feed grain.

"Now," Kurqôsz said, "Captain Gevlek has a raid to show us, from earlier this morning. I haven't seen it myself yet. Give him your attention."

They turned their awareness to that vast repository that was the voitik hive mind, and let the crown prince's deputy communicator focus their attention. A sequence of images began to run for them.

What they watched had been recorded by the eyes and ears of a supply train commander. It was a gray winter morning, and the train was proceeding slowly down a forest road. Occasional small snowflakes drifted reluctantly down, as if lost.

Abruptly a trumpet blared, snatching the commander's attention, sharpening his perceptions. The wagons halted at once. The commander was positioned somewhat back from the lead wagon; he'd decided it was the safest location. There were shouts from ahead, and within seconds, others from behind. With his mind, the commander called the system coordinator at headquarters, giving the situation and approximate location. That would alert road patrols, rakutur, that might be near enough to help.

The commander was on foot, of course, and his guard squad closed protectively around him. *Damn it,* he thought, *I can't see this way!* But he said nothing. As a voitu, he was a favored target. Often the raiders attacked the advance and rear guards to draw and engage the rest of the escort. Other raiders then emerged from the woods to kill the wagon horses. If they succeeded in killing and driving off the escort, they then looted some of the wagons, and set fire to the rest.

The shouting was much nearer now, some Hithmearcisc, some Vismearcisc. One of his guards, then another, fell from their horses. Both were to his right. With sudden decision, the commander gripped his trumpeter by a shoulder. "Stay!" he snapped, then broke between two mounted guards on his left and sprinted into the woods through old hard snow. He saw no one, and after fifty yards or so, stopped. Kneeling behind a large sugar maple, he looked back. The roadside undergrowth was too thick to see what was going on, but shouts and the clashing of sabers were mixed with the whinnying and screams of horses. These were not the noises of looting and burning he'd learned through the hive mind. Perhaps his escort would prevail. It was half again the size in recent use. He would, he decided, wait where he was till he knew.

Two minutes later the noise had changed to excited shouts in Hithmearcisc. Apparently the raiders had been driven off. A trumpet blew assembly. Rising, the commander trotted back to the road. The fighting was over. The mounted soldiers, riding back to their positions, seemed somewhat fewer. His trumpeter lay dead and trampled.

That, thought the commander, *could have been me.* To see better, he clambered onto a wagon whose horses were down. The driver lay back on one of the flour sacks he'd been hauling, a broadheaded arrow through his neck; the amount of blood was startling. Ahead and behind, the road was blocked by wagons. Many of their horses were down. He hissed an expletive. The sound horses would have to be unhitched, used to pull the dead and down animals out of the way, then assembled into new teams. Wagons without teams would have to be pulled from the road. Meanwhile the raiders . . .

The hive-mind recording stopped abruptly with a brief shocking pain exploding in the commander's neck, presumably from an arrow. Some ylf had stayed behind, concealed. To kill a voitu was worth more than killing a hundred hithar. It was worth dying for.

Lips thinned, Kurqôsz withdrew his attention from the hive mind. *And that,* he told himself, *was one of their less successful raids.* "How was this allowed to happen?" he asked.

"I do not know," the communicator answered. "Two companies of cavalry had passed down this road half an hour earlier, with scouts out on both flanks. At that time there were no raiders within two hundred yards of the road."

How does the enemy know where to be? Can there be spies among my hithar? But even if there are, how could they communicate what they know? Kurqôsz shook off what could only be another useless chain of unanswerable questions.

He looked around the table. "This column," he said, "was twice the size of any earlier column, with three companies of cavalry protecting it. Otherwise it would have been worse. We make adjustments, then they do. What we need to do is predict correctly how they will adjust, and take advantage of it. And make adjustments of our own that will bring predictable responses. Work on it!

"So far we have lost more than five hundred men dead or disabled, while finding eighty-six enemy dead and only twenty-seven wounded. They take their wounded with them whenever possible, and no doubt some of them die later. But the ratio of our losses to theirs is nonetheless unacceptable.

"Meanwhile, the construction of freight sleighs is proceeding. On snow they are much faster, and require fewer horses per ton of freight. But that is not a solution."

An officer raised a hand. "Yes, Neszkal?" Kurqôsz said.

"One solution might be to attack across the Deep River, and drive the enemy all the way back into the Western Empire."

The crown prince stared long at him, but answered mildly. "The ylver troubling us," he said, "are already living and operating behind our lines. If we advance farther, we will simply provide them with more room to maneuver, while requiring much longer hauls to supply our forward positions. No, that is not a solution."

He examined the officer thoughtfully. "I hereby assign you to produce a new strategy and tactics. Discuss your thoughts with General Orovisz. I want your analysis by tomorrow midday, and it must be more intelligent than the suggestion you just made." The crown prince paused before adding: "*Your* analysis. Do not abdicate the responsibility to someone else."

Kurqôsz's gaze held the officer for another moment before finishing. "And if I'm not satisfied, I will send you out with a supply train, for firsthand experience."

He looked around the table. "Now to go on to another matter. At breakfast I was informed that a force of dwarves, estimated at a brigade or more, was crossing the Pomatik River, as if to move up the Merrawin. Apparently they are not aware that we have powerful forces a few days north.

"Intelligence has interrogated knowledgeable captives, and one of the subjects explored has been the dwarves. They are considered dangerous fighters, and other nations prefer to trade with them, rather than fight them. At Colroi I decided to adopt the same policy. But unfortunately, our ignorance of Vismearc's political geography has made an enemy of them, and they have proven formidable.

"However, in the Merrawin Valley they do not have the advantageous terrain they had in the south. Also, they are on foot and short-legged, thus we have an immense advantage in mobility and freedom of maneuver. Just now they are in hilly terrain with considerable forest cover, but within two or three days they will reach country that is open and mostly flat. I have already ordered General Trumpko to send a battalion of cavalry and an infantry division, to engage and destroy them. The cavalry will arrive first, and harass them till the infantry arrives. Then decisive action will be taken.

"Incidentally, the dwarves are said not to have pikemen; a remarkable and serious lack. If the result is what I expect, this will be an extremely important victory for us. We will have wiped out an army which has enormous prestige in Vismearc.

"As support, I have ordered Prince Chithqôsz and his circle to accompany Trumpko's force. The dwarven trade embassy at Colroi seemed quite unaffected by our use of monsters and panic storms, but they may be susceptible to concealment screens. We will see."

Again he looked them over. "If any of you have questions or suggestions, now is the time to voice them. Before we discuss longer term prospects, and I assign further tasks."

❖   ❖   ❖

That autumn, during the Tigers' preparations for the expedition, the Cloister's teams of textile and garment makers had given their full efforts to preparing "rakutik uniforms." The actual rakutik uniforms they had as models were woolen, and presumably worn in winter. But the jackets were inadequate for living and fighting in the field in winter, and no one knew what their heavy field coats looked like, or even if they had any.

Macurdy had told the Sisters in charge to do the best they could. With his guidance, they created a winter coat design of their own—knee-length and fleece-lined, with large side pockets for gauntleted winter gloves. The exterior design and color resembled those of the autumn jackets.

They exercised the same creativity in producing winter caps—fleece-lined with ear flaps. The Tigers would wear fleece-lined versions of their own boots, and new, fur-lined mittens.

It wasn't as if they were going to stand inspection by the voitik crown prince, Macurdy thought.

Production took time, and he wanted his Tigers in action. So when they'd left the Cloister, only four companies of the 1st Cohort—what Macurdy called a "short cohort"—had been dressed as rakutur. The fifth company, still wearing Tiger uniforms, had been reassigned to the 2nd Cohort.

When they reached the confluence of the Pomatik River's Middle and North Forks, Macurdy sent the 2nd Cohort, six companies strong, west to the confluence of the Merrawin, with now full Colonel Horgent commanding.

Through the great ravens, he'd learned that the Asmehri scouts, and the Kullvordi and Kormehri, had reached ylvin lines. The Ozian Heroes would soon follow. He ordered them all to remain with the ylvin army,

west of the Deep River, till people from Cyncaidh's
raiders could brief them on their tactics and experiences. Finn Greatsword had cajoled a second company
of Asmehri out of the wofnemst. Both companies were
providing roadblocking teams, half using axes, the rest
protecting them.

The 2nd Tiger Cohort arrived at the town of West
Fork on the same day as the lead unit of dwarves. The
river was thickly ice-covered now. Rather than cross
where the dwarves planned to, Horgent led his force
another few hours upstream, and crossed there by night.
No snow had fallen since the river had frozen, so they
left no conspicuous tracks on the ice.

On the other side, they disappeared into the forest. Horgent had his orders and four great ravens. He
looked forward to what a Tiger would think of as the
experience of a lifetime.

Two days farther east, Macurdy's short cohort had
crossed before dawn, at the confluence of the North
Fork, and headed north. For a day and a half they rode
through rough, mostly wooded country, neither pushing their horses nor dawdling, and saw no one. Then
they entered the fertile, gently undulating North Fork
Plain.

Over the next two days they saw some furtive civilians, but no military personnel. Not one. The country
had been razed, as if a large force had ranged south to
loot and burn, and kill anyone they met. But the job
had not been thorough. Humans, and perhaps some
ylvin mixed bloods who could pass, had moved back
into villages and towns only partly destroyed. Macurdy
and his Tigers had spoken to none of them; their speech
would give them away as not rakutur. At night they'd
rousted people roughly from their shelters, slept in them,
then left at first dawn.

Vulkan traveled cloaked.

On their third and fourth days, they'd met three platoon-sized cavalry patrols, none of them accompanied by voitar. No one had hailed the "rakutur" in passing. In fact, the hithar had passed them apprehensively. This hadn't surprised Macurdy. He'd known only one rakutu, Tsûlgâx, but if Tsûlgâx was an example, the hithar undoubtedly feared them.

Now Macurdy sat his horse where a road crossed a modest rise. It was afternoon. He was waiting for Blue Wing, his Tigers behind him in a column of fours. Their horses' breath formed a cloud around them. In the distance, across snow-covered fields, lay the ruins of Colroi. A single unburned neighborhood remained.

The devastation had been blanketed and obscured with white. Its extent was suggested by the walls of scattered, burned-out buildings, presumably of stone or brick. The city had been large for Yuulith, but not as large as Duinarog, Macurdy decided. And unlike Duinarog, must have been built largely of lumber.

Clearly it had been burned by the invaders, not the ylver. The unburned section appeared to have been military, spared by the voitar for their own use. Most of its buildings were large. One had a tower. Others seemed to have been old barracks. Men could be seen on foot and horseback, moving among them.

Just north of the city, on a modest promontory above the river, was what must have been the imperial palace. What seemed to have been defensive walls and enclosed buildings, now were snow-capped rubble heaps. It seemed to Macurdy that to have wrought such utter destruction of a fortress, with the time and forces available, would have required explosives.

Or powerful sorceries. He remembered Felstroin's description of the great lightnings called down upon Balralligh. Concentrated and prolonged, they might have caused something like that.

When Blue Wing returned, he did not circle down

to Macurdy. It was best not to be obvious. Instead he flew at a few hundred feet, approaching from the west. Vulkan dropped his cloak, and the bird landed on his shoulder.

"Continue on the road," Blue Wing said. "The center of activity is in the unburnt buildings you can see. They include a stone building with a bell tower and guards, and a large stone stable across the street from it. Nearby to the east is a very large building by the river, also of stone. I do not know if it is the food storage building you asked about or not, but it is guarded, and has large haystacks outside. A number of wagons are parked there."

Macurdy gazed northward for another long moment, then turned to his trumpeter. "Let's move," he said.

The Tiger raised his trumpet and blew "ready," then "march." Macurdy trotted off, Vulkan invisible by his side. His cohort followed. This, he told himself, would be the voitar's biggest shock since the storm of darts, boulders, and water in the Copper River Gorge. Not in losses, but symbolically. For Colroi had been Kurqôsz's great symbolic victory, and it was some two hundred miles behind the front.

They rode unchallenged all the way to what had been tne main fire hall, and was now Colroi's military headquarters. As they approached it, Macurdy wondered if there'd be rakutur there. If there were, would they see through the pretense? But the guards proved to be hithar, humans, quite military looking, but inadequate for what they were about to experience.

Macurdy dismounted in front of their sergeant, who frowned, perhaps troubled by some anomaly in the "rakutu's" behavior or appearance. Macurdy drew his dwarf-made saber and ran the hithu through. There were shouts. While others disposed of the remaining guards, Macurdy and several Tigers pushed their way through the front door. Hithik administrative personnel took refuge behind furniture.

Three voitar were there, sabers drawn. Macurdy engaged one of them, leery of the voitu's reach and presumed training. Within seconds he'd cut his opponent badly. The voitu dropped his sword, and Macurdy ran him through. None of them lasted much longer, then his Tigers mopped up the staff.

No one, voitu or hithu, had rung the alarm bell, so Macurdy had one of his Tigers ring it. It was a lot quicker and less trouble than hunting down and rooting out the soldiers. Several hundred responded to the bell. When they found themselves attacked by what appeared to be rakutur, most tried to flee.

The Tigers killed those who didn't flee fast enough, and dug out and killed those who took refuge in buildings. The only Tiger casualties were three wounded, none severely enough that he couldn't ride. Most of the hithar had given up without a fight. Like a rat cornered by a weasel, Macurdy told himself.

Blue Wing had correctly identified the provisions warehouse. It held not only thousands of sacks of grain, but quarters of beef, large wheels of cheese in stacks, and loaves of bread. All frozen, of course.

First Company provided warehouse security guards. Platoons not on guard duty would move into whatever quarters their commanders chose. Some of those quarters, Macurdy supposed, would have stashes of wine, beer, or liquor. He reminded the men that unfitness to travel or defend the cohort because of drunkenness, was punishable by death.

Tiger punishments were commonly draconian.

Macurdy bunked with Vulkan in a single residence that seemed to have been that of the voitik commander. He took his boots off for the feeling of freedom it gave him, and lay back on the featherbed, hands behind his head. "I wonder what Kurqôsz will make of this," he said. "I suppose he'll see it in the hive mind."

«An event like this is likely to cause a vector change,» Vulkan replied. «In this instance, however, I sense no change yet.»

"You don't tell me as much as you used to. I hope I'm not missing out on too much."

«I will advise you when I deem it useful. So far your decisions have seemed quite suitable to the circumstances. Early on I did more tutoring, but now the need seldom arises.»

"The Bible says 'Thou shalt not kill.' "

«Indeed. And in general it is good advice. But that same venerable book proclaims as heroes many Hebrew warriors who took lives in wars. Neither the voitusotar nor any other ruthless conquerors can halt the evolution of consciousness indefinitely. Some may even accelerate it. But the Tao foresees the infinite vector sprays infinitely. And if the voitusotar prevail, the future will be ugly for a long time. That is why I was sent here. And why you chose to come.»

"I chose but you were sent?"

«In a manner of speaking. Your essence nudged you at critical points, but you the person chose freely, without knowing the circumstances. I also chose, but I knew something of what the stakes would be. And are. So for me the choosing was different, my decision a foregone conclusion.»

Macurdy frowned at the ceiling. Following Vulkan's meanings wasn't always easy. "You've mentioned other great boars," he said. "What are they doing?"

«One is on the other northern continent, far to the east of voitik domination. The voitusotar have designs there, too, where their rule would be as destructive as here. The third is near the western side of this continent.

If Kurqôsz prevails here, he will undertake to engineer something there.»

"And that's all?"

«Hopefully three of us are enough. At any rate, the sapient bipeds—ylver, dwarves, and ordinary Homo sapiens, along with the voitusotar—are responsible for their own futures. Their joint future. Humankind was and is an experiment. The others are separate experiments—variations on the theme. And though highly instructive, the experiment with the voitusotar threatens to be as unfortunate as the high trolls were in their time.

«Great boars were sent then, too. They worked with the dwarves; something retained in dwarven folklore. Which is, of course, somewhat embellished.»

Macurdy had nothing to say to that. With his hands still behind his head, he closed his eyes. He'd begun to drift off when Vulkan spoke to him again.

«You mentioned that I had not advised you for some while. Let me break the drought. A raider campaign is good work, but by itself it will not defeat the voitar on this continent. You are well advised to pass its leadership to others, and select a different activity for yourself.»

"A different activity?"

«Yes. Though the time is not yet upon us.»

"How about a suggestion? A hint, anyway."

«You will find it. It is only necessary that you be alert to the need.»

Great, Macurdy told himself. *I suppose I'll be awake half the night worrying about it.*

He wasn't though. Within minutes he was asleep.

In the iron frost of dawn, they loaded their pack animals with food from the warehouse. Finding a pile of pack saddles, they attached a number of voitik horses to their string, and loaded them too.

While his Tigers worked, Macurdy, via Blue Wing, let the ylver, dwarves, and others know about Colroi: a powerful symbolic victory. Cyncaidh reported sending several noncoms west across the Deep River, to personally brief the Ozians, Kormehri, and Kullvordi on voitik tactics.

Before midmorning, the 1st Tiger Cohort headed west across the plain, looking for a fight.

34

Battle of the Merrawin Plain

Despite his supply problems, the crown prince had been feeling rather buoyant since the news, that morning, of the dwarves' march northward. Despite their reputation, he could see no way they could survive the coming battle. They were used to lesser foes, he told himself, and overimpressed by their recent success. They might in fact fight well; it wouldn't surprise him at all. But they were badly outnumbered, they had serious tactical disadvantages, and they'd chosen the wrong terrain.

It was after lunch that Kurqôsz's good mood was soured. His communicator entered his office, seeming perturbed. "Your Majesty," the man said, "our occupation force at Colroi has been attacked, and may have been wiped out. By what appears to be a force of renegade rakutur."

"What!" The embarrassment of Colroi being attacked, the possibility that the garrison had been wiped out, the ambiguous "may have been"—it was

339

none of them that gut-punched Kurqôsz's equanimity. "Renegade rakutur?" he said. "That's ridiculous! The rakutur are our most reliable troops. And their entire battalion is based right here, carrying out patrol missions. My personal rakutur are within shouting distance of this building, right now. There are no other rakutur on this side of the Ocean Sea, except for Trumpko's detachment at Merrawin, and detachments guarding the various brigade headquarters on the Deep River."

"Nonetheless, Your Majesty, as seen in the hive mind, they look and fight like rakutur."

Together, the crown prince, his aide, and the communicator visited the hive mind to view the event. Kurqôsz melded with an officer's time track for maximum detail. And experienced a hithik corporal hurrying into Colroi's occupation headquarters, reporting a column of rakutur drawing up in front. "They're acting strange," he said. "They didn't respond when . . ."

He was interrupted by shouting in the street. Seconds later, intruders pushed through the door. Anomalies registered at once on the colonel's mind: The trim on their winter coats wasn't right, nor their cap emblems. Their leader had a saber in his hand, and the major had drawn his own. They traded strokes, the intruder's shockingly quick and powerful. The rakutu's saber sliced deeply into the major's upper arm, burning like fire, then thrust like an explosion between his ribs.

The experience kicked Kurqôsz out of the hive mind, cold and shaking. Even in a meld, the experience had been less traumatic for him than for the colonel, but it had shocked him severely.

After a minute, he returned to the event, this time without melding, in order to retain his own viewpoint and objectivity. The recordings ended with the death of the last voitu in the office. What happened afterward was speculation, but there was little doubt the base had been captured and looted.

Ylvin trickery! Kurqôsz ordered recon patrols sent toward Colroi from the Merrawin River base, each patrol accompanied by a voitu for quick reporting. *I need more information,* he told himself. *Then I will decide on actions.* Surely the ylvin tricksters wouldn't remain in Colroi. Where would they go from there? Balralligh perhaps? If they did, they were biting off more than they could chew, especially since Balralligh was warned now.

Nonetheless, a seed of anxiety had sprouted in the crown prince's belly. It seemed to him he was overlooking something. Somewhere along the line, something was seriously wrong, and he didn't know what it was.

He shook it off. Such thoughts were destructive. The ylver had counterfeited rakutur uniforms, that's all. And with them had gotten a battalion unrecognized to Colroi, where it had taken the garrison by surprise. It was a trick that could only work once.

Next was an update on the dwarven army. There had been no voitik observer; it had entered the hive mind verbally via General Trumpko, who had it from a patrol report. After crossing the Pomatik, the dwarves had started northward, on foot, in snow and hilly terrain. Their strength was estimated at eight to ten battalions, five to six thousand men.

The dwarves couldn't harm him without marching far to the north. And Trumpko's force was on its way to meet them: a long cavalry battalion—five companies—and an entire division of infantry, as ordered. Prince Chithqôsz and his circle accompanied its headquarters unit. The crown prince viewed Trumpko's force through his brother's eyes, as Chithqôsz paused on a low rise. A division in marching order was impressive—

18,000 officers and men. Add a long battalion of cavalry—600 men on horseback—to harass and distract them . . . Clearly the dwarves were doomed.

Yet he didn't feel the confidence and anticipation he should have. The anxiety that had grown out of Colroi still coiled in his belly like a snake. Colroi. There was something wrong there—something he hadn't put his finger on. So he returned to the hive mind, and viewed once more the forced entry, again without melding. But this time in slow- and stop-motion.

He saw again the face of the man who'd killed the voitu base commander. A face somehow familiar, but no rakutu's. The eyes and cheekbones weren't right. The other faces could pass, which was worrisome, but that one could not. He wished he could see their ears, but in the brief melee, none had lost their caps.

Another reconnaissance patrol had seen the dwarven army, on the Merrawin Valley Highway this time, emerging from the forest in a column of fours. Spied it from a distance and retired, seemingly undetected.

The patrol had left three men to observe from a copse. They'd watched till dusk, then ridden north to report the details. Its report had been encouraging. The earlier report—that the dwarves had no pikes—had been accurate. They'd be wonderfully susceptible to cavalry charges. And their mobility would be impaired not only by their short legs, but by the burdens they carried. Their packs alone were large enough that a human would find them burdensome, and large, recurved rectangular shields were slung on them. Some carried crossbows, some six-foot stabbing spears, and others two-handed battle axes. (They'd failed to notice that the axes were steel-handled, and tricked out with hooks.) A sheathed shortsword was fastened to each thick waist. And they wore knee-length hauberks that looked to weigh thirty pounds or more.

If their formation was broken, they'd be unable to flee.

Astonishingly they wore no coats, but none of the observers were troubled by this remarkable lack.

It was a bitter cold midmorning. Major Gert Ferelsma, hithik commander of the 4th Cavalry Battalion, sat in his saddle on one of the two highest points locally available. The dwarven legion had formed its defensive formation, a box with walls of spearmen six ranks thick. Its center was occupied by others, who presumably would provide both crossbow fire and replacements for casualties in the walls.

Their position was on a ridge. A low gentle ridge, but even so, to charge it on the long sides required riding or running uphill. With or without pikes, it wasn't something to throw cavalry at.

The dwarves waited stolidly. The major's spyglass showed their beards parted and braided, hanging to their thighs. Their torsos appeared thick, even allowing for their hauberks, and the quilted doublets they undoubtedly wore inside as padding. Their helmets seemed decorated—embossed or carved, though Ferelsma couldn't make out the details—and he wondered if precious metals might not be involved. It also seemed to him their heads were larger than the average human's. Their legs, he judged, would hardly be two feet long, and their hands hung to their knees.

Surely their minds were as different as their bodies, and he wished he knew what went on in them. He'd read the ancient description of the expedition to Vismearc, and been properly skeptical. Then the sea dragons had failed to materialize, and the man-eating birds, the bees large as sparrows . . .

But when Chithqôsz's army entered dwarven territory, its punishment restored credence to the tale.

Through his rakutik communicator, Ferelsma

recommended to Trumpko that they let the dwarves
wait there unmolested. After a bit the cold would weaken
them, numb their fingers and minds. When the infantry arrived, they could surround the dwarves and rain
crossbow bolts on them. By the time the infantry was
out of bolts, dwarven casualties would be high. Then
the spearmen could close with them. There was no
sensible reason to expend valuable warhorses and trained
cavalry in this situation. Save them to counter ylvin
raiders.

Trumpko acknowledged the recommendation without comment.

Ferelsma was not entirely happy at having a communicator. A few rakutur were born connected with
the voitik hive mind, and rakutur could ride. A con-
tingent of them had been trained as communicators
for hithik cavalry units. Most were with rakutik units
patrolling forest roads, but two had been assigned to
the Merrawin base, one of them to him. His rakutu
was tall by hithik standards—well over six feet—broad-
shouldered and muscular, and trained to weapons from
childhood. But more important, he was the general's
voice, and Ferelsma distrusted the general's, or any
voitu's, knowledge of cavalry warfare.

It was past noon when the first hithik infantry battalion appeared. It bypassed the dwarves, and took a
position to the south of them. Over the next two hours,
other battalions arrived and completed the closure.
Ferelsma and his battalion remained on their promi-
nence, out of crossbow range.

Trumpets called. The hithik crossbowmen cranked
and loaded their weapons, and held them ready. Ferelsma watched. Again trumpets called. The crossbowmen fired, sending a curtain of heavy bolts toward the
dwarven box. As quickly as they'd fired, they lowered
their weapons and cranked them again, bending the

steel bows. Again they loaded. Trumpets called, and they fired again.

The dwarves did not answer. They stood sheltered by their large shields, taking what came, glad for the warnings by hithik trumpeters. This continued for half an hour. They'd taken numerous casualties, but their defensive box had not shrunk.

Their shields, Ferelsma told himself, must be remarkably strong. But why hadn't they shot back? Meanwhile the infantry's supply of bolts had to be low. Supply wagons should have come up by then, but hadn't.

"Major!"

It was his communicator. Ferelsma turned to him. "Yes, Sergeant?"

"The general orders you to send a company of your people north, to learn why our supply wagons haven't arrived. I am to go with it. Quickly!"

A company, a fifth of his battalion. Ferelsma sent them, of course.

The company had hardly left when Trumpko's trumpeters ordered his crossbowmen to begin firing again. This time at will. Again the trumpets called. Now kettledrums began beating a cadence. The rest of the hithik infantry started marching toward the box, seven-foot stabbing spears gripped in hands that were numb and clumsy with cold. From every side, they advanced toward the box, in broad ranks not a dozen feet apart. They'd stood stationary so long, and gotten so cold, they stumbled at first.

Now the dwarves began shooting back, their bolts launching like great flocks of focused and deadly swallows. And dwarven crossbowmen "had the eye"; hithik soldiers began falling. Again trumpets called. The drumbeat accelerated, and the advance speeded to a run. The troops began to shout, to ululate. The hithik lead ranks reached the dwarven box, and began to pile up despite the drumbeat. But the hithar showed no sign of breaking off and retreating. As the men before them died, those behind pressed forward.

Ferelsma watched, awed. "Ensorceled," he murmured. A chill passed over him that had nothing to do with the weather.

A courier arrived, a long-legged voitu. "Major," he said, "General Trumpko expects us to be attacked by mounted ylvin raiders. Be prepared to engage them on my order."

The major felt a sense of relief. The waiting was over. He sent two of his own couriers to notify his company commanders. Then his attention went back to the struggle. The box hadn't broken anywhere. Soldiers were clambering over bodies to get at the dwarves.

The communicator's hand gripped Ferelsma's arm. "They are coming!" he said. "Over there!"

Ferelsma peered where the voitu pointed. A force of cavalry was coming into sight over a low rise—several companies, perhaps a mile away. He snapped orders to his trumpeter. The man blew a short series of notes, and the battalion adjusted its ranks, orienting on the enemy. Then, with another series of notes, the major led his four remaining companies at a slow trot toward them, forming ranks for a charge as they went.

The enemy had stopped, and sat waiting as if to receive his charge passively. Uneasy, Ferelsma wondered what that meant.

As the distant cavalry started toward him, Macurdy halted his force. His earflaps were up, exposing his steel cap, given him by Finn Greatsword at Macurdy's last visit in the mountain. A cap powerfully spelled. From where he was, he couldn't see the infantry battle, but Blue Wing could. The bird was flying a hundred feet overhead, calling down an occasional observation.

Horgent, with the 2nd Cohort, still waited to the south, out of sight but ready.

Invisible beside Macurdy, Vulkan spoke. «I sense sorcery in use. Be aware.»

What the hell am I supposed to do about that? Macurdy thought testily.

There was no sign of monsters. The oncoming hithar were still at the trot. He barked an order, and his trumpeter blew. With Macurdy in the lead, the cohort started toward the enemy.

With his hithar a quarter mile into their approach trot, the "ylvin" cavalry still stood stationary in a column of fours. Perhaps, Ferelsma thought, they'll turn and run. His own men rode knee to knee now. Then, finally, the enemy started toward him a file at a time, dressing their files into battle ranks.

Only after several seconds more did Ferelsma realize the enemy's first rank held bows. It commenced the gallop early, well before the ranks that followed, and well before his own. Unsettled by this, Ferelsma ordered the charge before he might have. Reaching effective bow range, the enemy's lead rank loosed quick arrows, one, two, three, then peeled off to the sides, riding furiously, still shooting.

Meanwhile the rest of the ylvin ranks began the gallop. At the ranges involved, hithik losses had been modest, but his people had no time to reclose their ranks effectively.

They clashed. The thunder of hooves was mixed with shouts, the clash of sabers, screams of men and horses. Riders passed through enemy ranks, then circled back; or milled, locked in combat till one or the other fell. Stricken horses ran in circles, some trailing entrails, some with a rider still aboard.

Ferelsma found himself engaged with what was surely a rakutu, whose strong teeth grinned at him

without humor. Treachery! Their blades locked at the
hilts. The rakutu's strength lent desperation to Ferelsma's arm, but not enough. He felt himself pressed backward. A long knife flashed, and abruptly time slowed.
The blade swept slowly, slowly toward him. Slowly his
mouth opened, sound swelling his throat . . . then the
blade struck his abdomen, bursting through coat and
underlying hauberk.

Time was normal again. He was slammed backward
out of the saddle. One boot caught in a stirrup, and
his horse cantered out of the melee. By the time it was
clear, Ferelsma was dead.

Horgent's great raven called, not in Yuultal, but in
a series of loud croaks. The sound could be heard a
mile. It was the signal Horgent had been waiting for.
His cohort was concealed in the largest draw the area
had to offer; not very deep, but deep enough. He signaled with a guidon, and they rode out in six broad
ranks. Ahead was a body of hithik infantry, facing away,
toward the action, oblivious of the Tigers approaching
behind them. Again the commander's guidon signaled,
and the cohort speeded up.

At about a quarter mile, a hithu looked back and
saw. The Tigers couldn't hear his cry, but they saw the
milling, the spreading disorder. Horgent's trumpeter
blew, and from their saddle boots, his Tigers drew their
heavy compound bows, already strung. A hithik trumpet sounded. At eighty yards, Horgent's trumpeter
answered, and stopping abruptly, the Tigers let arrows
fly; drew and shot again. And again, rapidly, till each
had fired half a dozen. Again Horgent's trumpeter blew,
and his ranks split, half going east, half west.

The hithar's regimental commander didn't realize
at first what Horgent intended. Then both wings of
the Tiger cohort turned north. Again he misjudged.
Only part of each wing dashed in on his flanks, and

only to distract and harass. The rest charged on toward the struggle at the north side of the dwarves' defensive box.

The men fighting there never noticed. First arrows, then sabers took them from the rear. It snapped most of them from their focus, fixed initially by sorcery, then by fighting. The unexpected strike on their rear disoriented and panicked them.

Only then did they learn how quickly dwarves can move, the attacked becoming the attackers, scrambling with axes and spears over windrowed bodies.

General Trumpko and his staff were ensconced on their little knoll, protected by two companies of infantry. He'd watched the destruction of Ferelsma's command, and realized now the danger he was in. Personally. His trumpeter blew the order for the division to disengage and reassemble. His men were willing, and the enemy was content to feed on stragglers and fringes, away from the crossbow fire of Trumpko's reserves. In twenty minutes his mauled division was moving again. Northward now.

Macurdy didn't even try for a count of hithik bodies. It seemed to him, though, that five thousand was reasonable. Strongarm had roll taken of his dwarves. The number of dead or unaccounted for was 560—the missing mostly under piled-up hithar—and 1,334 significantly wounded, many unable to walk.

The dwarves made camp, and their healers applied their talents to the wounded, wishing they could do more. Still, Farside medics would have been impressed by their effectiveness. Other dwarves salvaged crossbow bolts from hithik corpses, to replenish their supply.

Macurdy sent Tigers out to round up what horses they could catch, and to bring up pack strings. Pack loads were rearranged, and some goods cached, to free up additional horses for transporting wounded.

Dwarves don't ride well on full-sized horses; even
mounting is difficult. But pack strings and ingenuity
provided transportation for dwarven wounded, two
per horse.

Macurdy talked with Strongarm awhile, applaud-
ing the dwarves' performance, but not overdoing it.
They'd played their role superbly, and the hithik army
had taken a drubbing. But it wasn't a show suited for
repeat performances. The crown prince could replace
his casualties. Strongarm couldn't.

They agreed that Strongarm's legion should turn
west, cross the Deep River, and help the ylver when
the voitar attacked westward again. Tossi Pellersson Rich
Lode was on his way with two cohorts from the Diamond Flues. If both tribes agreed, they could fight
together as a legion.

As evening advanced, Macurdy and most of the
Tigers headed west. Behind them they left the dwarves
and the Tiger wounded. Along with three companies
of Horgent's long cohort as escorts, and to handle the
strings of "ambulance" horses.

As usual, the dwarves would draw on the Web of
the World for warmth and energy. The Tigers couldn't,
and the night threatened to be bitter cold again. Especially if it turned windy, Macurdy wanted them sheltered in the forest, where deadwood could be found
for fires. When Horgent and his advance companies
reached the forest, they'd cut firewood, and wait for
the dwarves. When Strongarm was ready to go on,
Horgent's men would escort them to the ylvin lines.

Through the great ravens, Macurdy notified the ylvin
high command of the battle, and told them to expect
the wounded. Then he led his 1st Cohort northwest-
ward, to make camp in the forest. From there they'd
head north, and join in the raiding.

❖   ❖   ❖

At his headquarters, Crown Prince Kurqôsz reviewed the battle. When he finished, his mood was foul. It was then he decided on decisive action. Extreme but decisive.

Certain conditions were necessary, and it was impossible to predict them more than two or three days in advance. But they would come. He'd already seen them several times in this miserable land. Meanwhile he'd continue to deal with the problems as he found them.

35

Prisoners of War

"A new raider force?"

"Without a doubt, Your Majesty, and they're not ylver. They don't have the same uniforms, and their tactics are different. If they qualify as tactics."

Kurqôsz's communicator, Captain Gorvaszt, reached to the appropriate memory track, taking the crown prince's attention with his own. The viewpoint was that of a voitik wagon master. This one preferred to stride alongside the first wagon in the train. Some fifty yards ahead was his advance platoon. Somewhere farther ahead, out of sight, were scouts.

In between, the road curved to pass a cedar swamp. From its dense green cover, horsemen exploded, charging the advance guard at close range. The platoon had no chance to meet them at a gallop; its horsemen were ridden down like straw figures in a tableau. Howling like lunatics, the raiders hurtled on toward the wagon train. Meanwhile the wagon escorts stayed in place, to protect against the expected attack from the flanks.

The voitu's bodyguards braced themselves, sabers bared. The voitu himself vaulted onto the first wagon, where he crouched low, taking refuge behind flour barrels.

It almost worked. The raiders, still howling, split into two streams and careened by, attacking the escorts. Thinking they were past, the voitu raised his fur-capped head above the barrels, to see. What he saw was a laggard raider, who without slowing, leaned impossibly to his right and struck with his saber. The voitu tried to duck away, and the raider's blade missed his neck, taking him across the side of the face, driving halfway through his head. There was blackness, a sense of duration without sight or sound. Then the voitu saw and heard again, briefly and without focus, while he strangled on his blood.

Kurqôsz jerked free. This was, he thought, intolerable. One of the problems was already clear to him: the hithik scouts had stayed *on* the road. Afraid of what they might find if they left it.

He sent Gorvaszt away, with orders not to disturb him for half an hour. Then he had his orderly bring lunch, and while he ate, mentally reviewed the overall situation. Henceforth, he decided, he'd settle for oral reports. It was unwise to repeatedly visit such events in the hive mind, even without melding. It gave emotionally disturbing views without context. After all, he held all of the Eastern Empire that was of much use. Adequate supplies still got through, and casualties were modest, given the size of his army. The only real battle had been with the dwarves, and while his casualties had been high, the dwarves had surely lost a higher percentage of their force than Trumpko had.

Meanwhile, he told himself, *I will send strong infantry escorts with the supply trains—spearmen and crossbowmen. Along with the cavalry. Let's see what the raiders think of that!* Orovisz could work out the details.

He'd just finished dessert—a cream tart with a

sweetened form of some astringent ylvin beverage—when there was another knock at his door. "Who is it?" Kurqôsz snapped.

"Captain Gorvaszt, Your Majesty. The half hour has passed, and I have an item you may find intriguing. From the Deep River Line. An ylvin page has contacted a flank post at the mouth of Piney Gorge. His master, an ylvin lord, wishes to speak with you personally."

"An ylvin lord? What about?"

"He didn't say, Your Majesty. Apparently something his master doesn't want his government to know. He may be our first ylvin traitor. The page claims to have crossed Deep River above the falls, then ridden south. I get the impression that his master may also have crossed, and is waiting in the forest."

"Hmh! Have him bring his master to the flank post. By supper. Is that feasible?"

"Just a moment, Your Majesty. I'll ask Captain Brellszok at the post." Kurqôsz waited. "He says his master can be there before dark. He will come by cutter with six personal guards and a hostage."

"A hostage?"

"Not one of our people, Your Majesty. Brellszok asked. It's one of his own."

Kurqôsz frowned down his arched nose. *Confusing,* he thought. "Make sure they are thoroughly searched. He is to bring the hostage, but no guards. Tell him I guarantee his safety. And Gorvaszt, I want a look at this 'ylvin lord' when he arrives at the flank post. But do not let him know."

Gorvaszt acknowledged the orders and left. *I'll send Tsûlgâx to fetch him,* Kurqôsz decided. *He is naturally suspicious, and has a nose for treachery.*

Raien Cyncaidh's cohort had suffered enough casualties that he'd consolidated its five fully-manned companies to four short companies, which operated in pairs.

The voitar had beefed up their escorts. The voitik command kept changing how they did things, and Cyncaidh tried to outguess and outmaneuver them with changes of his own.

With two of his companies, he'd positioned himself along a stretch of what he'd dubbed Road C. His bird had told him a major supply column, this time of sleighs, was coming west on it, having detoured from Road B, the major and most used road. With luck he'd get away with some sleigh-loads of hay and grain. It wasn't something he'd done before. Wagons weren't suited to off-road hauling.

The raiders had waited half a mile back from the road, for their bird to approve the situation. When they'd gotten clearance, they'd moved up. Then Cyncaidh had positioned his force far enough back in the woods to escape detection by the hithik scouts on the road.

Cyncaidh sat listening intently, his deputy and trumpeter beside him. Their horses' faces, necks and manes were white with rime from their own breath. His eyelashes were beaded with frost, his eyebrows crusted with it. They were at the east end of his assault line, where they'd be the first to hear the column. And nearer the road than the rest of his force was—less than twenty yards from it—screened by hemlock saplings growing on a large old windfall.

He didn't like waiting in such cold. It was hard on men and horses. Most of his ylver could manipulate their metabolism and circulation to some extent, to keep warm, but it drained their energy reserves. So they were under orders to use the technique only to keep their fingers warm, and in emergencies, their feet.

And just now their ears, for they'd turned their earflaps up, listening for the enemy's approach. Still, despite the general silence and his acute hearing, the sound of the column sneaked up on him. Suddenly he was aware of the plop-plop of hooves on packed snow.

The advance guard, he supposed. Quietly he drew his
saber. The hithar passed in front of him, well enough
screened by the hemlocks and roadside undergrowth,
that all Cyncaidh saw of them was movement. Then
came the chink of trace chains, and the squeak of run-
ners on packed snow in forty degrees of frost. He
couldn't hear a thing from the teamsters. They were,
he supposed, too numb to talk.

For long minutes the sleighs passed. Cyncaidh had
tensed. His right wing would attack the advance guard
at any moment. Then he'd . . .

He heard shouts from the head of the column, and
spoke a low word of command. His trumpeter blew a
long shrill note, and all along the road the ylver charged,
Cyncaidh with them. But as they plunged through the
roadside undergrowth, the column's escort surprised
them, meeting them not with the usual sabers, but with
seven-foot spears. A few of the raiders reacted too slowly,
and their horses were stabbed in head or neck, but most
reined back, briefly confused. At the same time, soldiers arose on the wagons, out of the hay or from beneath
tarps, crossbows in hand.

Cyncaidh felt a bolt slam through his cuirass, and
into his upper left chest.

The escort had never intended to fight with their
spears. They'd served mainly to halt the charging ylver,
making them more susceptible to crossbow fire. Fighting
in the saddle at a near standstill, spears were not the
weapon of choice, and the escort dropped them. Before
most of the raiders could recover their wits, the hithar
engaged them with sabers.

The ylver fought furiously and skillfully. Some killed
or wounded or unhorsed their opponents, some forced
them back. Others died. In the melee, the crossbows
had largely stopped. Cyncaidh's trumpeter and deputy
had hung back, as they were supposed to. They saw
their wounded commander defending himself against

a soldier. Then, deflected by Cyncaidh's blade, a powerful saber blow slammed his helmet, and he fell from the saddle.

The deputy saw the hithik rear guard charging up, shouted an order, and the trumpeter blew the quick notes of retreat. As best they could, the ylver disengaged and galloped back into the forest, crossbowmen sending bolts after them.

Nearly a hundred bodies lay in the snow, more raiders than escorts. Not all of them were dead.

The Younger Quaie and his party had met with a voitik officer the evening before, at the flank post. There'd been no actual negotiations. The voitu had asked questions, then presented terms. Quaie had accepted. He had nothing to negotiate with except his services, and at any rate he felt optimistic. He usually was, manically so, despite the mental abuse visited on him by his famous and sadistic father. Just now, in fact, he felt positively exhilarated; he would soon have the respect he desired and deserved. This voitik prince needed someone who knew the people, politics, and power sources of the empires and the Marches. And he was that man. As time passed, the voitu would rely more and more on him. He'd have rewards, power, people subject to him, whom he could do with as he pleased.

They spent a second night in the rude cabin assigned to them, and slept late. When Quaie awoke, his exhilaration had faded. Breakfast was more spare than he'd expected. After eating, he said good-bye to his bodyguards. That was the hardest part of the bargain—harder even than being searched. Then his new driver led them outside, and watched while they got back in the cutter.

Quaie felt alone now, exposed and anxious. His driver was a large, hard-looking, frightening man with a face seeming carved from pale, scarred stone. Even the voitik

sublieutenant who would accompany them spoke courteously to the creature.

For days, Quaie's hostage had traveled gagged and
hooded, nearly hidden beneath heavy furs. After they'd
crossed the river, Quaie had removed the gag; they
would no longer encounter ylvin couriers and other
travelers. Now, as the cutter moved smoothly away into
the forest, he smirked at her. "Soon you will meet your
new husband," he taunted. "And if you please him well
enough, who knows? He may not share you out."

She didn't answer. The Younger Quaie was well
known as susceptible to taunts, but infuriating him could
have no good result.

The cutter was drawn by excellent horses on packed
snow, and moved briskly. Here the countryside was a
fertile till plain, but very stony. Thus it was largely forest, with occasional farm settlements rich in stone piles,
rough stone fences, and stone foundations topped with
the charred remains of buildings. The voitu loped tire-
lessly ahead of them, eating occasionally from his pocket
as he ran. The creature impressed Quaie greatly; his
only stops were to turn his back to the cutter and relieve
his bladder. Quaie wished the voitu wouldn't turn away.
He wanted to see what the creature had.

Twice they met large mounted forces patrolling the
road. They wore uniforms like his driver's—quite different from those of the hithik soldiers at the flank post—
and their men looked dangerous. The fabled rakutur,
Quaie told himself. They must be.

The sun had set, and dusk was thickening, when
they rode into a large cleared area, perhaps a mile
square. Here there were no stone piles. Along the road
were only the stubs of hedges cut since the last snow,
and the charred remains of brush piles. In the southeast quarter of the clearing were buildings, a hamlet's
worth, with lamp- and candlelight burning in windows.

He was, Quaie realized, almost to the next phase of his great adventure, his new life.

As she got out of the cutter, Quaie threw the fur hood back from Varia's head, exposing her face. Then he gripped her arm needlessly. His strength surprised her. He'd always seemed smaller than he was. Now she realized his seeming weakness had also been an illusion. But not his mental problems; they were genuine.

Their tireless voitik sublieutenant entered the stone manor house ahead of them. Their driver herded them from behind. Varia found the rakutu disquieting. There was a sense of cruelty about him, and more unnerving, hatred.

The entryway opened into what had been a large parlor. Now it was a reception and office area, with numerous administrative personnel, and guards. As she entered with Quaie, eyes turned to them, but they were not challenged. They'd been expected.

The interior was rustic but well-constructed, with heavy, rough-hewn beams, and hardwood floors. The sublieutenant led them up a staircase. At the top, they turned down a hallway to a guarded door at the end. The voitu knocked. The door was opened by another voitu whom Varia realized was in early adolescence; a page or orderly she supposed. The sublieutenant ushered them in—Quaie first, then herself.

She knew at once which of the several voitu there was the crown prince. Even for a voitu he was tall, and his charisma struck her at once. Like the other voitar, his aura was strange, but it was a ruler's aura nonetheless. Like Raien's and Curtis's, and Sarkia's, but more intense than any of them.

He looked first at her, taking in her red hair and green eyes, then at Quaie, then at the sublieutenant. "Yes, Lieutenant?" he said.

The young officer bowed, a short half-bow. "Your

Majesty, I have brought the ylvin Lord Quaie. And his captive."

"Ah." Kurqôsz turned. "Lord Quaie. Remind me why you have come here."

Varia had already been impressed with the voitik fluency in Yuultal. She'd long since read of their hive mind; perhaps when one of them learned a language, it was accessible to all. All they'd need to do was practice using it.

"Your Majesty," Quaie said, "I am volunteering my services to you. I am expert in ylvin government and politics, and of course in the ways and attitudes of my people. In fact, during my fifty-seven years of life, observation, and study, I have learned much about all of Yuulith and its peoples. I can advise you and your generals on the most effective ways of dealing with them. And when your conquest is complete, on administering them with the greatest profit and least aggravation for Your Majesty."

"Hmm. Interesting. But as a person of power and position, why ally yourself with an enemy?"

"Why, it's clear that you will win. In Duinarog, the pessimism was so thick, you could cut it with a knife."

"Indeed? And your gift to me?" He turned to look again at Varia. "Why did you bring her?"

"As a token of my respect, and to demonstrate my knowledge and ability. She is the wife of Lord Raien Cyncaidh, you see, the Western Empire's most powerful duke, and the emperor's chief advisor. Yet I stole her without difficulty." He smirked. "She's very beautiful, don't you think? You may find her useful as a hostage. Or for your royal pleasure. Or both."

There was a sharp rap at the office door and, scowling, the crown prince turned to it. "What is it?" he said sharply.

The answer was in Hithmearcisc. "Your Majesty, an ylvin prisoner has been brought in. By his insignia, a general. He was wounded and captured while attacking a supply train."

Kurqôsz responded in Vismearcisc, seemingly for the benefit of his visitors. "A general? Leading raiders? Interesting. Is his wound serious?"

The man at the door switched to Vismearcisc to fit the crown prince's pleasure. "Your chief physician is with him now, Your Majesty."

"Your Majesty," Quaie interjected, "it is quite possible I can identify him for you." He had no doubt the prisoner was Cyncaidh.

"Can you now? Hmm." He turned to the door again. "Bring him in when Agrûx has finished with him. I want to see this general who leads his men instead of sending them. Either he has a poor opinion of his importance as a strategist, or a very high one of his importance as a fighting man."

He turned back to Quaie. "As for your gift, I already have ylvin women. Several of them, selected from thousands for their beauty. This one . . ." He gestured. ". . . is sufficiently robed, that all I can see is her face.

Kurqôsz paused. "But the crux of the matter is your qualifications as an advisor. Tell me about them."

Quaie began to recite a résumé. As he ran on, Varia was vaguely aware that it was almost totally false—his father's, not his own. His own acts, his abilities, even his evils were trivial by comparison with the elder. But her mind was not on Quaie. It was on the captured general. An icy fist had gripped her heart. *It's Raien,* she thought. *It has to be.*

There was another rap at the door, followed by a murmured exchange with the junior officer tending it. The young voitu interrupted Quaie's recitation. "Your Majesty, the ylvin general is here, unconscious on a stretcher. Agrûx is with him." He'd spoken in Vismearcisc. It seemed to be his master's choice this evening.

"Have him brought in." Kurqôsz turned to his aide, and gestured. "Clear that table for the stretcher."

Raien Cyncaidh's torso had been bared and bandaged. His face, always fair complected, was ivory white.

"I know him!" Quaie said.

The crown prince stilled him with an imperious gesture. "What are his wounds?" he asked the physician.

"A crossbow bolt struck his chest, Your Majesty, but his unconsciousness is from a heavy blow to the head. He will probably awaken from it before morning."

"Then he is not near death?"

"Seemingly not, Your Majesty."

The crown prince turned to Quaie. "Tell me his name."

"He is Lord Raien Cyncaidh of Aaerodh, Your Majesty. Gavriel's—the emperor's—chief advisor and sometime deputy." He pointed at Varia. "Her husband."

The crown prince smiled at Quaie. "I could as well have named him for you. He is not our first prisoner, you see, and we always question them. It is standard intelligence procedure, and occasionally recreation."

He pursed his lips in mock thoughtfulness. Quaie began to sense that he was in trouble. "I do not envision needing a viceroy. I will rule by force, not politics. As for an advisor . . ." Kurqôsz paused, watching emotions wrestle in Quaie's face. "I can smell liars," the crown prince said, "and liars make poor advisors. No, I have no need of your services."

Again he paused. "But I will reward you for your gift of the general's wife. Yes." He stroked his chin. "But what will it be? Hmm." He turned to the scarred, hard-eyed rakutu who stood behind Quaie, and spoke in Hithmearcisc: "Strangle him, Tsûlgâx."

Tsûlgâx reached a forearm across Quaie's throat and pulled him backward hard against him. The ylf's eyes widened, and he clawed at the rakutu's wrist and hand.

"You'll find it quick and relatively painless," the crown prince told him. "Merciful, compared to the death I will visit on Lord Cyncaidh."

The whole room watched till Quaie's heels stopped drumming the floor. When it was over, Varia looked pleadingly at Kurqôsz. "Your Majesty," she whispered, "please. Don't torture my husband, I beg you."

"My dear woman," he said. "Consider all the trouble he's been to me! It would be utterly immoral not to."

She ran to the table then, and turned to face the crown prince, her arms spread as if in protection, or supplication. The move captured every eye in the room. Tsûlgâx moved to get her, but his master stopped him with a gesture.

One of her hands rested on the knob of Cyncaidh's boot knife, concealed by the folded top of a heavy woolen stocking. "Please!" she said. "I beg you. I'll . . ." Abruptly she drew the knife, and turning, plunged it into Cyncaidh's solar plexus, thrusting upward, twisting. Blood gushed over her hand and wrist, then a fist struck her, knocking her to the floor. There, on all fours, she vomited. Tsûlgâx jerked her upright by the hair, to face the crown prince, her eyes wide with shock, mouth open, vomit on her chin.

Kurqôsz's eyes had widened. "Well!" he said. "We have a wildcat among us! Remarkable!" He laughed, the sound genuinely admiring. "You fooled us all with your act of the pitiful wife.

"You will pay me for that, you know, but not with your life. You are loyal and highly courageous, and you think quickly. An excellent bloodline. The pleasure of fathering sons on you will be my recompense."

To the crown prince, the death of the ylvin commander, and possession of his beautiful wife, were favorable omens. Quaie he'd already forgotten.

❖   ❖   ❖

Shortly before his orderly would have wakened him, Kurqôsz came awake on his own. And sat up abruptly with a new knowingness: Conditions would be right! Soon!

Without bothering to have Gorvaszt brought to him—it was a familiar channel—he reached through the hive mind to his younger brother. «Chithqôsz,» he said mentally, «come to my headquarters! As quickly as you can! With your circle. Leave this morning! I need you here!»

36

Decision

When Macurdy and the 1st Cohort had reached forest again, he'd divided its four companies into two independent forces. Blue Wing, through the great raven hive mind, had already called for another great raven to work with the second force. After that the two forces traveled north still as a unit, to the district through which the supply routes ran. There they separated.

Macurdy's first ambush was a success: somewhat costly, but less than he'd feared. They'd ambushed a company of rakutur patrolling the road, outnumbering the half-voitar nearly two to one. No prisoners were taken, and so far as he knew, none of the rakutur had run. All, or nearly all, had died.

As a side benefit, he and a few of his Tigers now wore the coats and fur caps of actual rakutur.

He'd known since his time in Hithmearc that the rakutur were the offspring of human women impregnated by voitar. Also, from his reading at the Cloister, he'd learned that after the voitusotar had crushed the continental ylver, there'd been a prolonged period of hunting down refugees, killing the men and boys, and making sex slaves of the women and girls.

It had been a period of considerable chaos. The voitusotar were in transition from being migratory barbarians to "civilized" rulers and administrators. The sex camps had been haphazard and unmanaged, and the voitik warriors ill-disciplined when away from their commanders. Thus numerous ylvin women had escaped. Those who could, then fled in small boats to Ilroin. Sometimes on their own, but often with hithar who hoped for sanctuary from the voitusotar themselves. Some had left pregnant, and later gave birth. And the ylvin attitude was that sound infants should be nurtured regardless of their origin.

Many or most—perhaps all—of the voitu-sired babies were red-haired and green-eyed, and rather like the voitar, had large flexible ears. Over generations of subsequent back-crossing with the ylvin gene pool, the "rakutik ears" disappeared by "genetic dilution," though contributing perhaps to the ylvin trait of pointed ears. But the voitik red hair and green eye traits persisted, manifesting infrequently but strongly. Sarulin, the founder and progenitor of the Sisterhood had had them, and according to tradition, so had her consort.

It seemed to Macurdy that Sarkia, at least, had seen the possibilities. The Tigers had probably been bred deliberately for rakutur traits—athletic redheads bred to athletic redheads, and the offspring graded according to "Tiger" traits. Those who met specifications would then have been segregated and trained. The breeding and genetic segregation records could probably be checked, if they'd survived Ferny Cove.

Varia had been interested in genetics and animal breeding when she'd been married to Will, back in Indiana. She might have drawn the same conclusions. If he ever got back to Duinarog, he told himself, he'd ask her.

At any rate, today the Tigers had proven as hard and strong and athletic as the rakutur, and seemingly better trained.

Rillissa, back in Hithmearc, had been a female rakutu, with Kurqôsz her father and some human woman her mother. In an old ylvin manuscript, he'd read that the rakutur weren't connected with the voitik hive mind, but Rillissa had definitely been. Some of the rakutur they'd just fought might have been, too. If so, the voitik high command knew of this battle. So when his Tigers had finished looting the rakutur's equipment and rations, and tethering the captive horses to a lead rope, Macurdy ordered them to move out.

His companies camped that night in the shelter of a dense stand of arborvitae—a "cedar swamp." Sentries were posted, the horses hobbled, and tarps strung up as lean-tos. Innumerable small warming fires were lit in front of them. They had no hay for their horses, but they did have corn and nose bags. And though few if any of the horses were familiar with arborvitae, after a bit some began to browse it. By morning many would, and take no harm from it.

Macurdy bedded down on the snow with Vulkan, without stringing a tarp. While waiting for sleep, he thought about Cyncaidh, whom he'd checked with the morning before, via the great raven connection. Each of the ylf lord's strike forces had averaged more than two raids a week, with casualties that were moderate for all the trouble he'd caused. Macurdy recalled his earlier doubts that the ylver could fight such a nonstandard war! So much for that worry.

He'd check with him again in the morning, he decided, and with the East Ylvin guerrillas. The Ozians were already in business, and the Kormehri and Kullvordi had left to begin harassing supply trains nearer the Deep River.

He'd thought about attacking Kurqôsz's headquarters, to see what would happen, and had brought it up with Cyncaidh the day before. The ylf hadn't liked the idea; Kurqôsz would probably have sorcerous traps in place. The thought was sobering.

Meanwhile, with Kurqôsz's army having difficulties, what sorceries might the voitu be cooking up to deal with supply train raids?

Macurdy was rather good at not worrying until he saw a handle for the problem. Rarely did unacknowledged tensions ambush him with an anxiety attack; ordinarily he trusted his intuitions rather cheerfully. So he didn't dwell now on the possibility of sorceries. It had been a long day in the saddle, walking in the snow occasionally to rest their horses. His thoughts soon bogged down in vague semi-dreams, and he slept.

He didn't waken for hours. When finally he did, it was to sit bolt upright, from nightmare. Slowly he got to his feet, walked off a few yards, and urinated against a red maple, the smell pungent in his nostrils. Then he returned to his place beside Vulkan's bristly bulk. Lying down again, he tried to call back the dream, and examine it. It seemed important— something about Kurqôsz—but beyond that it refused to show itself.

To hell with it, he thought. If it's important, the seeds are there. They'll sprout.

The next time he awoke, the sky was paling. Getting to his feet, he oriented himself, then roused his deputy, Captain Skortov, who sent an aide to roust the companies from their sheepskin blankets, and order the company officers and senior noncoms to a conference with the Macurdy.

While Macurdy waited, he described his intentions

to Blue Wing, and asked directions. "Backtrack into the hardwoods," the great raven said, "then keep the new sun off your left shoulder." He paused. "Riding Vulkan, you should reach Road B quite soon. Then go west until"—he paused; he still had trouble judging human travel time—"until sometime past midday. You'll pass four crossroads on the way."

His beady eyes studied Macurdy. "Just the two of you, going to beard the voitik troll in his lair. Hmh! I'd argue if I could suggest an alternative.

"Take care, my friend. I do not want to lose you. I hope you don't plan to knock on his door and introduce yourself."

Macurdy grinned ruefully. "Vulkan will cloak us. It seems to me his cloak will do the job even against voitar. When we get close, we'll probably leave the road, study the place from the edge of the woods. Then we'll decide how to go about it."

By that time his Tiger officers were arriving. When they were all there, Macurdy addressed them. "Tigers," he said, "I'm going to leave you on your own. Skortov will be in command. We can kill hithar and voitar and rakutur till spring, but if I can kill their leader, it'll finish this a lot quicker.

"He's likely to have his headquarters protected by major sorceries, so Vulkan and I are going to give it a try alone. Just the two of us; without even a horse. It's the sort of thing they're not likely to expect. If we don't pull it off, it'll be up to you. If you can bleed the voitar dry, that could win it. And if you can't bleed him dry, make him wish he'd never crossed the Ocean Sea."

It occurred to Macurdy that some voitik adept might sense the spells in his armor and saber, so before leaving, he traded the saber for Skortov's, and his hauberk and steel cap with two Tigers whose sizes matched his own. Then he shook their hands, climbed aboard Vulkan bareback, and left.

"What do you think?" he said to Vulkan as they left the bivouac behind. "Am I crazy?"

Vulkan snorted. «Not at all. I've been wondering when you'd make this decision. I'd almost decided to nudge you again.»

PART SEVEN
Climax And Aftermath

The greatest wizards and sorcerers of antiquity lived and studied under Sorthaelius Halfylvin at Beech Mountain. There a great library of magicks and sorceries was gathered, with extensive notes and commentaries by the masters.

Halfylvin was a powerful mage, but his greatest powers were of intuition, intellect, and discipline. He saw how things interacted, how matters remote to a problem applied to it, and how to test speculations.

He learned to enlarge greatly the power of circles, through configuration, amplification, and control. Configuration being how the members of a circle connected each with the others in the Realm of the Force. But perhaps his greatest advance was to create crystals of power. It is said that a crystal was formed layer on layer, each member of the circle contributing to the spell. Each such crystal contained the essence of each member's soul, harmonizing them all. And only they could use it.

Unfortunately the knowledge was destroyed by the earthquake and firestorm known as Fengel's Punishment.

From: *History of Magicks and Sorceries.*
Ylvin manuscript dating from
the fifth century before Exile.

37

SORCERY!!!

One of the powers Vulkan had that Macurdy didn't was an infallible sense of position and orientation. Thus they left without waiting for sunrise, and half an hour later reached Road B. Clouds were moving in, concealing the sun, and shortly afterward it began to snow. When it stopped, six hours later, the old snow had been covered by five inches of fresh white. It was the first substantial snowfall since the big storm in Eleven-Month. Meanwhile the air had warmed notably. At midday, it seemed to Macurdy, it wasn't a whole lot below freezing.

He preferred the weather they'd been having, bitter though it had been. With the new snow, Kurqôsz could order out his entire cavalry to hunt and track raiders. Though knowing the Ozians, Kormehri, and Kullvordi, they'd no doubt take advantage of it to lead pursuers into ambushes.

Cloaked or not, Vulkan too left tracks. They were not, however, the only cloven tracks. There were both deer and elk around, and to inexperienced observers, Vulkan's prints could pass for elk. Even as Macurdy thought it, Vulkan left the road, to parallel it forty to sixty yards back in the woods. In the woods, of course, the old snow had not been packed by traffic, and travel was somewhat slower. But cloven tracks that went straight down the road for miles might inspire curiosity.

It was late afternoon when they reached the big clearing. They examined the buildings from the forest edge. The row of cabins suggested the homes of tenant farmers or bonded help.

Now, of course, they housed soldiers. But by no means all the soldiers, for nearby were rows of crude huts under construction, and a short distance from them, rows of squad tents with the new snow swept off. But Macurdy gave the manor house his major attention. The number of people going in and out suggested considerable command activity.

Macurdy and Vulkan settled into a position sixty or seventy yards from the road, careful not to betray themselves by needless movement, or tracks to the road.

Near sundown he saw about twenty mounted men ride up to the house and sit waiting. Even four hundred yards away they struck him as rakutur, from their bearing. Then a voitu emerged from the house and began to lope down the road. The horsemen fell in on both sides and behind him. He ran fast enough, they spurred their horses to a canter to keep up, continuing almost all the way across the clearing. Then he loped his way back and forth on the pattern of farm lanes that from spring to fall gave access to different fields.

Macurdy guessed the time spent running was something under half an hour. And fast! Clearly the sonofabitch could outrun Gunder Hegg without shifting out of second.

When it was dark, Macurdy contemplated going to the house. He had no idea what he might accomplish, but he'd accomplish nothing sitting where he was. Still he didn't move, till across the clearing he saw northern lights begin to form an emerald curtain across the sky. He remembered a night in Bavaria then, and felt a sudden pang of urgency.

Quietly he told Vulkan he was going to the house by himself, under cover of his own concealment cloak. And kill Kurqôsz if he could. He'd hardly used his cloak since World War II, but he had no doubt he still could. He'd developed considerable confidence in it. A voitik master or adept might see through it, but he also wore a genuine rakutik greatcoat and cap. Hopefully they'd take him for one of their own.

Assuming the spell itself didn't give him away.

He had greater confidence in Vulkan's cloak, of course. He thought of it as bestowing actual invisibility, rather than simply making the wearer unnoticeable. But even it might not work against masters and adepts. And if someone saw through it, a giant boar with a rakutu on his back would draw serious attention.

He half-hoped Vulkan would suggest an alternative, or argue with him. Instead, the red eyes regarded him calmly, a pair of smoldering ruby coals. «I will monitor you,» Vulkan told him, «and if a situation develops, I will take the best action available to me.»

Macurdy took a roundabout route to the road, then strode down it into the clearing. He carried Skortov's saber, and the knife Arbel had given him, that had saved his life at least twice. They did not reassure him. As he approached the house, he saw that the entrance guards were also rakutur. *How,* he asked himself, *do I pass them? Even if they don't see me sooner, when I open the door, it'll take their attention. Then they'll see through the spell.*

As he approached, they showed no awareness of him. Their gaze was past him, fixed on something else, and pausing he looked back. A column of horsemen was trotting briskly into the clearing. At their front, enclosed by them on three sides, was a group of running voitar.

Macurdy stepped toward the house, then stood at attention a few yards from an entry guard. The approaching voitar would be his acid test.

The column reached the yard in perhaps twenty seconds, the mounted escort peeling off to the sides. The voitar slowed to a walk, and strode purposefully toward the entrance. Macurdy stood only a couple of yards out of their way. If they noticed him, they showed no sign of it, and when they'd passed, he fell in behind them. Their auras marked them as powerfully talented, but just now they were focused on something else. He had no idea what.

They pushed through the door, Macurdy with them. Inside was a vestibule with pegs on both sides, festooned with uniform coats. It opened into what once had been a parlor. Now it was an office reception area, with administrative personnel both voitik and hithik. And a pair of rakutur: security guards. No one challenged the voitar who'd come in, nor Macurdy, who at any rate would have seemed an attendant. Someone called "Attention!" in Hithmearcisc, and everyone stood ramrod straight, facing the newly arrived voitar.

Across the room was a wide staircase. His voitar were headed toward it. Another had just descended, and stood at attention. The leader of the group slowed and spoke. "Good evening, Captain Rissko! It's good to see you." The Hithmearcisc was simple and formulaic, well within the scope of Macurdy's limited knowledge.

"Good evening, Prince Chithqôsz!" the voitu answered. "It is good to see you, Your Highness." Then the voitar passed him, taking the steps three at a time. At the top they turned right.

Prince! But not the crown prince. This one he'd never seen before.

Macurdy was the last one up, and paused. The upper hallway had a short section to the right, and a much longer one to the left. At the end of the right-hand section was a door guarded by a rakutu, who was reaching for the door handle, as if to let the prince through. Meanwhile Macurdy felt seriously exposed to the voitar below. To stay where he was seemed unwise, and to turn right seriously dangerous, so he turned left.

Through the opened door behind him he heard a big voice. One he knew well: the crown prince's. "Hello, brother! I'm glad to have you here! You traveled quickly! I'm sure you . . ." Then the door closed.

Ahead of Macurdy were doors along both sides of the hall. If he could find a room unoccupied, and hide till late at night . . . But if the rakutu guarding Kurqôsz's office was paying attention, he'd notice a door opening, even if it opened inward. Of course, he might assume it was someone inside who'd opened it. On the other hand, if someone *was* inside . . . Macurdy heard footsteps on the stairs, and stepping quickly to the nearest door, opened it. Inward.

The room was not empty. A woman was there, garbed in a long shift. She turned, her face the color of bread dough. For a moment she peered uncertainly, then her eyes widened. For a long second Macurdy stood rooted to the floor, stunned. Then he raised a finger to his lips. "Ssh!"

Varia's knees had almost given way. She took an unsteady step backward and sat down on a chair behind her, staring at him. Carefully Macurdy closed the door. "Where can I hide?" he asked quietly.

For several seconds she simply stared, looking as if she couldn't breathe. Her eyes were darkly circled, as if from long weeping. Her mouth moved soundlessly, then she gestured. "Under the bed," she murmured, "or in the closet."

He frowned. "What's that?" He gestured at floor-length drapes hanging on one wall.

"There's a balcony, but the doors are locked." She hardly more than whispered it.

He went to the drapes and spread them a few inches. They concealed a pair of many-windowed doors. There was a simple latch, opened and closed by a doorknob, and a bolt operated through a keyhole. He wished he had the set of OSS lock picks he'd carried in Bavaria. But maybe . . . He could see the bolt through the crack between the doors. Deadbolt? Spring-loaded?

"What have you got that's metal and might fit between the doors?" he asked.

She took a clip from her hair, seemingly silver set with emeralds. "It's called dwarf silver," she said. "The same thing as platinum on Farside, I think. It's hard."

I'll take your word for it, he thought. All those books she'd read while married to Will . . . He wondered if she ever forgot any of it.

He carried a clasp knife. Now he forced its smaller blade between the doors, just above the bolt. Then he inserted the forked clasp of the hair clip, pressed it hard against the bolt, and pried. There was almost no room to work, but he gained a smidgen, and held it with the knife blade. Then got a new purchase with the clasp and pried again. And again. Something felt hot against his chest, but he ignored it. His nerves were stretched. He had no doubt whose room this was; Kurqôsz could walk in at any moment.

Once he lost it all, and started grimly over, but finally the bolt was clear. The two minutes it had taken seemed like five. "Push," he said. Varia pushed, and the doors opened. He sheathed his knife, then pressed the dead-bolt the rest of the way back with his thumb. It stayed. He drew the doors closed again, and closed the drapes over them.

Blowing through pursed lips, he handed Varia her

hair clip. "That's our escape route," he said, then paused, gazing at his ex-wife. On Farside still his wife. It took a moment to bring his thoughts back to the here and now. "I'll hide in the closet," he told her. "You stand outside it and tell me things I need to know. Close it if you need to."

She nodded.

The clothes hanging inside were too long to fit anyone but a voitu. Macurdy concealed himself well enough not to be seen at a glance. He'd get hot in there, dressed as he was, but it wouldn't do to take anything off. If he had to run for it . . .

"Have you got anything to wear besides that?" he asked Varia.

She looked down at herself, and shook her head. "Nothing for outside. They took my things. They're probably in the storage room down the hall."

He nodded. "We'll take some of Kurqôsz's, and shorten them so they're wearable." He paused. "How did you get here?"

She told him of her kidnapping, and that Cyncaidh was dead. She didn't tell him how; she couldn't say it yet, certainly not without breaking down.

Cyncaidh dead! The thought stopped him for a moment. *If we get out of this alive . . . Or maybe not. Maybe that's all over for her.*

She continued talking, sounding stronger now. "Kurqôsz has something important planned, for tonight or tomorrow night. He expects northern lights. Apparently they're important to his plans." She paused. "Can you feel it?"

"It?"

"There's a feeling in the Web of the World. Something ominous."

He had felt it, and blamed it on nerves. Which might be all it was, but now he didn't think so. "There are northern lights," he said. "Right now. So that means tonight."

"Probably, but not necessarily. On the Northern Sea, they often come several nights in a row."

"When do you expect him back? In here I mean?"

"It could be a minute from now, or hours. I've only been here a few days. But if tonight is the night he carries out his sorcery . . ."

Macurdy nodded grimly. If he simply waited in this closet, he'd probably be too late. "I guess you know why I'm here."

"To kill him," she said.

"Do you have any idea how I . . ." He paused, frowning. "Just a minute. Something's hot. In my shirt pocket."

He knew what it was. For months he'd transferred it whenever he'd changed clothes. His hand brought out the crystal Blue Wing had given him on the highway to Ferny Cove.

More strongly than ever, far more, it glowed in his palm.

They heard the latch; someone was opening the hallway door. Varia closed the closet and stepped away; Macurdy stuffed the crystal back in his pocket and drew his knife.

He heard her ask, "What do you want?"

Macurdy couldn't hear the answer. After a half minute of tension, he heard the door close, and Varia returned. "It was Kurqôsz's halfblood son," she murmured. "He does things for his father, who calls him Tsûlgâx; says it means 'most loyal.' In the old voitik language, from before they adopted Hithmearcisc."

Son? That's it! Macurdy thought. *That's the connection.*

"Tsûlgâx doesn't like me," she added. "His aura reflects a single talent, but I couldn't identify it. Now I think I have. He foresees danger to his father, through me."

"Good lord," Macurdy said. "He's hated me from the first time we saw each other. In Bavaria, during the war. I wondered why."

He paused, his mind staring briefly at nothing. "I need to talk to Vulkan about this," he said. "I don't see any way in hell I can for sure kill Kurqôsz soon enough. Set fire to the building—they'd probably get out. Walk down the hall, stick a knife in the rakutik door guard, then go for Kurqôsz—it might work, but it probably wouldn't, and I'd get no second chance."

He paused. "Just a minute. I'll see if Vulkan can hear me."

"No!" She almost hissed the word, her sudden intensity startling him. "Kurqôsz has his circle with him. If they're linked, and you shout psychically to Vulkan, they may pick it up."

Macurdy frowned. If Kurqôsz and his circle were cooking up some spell, he wondered if anything would distract them. Their attention should be heavily attached to whatever it was. But on the other hand, Vulkan had said he'd monitor him. If he was, and could reach him with his mind, he already would have. Unless it felt too dangerous. "Well then," Macurdy said, "I guess I need to use your balcony and go to him." He looked worriedly at her. "I hate to leave you, now that I've found you."

All she said was, "How will you get down?"

"Sweetheart," he said, "I was trained to jump from high places. And when I get back, you'll have to jump."

She thought back to her escape from the Cloister, twenty years earlier, when she'd dropped from the palisade. "Then go," she said. "I can do it."

He stepped out of the closet. The crystal had become so hot, he transferred it to a pocket in his greatcoat. Varia watched, her expression sober. Stepping to her, he drew her to him. "I love you," he told her. "I want you to know that."

"Come back if you can," she answered. "You lost Melody and Mary, and I've lost Raien. I believe now that we were meant to be together." She pushed away from him. "Go now."

He nodded without speaking, then turned and went out onto the balcony, closing the doors behind him.

The balcony had a simple vault roof, and this was the north side of the house. But he could have seen the aurora from any side; it was playing over the whole sky now. He could even hear it hissing, and wondered if the crystal made it audible to him.

The balcony railings were set into stone posts. Abruptly a powerful urge seized him. Reaching into his pocket, he took the crystal out. His movements quick but sure, he set it on a post, drew his saber, then smashed the pommel down onto the crystal with all his might.

It felt as if he'd hit a box of blasting caps, but without the sound! The saber rebounded, twisting in his hands, almost tearing from his grip. From somewhere he heard screams, whether with his ears or only in his mind, he didn't know or wonder. He dropped to his knees, and for a brief moment stared blankly, confusedly, out at the sky. The screams had stopped. He heard muffled shouts inside the building.

He knew what had happened, or thought he did. Still shaking, he got to his feet. A look around found a few small shards of the crystal on the post and deck. He brushed them together and threw them out into the snow. Then reentering the room, he went straight to the closet. From there he told Varia what had happened, then hunkered in a back corner with saber in hand. Without a word she closed the door.

A scant minute later, Kurqôsz entered the room, walked to the closet and opened the door. Varia told him he looked ill, and asked about the screaming.

He took out a thigh-length fur parka and fur-lined boots. "It is no concern of yours," he snapped, and stepped away from the closet.

There'd been too little time for Macurdy to stand and attack through the intervening clothes. And he didn't know if Tsûlgâx was in the room. That he didn't hear him meant nothing. Tsûlgâx spoke so seldom that at first, back in Bavaria, he'd assumed he was mute.

The hall door closed. A minute later Varia reopened the closet door. "They're gone," she murmured. "I was scared to death you might try to kill him. Tsûlgâx wasn't five feet away, with his saber in his hand."

Macurdy pushed his way out of the closet. His mind had moved to another possibility. "There's obviously a loft overhead," he said. "How can I get up there?"

"There's a storage room down the hall—a sort of a catchall. Kurqôsz's orderly took me there to find things I might want. It has a trapdoor in the ceiling."

"Good. The crystal I showed you was obviously a crystal of power. From a dead voitu. I smashed it on one of your balcony posts. That's what caused the screaming down the hall."

Varia frowned, puzzled.

"Kurqôsz and his circle will have another one," he went on. "Probably bigger; the one he had in Bavaria was big as an egg. I'm going to steal it, and the first chance I get, I'll smash it too. Without it they can't cook up any major sorceries, and judging from the screams, it'll lay them out."

"I don't understand," she said.

"His younger brother Chithqôsz is here, with his crystal circle. I followed them; it's how I got in. And the crystal I had . . . The dead voitu must have been one of them. And each of them would have part of his essence in it."

Her expression told him he'd thoroughly confused her. "I'll explain later," he said. "I need to move fast, before they get back. Which is the storeroom?"

Mentally she counted doors, then told him.

"Is there a candle I can take? Preferably one with a holder."

She took one from a shelf.

"Look, I'll be back in a little while. Be ready to leave."

He took her arms with his hands. "We're going to get out of here, and everything's going to be fine. But now I need you to open the door and step into the hall. Get the guard's attention so I can get out. And keep it long enough for me to get to the storeroom. I'll use a concealment spell."

She nodded soberly. Macurdy drew his belt knife, just in case. "Let's do it then," he said.

She went to the door, opened it wide, and stepped half out, clearing it for Macurdy. There was no guard at her door, but the guard down the hall fixed her with his eyes.

She sensed Curtis move out behind her, and called just loudly enough that the guard could hear. "Did His Majesty say how long he'd be gone?"

The rakutu scowled, saying nothing. She stood as if waiting for an answer, giving Macurdy time to get into the storeroom. Then she went back inside.

After closing the door quietly behind him, Macurdy lit the candle with his finger. The storeroom was long and narrow, with deep shelves on each side. He was surprised it wasn't fuller.

The trapdoor was large, and near the front of the room. A crude ladder leaned against the back wall. Snooping by candle light, the nearest thing he found to a rope was a long narrow drape, like those covering the balcony door. He put the candle on a top shelf, near the trapdoor. It occurred to him that what he had to do would be a lot easier without his coat and hauberk, so he took them off. Then he got the ladder, leaned it against the trapdoor opening, climbed a few rungs and pushed open the trapdoor. Next he put drape, coat and hauberk into the loft.

That done, he put the ladder back; leaving it under the trapdoor would invite trouble. The shelves were strongly built. Using them as a ladder, he reached sideways, got the fingers of one hand over the edge of the opening, and swung free. Then using both hands, he pulled himself up. It never occurred to him how few men, especially large men, could have done what he just had. Before he closed the trapdoor behind him, he reached out and got the candle.

The loft was a single room as long as the building, with a rough plank floor and no ceiling. Locating a joist by the nail heads in the planks, he followed it to the end, leaving tracks in the dust. A little beneath the ridge-beam was a small unglazed window with a louvered shutter, installed to ventilate the loft in summer. A ladder built onto the end wall gave access to it. Setting the candle aside, he climbed the ladder, opened the shutter, and looked out. This was the east end of the house; the other buildings were to the west. There seemed little likelihood he'd be seen, unless from the road.

He looked downward, and examined the outer wall. There was a vault-shaped roof a dozen feet beneath him, like that of the master bedroom's balcony.

The problems, as he saw them, were to get safely down onto the balcony roof, and from the roof get onto the balcony itself. And from there into Kurqôsz's office. There were other uncertainties: Was there a guard in the office who might kill him or raise an alarm? Might the rakutu outside the door hear him? Was the crystal even there? But those weren't problems. There was nothing he could do about them. Or about leaving the drape hanging down the outside of the house, like a flag shouting "something is seriously wrong here!"

Climbing back down the ladder, he got the drape. His hauberk he left where it was; it promised to be too cumbersome for things he had to do. He thought about abandoning his coat for the same reason, but kept it for appearances and its large pockets.

After tying the drape to the topmost step, he went back down the ladder and snuffed out the candle. The stub he put in a pants pocket, the candle holder in a coat pocket. Then he climbed the ladder again. Only then did he wonder if he could make it out the window. It proved by far the most difficult part of the project. First he dropped his coat onto the balcony roof. A couple of awkward, squirming, even desperate minutes later he was outside, clutching the drape, and lowering himself down the wall. His feet touched the balcony roof with a foot of drape to spare.

After putting his coat back on, he knelt and looked over the end. It scarcely overhung the balcony rail at all; a foot at most. He bellied over feetfirst. His feet found the rail and took his weight. Letting go the roof edge with one hand, he carefully reached upward and inward, finding and grasping a roof brace. Then he let go with the other hand, and hopped down onto the balcony—another remarkable feat taken for granted.

The easy part was the balcony door. He turned the handle and it opened. Inside he lit the candle and looked around the room. Bookshelves were built against the wall on both sides of the balcony door, their books gone. Now they held miscellaneous containers, loose goods, and weighted stacks of paper. Each side wall had a door. He examined the room no further, trying one of the side doors instead.

It opened into a smaller room. A slender metal tripod stood in the middle, topped with a black metal bowl, like the one he'd seen at Schloss Tannenberg. But that one had held a crystal. This one was empty. Next to it was a small stand, chest-high on Macurdy, holding a small casket of black lacquer. Macurdy unhooked its black-iron latch and lifted the lid.

There on a black velvet cushion lay the crystal, black as obsidian, reflecting the candle in his hand. It seemed alive, and he stepped involuntarily back. Like the one he'd destroyed, it was perfectly round, but much larger, the size of a goose egg.

Hesitantly Macurdy reached, then took it from the stand. The sensation jarred him. It was as if an alarm had sounded, silent but shrill. He shoved the stone deep into a coat pocket, beneath the mitten it already held, then darted from the room. There were shouts in the hall. Jerking the balcony door open, he stepped out, even as the hall door was being unlocked behind him. Vaulting over the railing, he landed without falling.

«I am with you. Hurry.»

Vulkan, there, invisible! They dashed around the corner to the north side. Varia was on the balcony. She saw Macurdy through his spell, but as she started over the railing, someone came through the curtains and pulled her back.

A third figure stepped to the railing. Kurqôsz! His glance took in Vulkan's massive bulk, but it was Macurdy he stared at. For a long two seconds their gazes locked, then Kurqôsz turned away, bellowing orders in Hith-mearcisc.

«On my back!» Vulkan's thought hissed in Macurdy's mind. He vaulted aboard him, and they fled eastward toward the forest, the boar sprinting faster than he'd ever carried Macurdy before.

Overhead, the aurora shimmered and pulsed unnoticed.

Their flight was not mindless however. Vulkan's course angled to the road, where the new snow had been heavily tracked by Chithqôsz and his escort. Within the forest edge, Vulkan stopped, and they looked back. Two figures were trotting to a point beneath Varia's balcony, where they stood as if studying the ground. Looking at tracks, Macurdy told himself.

Vulkan started down the road again at a brisk trot. Macurdy put a hand in his coat pocket. The crystal was noticeably warm. It hadn't been when he took it.

"Where are we going?" he asked.

«Hopefully where you can destroy the crystal. You will have to tell me.»

"What about Varia?"

«Your suicide will not benefit her.»

Macurdy's fingertips felt the crystal's glassy surface. Put it on a rock, he told himself, and hit it with another. But he hadn't seen a stone pile or boulder since the day before. Though he didn't know it, the locale was part of a postglacial lacustrine plain. The only stones were those brought in for construction.

"How much did you see or hear while I was inside there?" he asked.

«Much of it.»

"I suppose taking the crystal caused the alarm."

«Correct.»

And the crystal contained some of Kurqôsz's essence—his and all his circle's, woven together by who knew what spells. With Chithqôsz and his circle tied in. Macurdy was glad now for the hours spent in the Cloister library.

"When Kurqôsz left earlier, where did he go? Or didn't he?"

«He left the house with his circle. They went to the center of the clearing, where a pyre had been piled, and lit it. Perhaps you saw it.» Macurdy shook his head. «Then they sensed something amiss at the manor, and abandoned whatever they'd started to do.»

Macurdy put a hand in his jacket pocket. The crystal was distinctly warmer. "They're gaining on us," he said.

«Seemingly.» Vulkan speeded his trot a bit.

Before long they saw a solitary horse ahead, coming toward them with a hithik rider. A courier, apparently. "Stop," Macurdy murmured. "I'm going to steal a horse."

Vulkan stepped off the road and stopped. Macurdy slid from his back, willed his own cloak off, and stood waiting, a powerful figure dressed as a rakutu, with a hand raised in command. The horseman stopped, and Macurdy walked up to him. "Get down," he said roughly in Hithmearcisc. Hoping the order was too brief for his accent to be conspicuous.

With a worried expression, the soldier dismounted, letting the reins hang so the horse would stand. Macurdy stepped up to him and peered intently into his face. Then, as if to see the courier's features more clearly, he removed the man's thick winter cap—and slammed him hard between the eyes with the heel of his hand. The hithu dropped like a stone.

Macurdy turned to Vulkan. "I'm going to load him over your back. Can you keep him on board?"

«Hardly. I can carry him with my tusks, but neither fast nor far. And if he regains consciousness, I'll be unable to kill him. Killing an ensouled being is an act not available to me.»

Macurdy didn't hesitate. His thumb found the man's carotid, and he compressed it with force enough to crack walnuts. After half a minute he released it, and loaded the slack figure across the horse's withers. Then he swung into the saddle, and after recalling his cloak, he and Vulkan continued eastward side by side. A check found the crystal warmer than before. Kurqôsz, Macurdy decided, could run even faster than he'd thought.

Not far ahead they came to a lesser road that crossed Road B. On its surface, not a single track marred the morning's snow. Macurdy stopped. "I suppose," he said, "they can sense the crystal, and that's what they're following."

«I do not doubt it.»

"You turn south. They'll see your tracks, and probably follow them. I'll keep going east a little way, then circle north through the woods and head back to the farm. Where there are nice rock walls."

Vulkan answered by turning south and trotting briskly away through the virgin snow. For Vulkan's information, Macurdy continued his monolog mentally as he continued down the heavily tracked Road B. *When they realize they're on a false trail, it should take them awhile to sort things out, and I should be able to keep ahead of them. When I get to the headquarters clearing, I'll head for the woodpile and grab a splitting maul or single bit. Lay the crystal against a stone wall, and smack the sonofabitch.*

Then I'll get Varia out of there.

He didn't wonder how. A hundred or so yards farther east, he took advantage of a windthrown hemlock whose top reached the edge of the road. There he turned his horse northward into the woods, walking it along the very edge of the fallen treetop. If Kurqôsz got that far, he was unlikely to see the tracks.

When he'd passed the hemlock's uprooted base, he continued northward a ways, then turned back toward the clearing. He reached the virgin snow of the lesser road where a sleigh trail entered it from the west.

He took it.

With the help of motion sickness pills, Kurqôsz had learned to ride horses. Learned well enough to stay in the saddle at a gallop. Riding wasn't pleasant for him, nor were the pills, but it allowed him greater middle-distance speed than he had on foot.

Tsûlgâx rode ahead a hundred yards, and another rakutu behind. They were all the escort Kurqôsz had on this mad ride. The loss of his crystal had shaken him deeply, and he would not wait for a platoon to be called out and mounted.

It was Tsûlgâx who saw the tracks of cloven hooves turn south on the lesser road. He stopped, and when Kurqôsz got there, pointed them out. All three turned south then, following them.

Kurqôsz was queasy from the ride, and his senses somewhat dulled from the pills. If they didn't catch up soon, he thought, he'd get down and run awhile. They'd gone nearly half a mile before he realized something was wrong, and called a halt. Tsûlgâx rode back to him, his expression concerned.

"Are you all right?" he asked.

"We should not have turned. He must have thrown the crystal away, or hidden it. Near the crossroad. We are getting farther away from it."

He turned his horse then, and started back north, riding hard. *The crystal!* he told himself. *Follow the crystal! The thief, the tracks, are secondary.*

Macurdy had ridden half a mile up the sleigh trail, when he came to a three-sided woodsmen's shelter. In front of it lay a snow-capped heap of firewood blocks, with a splitting maul standing upright beside it. He stopped, and getting from his horse, stepped into the shelter. Inside was a split-log bench. A heavy steel splitting wedge lay on it, and he picked it up. It could almost have been made in Indiana; it had the familiar deep grooves on its slanting faces.

He knew at once what to do. Stepping outside, he lay the wedge on the battered maple chopping block, then reached into his pocket. The crystal was almost too hot to handle! Alarmed, he laid it hurriedly on a groove of the wedge, then reaching, took the maul and hefted it. Eyeing the crystal, he swung hard, overhead and down.

The heavy steel head slammed the crystal—and a shocking pain stabbed through Macurdy's skull! At the same instant he heard a terrible cry perhaps a hundred yards away. Dropping the maul, he staggered to the horse and pulled himself into the saddle. Then he kicked the animal into a canter, and lying low on its back, fled westward through the trees, toward the clearing.

❖   ❖   ❖

Kurqôsz lay shuddering and puking in the snow, with
Tsûlgâx and the other rakutu kneeling beside him. The
blow that had struck the crystal had hammered Kurqôsz
much harder than it had Macurdy, whose bonding with
it had been brief and superficial. After a couple of minutes, the crown prince raised an arm for help, and
Tsûlgâx hoisted him to his feet.

"He tried to destroy it," Kurqôsz croaked, "but it's
still here somewhere. Unbroken. Help me."

With Tsûlgâx supporting him, he hobbled on, the
other rakutu bringing the horses. A minute later they
saw Macurdy's tracks, and in another the shelter and
woodpile. They went to it, Kurqôsz scanning around
with his mind for the crystal. It took awhile to find it.
Instead of smashing it, the force of the hammer stroke
had sent it flying twenty yards, where it lay buried in
snow.

When he had it in his mittened hand, Kurqôsz raised
it to his forehead, closed his eyes and concentrated.
In his mind he saw a rakutu—no, a human or half-ylf
dressed as a rakutu. Saw the face from the crystal's point
of view. A face he remembered from the hive mind
scene, of raiders murdering the headquarters staff at
Colroi. And from somewhere earlier. He watched the
attempt to destroy the crystal, saw the hammer raised
and swung. And that was all. As if the sentience in the
crystal had blacked out.

He realized now what had happened to Chithqôsz
and his circle—those who'd survived the flood. This
same creature had somehow gotten Chithqôsz's old
crystal, and destroyed it. Crystals of power formed to
resonate with the circle leader, and his younger brother
wasn't hard like himself.

Turning, he gripped Tsûlgâx's shoulder. "I have seen
his face," he told him. "And I will remember. I will
hear him scream curses at the parents who gave him
life. He will beg me to kill him."

The second rakutu held out Kurqôsz's reins, but the crown prince declined. "I will run," he said.

Haltingly he started in Macurdy's tracks, while the rakutur mounted and followed. As he ran, he strengthened, his head clearing. He would, he told himself, have his revenge, but not tonight. First he would win the war, and he needed all his attention, all his strength, to control the forces he would use. His circle too would need to be clear-headed and strong.

So. Tomorrow night then. Tomorrow night he would win the war. The aurora would still be there for him; he sensed it with certainty. Slowing, he looked up. Through the leafless crowns of hardwood forest, he saw it flickering and pulsing. Victory and devastation would be the ultimate vengeance. He'd devastated the east with fire and steel. The energy storm he'd create tomorrow night would roll westward with far greater devastation. Where he willed, as far as he willed. Tomorrow night vast tongues of flame would lick the enemy army from the face of the earth, leaving not even bones!

Kurqôsz did not follow his enemy's tracks. He pressed forward toward the farm. That was where the creature was going, he had no doubt. Going to collect the ylvin lord's widow. A half minute more and he'd have taken her earlier; she'd have been over the balcony railing and gone.

At the manor, Kurqôsz posted guards inside every entrance, every ground-floor window. After working a spell, and showing them through the crystal what to watch for: a giant boar, and the face from the raid on Colroi. Kurqôsz was familiar with cloaking spells. Being warned, and knowing what to watch for, was half the task of seeing through them.

When Tsûlgâx was shown the face, he said a single word, a name: "Montag!"

Kurqôsz knew at once that Tsûlgâx was right. *Kurt Montag, the German half-wit!* But clearly no half-wit after all.

And Montag had been inside this house, inside his bedroom. Worse, inside his sanctum! Kurqôsz hadn't been aware of the drape hanging from the loft vent till he'd returned with the crystal. Things became clear then; Montag had bypassed the door guard by using the loft. Ingenious! Daring! What kind of man could even contemplate the act, let alone carry it off?

Before he put him to the torments, he decided, he'd sit down with him, question him. There were things to be learned from him, and at any rate the man would be interesting.

The realizations, along with his run in the forest, had fired Kurqôsz with a kind of manic exhilaration, though without canceling his wits. Back in the manor, he order the woman called Varia locked up with the other ylvin women. She was dangerous. He would still beget sons on her—this evening had added to his respect—but he would not have her as a lover.

Having had two long runs in the snow, Kurqôsz expected that when he went to bed, he'd fall quickly asleep. He was mistaken. There were things on his mind, demanding attention. Back in Bavaria, Tsûlgâx had said that Montag was dangerous, and should be killed. Tsûlgâx, with no access to the hive mind, and no apparent psychic talent. Only his hard, highly trained body and unbendable loyalty. But his concern over Montag had seemed ridiculous. *Perhaps,* Kurqôsz thought, *he has a talent that I do not: sensing future dangers. He warned me about the ylvin she-wolf as well.*

Tsûlgâx. What kind of father had he been to him? By hindsight, better than he'd realized, it seemed to him. He'd been kind, and not overly demanding.

He looked back then at Kurt Montag in Bavaria. Had there been signs he should have seen? That should have warned him? None came to him. He focused on the man as first he'd seen him: earnest, stupid, and lame. He'd even felt a certain fondness for the creature. Montag, whose psychic talents were strong only by comparison with the other Germans at the Schloss.

Unexpectedly, his concentration on Montag's face clicked in another picture from the hive mind, one Kurqôsz hadn't seen before: Montag wearing a peculiar uniform—baggy, and with many pockets. In Hithmearc, speaking to a guard corporal at the gate shelter! Montag, intelligent and self-assured, standing straight, and for a human, tall. *This* was the man in the raid at Colroi! No wonder he hadn't recognized him at first.

The corporal's trace in the hive mind ended with his shaking hands with Montag, and at the same moment a shocking pain in the abdomen. And unconsciousness. Kurqôsz scanned ahead. On that same day, the gate lodge had burned to the ground, killing all but one of the guards and hostel staff. Days later the gate itself had collapsed, seemingly destroyed, stranding Greszak and his staff on Farside. Too much had happened, in too short a time, and the corporal's trace had not been investigated. The assumption had been, the man had died in the fire with the others.

Montag! The human was more than intriguing. He was sinister! And how had he come to Vismearc? Perhaps Tsûlgâx was mistaken. Perhaps this man simply resembled Montag. But no, for that had surely been Montag in the uniform of many pockets. For it not to be him would require nearly impossible coincidences— a Montag in Bavaria, a lookalike in Hithmearc, and another here. No, all three were one man. Kurt Montag.

The crown prince swung his long legs out of bed, wrapped himself in his robe, and had the officer of the guard called. And Tsûlgâx. When they reached his room, he gave them only one order: "Montag must be taken alive! At whatever cost! Alive and sound! I have questions to ask him, and he must be able to answer. If anyone kills or sorely wounds him, except on my order, that person will replace him in the torments."

Macurdy was captured in the hour before dawn, but when Kurqôsz learned of it, he decided his prisoner could wait. He'd awakened with his attention on the coming night, and the sorcery he would work. It must have priority, even above Montag.

It was Tsûlgâx who reported the capture, and asked to be allowed to kill the German. His master's refusal so upset the rakutu, Kurqôsz feared his son's protectiveness might overcome his obedience. So within the hour, Kurqôsz sent Tsûlgâx off to Camp Merrawin, carrying a written order. He was to take command of the rakutur there—a "promotion" that did not fool Tsûlgâx. Nor did Kurqôsz suppose it would. But it enforced his restriction without the odor of punishment.

He'd always been a loving parent.

As soon as he'd sent Tsûlgâx off, Kurqôsz rousted his circle from their beds and ordered them out to run. "It will clear your heads!" he told them. Then he shook Chithqôsz awake, and ordered him to roust out his circle, sick and feeble from the destruction of their old stone. Kurqôsz himself led them all on a long walk, west out of the clearing, accompanied by two companies of rakutur.

The sorcerers finished with an easy, two-mile lope, by which time even Chithqôsz's circle was beginning to look functional. *I'll let them eat now,* Kurqôsz told himself, *then lead them in drills to renew their focus.*

❖   ❖   ❖

A few days earlier, he'd sent his third crystal circle to the forward lines at Deep River, to create an umbrella against the storm he planned. It was Chithqôsz's circle which would help "tap the aurora." (Actually tap the solar wind responsible for it.) Now he went over his plan with them.

It was midafternoon before he had the prisoner brought to him—hands manacled behind his back, for Kurqôsz recalled Montag's talent at casting small fireballs. His only other restraint was a rakutu standing behind him, ready to act.

But Montag had little to say, so Kurqôsz had him taken to the lesser of the two rooms flanking his office, where he was blindfolded, gagged, and bound to a chair. A heavy chair, bolted to the floor; he would answer questions later. The crown prince preferred to separate questioning and torture, but either way, he would have his information.

In his small prison, Macurdy was in the watchful care of a rakutu. At supper time the rakutu removed his prisoner's gag, and fed him—a cup of lentil soup, a small corn pancake, and water. Then he gagged him again. Macurdy was in blackness, for night had fallen, and the room's single candle and the snowlight through the window were too weak to filter through his blindfold.

He felt an impulse to meditate, something he'd seldom done since Varia had been stolen from him more than twenty years earlier. Being bound and gagged was not conducive to meditation, but he rationalized the impulse, telling himself it was something he could work at, to pass the time. It went surprisingly well. After a bit he reached a slow alpha stage, which was as far as he usually got. Thoughts, images, fragments of memories drifted through without taking root or lodging. Gradually even they ceased, and

his sense of time shut off almost entirely, though awareness remained.

After an indeterminate period, a drum began to beat.
In the next room. A small drum tapped with the fingertips in an intricate sound pattern; he could feel it
more than hear it. Kurqôsz, he realized. It was unlike
Arbel's drumming, which produced a reverie for healing. This . . . this sought to lure . . . not him, but something.

And now he sensed the crystal; it caught and held
his consciousness. The quality of blackness changed.
It was no longer an absence of light, but blackness as
a presence. He sensed the mind and will of Kurqôsz,
the synergistic minds and wills of his circle. And he
himself was with them, though not of them. An observer unobserved, for they were intent on their procedure.

The state was transitory. Abruptly he was outside
the room, in a night without stars, moon, or aurora.
There was no land, no trees . . . but gradually there
was light—a dirty magmic red that thickened, became
a vast, pulsing, plasmic energy.

Energy with a primitive but powerful sense of its
own existence, neither obedient nor resistive, but aware,
responsive. Responsive to the minds that acting as one,
ruled by one, enticed, molded, manipulated. The energy
plasma changed, its embryonic awareness unfolding and
growing. He felt Kurqôsz's intention flowing into it,
infusing it with something like intelligence . . . and
purpose!

From deep within/outside Macurdy, his essence
spoke. *Powerful! Must not happen, must not continue
to completion! Disrupt it! Disperse it!* An energy swelled
within him—a higher vibration, almost beyond bearing, more intense than the most powerful orgasm. His
follicles clenched, erecting his hair; he writhed and
thrashed on his chair. And with the energy came

intention surpassing anything he'd imagined, pure intention straining for release. *Now!* he thought. *Now!* It burst from the pit of his stomach—and the universe exploded. Minds screamed, their agony searing him. His own screamed with them—but in blind exultation, not agony.

38

Reverberations

Macurdy awoke with a groan. It was still night, but now he was on the ground. A fire was burning, tended by a woman. She turned and looked at him.

"You're awake!" Varia said. "How do you feel?"

He was covered with a blanket. With an effort he sat up, leaning on an arm. It seemed as much as he could manage. His head ached badly, and he was nauseous. "Not good," he answered. Then lurched to one side, vomiting thinly onto the dirt, a slime of gastric juices that burned his throat.

After a long minute he sat up and looked around. He was in a crude, three-sided woodsmen's shelter, like the one where he'd tried to destroy the crystal. His manacles were still on his wrists, but the chain connecting them had been cut.

"It's gotten warm," he said.

"Warm enough that the new snow is melting on the brush," Varia answered, then pointed upward. "Look at the sky."

Laboriously he got to his feet and stepped outside. With the branches bare, and the woods thinned by cutting, he had a fair view upward. The aurora was hidden by heavy, roiling clouds that pulsed with reddish light. It shocked him half alert, and he spoke in a near whisper.

"Where's Vulkan?"

«Here.»

Macurdy turned. Vulkan lay a few yards away. "What happened?"

«You will remember, when it's time. Suffice it to say, you aborted the crown prince's sorcery, and ended the voitik threat.»

Macurdy frowned vaguely. *Aborted? Ended the threat?* "How did we get here?"

«I will leave that for Varia to relate. It was she who handled most of it.»

"I was in the women's room," she said. "One large room. We had no idea what was going on, only that things had gotten strange. We could smell it. And it felt . . . as if something was wrong with the Web of the World, as if it was choked with something bad. Sorcerous." She looked at the sky. "It still does, but not so strongly.

"Then something hit like an earthquake. It didn't shake the building—nothing fell off the table or shelves—but we all felt it. I'd been standing, and it knocked me off my feet. After a minute there were shouts. Cries is the word. We didn't know what to think. We just sat there stunned, waiting for whatever would happen next. Pretty soon we heard people calling back and forth outside, in Hithmearcisc. I snuffed the lamp and opened the window drapes a little. Soldiers, including rakutur, were leading horses out of the stables, and riding away. Not in ranks, just leaving. As if fleeing.

"One of the other women tried the door then, but it was locked. I told her to stop rattling it. With discipline gone, as it seemed to be, I didn't want anyone reminded of us.

"The windows were latched too, so after things had quieted outside and I couldn't see anyone, I used a short bench as a battering ram, and knocked one of them open. Then I climbed out and dropped from the window sill. And found Vulkan waiting. He lowered his cloak for a moment when I got up. You can't imagine how glad I was to see him."

Vulkan interrupted. «I recommend you continue your account while we travel. The clouds portend a storm of worse than snow.»

Gathering himself, Macurdy followed them. Three horses were tethered to saplings behind the shelter. Two wore riding saddles, the other a loaded pack saddle. All wore nosebags, and were munching corn. He and Varia mounted, and the three of them left at an easy pace. Macurdy's headache made him reluctant to trot his horse.

They were on Road B before Varia continued the narrative she'd begun. "After I dropped out the window," she said, "Vulkan and I went in the front entrance together. Reception was full of corpses—voitar and a rakutu. No humans. Their faces were distorted; they looked terrible. Then I went upstairs, Vulkan with me. He told me where you were." She half grinned at Macurdy, riding beside her. "He broke down the door to Kurqôsz's office. Kurqôsz and his circle were in a side room, dead. They looked even worse than the voitar in reception. Their faces were more than distorted; they were dark and swollen, as if their blood vessels had ruptured. Their bodies looked boneless.

"Then Vulkan broke down the door to another side room, and there you were, with a dead rakutu. I almost died myself, before I saw your aura and realized you were alive."

Her expression changed. "You were the only one, you and the ylvin women. Everyone else had either died or left. The other women helped me get you over a horse. Then they headed west, toward ylvin lines."

Macurdy nodded slowly. "The dead rakutu must have shared in the hive mind. Did you find Tsûlgâx?"

"No. Apparently he left with the others."

Macurdy grunted. He couldn't imagine Tsûlgâx abandoning Kurqôsz's body.

A few hours earlier, not many miles south of the clearing, an entire cohort of Kullvordi rode through forest.

General Jeremid had been unwilling to assume that the voitik command center was unassailable. Even if the place really did have sorcerous defenses, it seemed to him it might be susceptible to surprise attack—a swift strike followed by an equally swift disappearance. So he'd left with his cohort, riding cross-country through the forest, planning to scout the place. Unless he found reason not to, he'd hit it. Raise all the hell he could, then run. Or if things went right . . . Who knew?

Again the sky was weird and beautiful with northern lights, a rare sight for Rude Landers. Two nights in a row now, he thought, and wondered what it meant.

Then something changed. The night took on a deeply ominous air. Evil, dangerous. Jeremid ordered a halt, and sent his bird to scout the place again. While he waited, he took his mittens off and shoved them in his pockets, then raised his earflaps. When the bird returned, it reported that everything in the clearing— everything but the sky—*looked* the same, but *felt* very very bad. In the vicinity, the northern lights had disappeared, hidden by thick serpents of cloud, writhing and twining in the sky. Like nothing he'd seen before, even in his species' hive mind.

"Sorcery is in use," the bird finished. "Big sorcery." Its voice was subdued. Ordinarily the great raven was self-assured, even haughty. Now it sat huddled and ruffled on a packhorse, utterly demoralized.

Jeremid ordered his men to make camp. Then,

leaving Colonel Tarlok in charge, he called a young officer to him, a young hillsman known as a daredevil. Like Jeremid when he'd been young. "Bring the best squad in your platoon," Jeremid told him. "You and I are going to examine the place ourselves."

They'd hardly left before something else happened. Nothing they could see or hear, but something *happened*. Jeremid felt it, and the others did too; he saw it in their eyes. But they rode on.

At the clearing's edge they stopped. There was no undergrowth there—cattle had grazed the bordering woods for decades—but night and the trees hid the patrol. The sky had stopped writhing. Now it brooded, flickered, pulsed, its clouds slowly roiling. They seemed too dense, too heavy to stay aloft. In the distance, soldiers emerged from the house, then from the stable, mounted their horses and left hurriedly. Neither in ranks nor singly, but in clusters, riding east on Road B.

Then nothing more. Jeremid had the patrol dismount, and they continued to wait. They saw no one else. After a while the lieutenant suggested he be allowed to ride in and see what he could find. Jeremid shook his head without looking at him. His gaze was intent, his senses acutely attuned to the scene in front of them. "We wait," he said. "Something's going to happen."

The air remained heavy with energy, and a towering, breath-suppressing sense of threat. But for a long hour, perhaps two, nothing happened, except that the sense of threat thickened. They watched mesmerized, almost unable to move.

Suddenly lightnings erupted from the clouds, monstrous blinding lightnings whose overlapping crashes drove the Kullvordi to their knees. The discharges continued for perhaps a minute, then subsided into spasmodic cracklings, and ceased. The air smelled strongly of ozone.

When Jeremid's vision recovered and he could think

again, the opening held no building at all. Not one. There weren't even rubble piles. Whatever was left, if anything was, was scattered.

Slowly he got to his feet. Their horses had fled. "Lieutenant," he said quietly, "it's time to walk." Then they started back westward to the cohort. It seemed to Jeremid the war was over, though how it had happened, he had no idea. Except that sorcery had been behind it.

Well before they'd walked the three miles back to the cohort, the sky had cleared. High in the ionosphere, the aurora still danced its stately dance.

As Macurdy, Vulkan and Varia traveled east on B, they heard great thunders to the west, brief but intense. Then the sense of threat dissipated, and in a surprisingly short time the sky was reclaimed by the aurora. Macurdy's headache died, and his mental processes regained their sharpness.

Before dawn they encountered scouts of an east ylvin guerrilla force. Their sergeant directed them to his captain. Over the weeks, the captain's command had accumulated heavy losses, and its two companies were down to eighty men. Two hours earlier they'd come upon an invader supply train, abandoned. Only its voitik commander remained with it, dead but apparently unwounded, his face a grotesque and blotchy grimace.

The ylf had no idea what might have happened. He only knew that he, his men and their horses, had been overdue for a rest. After selecting sixteen sleighs of food and fodder, he'd set fire to the rest, and was taking his loot to an old woods road he knew of. Macurdy and his companions were welcome to share.

Meanwhile his great raven notified Blue Wing where Macurdy could be found.

The woods road took them to an old forest burn, where there was lots of dense young growth for cover, and deadwood for fuel. There the ylver began erecting more effective shelters than they had previously. Sentries were posted, and a mounted patrol sent out. It was time, their captain said, to catch up on some serious eating and sleeping, but not to go slack on security.

The guerrillas were as impressed with Varia as with Vulkan. She was not only beautiful. She wore the rich fur robe and other expensive travel clothes that Quaie had provided. She'd gotten them from the storeroom before she left the manor house.

The captain gave his guests the best lodging available—an old hay shed, in a grove of young white pine just outside the burn. It had enough roof left, that inside, most of the dirt floor was bare of snow. It held no hay, but the captain had captured hay delivered for bedding.

By that time it was daylight. Over a hot bed of coals, Macurdy and Varia toasted hithik bread, spread it with captured hithik lard, and ate it with fresh, half-roasted hithik horse meat. Vulkan and Blue Wing preferred their meat raw. When they'd finished, Macurdy put chunks of pine stump on the fire, and watched flames begin to lick over them. He felt spent, used up, and almost fell asleep, but got to his feet instead. He still had things to do before he let go.

He went to the captain and was about to borrow his bird, when Blue Wing arrived. Through the great raven network, Macurdy made known to the entire army that Kurqôsz was dead of his own sorcery, along with some, perhaps many, of his voitar. The hithar, and apparently most of the rakutur, were still alive. Then he gave orders that went far beyond his authority, knowing they'd be accepted. Units were to probe the enemy positions on Deep River and in the Merrawin Valley, and let the ylvin high command know what they found.

As soon as he'd finished, Jeremid informed him that

Kurqôsz's command base had been demolished by great lightnings. The report made Macurdy's skin crawl. It occurred to him that the violent, sorcery-powered death of Kurqôsz and his crystal circle might have exploded with deadly force through the entire voitik hive mind, perhaps even in Hithmearc.

He returned to the hay barn, where he, Varia and Vulkan lay down on captured hay, covered with captured blankets. Macurdy gazed at the fire, then looked away. They weren't as mesmerizing by daylight as at night, but he wasn't ready to sleep quite yet.

"Vulkan," he said, "you told me *I'd* aborted Kurqôsz's sorcery. So I suppose that in a way I killed all those voitar. How in hell did I do that? I don't remember doing *anything*."

«Ah, but I *do* remember. I was with you, in a manner of speaking, monitoring your mind. I did not, and do not understand what was going on at all times, and eventually, sensing the approaching climax, I withdrew to avoid sensory overload. But I know enough.

«And you will remember when you're ready. Which I suspect will be while reviewing this life, after you've died.

«What you did was somewhat equivalent to lightning striking an electrical transformer. While the most powerful circle of sorcerers in the world was plugged into it.»

Electrical transformer? Macurdy was always struck by Vulkan's occasional allusions to things in modern Farside, but this took the cake.

Vulkan went on. «Kurqôsz and his crystal circle had gathered and were undertaking to manipulate forces of enormous power. And his control was still somewhat precarious. Your intervention disrupted the process, and the result was instantaneous.

«That at least is how it seems to me. As I said, when the time comes, you will know quite exactly.»

He paused. «And that is all I have to say—or *will* have to say—on the matter.»

Macurdy went to sleep contemplating it all, and never woke up till late at night. Stepping outside to relieve himself, he found the aurora dying in the eastern sky.

By midday, more news had spread via the raven network: everywhere contact had been made, all the voitar were dead. Without exception. The hithar were utterly demoralized. The only clashes had been with small groups of rakutur, disorganized, but still deadly. And reckless now.

39

Wrapping Up the War

In Yuulith, all but two of the voitar had died on that night of miscarried sorcery, and within fifteen days, all hithik forces had surrendered without fighting. The last was the most distant, the garrison at Balralligh. It surrendered to two short companies of east ylvin guerrillas, augmented by a remnant of Cyncaidh's ylver, included Ceonigh, his lordship's elder son. Having lost their bird, and unable to locate their cohort, they had joined the easterners.

Initially the rakutur had been more devastated by the loss of their masters than the hithar had. But on the night of the cataclysm, three companies on anti-raider patrol had retained discipline and organization. Over the next two days they'd found and attached most of the rakutur who'd fled Kurqôsz's headquarters.

Then they'd gone looking for trouble, more to die fighting than to win. And die they had, partly because of unit coordination by the great raven network. Over the next six days, the rakutur hunted raiders while the raiders dodged them, till enough raider forces had gathered. Then the short east ylvin force Macurdy had met, volunteered as bait, and the combined forces trapped the rakutur in the same large clearing where their crown prince had died.

The Ozians and Kormehri felt they hadn't gotten their proper share of fighting. So Macurdy assigned them to attack from the nearer forest margin. When they'd engaged and held the rakutur, the Tigers and Kullvordi charged from the farther margin, taking the enemy in the rear. Two green companies of west ylvin cavalry were posted to kill any who tried to escape. None did. However, the west ylver did bag some who got separated from the melee.

Despite near-zero temperatures, Macurdy's Tigers fought with hauberks uncovered, to avoid being confused with the enemy. The fighting was as desperate as any he'd experienced. He was glad he'd recovered his dwarf-made armor and weapons.

Small detachments of rakutur, totaling perhaps forty, had been assigned as guards for senior voitik officers on the Deep River Line. After the cataclysm, they crossed the ice and attacked ylvin positions. Their goal too was to die fighting, and they did.

Similar small bands from Camp Merrawin were hunted down and killed by east ylvin guerrillas. A small rakutik detachment had been sent to Colroi after Macurdy's successful raid, and they stayed put. Then the small combined force of east ylvin guerrillas and Cyncaidh's orphans reached there on their way to Balralligh. Badly outnumbered, those rakutur too attacked and died.

Emperor Morguil insisted the Congress of Decision be held at Colroi, his capital. Duinarog's Lord Gaerimor deferred to Morguil's wishes. Serving as

Gavriel's legate, Gaerimor had full authority to act in his name.

Most of the Rude Lands forces started home. However, from almost every kingdom that took part in the fighting, Macurdy took two short companies to Colroi. Short because of casualties. He also took both cohorts of his Tigers. All together, they would help Morguil and Naerrasil remember who had bled the enemy so badly.

They and the dwarves, for Aldrik Egilsson Strongarm also took two short companies, riding on sleighs that carried the army's hay supply.

Macurdy suspected that Camp Merrawin could house more troops than Colroi could. But he went along with Morguil's wishes, so long as the raiders were housed under roofs. They had, he said, spent too many nights freezing under canvas or the stars. Strongarm had also insisted on roofs for his people. "We didn't come here to be treated as poor cousins," he told Morguil. "And we killed far more of the boogers than yer army did."

Strongarm's strong right arm was without a hand since the Battle of the Merrawin Plain, while Morguil, who had no military skills, hadn't fought. So concealing his displeasure as best he could, Morguil deferred to the dwarf. Telling himself if he didn't, the dwarves would not attend the congress, and they'd hold it against him forever.

Lord Naerrasil deeply resented Strongarm's implied criticism, and with some justification. His east ylvin army had fought desperately at Balralligh and Colroi, and under terrible circumstances. He'd lost more men than all his allies together, though mostly by execution after they'd surrendered. But because of his defeats, and his contempt for the Lion's raider strategy, his reputation had suffered. Anything he said would be discredited.

❖   ❖   ❖

The disarmed hithar, under their own officers, were marched east to Colroi, herded by the remains of the Imperial East Ylvin Army, and units of the west ylver. Rations were short, and it was the prisoners who marched hungry. But there was little muttering in the hithik ranks; the voitusotar had long since taught them subservience. Eventually, to the compliant, they'd allowed privileges, but any hint of unrest had been punished with quick and ruthless cruelty.

At Colroi, Macurdy and Varia were given a room with an actual stove. Each had anticipated a period of adjustment, of getting used to each other. But the process proved painless. And Varia wore her hair in twin ponytails, as she had in Indiana.

The Congress of Decision was a lot smaller than Macurdy had expected. It consisted of Morguil and his advisors; Lord Gaerimor acting for Gavriel, with the general of the west ylvin forces as his aide; Macurdy acting for the Rude Lands and the Sisterhood, with Vulkan and Lady Cyncaidh as his advisors; and Aldrik Egilsson Strongarm acting for Finn Greatsword. Two hithar, High Admiral Vellinghuus and General Horst, were brought from Balralligh to answer questions.

As far as Macurdy was concerned, the principal issue was what to do with some sixty thousand hithik prisoners of war.

On the first morning, the status of allied and hithik military forces was reviewed. And Vulkan described the nature of Kurqôsz's final sorcery, an awesome assembling, molding and energizing of powerful elementals. Without saying how, he stated flatly that it had been Macurdy who'd caused its cataclysmic collapse, and by that one act had won the war.

❖   ❖   ❖

Subsequent discussions would be colored by the fact that two voitar in Balralligh had briefly survived the shocking event at the crown prince's headquarters. Both had died within two days, without emerging from their comas. But as far as was known, all the voitar at the crown prince's headquarters, Deep River, Camp Merrawin, and even Colroi had died instantly.

Macurdy and the ylver had assumed that the voitik hive mind was unaffected by distance. The two brief survivals seemed to contradict that. Admiral Vellinghuus volunteered that during the voyage, the voitar on his flagship had lost touch with their kinsmen in Hithmearc well before they'd completed the crossing. So clearly the attachment weakened with distance.

Even if only two at Balralligh had survived, for less than two days, and comatose, how many might have survived in Hithmearc, more than five thousand miles away? All of them? Most of them? Balralligh was less than four hundred miles from the event.

To begin with, it seemed irrelevant to the question of what should be done with the hithik prisoners. Morguil demanded reparations and vengeance for the terrible massacres, atrocities and destruction committed in his empire. Lord Gaerimor got Morguil's agreement to consider reparations and vengeance separately, starting with reparations.

Not only the Eastern Empire wanted reparations. Every Rude Lands kingdom that had sent troops wanted restitution for the expense, and something on the side.

But where would it come from? Certainly not from distant Hithmearc. The only voitik "wealth" at hand were (1) military equipment and supplies; (2) the ships of the voitik armada; and (3) the hithik prisoners of war. The value of military goods was of two sorts: their military value, and their value by conversion to civilian use. The main value of the ships was as merchantmen, but there were far more of them than all of Yuulith had use for.

The prisoners were of value primarily for labor.

Initially Morguil insisted that the disposition of hithik prisoners was the privilege of the Eastern Empire. They should, he said, be slaves. Perhaps half or a third could be set to work rebuilding his empire. The surplus would be auctioned to whoever cared to bid, to help finance that rebuilding. Selected ships would be taken over by the Eastern Empire as warships. The rest would be offered for sale. Voitik military equipment—that which couldn't be readily converted to civilian use—would be sold by the Eastern Empire as weapons, or melted down for other uses.

Strongarm objected instantly to the latter. It would swamp the market for metals—the heart of dwarven economy. Macurdy pointed out that so much weaponry could stimulate wars, an argument that brought strong agreement from Lord Gaerimor and, privately, from some of Morguil's staff. Macurdy then cited the Farside example of the American military in the Pacific Theater, where at the end of World War II, large amounts of ordnance had been dumped in the South China Sea, as being surplus to foreseeable needs, and expensive to transport and store.

Gaerimor argued against slavery. Use prisoners of war freely as forced labor, he said, but don't sell them. Both empires had enslaved conquered humans in the early days, and had still not fully recovered from the evil effects. "Let us not revive the practice," he finished. "If we do, it will be over my firm objections. And I promise you without reservation that Gavriel will agree with me on the matter."

Lord Naerrasil had kept out of the discussion till then. Now he spoke, caustically. "And what do you propose we do with the surplus? Execute them? Is that what you'd prefer? We can't afford to feed them." His voice dripped sarcasm. "Or perhaps the rest of you will send annual shipments of grain and cattle to feed them with."

Macurdy replied at once. His voice was matter of fact, but his blunt words were as undiplomatic at Naerrasil's, and more insulting. "Lord Naerrasil, I don't like your sarcasm on this subject any more than I liked it about my military proposals. You were wrong then, and you're wrong now. If His Majesty asked my advice, I'd suggest he fire you on charges of stupidity."

Macurdy's words shocked the eastern ylver attending, and Lord Gaerimor and his aide looked dismayed. Macurdy realized he'd overstepped. This was not, after all, some barracks or bar. He wondered if he'd endangered an agreement. But he continued. "Send the surplus prisoners back to Hithmearc. Then send the rest back when you're done with them. It's already obvious you can't get decent value for the ships."

No one replied to his suggestion, and Lord Gaerimor moved the meeting be adjourned till Three-Day. Morguil seconded the motion, and Gaerimor spent the next day with the eastern emperor trying to heal the damage. It had been Naerrasil's sarcasm, he pointed out, that had triggered Macurdy's insult. And earlier, at Duinarog, he'd insulted Macurdy very personally, on top of which, his criticisms had been proven utterly wrong.

"Frankly, Your Majesty," Gaerimor finished, "his lordship has long had a reputation for a quick and abusive tongue. And while he is your brother-in-law, you may nonetheless wish to speak to him about it. We do, after all, have agreements to work out. And Field Marshal Macurdy provided and led the actions that won the war. He bled, embarrassed and worried the voitar into undertaking a sorcery they could not adequately control. And then destroyed them with it. Without the Lion, it would be Crown Prince Kurqôsz, and not ourselves, dictating the peace."

He paused, giving time for his argument to sink in. Then added, "And almost surely, so powerful a psychic shock was felt even in Hithmearc. Felt sorely enough that I expect the voitusotar will leave us alone in the future."

Morguil was not as optimistic as Gaerimor claimed to be, but he let the matter lie. Instead he defended Naerrasil's criticism. "Marshal Macurdy," he pointed out, "is not only a commoner, he's a half-blood at best. That makes his insult far more offensive than it would otherwise be, and Naerrasil's considerably less."

Gaerimor regarded the argument for a long moment before replying. "That's true, as far as it goes," he said diplomatically. "But consider. In talent, Macurdy excels any ylf I know of in recent centuries. In that, one might say, he is more ylvin than we ylver. As for his common birth—legend has our aristocracies originating from commoners of great accomplishment. And Field Marshal Macurdy's accomplishments, both recent and past, abundantly qualify him as noble. If, unfortunately, somewhat rough-spoken." His lordship chanced a chuckle, to lighten the tone of the discussion. "As for a title, he has already been dubbed the 'Lion of Farside'; Gavriel routinely refers to him that way, as I do, and regards him very highly. I have no doubt he will confer a formal title on him, with a fief of some sort."

He closed his case with an oblique pitch to Morguil's well-known religious leanings. "It seems to me," he finished, "that the Lion is greatly favored by the All Soul. How else would he have been given such power, and so formidable a companion as the great boar."

Morguil chewed his lip thoughtfully.

Gaerimor left with hopes he'd see no more of Lord Naerrasil at the sessions, but Naerrasil continued to attend. It appeared, however, that Morguil had reprimanded him effectively. At any rate his lordship said little in open session, and when he did speak, he was stiffly courteous.

Over the next two weeks the congress worked diligently, and Macurdy saw the advantage in its small membership: there were fewer personalities and attitudes getting in the way. *Especially,* he told himself wryly, *when I keep my own damn mouth under control.*

In fact, both he and Morguil let Gaerimor run the sessions. Physically, Gaerimor looked like an affable but rather bland young ylf. But from his aura and knowledge, Macurdy guessed him at sixty years or more. Chairing the congress took a lot out of him. He became haggard, and Macurdy wondered if it was the onset of decline. His first task was to bring Morguil to the understanding that these annoying "others" around him had rescued his empire. And did not now owe him quick and easy recovery as well. Destruction was a reality of war, and recovery would require time, sacrifice, and continued privation, as well as much hard work.

After Morguil, Strongarm was Gaerimor's greatest headache. The dwarf knew what he wanted, was certain he knew what Finn Greatsword wanted, and was disinclined to compromise.

Eventually however, Gaerimor came up with a document that both Strongarm and Morguil accepted.

The keystone was disposition of the prisoners. For that, Gaerimor had adopted and adapted Macurdy's suggestions. The Eastern Empire would draw up a large rebuilding program, rough and quick. It would then estimate what labor was needed, and create the labor crews from prisoners, keeping in mind that they had to be fed and clothed to be effective. The surplus prisoners would be sent back to Hithmearc, on as few ships as could reasonably haul them. The ships would then return, if they were allowed to, to haul other prisoners when they'd completed their rebuilding tasks.

Certain other ships would augment the east ylvin merchant fleet. The rest would be dismantled, and the materials used for whatever domestic purposes were deemed appropriate by the Eastern Empire.

If the prisoner ships did not return, only then would prisoners become property of the empire. And they could not be sold, bartered, or otherwise exchanged. Except that they could buy their freedom if and when able, or receive it from the government.

The King in Silver Mountain would receive certain mining rights he'd long coveted, from the west ylver. Who in turn would receive favorable trading terms on several classes of goods from the Sisterhood, plus sixty percent of the backup cordage and canvas from the voitik armada, eighty barrels of tar, and one hundred of pitch.

That was just the beginning. Gaerimor had found something for everyone, in a maze of cross-arrangements that Macurdy didn't try to keep track of. Though Morguil's accountants seemed to, as did Strongarm. To Macurdy it was a monstrous version of some three-cornered personnel deals he'd heard about in baseball, on the radio back on Farside. Including versions of "players to be named later."

It seemed so complex, with some of the terms so ill-defined, or difficult to control, Macurdy couldn't imagine them being met. But it was an agreement, and as finally signed—organized into sections and subsections, with diagrams!—it looked useable. If the main features were more or less followed, it should work. He hoped.

Macurdy was responsible for the interests of the Rude Lands and the Sisterhood, and felt totally inadequate to the job. Fortunately, Gaerimor covered for him. The Rude Lands and Sisterhood received mainly trade agreements, but to Macurdy they seemed remarkably good trade agreements—well designed to fit their needs and potentials. And both empires honored the contracts Macurdy had made with Oz.

It was Morguil personally who'd brought up the one worrisome aspect of sending hithar home. It was a matter of the known versus the unknown. In Hithmearc, no one knew what had become of the armada and army, and if no one returned, they'd wonder why. After a while, they might assume that the hazards of the sea, Vismearc and war had claimed them. But returning the prisoners would expose the truth. And if the voitar in Hithmearc had survived the crash of Kurqôsz's sorcery, they might decide to invade again.

It was Strongarm whose viewpoint prevailed. "Considering what happened this time," he said, "they'd be daft to try." The conferees were not entirely reassured, but they accepted it.

The matter of vengeance barely came up again. When it did, Macurdy had the odd experience of finding himself and Naerrasil on the same side. Morguil let the subject drop. Dealing with reparations had been trouble enough.

The Rude Lands soldiers were to be paid by their own rulers, of course. But the raiders who'd ridden the long cold extra days to serve at the congress were rewarded with two hithik horses each, and the right to take whatever they wished from hithik officers, short of the clothes they wore. When the prisoners realized what was happening, officers passed their valuables to enlisted men. But the raiders quickly caught on and pillaged them all, officers and soldiers. And did quite well.

Macurdy, for reasons of his own, arranged a favor with the east ylvin Lord Felstroin, who had especially appreciated Macurdy's scathing of Naerrasil, and said

privately that if he ever wanted a favor done . . . Macurdy
jumped on the offer like a weasel on a baby duck. Felstroin, who was in charge of prisoner assignments, was
to watch for a bright young hithu of good character
who showed decent skill with Yuultal, and send him
to Aaerodh Manor.

That's where Macurdy would be, for he and Varia
remarried in a private ceremony presided over by the
Archbishop of Colroi. Lord Gaerimor and Sergeant
Ceonigh Cyncaidh stood as witnesses. This time it was
Macurdy who'd proposed. They were already married,
of course, had been since February 1930. But Farside
was in a different universe. They would live together
at Aaerodh. Ceonigh Cyncaidh, his lordship's eldest son,
was little more than halfway to thirty-five, his majority. Till then, her ladyship was the executor of the dukedom, the ducal regent so to speak.

And neither son was interested in agriculture.
Macurdy, on the other hand, was a farmer born and
raised, who wanted no more of war or the military. He
would manage the ducal lands.

There was no formal banquet celebrating the peace
agreement. There was no place to hold one, nor the
makings for anything suitably festive. So late on the
day of its signing, Macurdy went to Gaerimor's quarters to express his respect. He and Lady Cyncaidh, he
said, planned to leave the next day.

"Well then," Gaerimor replied, "let the two of us
celebrate." His lordship rummaged in a large wicker
hamper of rumpled clothing, and came up with a wine
bottle. "From Morguil, no less," he said grinning, "in
appreciation of my efforts."

Efforts, Macurdy thought. Judging by Gaerimor's
face, a strenuous effort. But however tired, the ylf
seemed in excellent spirits. He pulled out a shirttail
and wiped a couple of wine glasses with it before filling

them. "The quality is excellent," he commented. "I just tried it."

Macurdy sipped and nodded. "I wonder," he said, thinking of the agreement, "how carefully people will stick to the terms. With no enforcement arranged for."

Gaerimor laughed. "The needful thing," he said, "was to get a broad written agreement. Government and commerce are neither one entirely honest. But they involve continuous decisions, which can require a lot of pondering, weighing, and balancing. Our agreement provides the several governments with a fixed and reasonably clear reference of action. Wherever pertinent they'll tend to follow it, as the course of least effort. Fudging of course. And there is always the matter of relations between states, and concern over reputation and retaliation."

Macurdy nodded. "Another thing," he said. "I can't for the life of me see how you came up with all those agreement terms."

Gaerimor chuckled. "First you must know people. And next you need to read auras, which Lady Cyncaidh tells me you do very well. Something my own observations tend to confirm."

Again he chuckled. "And next I needed broad information and understanding about the various governments and their commerce. Many years in government posts provided me with a good foundation.

"And Strongarm, who has long served as deputy to the King in Silver Mountain, has remarkable recall. Quite reliable, too. I learned that by asking him questions whose answers I knew, or at least knew somewhat about."

Macurdy nodded. Gaerimor had twice invited him and Varia to supper in his quarters, and questioned him about various Rude Lands matters. Macurdy had concluded that Gaerimor knew more about the Rude Lands kingdoms than he did, though perhaps he'd filled a few holes for the ylf.

"And Morguil," Gaerimor went on, "when he evacuated the government from Colroi, took literally wagonloads of government records with him. Perhaps hoping against hope that someday the voitar would be driven out, and he'd have need of all those data. You'd be surprised how much of it there is. And when we had High Admiral Vellinghuus and General Horst brought here, I made sure they brought the armada's and army's records from Balralligh, to go with those from Deep River and Camp Merrawin. A treasure trove." He beamed at Macurdy.

Macurdy frowned. "And then what?"

"I read them, of course."

"Read them?"

"Not every word, obviously. Morguil's cache was categorized, of course. With most of it I did little more than look at major headings. If a heading looked hopeful, I explored the subheadings, and skimmed the contents of the more promising. Slowing here and there as appropriate. Fortunately his clerks were excellent penmen.

"The voitik records were much less complex but quite voluminous. I went through them with the help of aides provided by the admiral and general. It helps, of course, that their alphabet and numerals are recognizably like our own—a common origin, you know. And many of their words are similar, though the grammar is rather different. Most of the records are quantitative, and little grammar was involved."

His lordship had paused several times to sip his wine. It seemed to rejuvenate him. "That is one reason," he added, "that things went so much better after the first week. I'd developed a considerable sense of who had what, who might want what, and what was possible, you see."

Macurdy stared. "When did you have time to do all that?"

"Why at night, of course."

"Then—when did you sleep?"

"Every morning between four and six-thirty. Then I was pulled to my feet by my aide and orderly, stripped, helped or hustled outside, and rolled in the snow." He laughed aloud. "I believe they enjoyed treating an aristocrat and council member like that, once they got used to it." Pausing he added: "But tonight . . . Tonight, when you leave, I shall lie down and sleep till I waken. And woe to anyone who hastens the hour."

Macurdy considered a question, and decided to ask it. He didn't know much about ylvin sensitivities, but he couldn't imagine Gaerimor being offended by it. "It's amazing how you pulled it off," he said. "You didn't learn to operate like that overnight. How old are you?"

Gaerimor saw through Macurdy's verbal camouflage, and smiled amiably. "Eighty-seven years," he said, "most of them interesting, some of them challenging. I recommend old age highly. I should reach decline sometime over the next five years or so, and expect to enjoy that too. Not the decrease in capacity, or the eventual discomfort and pain. But the viewpoint . . . Ah, that will be interesting!"

He glanced at his clock. "And now, my honored guest, it is time for my overdue sleep."

Initially, in Duinarog, Macurdy had thought of Gaerimor as too weak to be War Minister, though Cyncaidh seemed to think highly of him. But here he'd quickly come to respect and admire the old ylf. And this night, when he left Gaerimor's quarters, it was with awe. He hoped he'd age half as well. A third.

Macurdy did some final things before leaving Colroi. He gave a copy of the Congress Agreement to Colonel Horgent, who was about to leave with his Tigers for the Cloister. Horgent would deliver it to Amnevi.

Then, via the great raven network, Macurdy summarized it for her in advance. And informed her he was herewith resigning as dynast, naming her as his successor. She'd have it in writing when Horgent arrived at the Cloister.

And the next morning, when the Tiger cohorts mustered to leave Colroi, he announced to them what he'd told Amnevi the day before. He had no doubt they'd support her.

PART EIGHT
Closure

Among human beings, pure love, agapé, is rare and mostly fleeting. It is sometimes approached, however, in romantic love, love of an offspring, a parent, a friend . . .

Ah. I see the term is unfamiliar to you. Agapé is love that requires nothing of the loved one, expects no reward, and imposes no conditions at all. The soldier who throws himself on a grenade to save his comrades may well be experiencing a flash of agapé.

By human standards, Mary's love for you approached agapé, and was remarkably constant. As was Melody's, and Varia's on Farside. You have been thrice blessed, my friend.

Vulkan to Macurdy,
on the highway to Teklapori
in the spring of 1950

40

Homeward

Macurdy and Varia left Colroi on two excellent horses—officers' horses that had crossed the Ocean Sea from Hithmearc. Macurdy's was exceptionally large; he'd been given the pick of the herd. Tagging behind were two remounts and three packhorses. As usual, Macurdy did without an orderly. For companions, the couple had Vulkan and Blue Wing.

They rode briskly southwestward, headed for the Pomatik River. The countryside was farmland, fertile in season, but now a bitter snowscape. There'd been a new spate of snowy weather, and nothing resembling a thaw. When the wind blew, the snow blew. Thus there were drifts for their horses to wade through. In this they had Vulkan's help, for the boar led, his powerful bulk breaking trail.

The only forest was scattered woodlots, kept by farmers, villages and towns to provide fence rails, lumber, and especially fuelwood. Almost the only remaining buildings were of stone, and they had been burned out. The countryside seemed totally abandoned. It had been heavily picked over earlier by hithik foraging parties passing through. Whatever locals had survived the ravaging hithar had since died, or fled south out of the country.

Blue Wing helped them avoid military company. When he spotted any, he informed Macurdy and Vulkan, who made any necessary course adjustments. The Lion had been enough in the company of fighting men for a while, even those he knew and liked.

Ever curious, Blue Wing questioned Macurdy from time to time as they traveled. Mostly about Farside, and what he'd done there during his years away from Yuulith. Varia, of course, listened in. More than a little of it she hadn't heard before.

She rode beside Curtis and a step back, to watch him without distracting him. He sat relaxed but straight in the saddle, watchful, totally in charge, but with no sign of arrogance. How he'd changed since she'd seduced him that night in Indiana! He'd been a man—what a man!—yet in important respects still a boy. All his twenty-five years had been spent with his parents. Doing man's work almost since boyhood, but their youngest child, the one at home. A mostly happy, full-grown child.

And of course, she told herself, *he's thinking how much I've changed.* While in Colroi, he'd been heavily involved with the congress. Living together at Aaerodh would complete the healing, the growing together. He'd get to know the household staff, the farm workers, the tenants. Deal with everyday life. In winter she'd teach him to ski the forest trails, show him moose, caribou, and, with luck, jaguar, her favorites.

In summer he'd learn how to farm in the north, and she would teach him sailing. They'd explore the shoreline, visiting the occasional fishing hamlets, and their people. Take him to Cyncaidh Harbor, and the best inn in the empire. They had twenty-five years, more or less, before decline hit her.

Meanwhile he began training her to draw on the Web of the World.

Like Varia, Macurdy had thought about the future, though not in such detail. This in connection with revisiting the past, remembering their brief married life on Farside. They could hardly go back. They'd changed too much, and this was where their children were. But this time they'd complete their lives together.

As they traveled, Vulkan spoke almost not at all. On their fourth night, as they lay in their tent, on and under ylvin furs, Varia commented on it in English. "His aura doesn't indicate unhappiness. It's as if he was meditating, with his body running on its own. Is he often like this?"

"Never for days on end before. When we first met, before I went back to Farside, he was almost talkative. He's told me since, he was excited to find me. He knew right away, he said, that I was his 'mission companion.' He's told me since that we were sent to Yuulith on the same mission." He paused, reflecting. "It seemed to me like a strange thing to say, seeing as how he came here a couple hundred years before I did. Besides, I knew why I'd come to Farside the first time: to get you, and take you home. Although when I was getting ready to leave, I did suppose I'd come back. I even wondered why."

Again he paused, this time longer. "And when I finally did, I knew he'd find me. At first he talked quite a lot again, telling me stuff he wanted me to know or think about. And asking questions, probably more for the things they brought to the surface than for my answers.

"He's never been big on idle conversation though. He's gone for hours sometimes without paying me any attention at all. I got the feeling he didn't want his thoughts interrupted."

She nodded. That was the feeling she'd gotten.

"And what you said about his body running on its own— He told me once that he can meditate while walking. He tells his body what he wants it to do, and then pretty much disconnects. Maybe goes off somewhere mentally, though I suppose he leaves some part of himself in touch. To pop him back if he's needed."

Again Macurdy reflected. "But this time . . . Might be he's getting ready to leave, now the war's over. Maybe I'll ask him tomorrow."

He didn't though. It seemed to him Vulkan would tell him when he was ready to.

Meanwhile the giant boar had hardly eaten since they'd left Colroi. He'd drawn energy from the Web of the World, and for other nutrients depended largely on reserves. Twice, when they came to an orchard, he'd paused to paw and root for frozen, windfallen apples, Macurdy and Varia helping, digging with mittened hands. That was all the food he'd had. He'd declined to share theirs, or the horses' corn, saying they didn't have any to spare. The supply situation at Colroi had not been good, and Macurdy had declined to take an inordinate share.

So when they reached the forested hills in the south, Blue Wing kept an eye out for game. The first day, he reported a small band of elk pawing for grass in a meadow. Macurdy stalked within bowshot of them, and hit a bull. The band fled into the forest, Vulkan following at a leisurely pace. The elk were in poor shape, and the one Macurdy had hit was now lung-shot. Not being pressed, it soon lay down to rest. When Vulkan arrived, it was barely able to get up. He knocked it back down and killed it with his tusks.

Macurdy skinned the bull, then sliced out some loin cuts for himself and Varia, while Varia made camp. They rested there throughout the day, while Vulkan, with the help of Blue Wing and assorted smaller birds, fed on the carcass.

After his initial feeding, Vulkan volunteered what he'd been doing these several preoccupied days: monitoring another great boar. Communication between them was not, he said, attenuated by distance. It didn't cross physical distance.

"Wait a minute," Macurdy said frowning. "Where is this other boar?"

«In Hithmearc.»

"Hithmearc?"

«Strictly speaking, it was initially well east of Hithmearc, but on the same continent. The region is savanna—in German you'd say *Waldsteppe*—grassland with scattered woods and groves, and woodlands along the rivers. The tribes there hunt, raise foodstuffs on small plots, and occasionally raid one another.

«They are animists, and regard my, um, kinsman as a deity. His experience and mode of life have been quite different than mine.» He paused. «While we were at Colroi, I asked him to find out if the voitar in Hithmearc had been affected by the event at Kurqôsz's headquarters.

«At the time, however, my kinsman was far away from the voitar, and the winter there has also been severe. Nonetheless, he agreed. So he's been traveling, and I with him, experiencing that part of the world.»

Again Vulkan paused, a pause which Macurdy realized was meaningful. «Today,» the boar finished, «we—he and I—finally encountered something pertaining to my question: report of a plague having swept the voitusotar. And of hithik uprisings against the survivors. The "plague" must be severe, or the hithar would not have dared.»

The next morning, Macurdy cut off some of the remaining frozen meat and put it in an empty corn sack for Blue Wing. Then they headed south again. A day and a half later they left the Eastern Empire, crossing the Pomatik River on the ice. There was a road along the south shore, and it soon brought them to a small village. They didn't stop there, but rode on west. Shortly after dark they reached a town—Big Fork—where a major tributary entered the Pomatik from the south. Another road ran south along the tributary, and at the junction stood a large, prosperous-looking inn. With a sign reading BATHS.

The stableman accepted the horses, but wanted nothing to do with Vulkan. He realized who Macurdy must be, and who Vulkan was, but he was adamant. Macurdy offered to stable the boar himself, feed and curry him, but the man wouldn't budge. He would not have the giant boar in his stable.

So Macurdy went in and described the problem to the innkeeper, who went out and reminded the stableman in no uncertain terms that it wasn't *his* stable, but the innkeeper's. Still the man shook his head. He'd quit, he said, if the boar was stabled there. Which would require the innkeeper to find another stableman at once, at night.

Macurdy defused the situation. "Is there another stable in town?" he asked.

There was, at the west end. "Well then," he said, "I'll take him there." Macurdy and Varia rode there with Vulkan, who was accepted willingly if warily by the owner-operator. Before Macurdy left, he had the man's promise to groom the boar.

At the inn, Macurdy bought a string bag of chicken entrails and organs for Blue Wing, the great raven's special order. Spreading his big wings, the bird transferred the foodstuff to the roof, to eat them in the lee of a broad, warm brick chimney. It was, he told Macurdy, where he would spend the night.

While paying for a room, Macurdy asked about the

baths. "My big bath's dry," the innkeeper said, "and not near enough hot water to fill it. If I'd known you were coming . . . There's folks would've come to join you in it, ask questions and hear about the war. But I've got three small baths, and enough hot water for one of them." He shrugged. "Not much good for sharing news or gossip—won't hold more than four people—but it's costly to keep water hot in winter. And *this* winter there's been little traffic, plus what there is don't have much money." He paused thoughtfully. "We heard, a few days back, that the war's over, and it was you that won it. So for you I'll fill one of them free."

"That's generous of you. We'd like that."

"We?"

"My wife and I."

"Together?" The man frowned. "Then I guess you won't want any company. Well . . ." He let it go at that.

After being shown the bath, Macurdy and Varia went into the taproom for supper. Word of them had spread, and the taproom was packed with folks who'd come in for a pint, to see the Lion for themselves, and ask questions. It took quite awhile to finish supper.

At length Macurdy excused himself, and he and Varia went to their room. There they dug out their cleanest clothes and went to the bath.

The townsfolk, walking home, tended to talk as much about the Lion's beautiful wife as about the Lion himself. A few had seen a Sister before, but this one, they agreed, had to be the loveliest of them all.

41

Hoofprints

The night after his father sent him away, Tsûlgâx had not camped. He'd kept riding, pressing hard. It was almost the only way he knew to travel when alone. Occasionally he ate saddle rations. He first realized something might be wrong when he came to a wagon train stopped in the road, its voitu commander dead. The mind of its senior hithik officer had been frozen with fear. Would he be blamed? He hadn't been able to decide whether to continue or turn back.

The corpse's grotesque features suggested it had died of something very extraordinary. Tsûlgâx ordered the wagon master to continue west. The hithu, of course, didn't argue. He gave orders to his trumpeter, the man blew the signal, and the wagons began to roll westward again.

The rakutu encountered another train about sunup. Its voitu had also died the night before. This wagon master had sent several of the escort back to Camp Merrawin with the body, and continued west.

Tsûlgâx rode on. It was evening when he reached headquarters at Camp Merrawin. There all the voitar had died, all at once, all seemingly in a terrible spasm of pain. Two of the rakutik guard had died at the same time, and apparently in the same way. Both of the dead rakutur, he was told, were cavalry communicators—connected to the hive mind.

Everyone there knew who Tsûlgâx was—who and whose—and as the senior rakutu, he outranked hithar of whatever rank. Thus he moved into the late General Trumpko's quarters and had a fire lit in the fireplace, while the rakutik lieutenant who'd been in charge briefed him on events.

Not much of it was useful. But there was, Tsûlgâx learned, a husky guerrilla held prisoner there, unwounded but confused, apparently from a blow to the head. Trumpko had ordered him kept alive for interrogation. Tsûlgâx had the captive brought to him, asked him several questions, and got no useful answers. He then ordered the man to strip, and when he was reluctant, slapped him with a sound like a pistol shot, sending him sprawling. "Strip him," Tsûlgâx ordered.

When the man was naked, Tsûlgâx looked him over coldly. "Tie him to a tree. As he is. Leave him there for an hour, then question him. If his answers don't satisfy you, leave him there till morning."

As the two rakutik guards dragged the half-ylf from the room, Tsûlgâx examined the man's sheep-lined farmer coat. In his mind, an idea had sprouted. He would, he decided, order the rest of the man's gear brought to him in the morning.

Then he went to the command messhall. Supper had been eaten, and the kitchen and dishes cleaned and put in order. Then the hithik kitchen staff had gone to bed. Tsûlgâx went to the mess sergeant and physically dragged him out of his blankets. "Stand up!" he barked.

Big-eyed, the man got to his feet, to stand there in his winter underwear.

"I am now the senior officer here. I've been riding for two days and two nights, eating saddle rations. Now I want a real meal. Hot! You have half an hour. If it is unsatisfactory, I will punish you personally."

The sergeant saluted. "Yes, Captain! Right away, Captain!" He looked around at the other kitchen staff, who were themselves out of bed now, and began snapping orders of his own. "Eno! Build up the fire! Oswal, bring the roast from the cold box! Fiskin, bring the pudding!"

Tsûlgâx turned and stalked from the room.

An hour later he fell asleep at the table, glutted. Informed by the mess sergeant, two rakutur supported him to the commander's quarters and got him into bed. He never knew it.

When Tsûlgâx awoke, fourteen hours later, he was ready to act. He knew that without the voitar, the hithar would not fight. Under rakutik pressure they might go out to fight, but they'd surrender on contact. He'd always known that, but the knowledge had been meaningless, because the voitar *had* been there.

Now it was pertinent. And at the same time unimportant to Tsûlgâx, because his goal had changed.

What he needed now was information. He didn't know how he'd get it, but it would come. He'd go out and let things happen, and it would come.

The mess sergeant was a resourceful man. Months earlier, foraging parties had brought him a number of ducks. He'd had a shed built for them, with nesting boxes and a brick stove. Thus the ranking officers sometimes got eggs for breakfast.

Given Tsûlgâx's disposition, his breakfast was to be prepared immediately when he got up, and served as quickly as possible. Even if it was nearly noon, which it was. Then he had eggs and bacon to start his day, and hot bread with butter. (The mess sergeant also had a cow shed.)

Not that Tsûlgâx savored his food. He ate quickly, voraciously, and carelessly. When he'd finished, he tried on the guerrilla's clothing. The breeches wouldn't do; the waist was all right, but they were too tight for his thighs and buttocks. The shirt was snug as well, so he had the commander's orderly—now his orderly—bring clothes from hithik supply. The plain brown hithik uniforms were less distinctive than rakutik uniforms.

The important items were the guerrilla's heavy farmer coat and cap. The cap wasn't designed to accommodate rakutik ears, but it was large enough to serve. His own boots and mittens he kept. They were warmer.

Given his now-assumed role as a guerrilla separated from his unit, a packhorse was an anomaly. He took one anyway. He didn't intend to get any closer to enemy troops than he needed to. And a packhorse would allow him to take an officer's shelter tent, an ax, abundant corn for horsefeed, and three weeks field rations for himself—dried beef, potatoes, bread, and lard.

By the time he was ready to leave, an outpost had reported an enemy patrol scouting the encampment. Tsûlgâx ordered the hithik General Gruismak to prepare a defense. He had no illusion that there'd actually be a defense, once he was gone, but the order was expected, so he gave it.

He himself did nothing till dusk. Then, still wearing his rakutik jacket and cap, he rode back westward. But not on the road. When he'd passed the last outpost and entered the forest, he changed into the farmer coat and cap, stowing his rakutik gear in a bag on his packhorse.

Mostly he stayed on or near Road B. Thus on the third morning, he knew when large columns passed

going eastward. Columns that could only be from the
Deep River Line. From the shelter of a tamarack fringe,
he watched across open bog as they passed: units of
armed ylver, followed by thousands of hithik prisoners, their hands tied in front of them.

Late that afternoon he reached the clearing. For
the first time in his memory, Tsûlgâx was astonished.
There weren't even rubble piles, only broken stones,
without one on top of another. There were, however,
dead horses and dead men, covered by new snow. He
brushed one off. A rakutu. A saber had struck him across
the back of the neck, above his cuirass, severing the
spine.

Tsûlgâx rode across the middle of the clearing. There
were many bodies toward the center, mostly rakutur.
But he felt no grief. Even among the rakutur he'd been
a loner.

And now he knew, really knew the situation. There
was not the smallest doubt that his father was dead,
and that only the hithar remained of his army. Tsûlgâx
spat in the snow.

He also knew, or thought he did, what had happened. The great sorcery his father had planned had
backfired, and Kurt Montag was the cause. He'd aborted
it the first night, had actually stolen the Crystal of Power.
On the second night he'd done . . . Tsûlgâx expected
never to know what. But even as a prisoner, Montag
had done something to cause this. Tsûlgâx had suspected
it when he'd encountered the second wagon train with
its voitik commander dead. Twice was no accident. He'd
known it at Camp Merrawin, when he learned that
everyone there, connected with the hive mind, had died
the same way.

Montag!

He didn't wonder how a physically and mentally
handicapped German had come to Vismearc. How an
inept psychic could block the sorcery of one whom the

hive mind had chosen the next Crystal Lord. Montag had come, and done whatever it was he'd done.

Nor did he wonder if Montag had died in the cataclysm. It was logical to assume it, but Tsûlgâx felt sure the German was alive. The question was where, and how to get at him.

The rakutu followed the enemy forces to Colroi. Their hithik prisoners far outnumbered them, but the prisoners had been disarmed, of course, and their officers segregated into separate encampments. Not that it made any difference; there was no fight left in any of them. Like most of the victors, they camped not in the ruins, but in the snowblown fields nearby, in squad tents. More snow had fallen, and when the wind blew, the snow blew, along the surface in a ground blizzard. It sifted into everything, including their tents. They were defeated and demoralized, and many were sick. They were fed twice a day: cornmeal mush with hard bread and lard for breakfast, and for supper, boiled potatoes with hard bread and lard. As bread was abundant, the prisoners would stash chunks of it in their jackets, to gnaw between meals with teeth that were loosening in their gums.

Tsûlgâx had no sympathy for them. They were hithar, no better than dogs.

Most of the ylvin army was camped in the open too. But their mood was grim, not demoralized. They were given more wood for their warming fires, and three meals a day, with meat or cheese, and beans.

Tsûlgâx knew, because he ate army meals, insinuating himself into raider mess lines. Always taking extra, and squirreling away what he didn't eat, to replenish the rations he'd taken with him from Camp Merrawin and used on the road.

Many of the raider forces wore uniforms of various sorts, but some, mostly ylver, were dressed in farmer clothes, with odds and ends of hithik uniforms. And single large mess crews served several units.

There were raiders with uniforms resembling the rakutur's. Some were dressed so much like rakutur, at first sight he thought they were. Turncoats! But listening at their fringe, he discovered they spoke Vismearcisc among themselves. They were, he supposed, some ylvin strain.

He did not live with any of them; he wanted no friendly approaches. His Vismearcisc was notably accented, and if they ever saw his ears . . . When speaking was unavoidable, he feigned a speech impediment, and impaired hearing. The surly personality was genuine. On his first night there, he'd snooped the ruins of Colroi, and selected a roofless, burnt-out brick shed to protect himself from wind. Then he set up his shelter tent in it, to protect himself from snowfall.

Between times he circulated on the fringe of things, watching for a glimpse either of Montag, his father's woman, or a giant boar. And seeing nothing. After several days he began to wonder if they were actually there, or if he'd assumed wrongly. But he continued as he was. From what he overheard, the purpose of this long cold wait was to decide on peace terms. So far as Tsûlgâx could tell, some general called the Lion was in charge. Why it should take so long, he had no idea. The enemy were the winners, after all. Tsûlgâx had no experience of government except the voitik imperial autocracy. He was not familiar with politics beyond differences of opinion. The voitik hive mind was not compatible with factionalism.

Another week passed, and several days more. It was Vulkan who gave Macurdy away. Tsûlgâx spotted the boar from a distance, beside a large man on horseback. Trotting through clots of soldiers, Tsûlgâx got nearer, improving his view. On the other side of the tall man was a woman bundled in furs. The man was in a uniform Tsûlgâx couldn't identify. And they were followed by packhorses and remounts; they were leaving Colroi. Along the road, men called and waved: "The Lion! The Lion!" It was the man with the woman and boar they were waving at.

Tsûlgâx couldn't see their faces. He speeded up, dodging among soldiers, trying to get a better angle. Finally he took a chance, crossing the road behind the threesome, guessing they'd turn south at the crossroads. They did, and he saw both of them from little more than a hundred feet.

There was no doubt. The man was Montag, and the woman was his father's woman, the one called Varia.

From there, with his speed, he might have—might have—taken them by surprise. Cut them off, and attacked with his saber. But there was the beast, the giant boar with its tusks. And soldiers on and along the road.

And this was the *real* Montag, formidable and dangerous. The lame German, slow, dull-witted and obsequious, had been a sham, a clever act.

He needed a horse again. He'd been required to turn his in to one of the horse herds, where they were fed and guarded. So he went to the sergeant in charge, and asked for one back.

"You need a note from your commanding officer," the sergeant said.

Tsûlgâx had no notion of how to write Vismearcisc, but he didn't argue. It would get him nowhere. Nor did he attack the sergeant, for there were other herd guards nearby. He simply nodded, stammered his thanks, and left.

He wasn't aware of the sergeant's gaze following him. The ylf gestured with his head, and spoke to one of his men. "Flann, take Cailon and follow that man. See where he goes—to what outfit. Then come back and tell me. There's something strange about him. No one talks like that without a harelip, and he doesn't have one." He paused, frowning. "I want to see what he looks like without a cap. See what his ears look like."

Flann's eyes widened, then narrowed. "Right away, Sergeant," he said.

The two ylver followed Tsûlgâx at a distance, to the nearby burned-out ruins, content to keep him in sight. Then they hurried to close the distance, and saw him enter a shed. Flann sent Cailon to tell the sergeant; then, slipping from cover to cover, he approached Tsûlgâx's lair.

As Tsûlgâx packed his gear, his mind was on Montag. The German had taken the south highway. He would too, watching for tracks leaving the road. If any did, and they included cloven tracks, he'd follow them.

When his gear was packed, Tsûlgâx wrapped it in his shelter tent, then lashed it onto a makeshift pack frame he'd made. He wished he had more rations. He would, he decided, go to one of the cook tents. Work or guard details often went there for early supper. He'd attach himself to one, eat, stash more food inside his coat, then try some other herd for a horse.

Pretending a speech impediment had been working. Now he'd try something more ambitious with it: claim he had a verbal order to ride somewhere; Balralligh. Hopefully that would get him not only a horse and saddle, but a sack of corn and a nosebag.

He shouldered his pack and went out the door.

"Hoy!" a voice called, and an ylf appeared around the corner of a building not thirty yards away. "The sergeant sent me after you. He says he's got a horse for you."

Tsûlgâx never broke stride, simply veered off toward the man. "Good," he lisped. "I knew he would change his thought of that." He didn't draw his saber till he was within three yards of the ylf. Then the move was quick. The ylf, however, had been distrustful, and his response was equally quick: he sprang to one side, and his saber was out almost as his feet hit the ground.

Tsûlgâx changed tack instantly. With the bulky pack on his back, he was at serious risk against a skilled swordsman. Instead he took off running, not toward the encampment, but eastward, away from it.

The ylf stared after him, astonished at the man's running speed. Even with a pack, he told himself, the stinkard could easily outrun anyone in the company.

Instead of giving chase, he turned and trotted off to inform his sergeant. Halfway there he met Cailon, leading four other men with a corporal in charge. He told them what had happened. Together they went to the shed and examined it, finding nothing of use. Then they followed the fugitive's tracks. His running strides were well more than an arm span long—six feet or more.

"Carrying a pack, you say?"

"A big one, corporal."

"That's amazing. He must be half voitu."

"That's what they say the rakutur are."

The tracks curved increasingly southeastward, then hit the east-west highway, where they were lost among others. The corporal stopped, "We might as well go back," he said. "It's a matter for the base provost now."

At the east-west highway, Tsûlgâx turned west, slowing to a jog, then a walk as he entered Colroi's unburned section. Best not to seem in a hurry. Beyond it was the great encampment. He'd been thinking in terms of waiting around for a meal, and to try stealing a horse after dark. Now he changed his mind. The sky was cloudy. Night might bring snow, and bury or obscure the boar's tracks. It was best to continue afoot. Montag wouldn't be traveling fast. He had packhorses and the woman with him. They'd camp early. He might even catch them tonight.

At the crossroads he turned south, as Montag had. When he was well away from soldiers, he again broke into a lope that, despite his pack, a cross-country champion would envy. At dusk he struck a large number of tracks that turned off westward on a minor road. If any were cloven, they'd been eradicated by horses, as they'd been on the highway. Nonetheless he didn't hesitate; he too turned west. If asked, he couldn't have said why. Half an hour later, several sets of tracks left the road. One set was of cloven hooves.

By that time Tsûlgâx was getting sore, stiffening up. He slowed to a walk, and before long was limping. In Hithmearc, running was almost as much a way of life for rakutur—even rakutik cavalry—as for voitar. He'd never found himself out of shape before, but he'd heard of it, and realized the source of his pain. Except briefly, he'd kept to a pace that didn't tax his strong rakutik lungs and heart; he'd thought that would be slow enough. But now his thighs hurt. His buttocks hurt. His calves and shins hurt. Severely!

Ahead and to his right, half a mile or so, was a sizable bivouac—two companies of Kormehri raiders headed for home, though Tsûlgâx didn't know it. It wouldn't have made any difference if he had.

Twilight had died, and their cooking fires were like small, yellow-red beacons in the night. He left the cloven tracks and angled toward them. Even though the night was cloudy, the visibility was good. The snow reflected what light there was, and formed an excellent backdrop for seeing. So he moved slowly, in a deep crouch, every step painful.

At two hundred yards he paused, sizing up the camp. A few men still stood or squatted by fires, but most were out of sight in their tents. Their horse herd was at the west end, almost certainly guarded. But with the war over, watchfulness was no doubt poor.

He'd seen a lot of those tents lately. Squad tents, but small. Crowded as they were, would the men keep their tack with them at night? If not, where would they keep it? If necessary he could ride bareback, but he'd never learned to control a horse with just his knees and weight. He'd need a bridle.

Later he could enter a tent and steal what he needed, but now the men would still be awake, talking. Meanwhile he'd scout the herd. He angled toward it, covering the last hundred yards on hands and knees, through dry snow that largely hid him.

There were no picket ropes. The horses were loose, their hind legs hobbled instead of their front, so they could paw the snow for grass. Thus they'd dispersed somewhat. Even allowing for packhorses, it was a very large herd.

He could see one mounted herdsman, and was sure there were others. One tent was larger than the squad tents, and stood a little apart from them, nearer the herd. A separate tent for the herdsmen? It seemed doubtful in so small a camp, and there was no dying fire in front of it.

Tsûlgâx was seldom emotional, but this sparked a moment's excitement. The one herdsman he could see sat in the saddle with his back to him. Even so, Tsûlgâx crawled to where some horses obscured the view. Then standing, he walked to the anomalous tent and ducked inside. The open door let in enough light to show him tack for several horses, and numerous sacks of corn, several of them open. It took him little time to gather a saddle and blanket, a bridle, nosebag and quirt. He also stuffed an empty grain bag in his coat, and took another one half full.

Then quietly but not stealthily, he lugged them limping to the herd. There he chose a large gelding, threw the blanket on its back and saddled the animal. It snorted softly, but stood relaxed. The unfamiliar saddle puzzled Tsûlgâx only briefly. Then he tied his bedroll to it with the sack of corn on top. He almost abandoned the pack frame, then put it on his back again, just in case.

"Hey! What's going on there?"

The voice was some distance off. Tsûlgâx didn't answer, didn't speed up. He gave the saddle girth a final pull, then stepped to the front of the animal and slipped the bridle over its head.

The call was repeated, less distant now. "You! What're you doing?"

Tsûlgâx buckled the throat latch and snapped the bit in place. Then he unbuckled and removed the hobbles.

"Sergeant of the guard!" The voice boomed it. "Someone's messing with a horse out here!"

Shoving the hobbles into the game pocket of his farmer coat, the rakutu pulled himself painfully into the saddle. Then he stung the horse's rump with his quirt, and dug its barrel sharply with his heels.

It started forward at a brisk trot, passing among other horses, which moved out of its way. When it reached the open, Tsûlgâx slashed it hard with his quirt. It broke into a gallop, its rider bent low over its withers, lashing it. Shouts from behind him energized his quirt, but the twang of a bowstring was far too distant for him to hear.

He steered the animal on an angle to intersect Montag's tracks, certain the herdsmen would pursue him. But he heard no more shouts, and shortly after he hit Montag's trail, heard a trumpet call. He looked back. There'd been the start of pursuit, but the riders had stopped.

For a moment they watched from a distance, then turned and rode back to their bivouac.

Kormehri companies were well disciplined, and these had more than enough horses—much of their herd was spoils, awarded them by the congress. And god knew how long it would take to run the thief down. They could easily wait where they were till noon the next day for the pursuit to get back, and then maybe empty-handed. Not that their commander thought all this out, but the rationale was there, behind his order to his trumpeter to call back the pursuers. The lost horse could be charged to whatever sentry the provost held responsible.

He might have decided differently had he known a sentry's arrow had struck the horse. It had been hit high on the rump, and there was not much bleeding. The drops of red—looking black by night—were not seen in the hoof-churned snow.

Tsûlgâx soon suspected, however, for after he slowed the horse to a trot, it began to limp. He looked back, and seeing the arrow, stopped to investigate. It had struck from long range, and penetrated only a few inches. Tsûlgâx tried to jerk it out. Fortunately for him, the horse's resulting kick only grazed him, the hock striking him with enough force to knock him down, but doing no harm. Limping, he had to follow the animal on foot a grueling half mile before it let itself be caught.

He didn't try to do anything more about the arrow, simply hauled himself back into the saddle and continued on Montag's trail. Later that night he passed near a large woodlot, and detoured into it to make camp. There he found a sugarhouse. Stopping by it, he buckled a nosebag of corn on the horse, and hobbled the animal. Then, with his fighting knife, he cut the arrow shaft short, hoping to lessen the movement of the head in the animal's croup. If the limp got too bad, he thought, he'd hobble it front and back, and cut the arrowhead out.

Finally he built a fire beneath the big cast iron sugar kettle, and made his bed. Being empty, the kettle heated red hot, and helped warm the shack. Twice in the night he roused, and built up the fire again. If it weren't for the pain that accompanied every movement, it would have been the best night he'd had for weeks. Instead it was the worst.

Meanwhile he abandoned the thought of catching up to Montag quickly. If it happened, well and good. But persistence was his strategy now. A lame man on a lame horse had no choice.

In the morning the horse seemed almost as lame as Tsûlgâx, who didn't try to hurry it. From time to time he got off and walked, limping badly, hoping to regain some mobility in his own legs, as well as rest his mount. They'd been on the trail about two hours when they passed his quarry's campsite of the night before. That evening, Tsûlgâx camped in a streamside woods, and rubbed the animal down with the empty corn sack. He himself was still about as sore and stiff as he'd been that morning.

Several days later, at dusk, Tsûlgâx reached the Pomatik. By that time he was walking naturally, with only a shadow of soreness remaining. The horse still limped, though perhaps not as badly. Tsûlgâx got down, removed saddle and bridle, then shouldered his pack. He left the animal with what little was left of the corn lying on the rubdown sack, and crossed the river on foot, at an easy lope. Ahead he could see the river road and a farm, the farmhouse showing candlelight at a window. He'd stop, make sure his quarry wasn't there, and beg a meal from the farmer. He didn't know what kind of police they had in this country—probably not much—but it seemed best not to murder anyone needlessly.

42

Confrontation

It was near midnight when Tsûlgâx reached the town of Big Fork. Its inn was dark, except for lamplight from the windows of a single ground-floor room. The kitchen, he supposed. He found the front door locked and without a knocker, so he pounded with his fist.

No one answered, and to waken sleeping guests by shouting and hammering did not suit his purpose, so he went to the stable. It was dark inside, but by leaving the door open, enough snowlight entered that he could dimly discern the layout. In the front was storage, and access to the hayloft. Beneath the loft, down each side, were narrow box stalls, dimly perceived. Body heat from the horses had warmed the place appreciably.

One of the front stalls held not a horse and manger, but a pallet on hay, and a man sitting up beneath blankets. "Close the humping door!" he said. "It's cold enough in here!"

Tsûlgâx spoke with his feigned impediment. "I can't see with it closed."

To the stableman, the intruder loomed large. So

he got to his feet; he was tall himself, and strong. "What do you want?" he asked.

"I look for man. Big, with beautiful red-hair woman. And giant swine."

"You mean the Lion of Farside. He's in the inn. But the boar's across town. I wouldn't stand for him in my stable."

The Lion. Tsûlgâx had never heard the name "Farside," but considering where Montag was from, the meaning was obvious. "What room?" he asked.

"How would I know?" The stableman gestured at the stalls. "These are the only rooms I got anything to do with. The roomers ain't much for conversation, but they don't argue or complain, either. And they don't leave the damn door open." He squinted hard at Tsûlgâx, trying to make out features. No way in hell in the darkness. "You a friend of his?"

"Yes. I from far place. In west. I was in war too."

The stableman took off his stocking cap and scratched shaggy hair. "In that case you can sleep in the hayloft. Got blankets?"

"Yes."

"If you need to shit or piss, use the manure pile out back. Now close the damn door!"

The trespasser went to it, but stepped outside before he closed it. *The horse turd,* thought the stableman. *The barn ain't good enough for him.* After a good scratch, he lay back down. He hated being wakened in the middle of the night. With all the hungry cooties, it took awhile to get back to sleep.

Tsûlgâx started back to the inn. The lamplight was gone from the kitchen windows. Then someone came around one end of the building and started toward the road. The rakutu cut him off, and the person stopped.

"You got bed I can rent?" Tsûlgâx asked, closing in on him.

The person was a kitchen boy in early adolescence, pale and worried looking. "I don't know," he said, then added, "we're closed."

Tsûlgâx leaned in the boy's face. "What room is Lion in?"

"Lion? The Lion of Farside? I— He— I don't know, but probably one of the single rooms in front. The rooms in back have pallets on the floor, several in each. I don't think he'd want one of them."

"Let me in. I pay. Stay in back room." The rakutu put a large right hand in a pocket. "Got money."

"I can't. It's all locked up."

Tsûlgâx's left hand shot out and grabbed the boy by the jacket front, jerking him close. This time when he spoke, he dropped the lisp. "You have key. Let me in." He glared intently into the boy's frightened face.

The lad nodded, scared half to death. "Yessir," he said, "since you're a friend of the Lion."

Together they walked around to the kitchen door, which the boy unlocked and held open.

"Go in," said Tsûlgâx, motioning.

"Sir, I need to go home. My ma'am'll worry if I . . ."

Tsûlgâx grabbed the boy's jacket again, thrust him through the door, then closed it behind them. Enough snowlight entered the windows to see by, dimly. "Get candle. Light it."

It seemed to the boy that something very bad was going to happen; he barely whispered his "Yessir." Taking a long splinter from a match pot, he lit it at the fireplace, and with it lit the large candle in a pewter candleholder. The man took the candle from him, then gripped the boy by the jacket again, this time a shoulder.

"Take me to stairs," the man said. "Do not fear. I not harm you."

The boy obeyed. When they got there, the stranger set the candle aside, grabbed him by the throat and crushed his trachea with his thumbs, holding him till he was surely dead.

Macurdy awoke slowly. For a moment he assumed Varia had lit their lamp, perhaps to use the chamber pot. Then realizing she was still in bed beside him, he sat up—to see a large figure looming over him. He felt the jab of a saber through the blankets.

"Lie back down, Montag!"

The order was murmured in thickly accented German. *Montag!* Macurdy's skin crawled.

"Curtis," Varia said muzzily, "is anything the matter?"

"It's Tsûlgâx," he answered.

She sat up as if propelled by a spring. "What?"

"He is right." Tsûlgâx spoke Yuultal this time. "He killed my father and stealed you." He did not remove his eyes from Macurdy's, or his sword tip from Macurdy's belly. "Get from bed, woman. Clothe yourself for travel. If you disobey me, or make difficulty, I kill your lover. Pin him to bed, then kill you. You follow my orders, you live. And he live for a while."

Carefully and without speaking, she slid naked out of bed. Tsûlgâx gave her not a glance.

Macurdy had examined the weapon threatening him. Single-edged. But even so, held strongly in a determined hand, with the point already in his skin, there was no chance in hell he could knock it away. The angle of thrust would drive it through his guts and into his chest.

"You think I killed your father?" he asked. "How could I have done that, tied and gagged, with a rakutu sitting by me?"

"It is no difference how. You killed him. I told him in Bavaria you were danger to him. Told him again at Voitazosz. He not believed. Now it is happened."

"You thought that even in Bavaria?"

"I never trusted Nazis. If you get what you want, you kill us all. And destroy gate."

"I was no Nazi. I was their enemy. A spy. The Nazis are dead now. My people destroyed them. We had a greater sorcery than the Nazis and their allies."

Tsûlgâx snorted. "Farside people no sorcerers. No . . ." He groped for the word. "No talent." Then he spoke to Varia without looking at her. "You ready to leave, woman?"

"I'm ready to scream," she said.

"Do not. It is no good. At first sound, Lion is dead. Then you. You do what I say, I not kill you."

Macurdy spoke as if Tsûlgâx's exchange with Varia hadn't occurred. "You loved your father, didn't you?" he asked.

"Don't talk to me about love my father! You love yours? My father always kind to me. To Rillissa and me, but more to me. Me he keeped by him. It all right that I not have hive mind. He kind to me anyway. He tell me, Tsûlgâx, we be always together, you and me."

"And you think I spoiled that."

"I kill you for it. But not yet."

"What do you have in mind? A fight hand to hand? Or a duel, with sabers?"

Tsûlgâx snorted scornfully. "Duel too quick. I . . ."

There was a noise from below, hard to identify. Tsûlgâx frowned. His eyes flicked aside for just an instant.

Varia heard it too. "Excuse me, Tsûlgâx," she said. "Shall I wear boots for riding or for walking?"

There was a hard heavy thudding from the stairs, then the hall. Tsûlgâx frowned, and the saber tip bit deeper as his eyes jerked toward the door. Macurdy tensed, readying himself.

Abruptly two hard hooves struck the door, driving it crashing out of the frame, and Vulkan's monstrous head and neck came through, great tusks clacking. Tsûlgâx jumped back, eyes wide, saber raised in defense. As he did, Macurdy threw off the cover and gestured.

Tsûlgâx screamed, throwing the saber from him. It landed on the foot of the bed, red hot, and the blanket began at once to smolder. At the same time, Macurdy rolled out of bed, into the knees of the distracted Tsûlgâx. The rakutu jumped back, drawing his belt knife as Macurdy scrambled to his feet. Another gesture, and the knife dropped to the floor—just as Varia, with all her strength, slammed the rakutu on the head from behind, with a heavy oak stool.

She'd always been strong; given the circumstance, her strength was tripled. Tsûlgâx fell. Ignoring him now, she stepped to the window and pushed it open. Then without pausing, she dragged the covers from the bed, flames flickering at one end. Wadding them roughly, she thrust them out the window, and they fell to the snowy ground. Then she poured the water pitcher onto the featherbed, which was beginning to smolder and stink.

There were excited voices in the hall. With Tsûlgâx down, Vulkan withdrew his bulk from the doorway and backed toward the stairwell. Wearing a nightshirt to his shanks, the innkeeper looked into the room. Guests peered in past him, their eyes on Macurdy, who was bent buck-naked over a figure on the floor. Before raising the unconscious rakutu, he removed the winter cap, exposing the ears. They were more than four inches long, covered with fine, curly red hair. The terminal three inches were free, voitulike.

Macurdy turned to the men in the doorway. "It's a rakutu," he said matter-of-factly. "Half-blood voitu. He's the son of the invader's commander, Crown Prince Kurqôsz. I didn't know he was still alive. He tracked me down to kill me, for revenge."

He turned to Varia. "I'm pretty sure he's dead. His skull's caved in, and stuff's run out his nose and ears."

Varia looked ill but didn't say a thing. Macurdy dragged Tsûlgâx into the hallway and talked briefly with the innkeeper, who dragged the wet and stinking feather-bed away, returning shortly with one in decent shape, and fresh bedding.

Bidding his host goodnight, Macurdy went back into his room and closed the door. With three volunteers, the innkeeper lugged the corpse of Tsûlgâx to the wood-shed. It would freeze solid by morning.

The next day, Macurdy arranged with the town magistrate for a funeral pyre for Tsûlgâx. He also hired the town's principal shaman to preside. When the magistrate asked why, all Macurdy could say was, he'd known the rakutu a long time, and owed it to him.

43

Love Stories

The next day at the crossroads, Vulkan said good-bye to Macurdy. «I discern no vectors that require my attention, and I am quite sure the voitik threat is past.» He paused. «I will not forget you, my friend.»

Macurdy felt very sober. "What will you do?"

«I will retire. I am done in the world, and I have been away from home a long time.»

Macurdy nodded. For Vulkan, retirement would involve dying, leaving his body and going—wherever it was he'd go. "Will I see you again?" he asked.

Vulkan transmitted a sense of grinning. «Of course. Though I will not be in the guise of a great boar. And you will not be in the guise of Curtis Macurdy. But we will know each other.» His eyes were red and his tusks fearsome, but his gaze was benevolent. «Do not dwell on the matter. When the time comes, it will seem entirely natural and good. Meanwhile think of me as I am now. And I will remember you as you are now.»

He turned to Blue Wing, who sat atop a packhorse. «And you, my friend . . . we too shall meet.» Then he met Varia's solemn gaze. «As for you, Varia Macurdy,

457

your strength is equal to your beauty. You have undergone much, survived much, and done nothing discreditable. You have my admiration as well as my love.»

Then the giant boar turned and trotted south on the crossroad, his brush of a tail skyward. As they watched, he winked out of sight. Macurdy wasn't sure whether he'd activated his cloak, or if he'd ceased to exist in Yuulith.

After a minute, he and Varia rode on westward, subdued and thoughtful. Their remounts and packhorses followed on the lead rope. Blue Wing flew ahead to scout. It was another cold day, though not cold enough that the horses were frosted with their own breath.

With the peace agreement signed, the great raven network had disassembled. But a precedent had been set, and the experience had enriched the great raven hive mind. Thus Blue Wing hadn't hesitated to relay a message for Varia, to the western emperor at Duinarog. She would, she said, appreciate a letter of credit, and gave her itinerary. Macurdy had already sent a message to Amnevi at the Cloister. He'd like payment for his services, if possible to be picked up at the Sisterhood embassy at Indervars. He'd suggested twenty gold imperials, a remarkably modest claim. He'd already informed her that he had married Varia, Lady Cyncaidh.

Upstream, the West Fork grew ever smaller. Within a few days, they'd crossed over into the Big River drainage, then rode south to Indervars. There they stayed a night at the palace, whose queen was a Sister. The next morning, the Sisterhood's ambassador gave Macurdy twenty gold imperials. After signing for them, he left again with Varia for Duinarog.

There was a lot of time to talk, to explore many subjects. Varia told him a great deal about Cyncaidh, whom she had indeed loved very much. She described in detail the ylf lord's rescue of her, and the long ride to Aaerodh. And their years together. Several times, in the telling, she shed tears, but none for having killed him.

It seemed to Macurdy the ylf would be a hard act to follow.

He in turn told Varia about Melody—how they'd met, their travels, their extremely odd courtship, and their months together on the farm in Tekalos. Her passion, her humor, her temper—her recklessness. And his devastation at her death. In the telling, he came to understand Melody—and the two of them together—better than ever before.

He also filled Varia in more fully on his years in Oregon, and in the army. And all one afternoon reminisced about Mary, Fritzi, and Klara, but especially Mary.

When he'd finished, Varia said it seemed to her that Mary was the great love of his life.

He didn't reply to that until that evening in the King's Inn, at the town of White Oak, in the Outer Marches. There they didn't have to spell the bed, the bedding, and the walls to protect themselves from vermin. The bedding was boiled after each change of guests. The bedroom walls and floors had been scrubbed with a liquid whose piney pungency was still discernible when they moved in. And with every change of guests, the thick featherbeds were spelled by an elderly half-ylf with a fair talent.

The food was superior, too.

But the high point was the bath. The King's Inn was famous for its baths. Varia had been there before, as Cyncaidh's captive. Twenty minutes alone in a bath, and getting clean clothes, had been a major step in her healing. At that time there'd been only two baths, but with the expansion of trade after Quaie's War, a short new wing had been built, all baths. The smaller, of which there were half a dozen, could accommodate four persons. The three larger, the innkeeper said proudly, seated eight each, and the largest, sixteen easily. When the demand was high, the water heaters burned upwards of two cords of oak a day.

Given the terrible winter, and the roads, there weren't many travelers. But what there were took the baths, if they had the money. If for no other reason than to soak in hot water after a day of freezing on horseback.

Varia and Macurdy spent a sybaritic hour in one. It was then he talked about Mary again. "You said she was the great love of my life. I'll tell you, it was beautiful being married to her. She was the sweetest woman, and the best human being on God's green Earth. On my dying day, I'll say the same thing. I wish . . ." Grief swelled, and he paused till it subsided. "She'd have made a wonderful mother."

They sat silent a long minute, holding hands and soaking. Then Macurdy continued. "While Melody, strong as she was, and tough, and weapons-skilled— she was the most . . . vulnerable's the word. She didn't hold anything back. To be loved by her, so wholeheartedly like that—that was a privilege. Sometimes it awed me. And humbled me."

He reached, touched Varia's cheek gently. "But when it's all over, and time to die, I have no doubt. It's you will be the great love of my life. The first, the last, and the greatest."

Then they donned their rented robes and went back to their room.

DAVID WEBER

The Honor Harrington series: *(cont.)*

Field of Dishonor

Honor goes home to Manticoreóand fights for her life on a battlefield she never trained for, in a private war that offers just two choices: deathóor a ìvictoryî that can end only in dishonor and the loss of all she loves....

Flag in Exile

Hounded into retirement and disgrace by political enemies, Honor Harrington has retreated to planet Grayson, where powerful men plot to reverse the changes she has brought to their world. And for their plans to succeed, Honor Harrington must die!

Honor Among Enemies

Offered a chance to end her exile and again command a ship, Honor Harrington must use a crew drawn from the dregs of the service to stop pirates who are plundering commerce. Her enemies have chosen the mission carefully, thinking that either she will stop the raiders or they will kill her . . . and either way, her enemies will win....

In Enemy Hands

After being ambushed, Honor finds herself aboard an enemy cruiser, bound for her scheduled execution. But one lesson Honor has never learned is how to give up!

Echoes of Honor

ìBrilliant! Brilliant! Brilliant!ìó *Anne McCaffrey*

continued

PRAISE FOR
LOIS MCMASTER BUJOLD

What the critics say:

The Warrior's Apprentice: "Now here's a fun romp through the spaceways—not so much a space opera as space ballet.... it has all the 'right stuff.' A lot of thought and thoughtfulness stand behind the all-too-human characters. Enjoy this one, and look forward to the next." —Dean Lambe, *SF Reviews*

"The pace is breathless, the characterization thoughtful and emotionally powerful, and the author's narrative technique and command of language compelling. Highly recommended."
—*Booklist*

Brothers in Arms: "...she gives it a genuine depth of character, while reveling in the wild turnings of her tale.... Bujold is as audacious as her favorite hero, and as brilliantly (if sneakily) successful." —*Locus*

"Miles Vorkosigan is such a great character that I'll read anything Lois wants to write about him.... a book to re-read on cold rainy days." —Robert Coulson, *Comic Buyer's Guide*

Borders of Infinity: "Bujold's series hero Miles Vorkosigan may be a lord by birth and an admiral by rank, but a bone disease that has left him hobbled and in frequent pain has sensitized him to the suffering of outcasts in his very hierarchical era. ... Playing off Miles's reserve and cleverness, Bujold draws outrageous and outlandish foils to color her high-minded adventures." —*Publishers Weekly*

Falling Free: "In *Falling Free* Lois McMaster Bujold has written her fourth straight superb novel.... How to break down a talent like Bujold's into analyzable components? Best not to try. Best to say: 'Read, or you will be missing something extraordinary.'" —Roland Green, *Chicago Sun-Times*

The Vor Game: "The chronicles of Miles Vorkosigan are far too witty to be literary junk food, but they rouse the kind of craving that makes popcorn magically vanish during a double feature." —Faren Miller, *Locus*

MORE PRAISE FOR
LOIS MCMASTER BUJOLD

What the readers say:

"My copy of *Shards of Honor* is falling apart I've reread it so often. . . . I'll read whatever you write. You've certainly proved yourself a grand storyteller."

—Lisa Kolbe, Colorado Springs, CO

"I experience the stories of Miles Vorkosigan as almost viscerally uplifting. . . . But certainly, even the weightiest theme would have less impact than a cinder on snow were it not for a rousing good story, and good story-telling with it. This is the second thing I want to thank you for. . . . I suppose if you boiled down all I've said to its simplest expression, it would be that I immensely enjoy and admire your work. I submit that, as literature, your work raises the overall level of the science fiction genre, and spiritually, your work cannot avoid positively influencing all who read it."

—Glen Stonebraker, Gaithersburg, MD

" 'The Mountains of Mourning' [in *Borders of Infinity*] was one of the best-crafted, and simply best, works I'd ever read. When I finished it, I immediately turned back to the beginning and read it again, and I can't remember the last time I did that."

—Betsy Bizot, Lisle, IL

"I can only hope that you will continue to write, so that I can continue to read (and of course buy) your books, for they make me laugh and cry and think . . . rare indeed."

—Steven Knott, Major, USAF

Robert A. HEINLEIN

"Robert A. Heinlein wears imagination as though it were his private suit of clothes. What makes his work so rich is that he combines his lively, creative sense with an approach that is at once literate, informed, and exciting."
—*New York Times*

A collection of Robert A. Heinlein's best-loved titles are now available in superbly packaged Baen editions. Collect them all.

EXPLORE OUR WEB SITE

 BAEN.COM

*VISIT THE BAEN BOOKS
WEB SITE AT:*

http://www.baen.com
or just search for baen.com

Get information on the latest releases,
sample chapters of upcoming novels,
read about your favorite authors,
enter contests, and much more! ;)